Shane Connaughton is an acclaimed novelist, screenwriter and actor. His screenplay for *My Left Foot* was shortlisted for an Academy Award; the film won two acting Oscars. His short film *The Dollar Bottom* (1980) won an Academy Award for Best Short Film. Originally from Cavan, Shane was brought up in a rural Garda station on the Fermanagh border. He is married with two grown-up children.

MARRIED QUARTERS

An insignificant Irish border village at the tail-end of the 1950s. The Sergeant is nervous. His men are lined up for inspection in the day room of the Garda station. Chief Superintendent 'The Bully' Barry is on the warpath, and any slip-ups will reflect badly on the Sergeant. But what can he do with the men under his command — all of them forcibly transferred from other more important stations in more important towns? On the cusp of manhood, his son is drawn in by these rough and ready men, stuck in this place and time, when all he wants is a chance to leave and start his life anew. Life at home in the station's married quarters is both comfort and knife-edged, ruled over by his by-the-book father and his gentle, emotional mother.

Books by Shane Connaughton
Published by Ulverscroft:

A BORDER STATION

SHANE CONNAUGHTON

MARRIED QUARTERS

Complete and Unabridged

CHARNWOOD
Leicester

First published in Great Britain in 2017 by
Doubleday Ireland
An imprint of Transworld Publishers
Dublin

First Charnwood Edition
published 2018
by arrangement with
Transworld Publishers
Penguin Random House
Dublin

This book is a work of fiction and, except in the case
of historical fact, any resemblance to actual persons,
living or dead, is purely coincidental.

A catalogue record for this book is available
from the British Library.

ISBN 978–1–4448–3831–2

Published by
F. A. Thorpe (Publishing)
Anstey, Leicestershire

Set by Words & Graphics Ltd.
Anstey, Leicestershire
Printed and bound in Great Britain by
T. J. International Ltd., Padstow, Cornwall

This book is printed on acid-free paper

For Elizabeth (Eilish) A. Moylett

Contents

O'Shea

His father had the men lined up in the day room. That morning the Sergeant in Tullyvin had telephoned to say Chief Superintendent 'The Bully' Barry was on the warpath. He was inspecting Tullyvin first thing and was certain then to head for Butlershill. That was his usual routine. Butlershill was last of the outlying stations. Any further North and you'd be across the Border and into Fermanagh.

The Bully didn't like Butlershill. He didn't like his father. His father dared contradict him on points of law. His father knew the law but it was The Bully who wore the Sam Browne belt. He had taken the Republican side in the Civil War. It was thirty-seven years ago but the political spite that was its consequence never withered. When at last de Valera came to power in 1932, The Bully joined the Force. His way to the top was mapped out. Dev needed the protection of his one-time trigger men. Europe was a cauldron of right-wing politics. With the growth of the Blueshirts, Ireland wasn't immune. The Bully feared neither man nor beast.

In the Cavan/Monaghan Division he was hated. He had been known to assault men who failed to answer correctly questions from the *Garda Síochána Guide*. The *Guide* was the Irish version of the English *'Police-Duty' Catechism and Reports*. One man who dared retaliate was

1

dismissed from the Force and along with his wife
and children had to scatter to England.

Over a snatched breakfast that morning his
father had pretended nonchalance.

'If he thinks I'm going to behave like a
whipped cur, he has another think coming. I'm
not one bit afraid of him. And never was.'

They could tell, though, he was apprehensive.
He hurriedly cracked his egg and swallowed his
tea at a gulp. And kept glancing out the window
for a sight of a car coming along the road.

Danny watched his mother brush his father's
tunic and, snaring the buttons in the button-
stick, brightly polishing them with a cloth grey
and powdery from years of Brasso.

He was home from college for the summer
and once more loved sitting with the two of them
in the kitchen. His father, as always, comically
trying to nail down the legal winds. His mother,
eyes twinkling with humour, as always, soft,
calm, loving, loved.

'Take your time, man. You know the
Catechism better than the same Bully. Go on,
have another drop.'

She poured his cup full.

His father told him to run down to the Widow
Smith and tell the men to report to the barracks
as soon as possible.

The barrack dormitory was too small to sleep
all the men. Four of them were put up by the
Widow. Guard Keogh, Guard Ryan, Guard
Ring, Guard Dempsey. These men were single.

'Then run fast as you can and get O'Shea.'

Guard O'Shea lived with his wife and eight

children in a thatched rented house nearer the village.

O'Shea himself answered when he rapped on the door.

'What the hell's up?'

'Chief Superintendent Barry. Inspection. Any minute now.'

'If thur's justice at all in Heaven, he'll crash into a stone wall and break his bleddy neck.'

His Wexford accent was scathing. Behind him children piled into the hallway. Further back in a small kitchen he could see Mrs O'Shea. Red-faced as usual, from cooking, cleaning, washing and blood pressure.

O'Shea was a tall man with 'a massive corporation'. That's what his father called a big belly. It made his uniform look ridiculous. He had a ferocious longing for pints of porter. A good few nights a week he could be found in Reilly's pub. His party piece was to ask for a raw egg, which he'd put into his mouth, shell and all, and munch crudely to bits. He'd spit pieces of shell with such velocity people ducked as if from bullets. Sometimes the yolk ran down his chin, merging with nicotine and porter stains, so that his face looked like a big plate after a fry-up.

Mrs O'Shea worked miracles to feed her flock and pay the rent.

He knew from his father O'Shea had recently applied to retire. Having served over thirty years he would qualify for a pension and a gratuity. He couldn't wait to get his hands on the cheque. He was going to have some drink that day and nobody better stand in his way.

'By Jesus, I'll drink the pump dry. I've a thirst on me I wouldn't sell for a bag of gold. Over thirty years serving this crooked, godforsaken dog's melt of a country, I've earned it. And sergeant, curate or craw-thumper better not try and stop me.'

He meant his wife. What would they do without his monthly salary? Where would she and her litany of kids live? *How* would they live? They had little or no savings.

The Sergeant was pleased he was retiring. It was his job to cajole men too fond of the bottle into finally leaving the Force. Or men who refused discipline.

The boy walked with him up the hill to the barracks. It wasn't steep but soon O'Shea was panting. His tunic hung open either side of his belly and with his big boots and reddish-blue face he was more like a clown than a policeman. A clown that couldn't escape the ring. Hemmed in by his large family, he escaped when he could through the bottom of a glass. But soon he'd be free. With a chunk of money in his back pocket.

'I earned every red cent of it. Shot out once and burned out twice. In the West of Ireland way before you were a gleam in your mother's eye. This present IRA campaign is a joke compared with what we had to put up with in the early days. A joke. The Bully Barry can kiss my FSA.'

'What's that?'

'My Free State Arse.'

He looked puzzled and angry. It gave him an odd innocence.

'For the love of God, no matter what your oul

4

fellah says, don't ever think of joining up.'

'I won't.'

When he glanced back down the hill he saw Mrs O'Shea emerge from the house carrying a white bucket. She was making for the spring well. Like chickens flocking round a hen, children scurried about and clung to her before she shooed them back inside. He liked Mrs O'Shea especially. Small, big-bosomed, clucky, she was as plump as a Rhode Island Red. And she always smelled of a pleasing mixture of baby powder and lavender. She constantly fingered through her stack of red hair. Her hair was still her glory.

He let Guard O'Shea plod on and went back down towards her. He'd carry the water for her.

'That man of mine, God protect us. What age are you now?'

'Sixteen.'

'Bless us and save us.'

The open well was in a scrappy piece of a garden just off the public road, beside the Methodist chapel. It was surrounded by rough stalks with rhubarb-like leaves the size of elephant ears. His mother called them Gunnera. The spring water was protected from the elements by a raised slab of stone the size of a cartwheel. At the lip of the well was a paving stone on which you kneeled to reach in with your bucket. It had the atmosphere of a sacred grotto. Some villagers believed the water was a cure for stomach ailments. He'd seen an old tramp bathing his sore feet in the well whilst praying with a rosary beads.

Mrs O'Shea wouldn't let any of the children near it. One of them had fallen in and had to be dragged out by the heels. Like a tadpole. She wouldn't let anybody but herself fill the bucket. The water was so clear, pure and dead still, were it not for a beetle flicking across its surface you wouldn't notice there was a well there at all.

When Mrs O'Shea bent forward to dip the bucket, her bosom filled her blouse.

She let him carry the aluminium bucket home.

'How's Mammy?'

'Grand thanks, Mrs O'Shea.'

'If she could get the chance to talk sense into Mister O'Shea. I can't, God help me.'

She always called her husband Mister.

Eight children. They came spilling out of the house clinging and dancing round her. As if she'd been away for months.

When he got back to the barracks, all nine men were lined up before his father. The four from the Widow Smith's and Guard O'Shea. And the four who slept in the dormitory — Guard Keegan, Guard O'Keefe, Guard Troy, Guard Brady. Keegan had been demoted from sergeant for hitting an inspector and was lucky not to have been cashiered. O'Keefe had little interest in police duties. He didn't have much time. He was running after local women or they were running after him. A widow. A waitress from the hotel in Cavan. A tinkerwoman. Guard Troy was twenty-seven, over six foot, with blue eyes and straight black hair. Found guilty of having a relationship with another man's wife in a previous station, he was transferred to

Butlershill — a punishment considered equal to the crime.

Guard Brady wasn't interested in police work. He'd joined up to save enough money to emigrate to Australia. Headquarters on hearing about his plans immediately posted him to the Border. Border duty and the Sergeant would soon force him out of the job.

The day-room window was open.

The room wasn't large enough for nine men to stand at ease in a straight line. Five stood along one wall, four at right angles to them.

'Attenshun.' His father enjoyed drill.

Shoulders jerking, hands behind backs, they drew themselves up without much enthusiasm. Guard O'Shea lifted his right foot and slammed it down on the wooden floor. He then burped. He kept his face straight but the others grinned. They knew he was deliberately mocking the exercise.

His father instructed them to march on the spot, swinging their arms vigorously at the same time.

'Quick march.'

O'Shea marched out the open door. Everyone laughed.

His father was angry. If The Bully Barry ordered him to drill the men, he wanted them to appear a disciplined force, not a pantomime shambles. His father was a serious policeman. Crime wouldn't be solved by uninterested fools. Order would be enforced by fit men acting in unison. The fact that there was little crime in the district made no difference. He still lived in hope

7

something big would occur. A murder. He prayed it would be soon. There were rumours hanging was going to be abolished. Murder without capital punishment belittled the crime.

O'Shea marched back into the day room, his heaving belly making a mockery of his uniform jacket.

'It's your own funeral, O'Shea. The Bully knows you've applied for retirement. To punish you, he could see to it that Headquarters rejects your request. You'll be forced to carry on here for a while yet.'

O'Shea was chastened. He was desperate to leave the Force. He needed that gratuity. He licked his lips.

'I'd go mad if I had to stay a day extra. It's no life for a thinking man, do you know what I mean?'

'It's no life for a drinking man.'

His father could give a cut when needed.

'I can't take much more of it. I do think we're not real. We must have fallen down be mistake. From the moon. Headquarters must think we're a flock a daws.'

His father looked at him like he'd gone soft in the head. Talk the like of that was so much *ráiméis*. A policeman's job was to hunt out clues. There were none to be found in philosophic ramblings. His father glanced at the open window.

The boy ducked away and went back to his mother in the married quarters.

She was putting turf into the range. She needed fire not just to cook but for the warm glow it gave the kitchen. Her heart needed flame. They had lived in the place for years and it was still as damp as the first day. The walls were painted the colour of wet cabbage.

'Where's Daddy?'

'In the day room, drilling the men.'

For the first time he noticed she was getting older. So was his father.

'Headquarters will close this place down as soon as the Troubles are over. We'll be shifted somewhere else. Or he'll be forced to retire. Headquarters don't care for him at all. He's done their dirty work all his life and they won't as much as say thanks. We'll buy a house in Dublin and live out our days.'

But would the Troubles ever be over? Men would police the Border for centuries to come. Men couldn't live without the hatred engendered by history.

He looked up 'daw' in the dictionary. It was Scottish in origin. The English had planted Scots all over the North to keep Ireland in London's maw. Their words had leaked on to the native tongue and the native tongue had become furred, corroded, with three languages. English, Irish and a smattering of Scots. Hills were braes. Babies were bonny. The local dialect was as indestructible as lichen on rock. 'That's an ojus horrid day. There's a hasky wind blowin' would flay you alive.'

His mother sat at the table turning her wedding ring round and round on her finger. Her eyes when she looked at him sparkled. She had gaiety. His father, she'd told him, was good-looking and charming when they first met. He was handsome still. But he had become stolid with years of hunting men and trying to put handcuffs round their wrists. Work was his life. He thought he was living life. What if life was living us? Maybe O'Shea was right. Maybe we did fall to Earth from another planet.

She smiled, opened a cupboard and took out the cake stand. It had two tiers, the one on the bottom a bigger circumference than the one above. Fitted to the top of a central stem was a delicate triangular handle. Underneath the bottom tier were three round shiny knobs acting as feet. It was supposed to be solid silver but when you flicked your finger against the fancy rim of the top tier it made a tinny sound. The cloth and Brasso were still on the table. She started shining the stand. Her hand brushed over and back in a blur. Sometimes she breathed over a particularly dull patch and buffed it with tremendous energy. Finished, she set it down. Admired it. It shone like silver. Everything around the place was like something else. But never the real thing.

As he did when a child, he flicked it. It rang with memory . . .

A Christmas Eve and outside on the windowsill a perfect parcel of snow . . . A sprig of holly above the tilley lamp . . . His father joining his hands in prayer before they ate . . .

'Thanks be to God.'

The cake stand shining like the moonlit snow . . . Like the Sam Maguire on All-Ireland final day.

It had been given to his parents as a wedding present. Apart from a soap bowl it was the last of their presents. A cake stand, a soap bowl, a carving knife and a matching fork with a finger guard. Some Wedgwood had been smashed in one of the moves to a new station and when they moved to Butlershill the same thing happened to a basin and ewer. The soap bowl was all that remained of the set. It was greenish in colour with two decorative black and yellow columns complete with clinging flowers painted on either side. His mother cried bitterly when she discovered the broken basin and ewer. Her own mother had given them to her. The last link with her past was in smithereens. The cake stand was the best thing she had left.

'You must be expecting someone.'

'Who knows?' She laughed.

A black car came slowly past the creamery and pulled up outside the barracks. The Bully Barry. The boy nipped outside.

The men in the day room had quickly formed themselves into the right-angled rows they had only just been practising. His father went out and greeted The Bully by the gate. Drawing himself up rigidly, he saluted him.

'Chief Superintendent Barry, you are very welcome.'

'Like hell I am, Sergeant.'

He was a squat man with powerful shoulders and a blustery red face. His nose had been broken by a rifle butt wielded by a Black and Tan in 1920. Concave as a result, he spoke with a forceful guttural snort. His accent was rough,

11

blunt and cynical. More sarcastic than perhaps intended. He looked like an ex-heavyweight boxer.

His father led him into the office. While they were in there discussing subversives and anonymous letters, the men in the day room remained at attention. They were as nervous as a bunch of schoolchildren.

O'Shea was finding it particularly hard. If he stood too long his swollen feet hurt. Whenever it was his turn to be BO (Barrack Orderly), he'd sit all day in front of the fire, only getting up to answer the phone. If he went out on patrol it was always on his bike. Come evening, a bar stool in Reilly's was his throne. He cursed the world in comfort. 'Shot out once. Burned out twice.' It impressed listeners. Fool though he might appear sometimes, there was a time when he was in the very thick of the action.

The Bully Barry, O'Shea, his father — they were men balled up in Ireland's history. They suffered every day her growing pains. The younger men they served with had no idea. They had never felt political flames licking their heels. They had never ducked an Irregular's bullet on the streets of Dublin or from behind a hedge on a quiet country road.

Peeping in the window, the boy could see O'Shea was boiling. He couldn't remain at attention much longer. He was mad enough to insult The Bully and ruin his chances of early retirement. Perspiration, from anger as much as effort, bubbled on his forehead. Taking off his cap he flung it out the window. It landed on the lawn.

The boy picked it up and handed it back in to Guard Troy. Troy placed it back on O'Shea's head.

'I tell you what we're going to do, Mick. And it's for your own good. And we haven't much time. You're going into the cell. We'll lock you in. You'll be out of The Bully's way. Come on, tippy-toe. Not a meg out of you. Sssh.'

Grabbing the big cell key, Troy and Guard O'Keefe bundled him out of the room and into the cell which was just along the tiled hallway. He didn't object. Anything to get off his feet. There was a wooden platform in the cell in the shape of a bed. He'd lie on that. The cell had a stout door with a massive bolt and a peephole. Also a big lock. The peephole was a small hinged hatch with its own bolt. But what would they say if The Bully queried his absence? They couldn't tell him they'd put him in the cell for his own good. A Guard arrested in his own station? They'd be cashiered, the lot of them.

Hearing the office door squeak open, they quickly formed up again. Without O'Shea's huge presence they seemed to have plenty of space. They waited. The Bully had stopped by the cell door. It was known locally as the 'Black Hole'.

'I'd like a look at the condition of the lock-up, Sergeant.'

'Certainly, sir. I'll get the key, sir.'

'I inspected Glangevlin last week. The cell had vegetables in it. And turf. And a woman's dress. And nylon stockings.'

When his father came into the day room, the men looked at him in such a horrified way he

13

knew something was amiss. They tried to mouth and mime to him about O'Shea's predicament. He took it they were scared of the coming inspection.

'Atten-SHUN.'

The cell key hung on a nail in the wall by the telephone. He automatically reached for it. It wasn't there.

'Where the hell is the key?'

Looking in the window, the boy sensed the tangible panic in the day room. So desperate were the men, an idea shot into his head. He raced around to the main door and went into the barracks. Chief Superintendent Barry stood by the cell door. He turned and looked at the boy. His uniform was light blue and finely tailored. There was a gold wire embroidered band on the peak of his cap. On each shoulder strap was a gold star and two gold bars on red ground. He wore a Sam Browne belt. Up close his concave nose made him look like a bat.

'Chief Superintendent Barry, may I ask you a question?'

His father came into the hallway. He was going to have to tell The Bully the key was missing.

'Who is this? He says he wants to ask me a question.'

'Oh, this is my son, sir.'

His father looked sick. The whole morning could end in disaster. He knew his father thought college was moving him a little further off. Making him a stranger. What on earth did he want to ask? Why? What was he doing in the barracks at all?

14

'Ah-hah. I was wondering. I hear you're a good footballer. They say you're a speedy buck.'
His father must have been boasting. His father was proud of him.
'We're studying modern Irish history.'
The Bully's chin lifted. His eyes danced. Modern Irish history? He *was* modern Irish history.
'What's your question?'
'Did you ever meet General O'Duffy? What was he like?'
The Bully's face clouded and he swung towards his father, fists up like a boxer ready for a fight. He gripped his upper lip with his lower teeth. He did look like a bat.
'Have you been telling him a load of nonsense about O'Duffy?'
His father held his hands out and shrugged.
'Hardly a single thing.'
'O'Duffy was Garda Commissioner until 1933. De Valera sacked him. He was on the side of big farmers and big business. The country was in ructions. He paid lads like yourself to attend meetings and attack Republicans. Ten shillings a meeting was a lot of money in those times. Your dinner thrown in as well. They wore blue shirts. They'd stop you in the street and ask if you were wearing your scapular. In Tralee one day I got a good wallop at him. Dev made Eamon Broy Commissioner. We scourged the Blueshirts. A lot of men in the Force were O'Duffy sympathisers. Am I right, Sergeant?'
This was a dig at his father. Most of the older Guards if not pro-Blueshirt were certainly

15

anti-Fianna Fáil. His father was. His mother wasn't. All her family had loved the 'Long Fellah'. De Valera. The calamity of politics forever sharpened family tongues. His father wasn't going to take the jibe.

'I served the democratically elected government. Didn't matter to me if they were bigshots or ex-gunmen.'

The Bully's forehead reddened. He clenched his fists. He was an ex-gunman. 'Dev was elected twice. In '32. And again in '33. We won. Didn't matter who you thought you were serving, did it, Sergeant?'

He stormed into the day room. He'd forgotten all about inspecting the cell.

The ruse had worked. For the moment O'Shea was safe. He went back out and round to the open window, standing to one side where he couldn't be seen. The station diary lay open on the table. It had a hard pale-grey cover and a blue spine. A white label read: 'Garda Síochána — Dialann'. The Bully examined it, snorting at the men as he did so.

'Stand at ease, for Jezus' sake. Who are you trying to kid?'

The diary was the soul of the Station: the catalogue of events, the daily history of plodding endeavour to weed out wickedness. Each man had to make an entry before going out on patrol. A brief description of purpose. Signed.

'9 A.M. Patrolling sub-district. Regular. Serving summons for cattle trespas on John Joe Sheridan, Clonandra. Signed, Guard Keegan.'

'I know you, Keegan. Hitting an inspector. By

16

God you won't hit me. You're signed out here. What's going on, man?'

Keegan was a rangy pale Corkman. Mature. He wasn't as nervous as the others.

'Yerra you know the way 'tis, Chief. I was just about to go on dooty, when the Sarge decided it was a drill morning.'

The Bully parsed the idiom for insubordination. Keegan's delivery was offhand, casual, too familiar. Gripping his upper lip with his lower teeth, he stared at the entry in the diary.

'When I was at school, Keegan, 'trespass' had two esses.'

His sarcastic tone was low and lethal.

'When I was at school it had three esses, sir.'

'I'm talking about the esses at the end. You've only got one.'

'It's hardly a hanging offence, Chief.'

His father was standing by the fire. Keegan was a volatile character. In his previous station an inspector had caught him sitting in the day room reading the *Irish Press*. A row ensued in which he punched the inspector. The thwartings of his superiors were as petrol to fire. His father, on edge, made futile circles with his hand. He feared Keegan was about to explode.

The tension was broken by a massive snore. The men glanced at one another. It had to be O'Shea. He'd fallen asleep in the cell. The Bully was both puzzled and suspicious.

'Is there a dog out there?'

The small room was thick with dark-blue uniforms. Bull's wool, the men called the material. Silver buttons. Black boots. Caps.

17

Batons holstered in shiny black leather cylinders. Handcuffs hanging from coat hooks, the keys dangling on thick green ribbon. Dusty files on shelves. Shiny whistles on silver chains. Ink. Nibbed pens. Blotting paper. The big map of the district on the wall and beside it a rainfall chart. The men, having broken their 'at ease' positions, gathered into the middle of the room. His father seemed lost. Like a man with a herd of cattle he could no longer control.

Guard Troy in the confusion slipped out the door. He had the key in his pocket. Quiet as could be, he opened the cell door and shook O'Shea awake.

'Mick, quick, quick, come on, don't ask questions, pretend you're sick or something. That's why you're late for duty.'

Returning to the day room he announced the noise wasn't a dog but Guard O'Shea pumping his bicycle tyres.

His father looked at Troy, utterly perplexed. He'd seen O'Shea earlier on. He'd drilled him with the others.

The Bully closed the diary and took up the *Garda Guide*. Nine hundred pages long. And though the hard cover was protected with an extra cover of brown paper, it was so thumbed from use, it was beginning to come apart. Snorting heavily, The Bully leafed through it.

'Sit down. Before you fall down.'

There was a collapsible wooden form and a few chairs. Troy squatted on the windowsill.

His father sat by The Bully, nervously rubbing his knuckles, one fist then the other.

18

'Guard Ring. You're called to the local pub. It's prohibited hours. A number of men are inside drinking. They give you their names and addresses. Except one of them. How do you proceed?'

Guard Ring was a Dubliner. The drumlins, byroads, lakes, accents, religions around Butlershill were foreign to him. They made him unsure. His innocent pale-faced expression made it seem he was always expecting a trap. The question asked was straightforward enough. But you couldn't be sure. He looked at the others. There was no indication that he was about to be tripped up.

'Come on, man, haven't all day.'

'I'd, yah knaw, sur, arrest the fellah who refused his name an' address. Take him up here and charge him, yah knaw? Tell the other ones I was going to summons them. Drinkin' after hours. Tell the publican he was goin' ta be, yah knaw, summonsed as well, sur.'

The Bully glowered at him. Ring twitched his fingers, his eyebrows. Waited. The Bully disliked Dublin. He thought it a second-rate city. Compared to Chicago.

'Good enough, Ring.'

The door burst open and O'Shea stood panting before them. Tunic open, tie askew, a bicycle pump in his hand, he was smoking. His hand shook.

'You look like a bloody haystack, O'Shea.'

'Sorry, sir. I had the diarrhoea. The wife says to me, lie in. But after a while I says I'd chance it. The diarrhoea — it's a divil.'

19

The Bully looked at him with disgust.

'Someone give him a chair. And put that fag out.'

Taking a final drag, he tossed the cigarette into the fireplace. A fire of newspaper, twigs and turf had been set. It wasn't to be kindled until November. Regulations forbade it. It was littered with butts and half-burnt matchsticks.

'Pull yourself together, O'Shea, or I'll have you transferred to the arsehole of Donegal for the rest of your days. You're no longer worthy of that uniform.'

'Shot out once, burned out twice.'

'That cuts no ice with me. A lifetime ago. Look at the state of you. A laughing stock.'

'I've applied for retirement, sir. You know that.'

'Until it's granted, you'll behave according to regulations or you'll be dismissed.'

'I didn't touch a drop the whole of Lent. Ask any of the lads here and they'll swear it.'

The men mostly looked at the floor.

'I don't care what you did in Lent. We're a police force. Not a religious order. Patrolling that Border, catching subversives. That's our aim. We can't afford passengers. You're supposed to keep their noses to the grindstone, Sergeant.'

'I understand, sir. But I don't run a reformatory.'

His father's cold eyes looked at the Chief. Chiselled cheek-bones, firm lips, tilted chin, strong shoulders, long legs, big boots, hard knees, raw fists, dark hair going grey in the service of his country, the Sergeant was all of a

20

piece; he'd back down to no man if he thought he was in the right. The men watched him, riveted. This had the makings of an exciting row.

The Chief Superintendent, for all his power, wasn't prepared to hold his gaze. He licked his index finger and thumb and opened the sticky pages of the *Garda Guide*.

Without looking at him, he addressed Guard O'Keefe. O'Keefe was from County Offaly.

'What's the difference, O'Keefe, between an idiot and an imbecile?'

O'Keefe's head shot back for a moment, like a startled cockerel. Was he being insulted? The best policy was never give a straight answer. That way you couldn't be pinned down.

'An idiot pays the asking price. An imbecile pays twice the price.'

He grinned. So did the men. It wasn't the forensic answer The Bully was looking for. It was a pub quip. O'Keefe looked sheepish but had an insolent mouth and cunning eyes. He was reputed a great man to fool women.

In the grate the old newspaper, matches, turf, began to smoke. A flame stabbed upwards, withdrew, quickly stabbed up again.

The Bully slapped the *Guide* down on the table. He had little interest in O'Keefe and the present generation. He knew O'Keefe to be interested only in hurling and dancing.

It was O'Shea he had in his sights. He opened the diary again and squinted at an entry.

'This is your scrawl, it is, isn't it?'

O'Shea flinched.

'A blind spider coming out of an inkwell

21

would be more legible. The hand indicates the mind.'

O'Shea's face clouded.

'Name a ruminating animal.'

O'Shea looked stunned. A what animal? He grimaced, scratched his chin, scratched his knees. He couldn't think straight. He crouched over and rubbed his forehead with his fingers. He straightened up. He was in agony. This was persecution. He just wanted to retire. He looked into the fireplace. The scrunched-up newspaper was beginning to burn.

'A room-in-atein' animal. Roominatein'? A dog, sir.'

A satisfied explosion of anger erupted from The Bully. A fierce guttural growl, chilling every heart within hearing. At the same time, with a powerful flick of the wrist, he contemptuously threw the diary into the fire. It stuck at an angle tight into the grate. Flakes of soot fell. The flame in the grate fattened as it immediately bit at the soft pages between the hard covers. Smoke crept out from under the book, swirled over it and up the chimney. The faded grey-blue cover was already darkening. The men, shocked, stared. This was sacrilege. This was Moses down from Sinai, breaking the tablets of testimony and burning them. To damage the diary was a crime.

O'Shea, shaking with nerves, his great belly heaving, moved to retrieve it from the flames.

'Don't touch it.'

His father's command was softly spoken but firm. O'Shea dithered between Sergeant and Chief.

The diary, cornerstone of legal activity, litany of the law, was burning.

The Bully, red eyes glaring, looked to his father. He might as well have been staring at stone. And the others wouldn't move without his say-so.

Jumping to his feet, he grabbed at the diary with the tongs and awkwardly lugged it on to the hearth. He'd had to back down. The Chief had to back down to a Sergeant.

The tongs, big and black with powerful shoulders, was government issue from the time the Royal Irish Constabulary ruled. For a moment he wielded it in his fist as if he was going to cleave somebody. Despite the grand uniform, Sam Browne belt, gold-braided cap, he looked like a savage with a claymore.

He placed the tongs back in its customary position leaning against the mantelpiece, steadying it with a nervous hand. Slapping the scorched diary down on the table, he dated it, signed it.

'C-Supt 9.7.59.'

He had been bested right enough. Bested. The damn Sergeant would never be forgotten in Monaghan/Cavan Division.

Butlershill. It was a cold outpost. Strangled by the Border, woods, lakes and drumlins, the light was dark, the air sharp, the prospect dismal. The members disenfranchised malcontents, full of grievances, dreaming of escape. The Sergeant an encyclopaedia of the law, garnered from experience not bookish accomplishment. And deep down, still a Blueshirt at heart. The sooner the present IRA campaign could be brought to a stop the better. Transfer the lot of them and close the place down.

'That's it for now, Sergeant. Thank you.'

He made for the door.

The men grinned behind his retreating back. His father quietened them with a rigid wave of his hand as he followed The Bully out.

'Well, till the next time, sir. Goodbye now, thank you.'

The Bully flicked his Sam Browne belt with his thumb.

'I'm the one wearing this. And don't you forget it.'

Getting into his car he drove away. Like a squall of rain, the inspection had ended abruptly.

A scatter of scald crows crossed the barracks and into the wood. Black and grey. The grey was the same grey as the station diary. They could have been the burnt bits of it blown on the wind.

His father grinned.

'You got a good eyeful anyway.'

'I did.'

As he passed the open window on his way round to married quarters he stopped and listened to O'Shea.

'Bejapers, lads, I'm a feckin' nervous wreck. We could all do with a stiff drink. Blast him anyways, may he die roarin'.'

★ ★ ★

One o'clock. His mother would have the dinner on the table. Married quarters was separate from the barracks but only just. On the other side of a bedroom wall was the day room. In bed at night you could hear the telephone ringing. Or the BO winding it up to make a call.

The mystery of his mother was her gentleness. He watched her stir, without fuss, a pot of stew on the range. If his father was ever called upon to do it, he'd churn at it efficiently, beating it into submission. She tried to keep their side of the bungalow building warm. The range was smoky and of a winter's night the chimney a gut howling in an agony of wind. They had electricity now. It was a mixed blessing. Bulb light showed up all the damp defects and flaking paintwork. And still no running water or bathroom. Yet when his mother opened the door of the range so they could see the glow and they sat either side of it, there was nowhere else he'd rather be. He often wondered would she still be alive come the year 2000.

A tillage book sat on top of the sewing machine. The Guards visited every house in the district taking details of land, crops, animals, fowl, even the number of eggs laid. Beside it was a Register of Householders. In this book was recorded the bare details of every family — townland, names, birthdays, occupations. The head of the household was entered as 'Farmer' or 'Labourer' or 'Blacksmith' . . . The wife was entered as 'Home Duties'. His mother didn't have a penny to her name. Most of the women were the same. He'd heard O'Shea say in the pub one night, 'You could buy half the women in the country for a handful of cash.'

His father came into the kitchen and hung his uniform jacket on a nail driven into the side of the crockery dresser. The dresser transferred with them from place to place. It was painted crow grey. The kitchen walls were public-works green. The floor was covered with the same blue lino he helped his mother put down years before.

His father had a triumphant smile. A shy, pleased smile. He had an ambiguous view of The Bully. It was The Bully who had forced him to study for the sergeant's exam. But for that he'd still be an ordinary Garda. On the other hand if he hadn't been promoted they'd still be living in the town they had lived in for fourteen years. Where their son was born.

They had moved when he was young. He had lost his friends. He knew he'd miss them all his life. The day they moved was the day pain entered his stomach. Being away at boarding school was by comparison no pain at all.

'Well,' said his mother, 'how did it go?'

She spooned stew into three bowls. Willow-pattern blue. A quaint bridge, an Oriental woman, a tree, a river winding.

'I didn't let him walk roughshod over me anyway.'

'How about O'Shea? Have they granted him retirement?'

'I wouldn't be one bit surprised if they didn't keep him dangling on for spite.'

'God help him. And her. And their lovely children.'

His mother found good in everyone. His father was paid to look for the bad.

'He's a desperate character. He says he's going on the batter tonight. No use me trying to advise him.'

★ ★ ★

That night the boy went down to the village. There was a light on in O'Shea's house. The curtain wasn't drawn. All the children sat round the kitchen table — a confusion of annuals, comics, pens, pencils, rulers, toys. Mrs O'Shea sat by the fire darning socks. The fire having died down she had her sewing box and a pile of socks sitting on the range. The pram, with the baby in it, was facing the window. The baby sat propped up waving a teething ring. It too was the colour of the station diary.

He went on down and into Jim Reilly's pub. He helped out whenever he felt like it or whenever Reilly needed him. Either behind the bar or filling bottles with porter. He stuck a Guinness label on each bottle: 'Bottled by Jim Reilly, Butlershill'. And underneath: 'Who bottle no other stout or porter'.

Guard O'Shea, on a high stool at the end of the bar, was staring into his glass. There were three other men there. One of them the blacksmith. After a fiery day in the forge his fierce thirst needed quenching.

'Give us another bottle there, gauson. Quick as you'd pull the drawers off a hoor.'

The two other men were middle-aged brothers. Unmarried, they lived together but rarely talked to each other. One of them was

27

threatening to shoot O'Shea.

'I'll shoot yah.'

'Why, Chisholm?'

'That's why. I'll just fuckin' shoot yah.'

He claimed he'd been a cowboy on the Chisholm Trail. He could turn violent in drink. O'Shea's strategy was to humour him.

'What if I shoot you first?'

'You'll not be fit. Yiz are no good. I'll shoot yah.'

'Why, Chisholm?'

Chisholm, irked at such an unreasonable question, let out a grating 'agghh'. 'No reason. I'll just shoot yah. Yiz never done anything for me. I'll fuckin' shoot yah.'

His brother, face screwed upwards, as if staring at a star, didn't say a word.

Chisholm walloped the bar with the flat of his hand. O'Shea took a deep slug that sunk the white collar of his porter deep down into the glass.

The boy poured bottles at their command. The blacksmith was a rough drinker. But merry. O'Shea had a huge belly to fill. He went about the task steadily. Four bottles an hour.

'Get me two eggs.'

He nipped over to the grocery counter. O'Shea held the eggs in the palm of one hand.

'I'll get me gun and I'll just shoot yah.' Chisholm's tone was matter-of-fact reasonable.

Jim Reilly, the publican, came in from the back kitchen. He immediately saw the eggs.

'You're not going to ... ? God grant us patience. You'll clean up, I'm telling you.'

28

'Shot out once. Burnt out twice.'

Chisholm took a vicious swing at O'Shea. The blacksmith blocked the punch with his forearm. Reilly bustled round from behind the bar and gripped Chisholm by the back of his red neck. O'Shea deftly smashed the two eggs on Chisholm's head. Yolk bled from his hair down over his eyes on to his unshaven face. Reilly threw him out the door.

'Fair weather after you,' O'Shea shouted, 'and speed to your heels.'

Chisholm's brother, known as 'Squealer', looked at Reilly.

'Agh. Squee-squee. Ee. Naah-nah. No-no nee . . . the like a-a-a-a tha-tha-t.'

He drained his glass and went out. Squealer lived so close to his animals he mostly sounded like them.

Reilly disappeared into the back kitchen. O'Shea asked for two more eggs. A party of men came in. Hunters. One of them had a beagle on a length of binder twine.

'Howaya, Guard? How's she cuttin'?'

'Like a mowing machine.'

He uncorked six bottles. A glass of stout was a priest. A black suit and a white collar. Or a nun. A black habit, a white wimple. A perfect symbol of the country. One of the hunters, uninvited, started singing.

We hunted wee puss round the rocks;
We chased her through the whin.
We didn't kill her; if we did
What would we hunt for then?

29

He paused for a drink. A deep swig between verses. Sighing with satisfaction, licking his lips, he said, 'This porter's powerful. It's too good to share with a stranger.'

'Puss' was the hare.

O'Shea wore a white shirt, a red gansey and his uniform trousers. Strictly speaking, wearing any part of the uniform in a public house was in breach of regulations. The beagle, covered in mud, lay among the men's feet under a table.

Before the boy came home from college they'd read *Love's Labour's Lost*. Reilly had said, 'God grant us patience', and O'Shea shouted after Chisholm, 'Fair weather after you.' The expressions were Shakespeare's. He could have heard them in a setting similar to Reilly's bar. In Stratford. Or along the Thames. Clothes changed, that was all.

O'Shea put an egg in his mouth and chomped it. His red cheeks ballooned, then, like a boil bursting, exploded. Bits of shell and yolk spattered into his glass and on to the bar. The men looked at him with disdain and amusement. They'd seen him do it before. A string of yolk spanned from his chin to his neck. He took a glug of porter, swigged it round his mouth. The blacksmith jumped off his stool out of the way. A yellow and black gob, thick with shell, shot-gunned to the floor. The hound got up, sniffed at it, but went back under the table without risking a lick.

The boy got a bucket of water and a cloth and cleaned up.

'I suppose you'll tell your father every little

tittle-tattle. 'Guard O'Shea was drunk again in Reilly's and him not in mufti.''

'He knows anyway. He looked in the window a minute ago.'

'A hungry eye sees far. Nuthin' escapes that bleddy man.'

He rinsed the cloth out in a basin of cold water. Then he got a kettle of boiled water from the kitchen and poured it into the bar bucket. He put new corks in and put a cloth over them to keep them down in the water.

'What are you going to do when you retire? Where will you go?'

'You're too young to be asking questions the like a that. You heard the women talking.'

He wiped his mouth with his hand. He slicked at his dark-grey hair with his fingers.

'Why did you answer 'dog'?'

'Gimme me hard-earned gratuity and I'm off like a redshank. There's got to be something else.'

'I'm beginning to like it. And we've got a good minor team for the summer.'

'No, not just the place. Trapped at the bottom of an ocean of stars. Billions a miles from whatever it is. With a wife and a load of kids, not their fault mind, and the eejits running the country on top of your head all the time.'

O'Shea looked deep into his emptying glass. His chin jutted out square and strong and stubbly. A bit of shell stuck to it.

When he talked he had an amused expression. As if a joke was being played on him. On everyone. Even on The Bully.

'By the Lord Harry, I'm going to drink Lough Erne dry.'

Lots of drinkers said the same. But Lough Erne was never empty. Even in a dry summer.

By the end of the evening he'd uncorked seventy-two bottles. O'Shea alone had drunk over a gallon. When they'd all gone home Reilly came out from the back kitchen and counted the takings.

Ten pennies a bottle. Three bottles a half-crown. Three pounds in total. A small fortune. Reilly gave him a half-crown.

He went home. O'Shea's house was in darkness. Over a gallon of Guinness. Sixteen, seventeen bottles. Fourteen shillings and tuppence. Multiply that by three or four nights a week. His salary a month was about thirty pounds. How could he afford to do it? What would he do if they allowed him to retire?

High in the darkness the moon was big and still as a half-crown on a mantelpiece. Light spilled on slate roofs, on the Widow Smith's thatched roof, on the trees inside the demesne wall, on the still face of the spring well under its canopy of rounded stone. He paused to look at the galaxy of stars so far away and dead but never buried. A star fizzled and fell. A soul gone to purgatory.

A baby began to cry in Guard O'Shea's. A corncake grated out a mating call in the swampy land behind the barracks.

★ ★ ★

A few days later his father had a call from Divisional Headquarters in Monaghan town. They'd heard O'Shea's request to retire had been granted. Someone had phoned them from Dublin. The Bully was already making jokes about it.

'He'll have all the time in the world to teach dogs how to chew the cud.'

O'Shea came round to married quarters. His mother made tea. His father shook his hand.

'God direct you, Mick. May you have a long and happy retirement.'

'Thanks, Sergeant. When do you think the cheque will come?'

'You'll get the letter, don't you know. Informing you of the decision. Then you'll be told how much exactly, to the penny, your pension is going to be.'

'I haven't opted for the big gratuity. The missus wants a good pension. And a small gratuity.'

'Yes, I know. That's wise. If I'm not mistaken, you'll be getting a cheque for five or six hundred.'

O'Shea grinned and danced his boots on the lino.

His mother baked bread, strong arms flaky with flour, fingers gooey with dough. A good fire blazed in the range. She'd call him when taking the bread from the oven and give him first slice. With country butter and plum jam. The bread was her body. Warm, tender, sweet. Until he went away to school, aged fourteen, he slept in her bed.

He ambled down to the village. Knocked on O'Shea's door. Mrs O'Shea invited him in when he told her that her husband's request had been granted. She was baking too. All the women baked. She was wearing a white calico apron. On the kitchen table were spoons, flour, a big bowl, a tin of Royal baking powder, margarine, salt, a knitting needle, a jug of buttermilk, strips of brown paper greased with butter. The table oil-cloth was patterned with blood-red roses.

'He'll be happy anyway. At last. Thank God.'

The baby was in a pram, sucking milk from a Guinness bottle with a teat.

'Will you go back to County Wexford?'

'Wexford? Sure we have nobody there any more. Them that's not dead are in America long since.'

She put butter and brown sugar in the bowl. And mixed them with a wooden spoon. A segment of the bowl near the bottom was flat. So the bowl could be safely tipped on that side when mixing the ingredients. But sitting beside the fire, she held the bowl between her thighs. Her heat melted the butter. She was making a fruit cake.

'Will you stay on in this house?'

'Oh no. Mister O'Shea wants to get away. A town. With good schools.'

'We'll be leaving too, I suppose. Some day.'

'How much do you think the gratuity will be? Did your father say anything?'

'I heard him talking to Mammy. He said it could be as much as nine hundred.'

'Well, he's earned every penny of it. Shot out

once and burned out twice. He's going to buy us a television set.'

'You can get good reception if you live near the Border.'

'That's the whole thing. Where oh where are we going to live?'

The more she beat with the spoon, the more the colour of the butter and brown sugar lightened. A tanned colour, like her powerful legs. Like the baby's rubber teat.

She started humming, then sang softly. His mother said she'd stand in the snow listening to her. 'Who's sorry now? Who's sorry now?' Connie Francis.

Her children rushed in from the back garden where they'd been playing. They stood clumped in the doorway, beaming happily at her happiness, though the song was sad. She allowed them to wipe their index fingers inside the bowl. Dipping her own finger in, she then let the gurgling baby lick it.

He blushed when she saw him looking at her legs. At the span of her white petticoat. The children dragged him out through the scullery to the garden to play 'Queenie'.

Queenie, Queenie who has the ball?
Are you short, are you tall?
If you're hungry give a call
And you're the one with the ball-i-o.

He threw the ball too hard over his shoulder. It shot out into the wilderness at the rear of the small garden. They laughed as they milled about

35

searching for it. The younger ones started shrieking. A stretch of ground the length of the village was covered with the coarse plant some locals called wild rhubarb. Others said it was butterbur. If you touched it roughly it could be worse than nettles. Soon they were hopping about and rubbing their bare legs with dock leaf.

★ ★ ★

They would leave the village. The O'Sheas. All of them. They'd be missed in school, they'd be missed in the chapel on Sundays, they'd be missed playing on the village green. They'd leave a gap in the life of Butlershill that would never be filled. Eight of them and their parents. That was the life of a Guard's family. You went where you were transferred and when no longer needed you went.

Word spread that O'Shea was retiring. He still went out on patrol but never summonsed anyone. Pending cases would mean he couldn't leave until they were processed in the District Court. Cyclists without lights and drinkers who weren't bona fide knew they were safe from him. They only had to worry about the Sergeant.

The younger Gardaí manned the Border. They didn't much concern themselves with ordinary crime. They stood at bridges, crossroads, down laneways, at all hours, in all weathers, watching for IRA men. The IRA came from down South and crossed the Border to blow up Customs and Excise posts. And police stations if they could.

Retirement rumours became fact when at last the confirmatory letter for O'Shea, from

36

Headquarters, arrived. It was followed by another a few days later, detailing his pension and gratuity. Eight hundred pounds. All his. Eight hundred pounds. A small fortune. As good as a win on the Sweepstake. His spirits soared. He lived in a swelter of good humour. He told everyone he was going to miss the place. The people were the best he ever had the pleasure of serving. Eight hundred pounds. He'd be sorry to leave the job. He'd enjoyed every day of it, alongside the finest bunch of men you'd meet the length and breadth of the world itself. He told his wife that once the money arrived, eight hundred pounds, their life was never going to be the same again. They'd be on easy street. Yes, he was getting her a television set and then he was going to buy a car. And his eldest son and daughter were going to go to the best schools in Dublin. As boarders. Eight hundred pounds. And a fat pension every month.

The boy's mother invited Mrs O'Shea to the barracks for tea. He laid the table for them, putting out the best crockery. A mixture of Arklow and Belleek. As soon as Mrs O'Shea sat down, she started telling them about her fears. There was no knowing what her husband would do once he got his hands on the money. The eight hundred. If they weren't careful he'd go through the lot in a couple of months. They'd end up on the side of the road.

His mother sat in to the table and, after slicing a currant cake, rested her hand on Mrs O'Shea's hand. Mrs O'Shea blinked to hold back the tears. Earlier he had watched his mother dab

Yardley perfume behind her ears and on her neck. Mrs O'Shea smelled of lavender. They both wore white blouses. Mrs O'Shea's red hair hung over her shoulders. His mother wore her hair up. The grim, damp atmosphere of married quarters had turned exotic. The flames from the range twinkled on the silver spoons and danced slowly in the glass doors of the old dresser. He filled their cups with tea, then sat in the shadows over by the sewing machine. Pretending to read a *Sacred Heart Messenger*.

'Between miscarriages and babies . . . it's been a struggle, I may as well tell you. Mick is a man can't manage money at all.'

His mother felt she had to reveal something of her own life. It wouldn't be fair otherwise.

'Bernard wanted more children. It wasn't to be. God makes the back for the burden, I suppose. All our eggs are in the one basket.'

They turned and looked at him, their heads sideways, smiling, like a pair of saints.

They held hands and wept but not for long.

'He came in the other night and says he wished he'd studied and he'd be retiring now, on a Superintendent's pension. Men. God forgive me.'

They began to laugh. They couldn't stop.

'Dreams they won't make come true. Because they can't.'

'If he had a penny for every bottle in his belly, we'd have more money than the Commissioner himself.'

The cover of the *Messenger* was blood red. As if the Sacred Heart was bleeding all over it. Mrs

O'Shea's hair was rhubarb red.

'Come on — we're not in the poorhouse yet. Take another slice of cake.'

His mother was good company because she liked company. She had the knack of setting people at ease. His father, if anyone called and she wasn't there, would sit with his legs crossed, his big boot bouncing up and down, seconds seeming like minutes, as he struggled to appear relaxed, talking nervously: 'Well now . . . she should be back soon. I don't know where she's . . . Let me see now. That's a grand day, anyway, TG.'

The boy went down to his room and started relearning the first few pages of *Caesar's Gallic War*. 'Gallia omnis est divisa in partes tres . . . ' His mind stayed in the kitchen. He hoped he'd never burden anyone he loved.

★ ★ ★

O'Shea, counting down the days, took life handy. The cheque would soon be in his grasp. Eight hundred pounds. He sat in Reilly's most nights but took it easy. A few bottles, no more. He told Reilly he was saving himself. But as soon as the gratuity arrived, then, by the Lord Harry, was he going to have a skinful!

'Over thirty years at their beck and call. Hardly a day without some jumped-up whelp with a few stripes or a Sam Browne belt giving you gyp. Or a gang of go-boys if you looked crooked at them. I've done my duty to the letter and no one can deny it. Who put the bread on

39

the table? I did. Have I earned a drink or haven't I? Shot out once and burnt out twice.'

Reilly looked at him but didn't say anything. O'Shea winked at his glass of stout. Winked at his own soul.

'How were you shot out, Guard O'Shea?' asked the boy.

'Did your oul fellah never tell you?'

Reilly went into the back kitchen. He had a rasher and sausage frying on a pan. Reilly had promised him a few bob if he swabbed the place down and filled enough bottles to stack the shelves. The Sunday would be busy. There was a football match on.

'I was BO one night in a barracks up in the arsehole of the County Leitrim. The Free State wasn't long in it. The country was full of guns. Every Tom, Dick and Harry had a parabellum.'

He held his fist out, extended his index finger, cocked his thumb, paused, then mimed pulling a trigger.

'They were going around robbin' post offices and banks. Irregulars. Ex-IRA who refused to accept the Treaty in '22. One of them called himself 'General'. He was heard roaring in town one time he was going to blow us out of it. Dynamite the barracks. This night anyway, the wind howlin', the rain comin' down in buckets, me on me own in the Station. I decided to get the tin bath we had and have a good soak in front of the fire. I boiled up kettles of water. And at last in I got. I heard a lorry pull up outside in the street. Bejesus, next thing all hell breaks loose. A bullet shatters the day-room window.

Missed me be inches. A shower of glass cascaded over my head. 'Come out, yah Blueshirt bastard.' The 'General' shouting. 'Up the Republic.' Trapped, trapped. Next second, Jesus, Mary and Joseph, they flung a bomb at the front door. I can hear the ringing in me ears to this day. Plaster coming down, the door in splinters, a big chunk of the main wall destroyed. The oul bath being a tight fit, I was wedged in. I had to toss meself and it over on the side to get out of it. A mad scramble on all fours to find me trousers. I dived out the back window into the garden and, naked as a newborn babe, away with me like the hammers of Hell across the fields, bullets pinging round me in the pitch-black night. I crashed into a feckin' donkey, nearly bruk me leg. I heard a rumour after, that The Bully was one of them. It was before Dev got power, you see. And she's going to try and stop me having a drink when me gratuity comes? Have I earned it or haven't I? Hah? Hah?'

'Mrs O'Shea, you mean?'

'Who else? You're only a whippersnapper, you know nothin'.'

His chin stuck out, grim and stubbly. Face red with a touch of blue on his lips and nose. Chest round as a tar barrel. He looked big and fierce enough to pull a plough.

'What happened the donkey?'

'What? Bejesus, you're some gink. If I'm any judge you'll end up a teetotal civil servant. Or a priest. Sure as soot up a chimley.'

Gripping his glass of stout around the waist with finger and thumb, he drained it dry. A

41

dainty gesture, as if he was sipping sherry. When he stood up, his head wasn't far from the ceiling.

'Oíche mhaith. Take it handy.'

When he pulled the door open to leave, it stuck for a second, then scraped shut of its own accord along the worn flagstone.

Reilly at the end of the night came out to count the takings.

'He's a decent man. He'll be missed.'

★ ★ ★

The postman delivered mail to the barracks every morning at 10.30. He usually went right into the day room and handed the letters to the BO. The Sergeant informed him that for the foreseeable future he was to hand all mail to him personally, in his office. The office, a small room with a collapsible table and two chairs, was just inside the hall door.

Each morning O'Shea arrived in the barracks at 10.35.

'Has it come?'

'No, Mick, not today.'

'Feck them anyway.'

Two weeks went by and still the cheque hadn't arrived. Each morning the stubble on O'Shea's chin grew darker. As if his temper was colouring it.

'By the Lord Harry, if it doesn't come soon, I'll go up to the Phoenix Park and choke it outa them. I'll kick the lard outa them. The bleddy rotten basturds.'

'Now, Mick, don't do anything rash. It'll be

here any day. Have you decided what you're going to do with it, when it comes?'

'Have a bleddy good drink for a start.'

His father didn't approve of men pouring hard-earned money down their gullets. He worried about Mrs O'Shea and the children. One evening he offered up a decade of the Rosary for her intentions.

'Let us offer up this Second Mystery — the Scourging of Our Lord at the Pillar . . . '

'One of the boys at school said to the priest, 'Nelson's Pillar?' '

They were kneeling, resting elbows on chairs. His father turned and looked at him.

'That's not funny.'

He turned back to his rigid stare at the picture of the Sacred Heart above the mantelpiece. A black cross sprouted from the heart. There was a crown of thorns on the head and thorns binding the heart. And nail wounds gouged in the open hands.

'Our Lord Jesus Christ was scourged on Pilate's order. He received five thousand stripes.'

'Who was counting?'

'It was revealed to St Brigid, if you must know. Smarty.'

Were he younger he might have received a stripe of rosary beads across the head. His father's tunic had three stripes. It hung on the back of the door.

'We are sorry, O Lord, for irreverent interruptions, forgive us, O Lord. We offer this decade to you, Lord, for the intentions of Mrs O'Shea and family. God direct them, we implore

Thee. Especially Mick. Our Father who art in Heaven . . . '

'God help them indeed,' his mother interjected. 'When he gets the money it'll burn a hole in his pocket. As sure as there's cotton in Cork.'

When his father prayed aloud, he always tried to work in 'We implore Thee'.

★ ★ ★

Next day O'Shea walked about the village in full uniform. He strolled across the green to the pump. Removing his cap, he lowered his head and pumped the handle. Water splurged down, splashing his boots as he drank deep.

He had a powerful swallow. Deep within, consuming fires had to be quenched.

Wearing bicycle clips revealed the full size of his big boots.

People peeped out at him from behind twitching curtains. Chisholm, the rough drinker from Reilly's, came riding into the village on a straggly brute of a piebald mare. He was heading to the blacksmith's, seated askew, holding on to the mane with one hand. Though broad daylight, he was already drunk. Chisholm and his brother brewed their own potcheen.

'Fuck yah. I'll shoot yah.'

O'Shea wiped his mouth and fixed his cap in place.

'And you'll not be fit for to do anythin' about it. I'll just fuckin' shoot yah.'

'Why, Chisholm?'

'No reason. I'll just shoot yah.'

O'Shea stomped across the green, grabbed him off the mare and, holding him by the shirt front, punched him on the jaw. From his great height and massive stomach, fists hanging loose, he stared down at the prone, dazed Chisholm. It seemed as if he were already regretting his action. What if he was reported to Headquarters? The mare turned her slabby neck to gaze in wonder at her burden now sparked out on the grass.

O'Shea grabbed Chisholm by the arms, hauled him to his feet, then lumped him up on to the mare like a sack of spuds. Head and arms hung down one side, legs the other. The horse, prompted by a slap on the rump, took slowly off in the vague direction of the blacksmith's. A drop of blood hit the road.

'Fuck yah,' Chisholm muttered, 'and doubled fuck yah. Fuck yah from a height.'

O'Shea turned away and headed for the railway bridge. Leaning on the parapet, he stared down at the permanent way, now overgrown with weeds, grass, and strewn with used tyres and rubbish. The last train had run three years before.

Straddling his bike, one leg on the road, watching, at a loose end, the boy decided to ride up and talk to him.

'Why did you do that, Guard O'Shea?'

'He had it coming to him a long time.'

His face, fresh shaven, was dark blue, eyes raw red. A thick slice of hair bulged out from under the peak of his cap.

'He hit many's the innocent bystander, the

45

same Chisholm. He got his comeuppance.'

Along the chapel road, they saw the mare turn down the path to the forge. Chisholm on her back was as relaxed as if he were lying on his belly on a sofa. Potcheen with a punch on the jaw was a great pacifier.

Mrs O'Shea came along the road, pushing a pram, the children following behind like so many ducklings. She was wearing her good brown skirt and white blouse. The children were in an assortment of ganseys, frocks, short trousers, brown sandals, white plimsolls. Their legs were bare and skinny. Like his own used to be. When they got to the footpath, she heeled the pram on its back wheels the better to land the front wheels on to the steep pavement. They headed for Tully's shop. Tully, on his way out, raised his hat to her. She said something to him. They laughed.

O'Shea watched them, then, looking bleakly along the railway cutting running into the empty hills, said, 'No trains — no way out.'

'You'll be able to buy a wee car when your gratuity comes anyway.'

'You're like a fourth stripe on your father's sleeve. Following me about. I'll be glad to see the back of ye. He'll certainly be glad to see the back of me. Another poor fool consigned to history.'

'That's not true. He offered up a decade of the Rosary for your intentions the other night.'

O'Shea, face blank, stared at him.

'By the living jingo, if it doesn't arrive tomorrow morning in the post, he'll need to be offering up a decade of the Rosary for himself.

46

The Bully is keeping me hanging on deliberate, so he is. I hear he's in Cavan town tomorrow. I'm goin' in. I'll pull the fucken balls off him, so I will. And hop them down the street.'

'Oh.'

He drummed on the parapet with his fists.

'They even take back the bicycle clips. Imagine that. When you retire.'

Hands behind his back, he walked out the Border road. He seemed to be strolling about, trying to keep himself occupied. Trying to keep out of the pub. Trying to hold himself together until he got his hands on the money. Trying not to blow up before it reached him. He was over sixteen stones. It took him a good while to disappear along the road. There was a lot of material in his uniform. Bull's wool for a bull of a man.

Sitting on his bike, the boy freewheeled down off the bridge and into the village. Mrs O'Shea was coming out of Tully's.

'Where's that man of mine gone?'

'He's on patrol, I think. He didn't have his bicycle. Though he was wearing his clips.'

'You don't miss much, do you?'

When in uniform, a Guard wasn't supposed to wear bicycle clips without having a bicycle with him. That was the regulation.

The baby in the pram now shared the space with a batch loaf, block cheese, Lough Egish butter, tea, sugar, salt, a flitch of bacon, loose sausages, a bag of flour, milk, shoe polish, bootlaces. Tully would miss them. Mrs O'Shea spent a lot of money in his shop.

He walked with them back to their house. They were all chomping happily on bullseyes or lollipops. One of the girls puffed on a liquorice in the shape of a tobacco pipe. The eldest boy had a bar of slab toffee which he tried to break against the demesne wall. The wall kept the village out and Lady Sarah Butler-Coote and her Anglo-Irish world in. Crumbling in places, it was being eaten alive by ivy. Time was doing the same for Lady Sarah.

When they reached the house, the children made him play football. They kicked a tennis ball over and back across the road. The little ones sat in the road. If the ball hit them they laughed. Only one car interrupted them. Tully trying out his new second-hand hearse.

★　★　★

Late next morning his father came charging into the kitchen. He had a brown envelope in his hand.

'Quick, quick. Slip down to Mrs O'Shea. It's the cheque. The gratuity. O'Shea is in the WC. Quick.'

The WC was in a small shed out the back. There was just enough space to sit over the Elsan can. Jeyes fluid, Sweet Afton and cut-up sheets of the *Irish Independent* kept the odour down. When the can was full, the contents were buried down the bottom of the garden. The BO for the day dug the hole.

It was the same routine in married quarters. The two lavatories were separated by a wall. The

48

same wall separated the gardens.

The Elsan job was his now. He took the cue from his mother.

'Time you buried the dead.'

He ran out the front gate and down the hill. Mrs O'Shea answered his knocking.

'What on earth's the matter?'

'Daddy said deliver this. It's the gratuity.'

'The gratuity?'

'The gratuity.'

Ripping off her apron, shrieking, grabbing her coat and hat, she snatched the envelope out of his hand and fled down the village. As if she had been dreading the moment.

'Help the big ones look after the little ones,' she shouted back to him.

Fixing her hair with one hand, putting her hat and coat on with the other, she waddled away quick as a goose chased by a gander.

She rushed into Tully's shop. Soon his car drove out over the railway bridge. He was pretty certain she was in the passenger seat.

He was torn in two. What would O'Shea say? The letter was his. Why hadn't he given it to him? He did say to Mrs O'Shea, 'Daddy said deliver this.' He could argue he presumed she was going to give it to her husband. He wasn't to know he wasn't at home.

The baby was asleep in the pram. He wheeled it outside. It was going to be a warm day. He got the other kids to bring out three-legged stools and a cushion. They hunkered around the door, giggling, and cheered when he said he was going to tell them a story. Next door a one-legged man hung out a birdcage. The captive goldfinch started singing. The sun was rising over the demesne and spilling through the trees. He'd tell them the story of Gabby the Goldfinch.

'Once upon a time there was a gol . . . '

O'Shea came running down the hill. His tunic was unbuttoned and the front part of his shirt flapped outside his trousers.

Even before he got to them he shouted, 'You were told to deliver it to me. Personally. Have you still got it?'

'I delivered it to you, Guard O'Shea. But you weren't in.'

Going into the house he scattered the children like a wind through chaff. Barging and bumping about from room to room looking for his wife.

'Where the hell is she?'

'She went down the village. I think she's gone somewhere with Mr Tully.'

He let out a terrifying roar.

'Agh no, the stupid feckin' blithering bitch. You've done for me, you whelp.'

'But I . . . you weren't here, when I . . . '

His eyes were furious red gooseberries.

'I've a good mind to lacerate you.' He clenched his fist. The one that knocked out Chisholm.

The children started crying.

'Don't, Daddy, don't.'

Belly heaving, face a lather of sweat, he headed for the village. The sun rose above the trees. The village green came up velvet.

★ ★ ★

50

Mrs O'Shea had gone to Cavan town. Later on he heard her tell all to his mother. Tully had given her a lift. In Cavan she went straight to the 'Tangler' Smith, an auctioneer. He took her to an empty house on the top of Doonan Hill — the steep drumlin leading up from the main thoroughfare. The house had six rooms, a kitchen, an indoor lavatory, running water, electricity. The rooms were small and badly in need of repair and decorating. She noticed a dull stain at the bottom of the stairs. Like oil had been spilled or something. No bother. Perfect. And she could move in next day if she wanted. She was thrilled. The Tangler told her the price was seven hundred pounds.

'Thanks be to God and his Holy Mother.'

At last a home of their own.

They went to the Bank of Ireland. It was where the Garda cashed their cheques. The manager knew her husband. She handed the cheque over. The Tangler and the manager did the deal. They understood her desperation.

'I know the house,' the manager said. 'Old Nan Gaffney lived there all her life. Until she fell down the stairs and broke her brains. It's a lovely house. You'll be very happy in it.'

Before she left town she bought a bag of gobstoppers.

She walked out the road into the harsh countryside. If a car came she'd hitch a lift.

In her absence, O'Shea went on a mad tear. He'd show her. It was his money. His hard-earned money. After all he'd done for her! In the heel of the hunt, she'd stabbed him in the heart. Deprived him of a celebratory drink. A revenge drink. Revenge for over thirty years at the service of crooked politicians and conniving craw-thumpers. He'd show her. He'd show them all. Drink? He'd show them drink. He'd show them paralytic, scutterin', seesaw marjorie daw, roominatein', fuckin' drink.

In full uniform he sat in Reilly's bar. Plus bicycle clips. One bottle after another. Like a man newly clambered out of the pit of Hell. He paid for the first fifteen bottles. He'd owe for what was to come. He had the money. His wife had it. He'd deal with her later. He was in uniform but no longer a policeman. They could do nothing to him. He was finally free.

'The thirst I have on me, I'd drink it out of a piss pot.'

Word spread round the village O'Shea was on an ojus jag entirely. There was no knowing what he'd do. A woman sent her husband into the pub to buy a box of matches. To see what was going on. When he came back out, he told the gathering neighbours O'Shea was threatening to burn the whole place to the ground. He was on a horrid batter altogether. There was no holdin' him. He'd drunk so much Reilly was nearly out of porter.

They crowded closer round the door when O'Shea started singing.

At the siege of Ross did my father fall
And at Gorey my loving brothers all
I alone am left of my name and race
I will go to Wexford and take their place . . .

His voice was a fine and deep one. The notes rose from his belly well rounded and washed in stout. He had a big face but a small mouth. Especially when he sang. Then the opening in his lips was no bigger than a shilling. Yet the words soared round the pub and out into the street like pigeons escaping into the wood.

A verse or two before the Croppy Boy met his shocked end, he somehow exited Wexford to emerge seamlessly in completely different territory — where he had no bags and baggage to slow him down.

A Cliff Richard number.

The man who bought the matches, annoyed, whispered loudly to the others, 'Ah, he's made a bags of it.'

O'Shea and his wife sang every year in the village concert. Their party piece was a sweet rattle through 'Ave Maria', 'The Stone Outside Dan Murphy's Door' and 'The Boys Of Wexford'.

'Yes, I'd stand in the snow listening to the pair of them,' the boy's mother always said on the way home.

★ ★ ★

All day he was in a tangle of emotions, keeping an eye on O'Shea in Reilly's, looking after the children and praying Mrs O'Shea would return soon. The children were golden. They spent most of the day laughing, playing and searching for sweets.

At long last, their mother, having walked for

miles out of Cavan, got a lift home in a lorry. A cattle dealer dropped her right outside the house. The lorry was loaded with bawling beasts. Desperate dripping mouths stuck out from a lengthy gap made by a missing plank.

The children flocked round her like excited puppies, tugging, embracing, gripping her hands, clinging, holding the baby up to her face. She gave them the gobstoppers. They didn't have a care in the world. She removed one of her shoes. A heel had come off.

'Where is Mister O'Shea?'

'In the pub.'

She smiled and went inside.

He called after her. 'I'll go now, Mrs O'Shea.'

She stood down the hallway. Looking sad, apprehensive, fatalistic. Like all women with raging men — accepting. But somehow content. There would be no surprises. Sad-looking women looked beautiful. Like statues of the Blessed Virgin. They knew the folly of the world.

'Your dad is a good man. Only for him. I've bought a house. We won't be on the side of the road anyhow.'

His father had planned the cheque business. He went home. His mother was delighted. His father came into the kitchen. He was smiling his shy, boyish, pleased smile. He always smiled like that when he achieved something of which he was proud.

They had tea and then he told his parents he was going to Reilly's. To see the lie of the land and to earn a few bob.

O'Shea was crouched over at the bar, nursing

his latest bottle. He didn't seem to notice him. He was growling to himself.

'I've got a thirst on me I wouldn't swap for a bag of gold. And I don't care who knows it.'

The boy cleared the bottles and wiped down the counter.

'She thinks she's pulled a fast one, hah? You wait. I've bet better men than The Bully Barry. Think I'm afraid of him? He's a bully, that's all he is. A bully. All them days I put in. All them nights in the pissin' rain. Am I a dog? At every pipsqueak's beck and call. I arrested more criminals than the whole lot of them put together. The Sergeant? Hah! I was never a novena man. Holy Hour of a Sunday man, yes Father, no Father, forgive me all my sins. Ruined me feet tramping the country to keep them safe in their beds. If you said boo they'd threaten to send you to the arsehole of nowhere. They'd put the block on you. The rotten bastards. I was proud to wear the uniform. She's landed me right in it. My money. Did I earn it or didn't I? Where the hell did she go?'

He shouted for two eggs. It was a half-hearted cry. The door opened and Chisholm came in. O'Shea glanced at him but didn't seem to register who it was. Or if he did he didn't care. Chisholm sat along the bar and ordered a bottle.

The boy held the neck up to the corkscrew and pulled down the handle. He smoothly poured the porter into a glass. The colour of bog water.

'Shot out once. Burnt out twice.'

'I'll shoot yah. I'll fuckin' shoot yah. For what

55

you did to me the other day. I'll just . . . shoot yah.'

Chisholm's horse, tethered outside, looked in the window.

O'Shea got to his feet and, puffing his cheeks in and out, made for the door.

'We'll see now what she's got to say for herself.'

He followed him out and watched as he crossed over to the village green, where a boy happened to be playing with a rugby ball. The boy was on holiday from Enniskillen and was staying with his sister. Only a Protestant would have a rugby ball.

O'Shea laughed when the boy kicked it high into the air, and when it came down and bounced near him, he lurched towards it. Falling down on all fours, he crawled around laughing. The ball was about five yards from him. Still on his knees, he scrambled to it and lay on it, like he was hatching it. The boy was afraid to go near him. Getting to his feet, he steadied himself, gave it a crooked kick and once more fell over. He rolled on the ground laughing, then stopped and sobbed once or twice. On his back, he furiously kicked his legs in the air and waved his arms in anger.

Villagers watched, horrified. They'd seen much, but never a policeman in full uniform cavorting round the green like an upended demented cockroach. Or like a horse who, released into a field after a hard day between the shafts, gallops down the meadow and enjoying the sense of freedom rolls around on the grass kicking his heels.

'Guard O'Shea, can I help you?'

'No Guard no longer. Little twister. Yes, you, you were part of it.'

He hated being called a twister.

'Your wife is back home now.'

★ ★ ★

A few days later a cattle lorry pulled up outside O'Shea's. It was the lorry in which Mrs O'Shea got the lift the day she bought the house in Cavan town. The owner had washed the cattle dung out and spread straw on the floor.

The boy helped them load up their belongings. Chairs, tables, beds were hard things to pack. Anything with legs. The last items loaded were a gramophone with a big horn loudspeaker and the pram. They put the gramophone into the pram.

O'Shea got in beside the driver. Between his boots he gripped a last bucket of water from the spring well. Mrs O'Shea and the children were driven away by Tully. His car was just about big enough to squash them all in.

That evening when they were having their tea, his parents were subdued. His mother would miss Mrs O'Shea. She'd miss the children especially. The village was already a quieter place.

'Well, you got rid of him at last.' There were tears in her eyes.

'He had to go. Half the time he was a disgrace to the uniform.'

His father thought by the book, acted by the book. Serving your country, there was no time

57

for sentiment. The country had been carved out of the bodies of men.

★ ★ ★

A fortnight later Butlershill played a match in Breffni Park in Cavan town. He was selected to play in goal. After the game, muddy boots in hand, he wandered down the town, looking to buy an ice cream. He came across O'Shea pushing a handcart. He was trying to get it up Doonan Hill. Way up to where they now lived. The cart had two shafts, two stout wooden legs and two spoked wheels with iron rims. On it was a massive oak dresser with a mirror. And a television set as big as an armchair. O'Shea looked strange in ordinary clothes. He was wearing a cloth cap, an unbuttoned shabby gabardine coat, grey trousers and sandals. He didn't look half the man without his uniform. Even his belly looked shrunken. The boy crossed the street.

'Mr O'Shea.'

He didn't answer. He was puffing and perspiring, his face a vivid red blotched with blue. His eyes were sad, angry, puzzled. Somehow, it was a betrayal, the end of his days.

He helped him push the cart up the hill. It wasn't easy. The dresser was bigger than a double bed and much heavier. It was tied crudely on to the cart with ropes. As was the television.

The hill was so steep, the further they went the harder they had to push.

58

He edged the cart into the gutter kerb, where it came to a stop. O'Shea was looking in need of a breather.

Leaning heavily on the shafts, he stared long and hard up the hill. Smoke came out of the chimney right at the very top.

'Never have your boot off their arses, except when you're swinging it.'

Eventually, they started pushing the load again.

Keegan

Word spread quickly: Guard Keegan had a girl-friend. She was from Belturbet. Butlershill was in the same parish as Belturbet, but they had little else in common. Belturbet was a town. It had twelve pubs, shops, a courthouse, a bank and the Erne Cinema. Its annual agricultural show was famous. To those who went to it. Duffy's Circus visited every year. The main street on top of the town was called the Diamond. The Erne River, brimming with trout, ran at the bottom of the hill. They had tourists every summer. Fishermen.

No one could say for certain who the girl was. But Guard Keegan was courting. And she was definitely from Belturbet. There was a dance in the cinema one night and he was seen slipping down to the riverside afterwards. There were benches there. There was a walkway along the riverbank. Men and women arranged to meet down there in the darkness. Daylight gossips could torpedo a relationship. Couples tried to keep their lives private until certain enough to face family and friend.

The dance was on a Sunday evening. By the Monday morning, people were talking. Farmers at the creamery talked of nothing else. Keegan was caught at last. Apparently nabbed by the Gaffney one in an old-time waltz. Nora Gaffney. She was good-looking. Despite walking with a slight stoop. She worked in the courthouse. Men referred to her as the Gaffney one.

The creamery was just across a small field from the Garda Station. Each morning a queue of farmers waited with their milk. A tangle of horses and carts, a few tractors and trailers, one pickup truck, backed right out on to the road. A few farmers walked it, carrying their milk in buckets.

Creamery cans were lifted on to a high platform. Before being emptied into the stainless-steel receiver, the milk was tested. The creamery manager took a sample from each can with a shiny dipper and poured the sample on to a steaming hot pipe. The dipper was shaped like a candle-snuffer. If the milk curdled, it was deemed sour and rejected. If fresh, the cans were emptied into the receiver, the milk inspected and weighed. A gallon of milk was just over ten pounds. Once released into the system the cream was separated, leaving the skim for the farmer to take home. The cream was three and a half per cent of the milk.

It could be a slow process. But the summer morning was warm. Another hour or two and mown hay would be dry enough to start turning. Guard Keegan and the Gaffney one would fill the time. How the hell did she nab him? Many's the woman failed. Keegan was a tricky hoor. He owned a black Volkswagen car. Women liked a man with a car. That was a fact.

The creamery ritual was as good as Sunday Mass for meeting friends and hearing scandal. The farmers shouted and laughed. The creamery manager shouted and swore and fought with those who refused to accept their milk had failed the test.

Chisholm Flood and his brother, Squealer, collected milk for various neighbours. They were paid one penny a can. The milk was left out at the end of a lane or on the side of the road. The creamery was shut on Sundays. If the cans weren't left standing in the cool of a river or a spring well, come Monday, if the weather was humid, the milk could have turned sour. For the moment talk of Guard Keegan and the Gaffney one ceased. Jim Dolan, the manager, had just rejected Chisholm's milk. Chisholm started roaring. His brother, who rarely spoke, squealed his support. He sounded like a stuck pig. It had the makings of a royal row.

The boy found himself in the middle of it. His mother had sent him over with a jug to get cream. For after-dinner dessert she was making a rhubarb pie. A jug of cream was half a crown. He had gone up the steps of the high concrete platform on which the farmers placed their cans. He had a perfect view of both inside and outside the creamery. He was so close to Chisholm, he could see his spittle spattering the manager.

'Yah quilt yah, Dolan, don't try that one on me. There's not a hate wrong with that milk. I'll fuckin' shoot yah.'

His brother squealed agreement: 'Eek. Agh. Eekek. Squee. Agh. Eek.'

'Shut your mouth you unless you've something to say.'

'Don't talk to me brother like tha'. Yah feckin'

runt yah. Are yah akcep'in' this milk or not?'

'Are you blind, man? Look. Curdling. Sour as be damned.'

The sample poured on the hot pipe trembled, wrinkled, looked dead and flaky.

'It's sour, okay, Chisholm.'

'Who the fuck is aksin you? You shouldn't even be up here. Go home to Hell where you belong. Fuck you and your oul fellah. An' all the other big boots as well.'

Chisholm's face was a raging fire of emotions.

Dolan took the lid off the last can.

'Oh, Jesus, what's this?'

A dead kitten floated on the top. Two snails as well. If the lid wasn't secured properly, cats could get in. Snails loved milk.

'It's only a cat. It could have been a rat.'

'Take these cans away to Hell, man. Before I call the Guards. Rotten. Every drop of it.'

Chisholm looked genuinely shocked at being rejected and threatened with the law. As if he was the victim of a grave injustice.

'Eek. Agh. Eekek. Squee-squee. Agh. No.'

'Shut up you, Squealer.'

'Don't talk to me brother the like a tha', I towl yah.'

Squealer had a head like a block of timber. It was said a schoolteacher broke his knuckles on it. His face was as big as a council shovel. He wore a dirty brown ragged gansey on his otherwise bare chest. His torn muddy trousers were held up by braces secured to the trousers with a safety pin and a nail. His wellingtons were sawn off at the ankles.

63

Dolan, the manager, though thoroughly disgusted, tried to be calm and reasonable.

'Come on, Chisholm, I deal with you the same way I deal with everyone. Fair is fair. Come on, away you go, sorry, has to be done. Rotten sour. A cat? Snails? All these men behind you are in a hurry. Now feck off like a good man.'

Chisholm looked at the cans for a moment before exploding into action. His brother helping him, he upended all seven cans, spilling every drop of milk out on to the platform. Farmers jumped back to avoid the white deluge splashing over the edge and down the steps on to the ground below.

Guard Keegan, BO for the day, heard the ensuing hullabaloo. Stepping out to see what it was all about, he went to the strands of wire separating the Garda station from the tiny field between it and the creamery. The field was owned by Lady Sarah but was known as the creamery field.

'Less of the bad language, it's too early for that carry-on,' he shouted, as much to the manager as to Chisholm.

'Did you see what he's only after doing?' Dolan shouted back.

'I'll do it again, only next time it'll be over you, yah hoor's melt. I'll shoot yah.'

'Hey, hey, that's enough. If you can't keep a civil tongue in your head, there's a cell here where you can cool off.'

'What's it got to do with you? Keep your snout to yourself and your hands off the Gaffney one. The Gaffneys are respectable people. You tried to

64

get the hand up last night. You were spotted. Dark and all as it was. Feck off before I wrap your windpipe round your knees.'

Squealer joined in.

'Eekughekeekekaghcksquee-squee.'

His hair was rust-coloured and in short tufts round his skull, as if it had been badly cut with a sheep shears. His cheekbones were hairy, and hairy sprouts grew from his ears. It looked as if he had eyebrows everywhere except over his eyes. It was said he could lift a pregnant sow clean off the ground.

Guard Keegan's face was naturally pale. But even from the creamery it could be seen to redden. Chisholm's onslaught had taken him by surprise. Keegan had a dangerous temper and for a moment ducked through the strands of wire to cross the field and confront Chisholm. His better judgement prevailed. Why make a fool of himself in front of all the farmers? Besides, regulations forbade a Barrack Orderly to desert his post. He retreated into the day room.

Already the creamery boilerman had begun slooshing down the platform steps with buckets of water. Chisholm flung the empty cans and lids into his cart and flapped at his piebald mare with the reins. Despite the shouting and swearing and being splashed with milk, she had remained, head down, placid throughout. Humble and indifferent to the angry voices.

Squealer shouted back at the manager, 'No neeneeneed forthatha like a-a-a-a don. Eek. Squee-squee.'

Chisholm whacked the horse's rump. The cart

65

lurching, his brother stumbled against the seat board, falling backwards to the floor amongst the empty cans, feet sticking up in the air. Dolan and the farmers cheered.

The boilerman filled the boy's jug with cream. It ran smooth as altar marble, soft as flesh. He went back across the small field to the married quarters. His father rented the field from Lady Sarah. He sowed corn. For the hens. It was a lot of work for a few bags of oats. It had to be reaped with a scythe. Brought up hard on a small farm in Galway, his father knew the value of land. Apart from investigating crime, he was only happy when his boots were walking on clay. Land was a way to get even with the past.

The corn was up to his waist. It was turning gold. It was alive with bees, moths, spiders, red beetles, pigeons, finches.

The day-room window was open. He stuck his head in.

Keegan was reading a book.

'What's the book?'

'*Crime and Punishment.* I thought it was a whodunnit.'

'What is it, law?'

'It's Russian. Doctor Evski. The names are a curse. You're in trouble, boyo.'

He didn't know why but he felt instantly guilty. In a Garda station guilt was oxygen.

'You've been picked to play on Sunday. You'll be playing alongside me. I've bet five pounds with 'The Whin Man' McNally I'll score a goal against him. He's only got one arm.'

They were playing Drung, a neighbouring parish.

'How can he play with only one arm?'

'He catches the ball one-handed. He hits you a box on the back of the head first, then grabs it. He lost it in a sawmill. You better not let me down. A fiver. It was him gave me this book. I caught him driving a car. He steadies the wheel between his knees and changes gear with the one hand.'

Keegan was a strong man. He played football like it was rugby. He flung men around as if they were rag dolls. It would be mayhem with The Whin Man.

'Why is he called that? Whin Man?'

'He can pull a whin out by the roots with his one hand.'

He'd have to keep out of his way. And Keegan's way. He could get crushed between them.

'What about the Gaffney one? Is it true?'

Keegan hadn't taken his eyes from the book all the time he'd been talking to him. But now he did. His eyes were pale blue, unblinking. His face was pale, his hands were pale. Except the nail on his right index finger. That was black.

'I don't pry into your private affairs.'

The tone was narrow, curdling. Sour.

'If only I had private affairs. I was just going to ask . . . . How do you do it? Like, how do you get the hand up?'

The book closed around his deep dividing black-nailed finger. He came to the sash window and bent to him.

'The term 'the Gaffney one'. It's demeaning of the person concerned. Nora is her name. Do

67

people ridicule her just because she's got a hump?'

'Ah . . . I . . . I was just . . . like, wondering, what do you do with your hand, if, when, you actually do manage to get it . . . up?'

'Get your hand up to the ball on Sunday. And pass it to me. That's all you've got to worry about, boyo.'

'Right, sorry.'

★ ★ ★

His mother was waiting for him.

'Guard Keegan has a girlfriend.'

She was pleased. She liked Keegan. She hoped he would settle down with a nice girl. He was an intelligent man with a college education and had seemed set for a great career in the Garda, having passed the sergeant's exam before his thirtieth birthday. Initially stationed over in the West of Ireland, he had made enough of an impression to be posted to the Midlands, not far from Dublin, and the future had looked bright. He was a certainty to be promoted up the ranks.

Then he hit a superior. An Inspector. They took his stripes and transferred him to Butlershill.

His father wouldn't reveal the details. He was tight-lipped about official business. A secret spilled was an excuse for Headquarters to get revenge. Didn't matter for what. They'd invent something. Dublin was the 'Department of Spite'.

His father was tight with his own feelings too.

68

He showed little if any. There was anger. But was that the same as feelings? For a lot of the time, their lives were set rigid as a wheel frozen in ice. They were stuck. Waiting for a thaw.

His mother wanted to invite Keegan and Nora Gaffney to married quarters. To tea. That's what one did. The nuns in Gortnor Abbey had taught her the rules of happy domestic life. Include the courting couple in family life. Show them by example the warm normality awaiting.

His father wouldn't hear of it.

'It's much too soon for the like of that. Wait 'til it's a sure thing.'

★ ★ ★

He borrowed his father's bike and rode to Belturbet. He wanted to get a look at Nora Gaffney. He didn't quite know why. He wanted to see what Guard Keegan was grappling with. A man and a woman meet up and decide to spend the rest of their lives together. Why? You'd have to have a load in common to take such a risk.

He rode out the Border road and was careful not to put a strain on the gears going up hills. His father didn't want him to change gears at all. In case the cable snapped under pressure. He kept it in second, not daring to change to third. His father mending anything broken was to be avoided. Repairing shoes and boots, punctures, fixing frayed gear cable, replacing the shaft in a spade — they were all a curse, unfair. Unsafe. His big wooden workbox was a tangle of needles, knives, sparables, glue, chisels. Every item capable of exacting the bloody revenge of a malevolent fate. Even the glue. One time he managed to glue two needles together. Trying to separate them he pierced under his thumbnail. For the guts of an hour he bumped round the kitchen in howling agony.

'For goodness' sake, why don't you pay the cobbler to sole your boots?'

'That's the last thing I'd do.'

'The last is his life. It's only a few pence.'

'I'm glad you think money's so cheap.'

'You'd try the patience of a saint.'

'You have a big opinion of yourself.'

'I never said I was a saint. And you certainly aren't.'

His parents usually bantered their way back to calm.

When he reached Belturbet he walked up the steep hill to the Diamond. The courthouse commanded the view. He sat on the steps whilst holding the bicycle upright, fiddling with the gears, pretending there was something the matter. Nora Gaffney worked for a solicitor. She was sure to come out for her lunch or maybe with letters for the post office across the way. Six streets led into the Diamond. Heart and hub of the town, it was an attraction in itself. The sun shone, the steps were warm, a mongrel and his shadow nosed along the cobbled gutter. He shooed it when it approached and lifted its leg against the back tyre. A hefty tinker woman emerged from a shop. She had a massive posterior and matching bosom. Her skirts and shawl were all the colours of the rainbow, plus black.

'Lave him alone. He won't bite ye, so he won't.'

She waddled down Bridge Street, the dog at her heels. Men's hobnailed boots.

A man emerged from a pub. He walked into the middle of the Diamond, forcing a car to stop. Putting his cap down, he stood back a few yards, paused, then went head over heels on the road, judging it so perfectly, his head ended up in the cap. The driver, as he steered past, beeped the horn by way of applause.

The man turned towards the boy, grinning, a cigarette between his teeth. With a twitch of his lips the cigarette vanished into his mouth. Smoke came out his nostrils.

He laughed at his antics.

'Are you a clown?'

'Aye. One night only like Duffy's Circus. Tumbling the wildcat, that's me.'

Laughing eyes, carefree of concerns. Dusting his tartan cap against his arm, he followed the tinker woman down towards the river. His frame was lithe and light. Agile on his quick feet in white plimsolls. Canvas trousers.

A young woman with a parcel and brown envelopes came out of the courthouse and crossed over to the post office. He hadn't heard her coming. He only saw her back. She had a stoop. The Gaffney one. Had to be. Nora Gaffney. She wore low shoes and a black tight skirt with a kick pleat.

He'd get a full look at her when she came back. The post office was a brick building with the date 1904 AD raised in stone above the door.

71

The town was founded in 1613 by Planters, under a charter from King James. The natives — quagners, gudgeons, Papists, Sabbath-breakers — took centuries to come into their own. Quagners lived on quagmires. Bog trotters. The Red Bog was still being worked. He helped his father cut turf there.

History was great but did it give you a clue what to say to a woman you'd never met before?

She emerged into the sunlit Diamond, pausing to let a cattle dealer pass. He had his stick across his shoulder blades, held in place either end by his big fists. It exaggerated the size of his chest and gave him a stiff, swaggering walk. He said something to Miss Gaffney. Whatever it was, she shot away from him and walked in close to the walls of the shop buildings. The stoop added to the furtiveness of her scurrying steps. Before crossing over, she waited on the edge of the pavement for a horse and cart to rattle past. Her hair was blonde, her face sharp, attractive.

He bent to his front wheel as if examining it for a puncture. She was approaching. He had to say something. But what?

She glanced at him, face cocked sideways, as she reached the steps.

'My mother would like to invite you and Guard Keegan to tea.'

She stopped on the top step, surprised and suspicious. Was he being smart or in earnest? She had no idea who he was.

'What's your mother's name?'

'Mammy.'

Momentarily startled, she laughed outright.

Then seeing his serious face, she looked kindly at him, before turning away in the big doors of the courthouse.

He jumped on the bike and rode like hell out of the town. He'd made a complete fool of himself.

She was bound to tell Keegan. He'd be accused of putting his nose in where it wasn't wanted. Why had he done it? To find out what it was she had that Keegan wanted? He surely wouldn't have ridden all the way to Belturbet just to see her hump? She was no Quasimodo. Or Richard III. It was a stoop more than a hump. When Keegan found out he was quite likely to clatter him.

Coming past the Leggykelly pub, the gear cable snapped. He was booting along in top and it couldn't take the strain. He had to walk the rest of the way home. Out of Cavan into Fermanagh, out of Fermanagh into Cavan. The road was potholed, boggy, sunken, like it had been heaved by an earthquake. A strange unsolvable political equation of a road. Loved only by dandelion, haw and smugglers.

His father, when he saw the broken gears, sighed heavily and twitched his lips in a smile but didn't get angry until he went to repair the damage. He tried to rejoin the cable and when that didn't work, his blunt hands blundered into spasms of awkwardness, until his spirits and temper snapped and frayed like the cable itself.

'Didn't I tell you not to change the bleddy thing from second?'

'I'm sorry, Daddy.'

'You are in me hat.'

Everything about the old Rudge was heavy. The chain was encased, the frame stout, the saddle leather underpinned by big grunting spring coils. The wheels were strong enough to withstand sacks of flour, turf or potatoes carried on the bar. In fact it was like his father. Indestructible. He nicknamed it his 'Tin Lizzie'. The gears, though, were like his father's heart. Delicate, moody, sensitive to pressure, afraid of the Cavan hills.

★　★　★

He avoided Guard Keegan until the football match on the Sunday.

They togged out in a hayshed across the road from the pitch. Keegan stripped to his underpants and executed some squats and arm-winding exercises, puffing his cheeks in and out as he did so. His chest and back were hairy black. His skin was white as snow. Well over six foot, he was carved out of Nature like a Roman soldier in the Stations of the Cross. The rest of the team dodged about the shed half shy of their bodies. Most of them were butty, with gnarled knees and legs like lumps of bog oak. One of them wore a scapular under his jersey. He adjusted it on his breast and up his back with one hand, as he blessed himself with the other.

Their captain and trainer, 'Stumps' Gargan, came in, followed by the referee. Stumps had ridden on his bike from Dublin, where he worked in a pub. Eighty miles. He announced that the referee, having forgotten his watch, needed to borrow one. Keegan gave him a loan of his. It was supposed to be gold, won in a seven-a-side tournament the previous summer. A set of watches was a prize worth the winning.

A blue-and-yellow striped tie hung from a wooden peg sticking out of the shed wall. The peg in previous days was used for hanging up a horse collar. The tie had been there since 1947. The owner had forgotten it after a match. He emigrated to America and had been killed working on the railways. The tie was his memorial. No one mentioned his name but everyone glanced at it before leaving the dressing room. The pious ones mumbled a prayer.

They crossed the road outside the shed and entered the field. A large crowd had gathered. Playing Drung was the match of the year. Drung were already out kicking about at the far end of the sloping field. They'd changed along the hedge. The field was covered in rushes and ragwort but most of the playing area had been mown. Six cows grazed behind one of the goals until they were shooed away. Most of the crowd had come on bicycles. The bikes lay tangled in confused piles, pedals through spokes, handlebars locked in confusion.

Keegan grabbed him by the back of the neck.

'Mind your own cork. Nora Gaffney phoned me.'

'I'm sorry. I don't know what made me do it. I'm sorry, Guard Keegan.'

'The name's Ted. When we're playing football. Grow up. Pass me the ball. If you get it. Now feck off and don't get in my way.'

The referee blew his whistle. The teams lined up; the ball was thrown in. Keegan jumped high for it and broke towards the Drung goal.

He ran into his corner-forward position and waited for Keegan to kick the ball in to him. When he did, he ran towards it — it bounced perfectly in front of him. As soon as he grabbed it, he was slapped so hard on the ribcage by The Whin Man McNally, he dropped the ball and sunk winded to the boggy ground. He stared at the soft brown earth. So soft he could have dug his own grave by hand. One arm of McNally's jersey was tied up in a knot. Like a stallion's tail.

'Get up outa that,' Keegan shouted, 'and go and mark your man.'

His 'man' was a youth like himself, another college boy.

Keegan and McNally stood shoulder to shoulder. If the ball came anywhere near them, they blocked, dragged, swung out of each other, grinding their teeth with effort. The first time the ball came in really high, as they jumped for it The Whin Man hit Keegan on the back of the neck with his fist and, to the cheers of his supporters, hoofed the ball about sixty yards down the field.

They were a carnival of bone and boot clashing over a capricious bag of wind. As well as the strength of contending bulls, they had the humour of clowns playing to the gallery. The spectators laughed, cheered, urged them on. Everyone knew about the five-pound bet. A fiver was a week's wage. It added great spice to the game.

76

Just before half-time he managed to get his hands on the ball. Side-stepping his marker he raced towards the goal. As he was about to shoot, The Whin Man made a drive at him but he slipped the ball to Keegan. Keegan joyfully buried it.

Mayhem instantly erupted. McNally ran to the referee, claiming Keegan had pushed him in the back. The other players crowded round and soon opposing spectators invaded the pitch. Chisholm Flood and Squealer were in the thick of it. Chisholm especially loved a fight at a game. A scatterin' match, he called it. Players and people were bound in a revolving wheel of flailing limbs. So close to each other, arms and fists blurring like spokes, they moved round the centre of the pitch in a tangled colourful circle. Squealer rapped men on top of their heads with his knuckles. His own supporters as well as the opposition's. Somewhere in the middle of it all, the referee, furiously blowing his whistle, tried to restore order. The Whin Man, his one arm whirring like a propeller, tried to land a blow on Keegan. Keegan ducked and countered with a jab, just as the referee stuck his arm out between them, trying to separate them. Keegan's blow landed on the ref's wrist, smashing his own watch to pieces. The gold watch he'd won in the seven-a-side tournament. He let out such a roar of grief and fury the spectators, scared, scattered back and the melee ceased. Apart from a few torn shirts and jackets, not much damage had been done. It had been an enjoyable interlude.

Keegan couldn't blame the ref. He himself

had caused the damage. The ref ruled his goal legitimate but the fiver he won wouldn't compensate. Made in Switzerland. Magnetic. Waterproof. Most of it now lying in bits all over the cog-marked ground. It wasn't the gold; it was the winning of it. It wasn't real gold. It didn't matter. It was a symbol of triumph. It shone brighter than the silver sergeant's stripes they stripped from him when they demoted him for hitting the inspector. The watch had stood for part and proof of his worth.

The ref blew for half-time. They sat in the hayshed eating blood oranges. They were happy; they were winning. Keegan took his jersey off and, bunched in his hand, used it as a towel to wipe the sweat from his chest and face.

'I'm having no luck at all,' he said.

They sensed he wasn't only talking about football. His body was pale, defined, like a sculpture in a museum. His head was noble, erect. Like a handsome boxer posing before a fight. His eyes were cold, blue, sad. He kept his own counsel, not joining in the boasting and banter. He wasn't one of them. He was from away down South. His teammates, who had gone to school together, grown up together, had accents completely different and their peeling skins were a mixture of red and brown from working at the turf and hay.

He left them to it and went back out. He wanted a few minutes on his own. To psych himself up.

A spectator shouted encouragement: 'Good cawdee, keep at it.'

The fellow marking him ambled away from his mates huddled along the hedge and came to him. He had finished college and was in his first year at university.

'What's it like?'

'Ah the best. Going to the pictures. Horsing about. And reading oul books. I'm doing law.'

There were few books at home. His father didn't read anything bar the *Irish Independent, The Wide World*, the *Reader's Digest* and the *Sacred Heart Messenger*. There was no library near them or a bookshop selling anything other than stuff for exams. You never saw anyone reading a novel. Only Keegan. And the latest one was thanks to The Whin Man McNally. And that because he thought it was a crime manual.

There were plenty young women watching the game. Football was an opportunity to see the cream of the parish stripped for action. Candidates for marriage could be marked down. The constantly encroaching crowd was kept off the pitch by a man with a stick, which he walloped against his wellington boot as he hurried up and down the sawdust sideline. The gesture was desperate and vaguely threatening.

'Get back the hell, get back there.'

There was a youngish woman sitting sideways on the carrier of her bicycle in a corner of the field. She was on her own. He'd never seen her before. It certainly wasn't Nora Gaffney.

His father wasn't at the game. He was in Dublin having a barium meal test on his stomach. He'd been feeling queasy lately. He'd eaten cheese which hadn't agreed with him.

'I find cheese binding.'

Having bombarded Headquarters with his anxieties, they summonsed him to hospital.

He was a hypochondriac. Like all sergeants. Food could often be criminal. Even the best of grub couldn't be trusted.

'Some germs can survive in boiling water. Look at all them creatures in hot African rivers.' *The Wide World* was full of lurid tales about man-eating animals and poisonous insects.

The game ended. Keegan gave him a shilling. He also gave him the Russian book.

He rode home but stopped under a plum tree and started reading. The front cover was missing and there were car registrations written in puce pencil inside the back. The story seemed to be about a student. On the bottom of a page Keegan had written, 'Jas. Collins, driving a car without insurance'.

The plums were dark red, plush. They wore a passionate breath on their skin which came away on your fingers.

★ ★ ★

His mother was always relaxed when his father was away. They didn't have dinner. They drank tea and ate a fry and homemade bread and afterwards a currant cake. And talked. She always returned to Mayo. It was more alive to her than the kitchen they sat in. It danced in her eyes brighter than the flames in the range. At boarding school in Gortnor Abbey. Swimming with her friends in Lough Conn. Memory was

80

misty and magical. It turned the black clouds blue. Mayo was an architecture more solid than the bungalow barracks.

'We loved when a foreign ship came up the Moy. The brown eyes of the sailors. They had come from a warmer world.'

'Did the life you had prepare you for this life?'

'Are you saying I pulled a short straw? Daddy is such a good man. I was lucky, I suppose. God wouldn't give us our cross if we couldn't carry it.'

She was tall, well built. Happy eyes open all hours for fun. He knew little of women but he knew to be gentle was the only thing. She sang Gilbert and Sullivan.

On a tree by a river a little tom tit
Sang willow tit willow tit willow . . .

She made jam in a big copper saucepan. He licked the wooden spoon. The sweetness was ingrained and would never be obliterated by time. Her soul was in her hands.

She told him to go round to the day room and tell Guard Keegan she wanted to see him.

When Keegan came to the door she said she wasn't going to take 'no' for an answer. He and his girlfriend were coming to tea the following Sunday and that was that.

'It's no trouble at all. I'm glad you're thinking of settling down. It's only right we introduce ourselves to the pair of you. Make her feel at home. Say you will, Ted, say you will.'

Keegan didn't want to hurt her feelings. He

accepted the invitation.

'You and your fiancée, Ted.'

'I wouldn't go as far as that.'

'No? Nora anyway. The Gaffneys are a lovely family. I met her mother in Lough Derg.'

Lough Derg. A penitential island where middle-aged women went to suffer for their sins and have respite from the difficulties of married life. It was also a popular place for younger women looking for husbands or asking God were they marrying the right man in the first place. They went around in their bare feet for the best part of three days, got little sleep and ate only dry toast or Lough Derg soup — hot water with salt and pepper. Despite the rain, his mother looked on it as a weekend holiday. A religious comedy. She never stopped laughing. People followed her about and tried to befriend her.

'Honest to God, every second person I met was married to a drunk, a gambler, a wife-beater or a hoor-master. If you ask me, the country is half cracked. Daddy's so good. He never once hit me.'

It was an astonishing thing to say. As if to hit your wife was a normal thing to do. He couldn't imagine being married. He didn't know the rules.

The coming visit of Keegan and the Gaffney one sent her into a domestic spin. He helped her with the dusting and polishing, the mopping of the lino, the shining of the hallway tiles, the reordering of the hat and coat stand, the polishing of the sewing machine, the cleaning of the dresser's glass doors. The removal of his

82

father's gardening boots from the sewing-machine treadle. He must have wiped the red globe of the Sacred Heart lamp ten times. When the wick burned, the glowing light looked a living thing. The draught in the room moved the flame as if something inside was breathing. When the oil ran out, it looked a shabby artefact. Like seeing up a magician's sleeve. It was his job to quickly refill the paraffin. Reality was unbearable. There wasn't a cobweb left in the house. He murdered spiders by the dozen.

There was an L-shaped lawn flanking married quarters and the day-room side of the squat square building. He cut the grass with the useless lawnmower but couldn't locate the rake in the tool shed. The shed was a dark confusion of tangled spades, shovels, forks, graips, a sledgehammer, saws, ropes, a pickaxe, a crowbar, a yard brush, dozens of broken wooden handles. He strung a rope across part of the lawn and managed to find the two tennis rackets and a ball. His mother was convinced Nora Gaffney could play tennis.

She'd played tennis at Gortnor Abbey and with his father had belonged to the tennis club in their previous station. But since she'd come to Butlershill she'd never hit a ball or gone for a swim despite the many local lakes. You played tennis with friends. She had no friends now. Her wings had been clipped. She was in a cage now. So was his father.

So was he.

His father still wasn't convinced inviting Keegan was a good idea. He wasn't sure either about how they were going to deal with a woman with a hump. He couldn't understand why Keegan would go out with such a person.

'Oh, catch yourself on, man. In Ballina there was a man who married a girl with one eye and a leg a good deal shorter than a walking stick.'

'She must have been wealthy.'

'People marry for love, you know. Keegan must see something in her. And she in him. That's how the world turns.'

She'd never give up on people. Every heart could give a push to the wheel.

'What's the point of expecting her to play tennis? And she with an impediment not conducive to either skill or mobility.'

'A slight stoop is no impediment to anything. You'd swear she was a camel the way you're talking.'

★　★　★

Keegan arrived on the appointed day at the appointed hour. He had a woman with him but it wasn't Nora Gaffney. When they came into the kitchen, his father looked her up and down, wondering what all the talk was about a hump. She manifestly didn't have a hump, a stoop, a crouch. She was on the small side but perfect in every way and good-looking. And smelling delightfully of perfume. And she had a gap between her two front teeth that gave her a singular appearance. It gave an edge to her smiling face. A friend at school told him women with front teeth like that were sexy as a

84

nanny-goat on a May morning. She was certainly a sight for sore eyes.

His mother was completely bamboozled as Keegan introduced her.

'This is Paula Cartwright. Paula, this is Bernard and Lizzie . . . and the boyo himself.'

They looked at him and laughed.

'I have to say there seems to have been some misunderstanding about . . . identities,' his completely puzzled mother said.

'Didn't I tell you you were jumping the gun?' His father was trying to be pragmatic but he was already nervously rubbing his knuckles.

'I never went out with Nora Gaffney. By mistake she asked me to dance one night. It was a Ladies' Choice. She meant to ask a different man. But he was taken up by another lady and rather than walk off the floor alone, she asked me. I obliged. The rumour spread. The fact is, me and Paula have been going out for weeks. Paula is from Cootehill.'

'Be the holy,' said his father, 'you're the cool customer. Sit down let ye, take the weight off your feet. You're very welcome, Paula.' His father liked her. The skirt, the jacket, the high heels, the pointed bosom, the gap in her shiny teeth.

When she told them she was Dr Cartwright's daughter, his mother was delightedly impressed. Smiling, fussing, she began to wet the tea. Her own brother was a doctor. Her face shone with excitement. She and Paula would have lots to talk about.

'Oh, Dr Cartwright, you don't say? Well now, imagine.'

Magically the table filled with salad — lettuce, scallions, tomatoes — 'That's all our own, Paula' — ham, beetroot — 'The beetroot is our own as well, Paula' — eggs . . .

'Are the eggs your own too?'

'No. The hens laid them.'

They looked at his deadpan face. Then laughed.

His mother finally plonked the gleaming cake stand on the table, a rhubarb pie and the good china jug brimming with fresh cream.

Keegan was wearing slacks, brown shoes, an open-necked white shirt and a Donegal tweed jacket. He couldn't connect him with the Keegan who wore a Garda uniform; the Keegan who was a savage on the football field. You could smell his Old Spice aftershave and the Brylcreem on his jet-black hair.

'What do you do yourself, Paula?' his father enquired.

'I'm a teacher.'

'Oh, good, grand. I often thought maybe I should have done the same thing myself. A teacher. Or a chiropodist.'

The boy and his mother exchanged looks. They'd never before heard him mention either. Whatever about him being let loose in a classroom, the thought of him being anywhere near a person's foot with a blade was just too funny. And horrific. Whenever he attended his own toenails and bunions, he invariably drew blood.

Keegan looked at him with a straight face. You could tell he was thinking the same thing as they were. So was Paula. A chiropodist? The Sergeant? Those big awkward hands . . . thumbs that could throttle a goose.

His father, nervous in social situations, was apt to say the most outrageous things but such was the simple way he said them, you couldn't doubt he was speaking true. He looked too handsome and far too straight to be fanciful.

Keegan bit into a scallion. Then he dipped the end into the salt cellar and bit again. His mother noticed and didn't approve. That's the way germs were spread. Paula noticed. Smiling, with the end of her knife she transferred salt from the cellar on to Keegan's plate.

Keegan paused in his chewing. His face darkened but then he smiled a lopsided smile.

His father was tucking into the beetroot. His lips were raddled. Like he'd cut himself shaving. As always, he ate with gusto. Food was revenge on a cruel history.

'Did you fetch Miss Cartwright in your car?' he asked Keegan.

'No. The Doc gave her a lift.'

'How will you get back, Paula? Ted is on duty this evening.'

'Oh for goodness' sake, O'Hay, she's only just got here.'

Who or what O'Hay was, he still had no idea. He knew where chiropodist came from. The Greek. *Cheir* — hand. *Podos* — foot. From hand to foot.

Paula's eyes were rarely off Keegan. Any time he looked at her she smiled, eager to please him.

The boy couldn't help looking at the gap in

her teeth. Then there were her pointy breasts. His mother's bosom was round as the breast of a clocken hen. Paula's were taut under her blouse. He thought of the warning on certain packaging: 'Handle with care'. He definitely could see the outline of her nipples. Like thimbles.

'Well, Ted, I'm so pleased you and Paula are here with us. You're a lovely couple. Who knows . . . '

She let the words dangle. Paula, pure as a saint, smiled demurely and looked at Keegan sideways and simpering. Keegan played with a knife. Then picked crumbs off the table-cloth. He looked at the wall by the window.

'Is that damp, Sarge?'

'Bedad it is. I think when they built the place they used sea sand.'

'It's an uphill job, Paula, it makes you not want to get good furniture. Mildew everywhere. At least we have electricity now.'

Keegan looked around at the other walls. He noticed the dresser, the sewing machine, the armchair with the big rip partly hidden by a cushion. The dangling lampshade and bulb. The old swan-necked tilley lamp was still on the wall over the table. Each item grew shabbier in his stare.

'When it's not your own house, why bother?' Paula said. 'I can understand.'

'Isn't that what I'm saying, Paula?'

'It won't be for always,' his father said defensively.

Keegan was in the full of his powers and had the air of someone who didn't have to care a straw for domesticity. He leaned back in his chair and cut himself another slice of rhubarb pie. He lifted a piece of it into his mouth with his knife. Everything he did was definite. He looked at Paula like she was a child.

'I don't think married quarters is my cup of tea,' he said.

Paula stopped smiling. His mother looked at him, her eyebrows raised.

'People don't know what they want until they've got it. Or lost it. Isn't that right, Paula?'

It was plain that, whatever her strengths were, Paula was no match for Keegan. She went very still every time he looked at her. As if wondering what his mood was now. She was younger than him too.

The Whin Man McNally could barely handle him; how could she?

He wanted to defend their humble sticks of furniture. They had the hidden added value given by his mother's hands. Surely Keegan could see that the cake stand, silvery and delicate, was a thing of beauty? Keegan didn't know the magical light they got from the tilley lamp before electricity came. He felt like telling them about it. A new mantle was drab and lifeless as a dress on a coathanger, but when transformed by methylated spirit, paraffin vapour and a matchstick, it turned into a hive ball of sighing light that hid the ugliness of things and painted the humdrum kitchen a creamy buttercup gold. Electric couldn't compare. The tilley would never be lit again. It would be taken down one day and thrown in the shed.

They sat in silence round the table. They were like characters in a play. All of whom had forgotten their lines. His mother looked to him, her sad eyes still open for business.

'Guard Keegan, how did you . . . actually . . . hit the Inspector? Why did you? He must have really hurt you to make you do it.'

Now everyone started talking at the same time. His mother was shocked. His father was angry. Paula was spluttering as she tried to gauge Keegan's reaction. Keegan himself slapped the table with his hand. Then he started laughing.

'It's none of your business,' his father said.

'None whatsoever,' his mother added.

'What a question,' Paula said, dusting down her pointy breasts.

'No one knows the real reason,' Keegan said, 'not even your father.'

Now the silence was so total they could hardly breathe. The air was frozen and crystal clear. It was like an icy morning out on the hills. When a great way off you could hear a beast break the rim of a frozen pothole with its hoof.

'Your dad only has the rough details. I hit him in a fit of temper whilst refusing to be disciplined.'

'There's nothing more to be said, Keegan.'

'There is, Sarge. He says to me, concerning a burglar in the area, 'With the help of God, we'll catch him.' 'I didn't think we had a member of the Force called God,' I says. 'If we did, he'd be better than Sherlock Holmes.' 'Don't blaspheme,' he says, his face red as a turkey cock, 'God will not be mocked.' 'You might get a terrible land one day when you discover there's no such thing as God,' I says. I knew him to be a right Holy Joe, you see. He ran across the day room and stuck his face right up close. I hit him a clatter.'

Paula's face drained like someone had pulled her inner plug. His father realised that Keegan was indeed even deeper than he appeared. Headquarters didn't put the bit about God in the reports. They probably took advice on it from a bishop.

'God protect us from all harm,' his mother said, her eyes raised to the yellow ceiling. He could tell she was pretending to be more shocked than she was. She knew religion where men were concerned: most of it was lip service. His father, though, believed and was afraid of every word. He never doubted there was a Hell and it was full of burning bodies. He never looked into a fire but he saw frying souls. And he definitely didn't want to join them. Paula was looking at Keegan, her lips trembling. She wasn't quite sure what he believed but she was afraid for him. For them both.

Keegan laughed and took another slice of pie.

'You're as tasty a cook as ever there was, missus. It was worth losing the stripes. Oh a real Holy Joe of an oul cod.'

Paula tugged down the end of her skirt and stared at the lino. His mother, a habit she had, rubbed the face of her gold watch with her little finger. His father had bought it for her on their honeymoon in London.

'Do you like Kathleen Ferrier, Paula? 'Blow

The Wind Southerly'.'

'My father likes her. If she ever comes to Ireland I'd love to see her.'

'She died six years ago.'

'Oh. Of course.' There was no of course about it. She had chanced her arm.

'A voice to make the Angels jealous. God gave her the notes and she sang them back to Him.'

His mother looked like Ferrier. A strong body, clear face, honest eyes, short hair. A slender upper lip shaped like a perfect bow.

'Sometimes I think Ireland is such a higgledy-piggledy amateur kind of a country, what do you think, Paula?'

They looked at her, wondering what she meant.

'I couldn't, for shame, show you the sitting room. You couldn't swing a mouse. Our suite of furniture doesn't fit. The fireplace is no bigger than a crow's nest. If this is the best the Board of Works can come up with, they must have been born in burrows and blind as well as stupid.'

Keegan stood up.

'Begad, missus, you must have got out on the wrong side this morning. Don't worry about it. None of us are here for ever.'

'Well, that's true,' his father said. 'A Garda station isn't a life sentence.'

'It only feels like one,' Keegan said.

Paula glanced at Keegan and laughed happily when she saw his pleased look.

'Come on, boyo, I'll give you a game of tennis.'

They went outside. Paula slipped her shoes off

and left them sitting prettily on a windowsill. She skipped across the mown grass and hung her jacket on a fence post.

'I'll play the two of you,' Keegan said.

'We've only got the two rackets.'

He served an easy underhand ball to Keegan, who whacked it so hard it soared skywards before coming down somewhere in the swamp way beyond the vegetable garden. It was too wet there and stinky to bother searching for it.

'Have you not got another ball?'

'No.'

Paula picked up some grass and threw it over Keegan's head, then ran away. He chased after her, caught her round the waist, lifted her up, swung her around before flopping her flat down on the ground like she was a rag doll. He'd seen him doing the same thing to footballers.

Her legs kicked up and he saw her suspenders and a fleshy spark of thigh.

Hearing the merry shrieks, his mother came out and standing on the doorstep watched as Keegan threw grass all over her hair and down the back of her blouse.

'Stop, Ted, stop it, you brute,' Paula shrieked excitedly.

Keegan hauled her up and gave her a slap on the bottom, then playfully ran away from her. Combing the grass out of her hair with her fingers, she said, 'I'll get you for that, mister.'

They went and leaned on the wall at the front and Paula lit a cigarette, took a puff and offered it to Keegan. He dragged the smoke deep into his lungs. They stared at the road. It lay between the grass verges the colour of a basking pike. Lady Sarah's demesne of trees and rolling hills was inside an eight-foot-high wall. Part of it was broken down by an age of ivy and children climbing over that spot to play among the Scotch pine or go fishing in the lake.

Paula slapped Keegan's wrist. He grabbed her hand and, squirm and twist as she might, she couldn't free herself. Keegan knew how to handle women. He pulled her tight to him, still holding her wrist and head on his chest. All she could do was look up into his face. He let her go. Paula Cartwright, it was plain, couldn't stay Keegan's hand.

She was a mixture. Saint and minx. And snared.

'I like your parents,' she said, 'they are good people.'

'I quite like them too.'

They laughed. He fetched her shoes and jacket. She wriggled into the high heels, briefly admiring her feet as she did so. Keegan stared at the empty road.

'You'd hate to end up in a life like this, though, wouldn't you?' he said, as if to himself.

They heard an engine approaching up the hill from the village. Keegan, immediately alert, went out into the road. It was Mr Tully in his hearse. Keegan stopped him with a raised hand. He was on his way to a removal in Cootehill.

'That's what I thought,' Keegan said, leaning in the driver's window. 'I got wind you were doing that particular death. Paula Cartwright here, Dr Cartwright's daughter, wants a lift home. I'm going on duty' — he pronounced it 'dooty'. 'Could you drop her in Cootehill like a good man?'

Tully looked out the driver's window. His coat, tie, hat, hearse were so black, his shirt and loose false teeth seemed extra white. He looked like a coot on dark water. Paula's face puckered, on the verge of tears. She stared angrily at Keegan. Surely he wasn't going to subject her to the indignity of a seat home in a hearse?

'In you get, darlin', ring me tomorrow.'

'A pleasure, Miss Cartwright,' Tully said, looking her up and down and liking what he saw. 'In you get, daughter. I'll have you home in two shakes of a lamb's tail.'

She had no choice but to get in beside him and sitting tense, staring straight ahead, was driven away. A whiff of perfume was all that was left of her. The boy wanted to run to her and say goodbye and touch her and say kind words but he was afraid of Keegan, afraid of his own emotions.

Was he going to get on his bike some day and ride all the way to Cootehill just to get another look at her? 'Catch yourself on,' he warned himself. Only eccentric bachelors did the like of that. He sensed he'd never see her again. The strange loneliness within him went deeper than the rings in an oak.

Keegan exhaled, his cheeks puffed as if blowing on a trumpet.

'What do you believe in, Ted?'

'Call me by my name on the football field, nowhere else. What do you mean — believe?'

'Well . . . God? Politics?'

'Believe one you might be a fool, believe the other and you're definitely an idiot.'

He cheerfully rubbed his hands together.

'Time for a quick gulper. Don't tell your oul fellah. I'll be back in a minute. I used to be called Sergeant Keegan one time.'

'Do you get the . . . hand . . . up, like, with Paula, Guard Keegan?'

He flinched, expecting a blow. Keegan smiled.

'You like her, don't you, boyo?'

Everyone called him boyo. Even the college principal.

Keegan headed for the village and Reilly's pub, a spring in his step. He watched him disappear down the hill.

A weather-beaten man on a crock of a bicycle approached. The brake blocks worn down, he stopped by dragging his boot along the road. He had a load of rolled-up posters tied on the carrier.

'We're Batty's Circus. We're coming next week. Stick that up for me, will you, like a good lad?'

He was wiry as a weed and with a hungry face. He wore a black beret and a blue-and-white striped knitted jersey under his jacket.

'We're a small family circus. We're not like Duffy's or Fossett's. They wouldn't come to a place like this. We've got a fierce gorilla. He nearly tore a woman in two last week in Gowna. Tell as many people as you can. All your friends.'

The poster was green with black print. 'BATTY'S FAMILY CIRCUS. CLOWNS.

ACROBATS. FIERCE GORILLA. BELLA GOLD STRONGEST WOMAN IN THE WORLD. ADMISSION 6d. Is. 2/6. Children half price.'

'We've got a contortionist who disappears up his own arse.'

'Go way?'

'No, I've only just got here.'

A tobacco pipe stuck up out of his boot.

'They can pick your pocket but they can't pick your boot.'

He jumped on his bike and rode down into the village. He was sure to meet Keegan.

He secured the poster to the creamery door. If the manager didn't remove it, all the farmers would see it next morning. Life in a circus must be tough, when you had to hide your pipe in your sock.

His mother was much exercised by Keegan and Paula. His father sat in the armchair reading the *Sunday Independent*.

'He doesn't give tuppence for Paula. Not two hoots. He no more cares about her than the Man in the Moon. The way he threw that grass over her. Upended her on the ground.'

Paula's suspenders were fantastic. Alive. The only other ones you'd see were hung out half hidden on clotheslines at the back of houses. A friend at college smuggled the *News of the World* in sometimes. You might see an advert for them there.

His father flapped the newspaper into readable shape.

'They didn't take the stripes off him for

nothing. If he doesn't shape up soon and pull himself together, I'll see to it he's on his way out of here or out of the job entirely.'

His father hadn't liked what he'd said about God, and his mother didn't like the rough familiar way he handled Paula. She couldn't stop protesting on her behalf.

'Tossed her up in the air, grass all over her. Her unmentionables fully on show for all the world to see. That's acting the animal altogether. And sending her home in a hearse? Oh, not tuppence.'

'Your cake with the caraway seeds was lovely, Mum.'

'Was it? Thanks. Dr Cartwright's daughter. She's too good for Keegan. Did you notice he couldn't relax at the table? He wanted to be out of here as soon as decently possible.'

'There's a bit of the corner-boy about him all right. Will he get his stripes back? I have me doots, as the Scotsman said.'

His Scotsman was never convincing but was a favourite saying of his father's.

Standing up and buttoning his tunic he then fiddled with his whistle and chain so it was in regulation order as per the *Garda Code:* 'Chain hooked to the shank of the second button . . . brought across horizontally and whistle placed in left-hand pocket.' Getting his cap from the back of the door, he headed out on patrol. He was only truly happy when walking the sub-district.

His mother was right about Keegan not relaxing in the kitchen. He didn't seem to relax anywhere. As if he had too much nervous energy and strength to be contained by drab domestic walls or a dark-blue uniform. He looked like a man born to captain a pirate ship. The ocean could contain him. Maybe a woman couldn't. His mother contained his father. Most of the time. His father wasn't one to relax in domestic situations. If he sat back and crossed his legs, a booted foot wagged continuously. He rarely removed his tunic. Sometimes when out on his bike, he'd dismount and, one hand on the saddle, the other on the handlebars, stare down at a river or into the distance at a lake. That was as relaxed as he got.

★   ★   ★

The following Saturday, as advertised, Batty's Circus rolled into the village. They had three horse-drawn caravans, a loaded horse-drawn wagon and a wagon with the bars of a cage painted on the sides. Diagonally across the bars were two black words — 'FIERCE GORILLA'. The horses were piebald, the paintwork on the wagons peeling. The men holding the reins were thin as the horses. A girl drove the gorilla wagon. She was brown and pretty with flashing eyes. Humans and animals looked tired and hungry. A beautiful white pony was tethered on a long rope to the rear of the gorilla wagon. A goat on a short rope was tied to the axle. There was a pothole in the middle of the road. The far wheels of each wagon hit it. As they clopped, clattered, rumbled past the Garda Station it started raining.

It rained so much, that evening's show was cancelled. It was announced there would be a matinee on the Sunday followed by the evening performance.

The village green turned quagmire. Hooves and feet churned up the ground and round every tethered horse the grass was mashed to a brown sludge. Potched, his father termed it. It reminded him of the smell when the men dug a fresh grave in the cemetery. In pouring rain the circus family hammered in poles and tent pegs and hauling on ropes managed to raise the big top which wasn't big at all. It was old, torn, patched brown canvas that let in as much water as it kept out. The crows in the big trees inside the demesne wall, subdued by the rain, made an occasional sardonic caw. As if they'd never witnessed such a strange human collection on the ancient village green.

No one had ever heard of them. Batty's. The very name was ridiculous. Keegan told his father they were from Kildare and hadn't two pennies to rub together. That much was obvious. They looked only a rung or two up from tramps and peddlers. Village children asked one of them what time the gorilla was going to be fed. They were told that 'Bertie' had been fed already. He ate a sack of bananas and was now asleep. He could be seen after the matinee for a penny. Adults tuppence. The circus men were thin but wiry and light on their feet, like boxers. Drinkers in Reilly's pub peeped out the window hoping for a look at the gorgeous girl. She obliged a few times going from caravan to caravan, her dainty bare feet trying to avoid the puddles. If the circus was as good a show as she was, it might be worth paying the admission price.

The village was soaking wet. The sky had turned wet pewter. The light dripped dark instead of bright. The tent looked bedraggled, sad, without a hint of magic. Sometimes when it rained like this, villagers feared it might never stop. The river at the bottom of the gardens began to slop and gurgle and race towards its meeting with the Finn.

That night as he lay in bed he could hear through the wall the phone ringing in the day room. Keegan answered it. He listened to him remonstrating with someone.

'It's only over if you want it that way. No worry to me.'

It had to be Paula Cartwright. The phone was slammed down. It rang again.

'Yes?'

He listened for a long time, as on the other side of the wall Keegan listened without saying a word. In the still raining darkness he could hear him eventually, wordlessly, putting the receiver this time gently down. At night a bed was brought into the day room and placed near the telephone. He heard Keegan's boots hitting the floor. The springs of the iron bed creaked under his weight. Soon he heard him snoring. Paula's heart was crushed. Relationships could change as quickly as the weather.

★   ★   ★

The next day Jim Reilly wanted him in the pub. He had to fill dozens of bottles, label them, crate them. He did it in a shed out the back. When he carried them into the bar, Keegan, in uniform, was having a drink. Being a Sunday afternoon the pub was shut. It was still raining. Keegan was alone in the pub, drinking and talking with Reilly. The Munster hurling final was on the wireless and he was going to listen to it.

'Did you read that book I gave you?'

'I did.'

'Jesus. You're a better man than me.'

'What do you think of the circus?'

'The fellah who owns it, he was in here a while ago. He's a respectable man, so he is. He's travelled the world. But had to come back to Ireland. He used to be a lion tamer. A lioness bit his hand off. Then a horse trampled on his foot.'

He slowly poured a bottle of Guinness into his glass. The one delicate action men had mastered.

'The policeman is stupid on purpose. He knows what he's doing. That's how he trapped your man.'

Keegan was talking about the Russian book.

Just before five o'clock he brought the last crate of stout in and told Jim Reilly he was going over to see the matinee. Despite the rain a good few children had gathered and some adults. An old woman had an umbrella up and a man sat with a copy of the *Anglo-Celt* on his head. You could hear the drips hitting the paper. Squealer Flood was there. He looked soaked to the skin.

The white pony burst into the ring, ran briskly around, stopped abruptly, turned and ran round the other way. The gorgeous girl, wearing a fluffy white tutu, entered and, running alongside, sprung on to its back. Then, arms outstretched for balance and applause, she stood on its back. She was light and graceful as the angel on top of a Christmas tree. She had to keep adjusting her feet as the pony cantered, its hooves churning up a perfect circle of mud. After a few circuits they left the ring. No one applauded. Apart from a young woman sitting on her own.

A limping elderly man, dressed in a red coat, top hat and jodhpur breeches and boots strode into the ring. He cracked a whip. Where his left hand should have been was a hook.

'Boys and girls, genties and ladlemen, welcome to Batty's Circus.'

A clown entered playing an accordion, a drum, cymbals, bells and a tin whistle. Wearing gigantic boots he padded round the ring splashing as much mud as he could on the children in the front row.

The gorgeous girl returned, this time wearing a sparkling leotard. The man with the newspaper on his head gave a wolf whistle. Swift as a spider she sped up a rope and carefully seated herself on a trapeze. It was only moderately daring, as the big top wasn't very high. Swinging over and back, a beautiful pendulum, her slippered feet hit a bulge of rain that had collected on the outside in a slack stretch of tent. The upended water ran free and down along the canvas in a furtive rush.

After hanging by her hands, her ankles, her teeth, she slid back down to earth and, though her dainty feet were in mud, gracefully bowed.

Across the other side of the ring, the woman sitting on her own applauded. He was sure he'd seen her before. She wore wellington boots and a white mackintosh. She had bluebells in her hair.

The ringmaster announced that Bertie the gorilla was about to enter.

'Boys and girls, genties and ladlemen, do not throw any nuts or bananas, as he gets very angry if they hit him. If you are kind to him, he will be kind to you. In fact he will shake your hand and let you stroke his head. Bertie has come all the way from Africa, so please, let's give him a big Irish welcome.'

The children clapped their hands as the gorilla bounded into the ring carrying a chair. He sat, scratched under his arms, grinned, produced a banana, munched at it skin and all, then balanced the chair on his chin. The children started booing. It was obvious Bertie was a man. He wore black trousers with a bit of rope for a tail. His long black hair was slicked down over his forehead and eyes, which didn't look at all believable. He wore a black tailcoat and on his feet crude clumps of brown fur. His grimacing was good and his 'uh-uh' grunting, but the children were furious. They had been sold a fierce gorilla and what they had was a silly human pretending. A girl threw a bullseye. Bertie caught it and stuck it in his mouth. A boy threw a lump of mud. Others joined in. Squealer Flood squealed in delight. The ringmaster cracked his whip and Bertie gambolled out of the ring to safety. As he exited, he cheekily raised one leg and wagged his rope tail.

The woman sitting on her own laughed. He knew he'd seen her before. It was the Gaffney one. Nora. She looked nice. What was she doing there? Why had she come from Belturbet on such a wet day?

People were trapped in a uniform of skin. Life was a penny with two heads. You could toss it all you wanted but it always came down the same. A circus was for the imagination. For a few moments watching a girl on a trapeze you could fly with her.

Bella, the strongest woman in Ireland, stomped in with a long plank. She wore a leopardskin outfit and tights and had leather bands on her wrists and a massive belt round her belly. Her bosom was nearly as big as a bag of hay. Her powerful muscular legs rubbed against each other. When she called for volunteers from the audience, two children jumped forward. She sat them on either end of a plank and easily raised them above her head. The more you looked at her, the more you noticed she was quite possibly a man. The bosom looked ridiculous and her dark face needed a shave. In Batty's Circus, nothing was as it seemed.

Keegan raised the entrance flap and stepped into the tent. With barely a glance at anyone, he stumbled straight into the middle of the ring. Still in his uniform, he was stocious. He'd never seen him in that state before. He could take a drink but was never a drunk. Bella, the strongest woman or quite possibly man in Ireland, fled. A Garda in the middle of the ring was either going to arrest her/him or someone else in the troupe.

Or he was deranged. Keegan, as if hypnotised by the big waddling retreating figure in tights, looked lost, robbed of action. Bemused, he swivelled and stared at the sparse audience. As if meeting them in a dream. His face was pale as whitewash. He flung his cap up at the trapeze. When it came down, the peak stuck like a blade into the mud. He didn't even wipe it as he placed it back on his head. He had been in Reilly's all afternoon, listening to the hurling match and drinking. The two children who had been raised up on the plank of wood, now abandoned, didn't know what to make of him. They held hands, frightened. The few grown-ups were scandalised. This was a disgrace. A Garda, maggoty drunk, in uniform, staggering about in the middle of a circus.

Pulling himself together, crouching slightly, stock-still, hands hanging down by his sides, puzzled, Keegan started singing.

How oft do my thoughts in their fancy take
    flight
To the home of my childhood away
To the days when each Patriot's vision
    seem'd bright
Ere I dream'd that those joys should decay
When my heart was as light as the wild
    winds that blow
Down the Mardyke through each elm tree
Where I sported and played 'neath each
    green leafy shade
On the banks of my own lovely Lee . . .

It was a song from his native county. They must have won the hurling match. He sang as if his head was full of pain, his eyes fixed on the tent above the trapeze. His tenor voice was a good one. Full of music, desperate longing. His back was to Nora Gaffney. Before he finished, she got up and seeing a loose flap of canvas, slipped out under it. Perhaps she had arranged to meet him. If so, she wasn't going to be disgraced. He stopped abruptly. Still as a statue he stared at the ground. He moved his right foot as if examining his shoe for mud. He walked slowly as if he was living out a nightmare.

Locals would inform the Sergeant. The Authorities in Dublin. He would never get his stripes back now. The circus folk peeped at him from their dressing area. They were afraid to go near him or stop him. He had invaded their space but, drunk or sober, he was a policeman and dangerous. There was no knowing what he'd do next. His eyes burning fiercely, he looked mad enough to tear the tent down. The ringmaster, parting the dressing-area flap with his hook, shouted, 'Boys and girls, ladies and gentlemen, there will now be an interval. This way, please, to see Bertie the gorilla.'

Keegan growled, cleared his throat and spat on the grass.

'We're all bloody gorillas,' he said quietly.

Seeing the boy sitting by the entrance, he made straight for him.

'Here, boyo, go over to Reilly's and get me a Spanish onion.'

He wanted the onion to kill the smell of the

alcohol. He would soon have to face the Sergeant. He was on duty at seven o'clock.

It was still raining. The sun was drowned. It was dark as winter. He knocked on Reilly's door.

'Guard Keegan wants a Spanish onion.'

'Holy Jesus. Wait 'til your father finds out.'

There was a bag of onions inside the door. Reilly gave him the biggest one he could get. He brought it over to Keegan, who straightaway ripped the peel off and, eyes watering, munched into it as if he were starving.

When he went home his father was on the phone. He rapped on the window when he saw him, beckoning him into the day room. Though he'd already been told about it — a busybody had phoned — he asked all about Keegan's shocking display. The boy didn't like telling him anything. He didn't want to add to Keegan's troubles.

'Chief Superintendent Barry is coming out first thing in the morning. So you may as well tell me the truth. He was drunk in uniform, yes? He did invade the circus, did he, yes?'

They went round to married quarters. His mother had the tea ready. She was upset about Keegan.

'Poor Ted. He'll surely be sacked, I suppose.'

'I didn't know you were so fond of him.'

His mother's eyes narrowed and she went silent.

Keegan was a loose horse. There was no way of knowing when he was going to kick his heels. But there was something sad about him. His mother definitely liked him, though she didn't like the way he treated Paula Cartwright.

'He's a fine man. There's so much good in him. If only he . . .'

'If ifs and ands made pots and pans, there'd be no need for tinkers.'

His father was looking forward to the inquest with The Bully Barry. They'd haul Keegan over the coals. He'd be eventually sacked or transferred. He was an utter disgrace to the uniform. If the white circus pony had burst into the day room, kicked the table over, chewed up the diary, then trotted off, it wouldn't have been more extraordinary than Keegan's entrance into the ring.

* * *

Next morning it was still raining as the circus left the village. The caravans had to be shouldered out of the muddy ruts on to the road. Mr Batty, stout as he was, sprung nimbly up on to the leading caravan and took the reins. The white pony had been loaded into the gorilla wagon. The goat was tied to the axle. As the horses moved off, the village children started booing. The gorgeous girl was the only one who looked at them. Her comrades, pretending not to hear the cruel jeers, stared straight ahead.

It was the poorest circus they'd ever seen. But for all that, when they'd gone, the village seemed even lonelier. The crows cawing in the big trees made a mournful racket as if they too were sad.

The white pony had imprinted a perfect muddy circle on the green. That was all they left behind.

The rickety procession of rumbling wagons hadn't passed the Garda Station when the rain stopped and the sun reappeared. Refreshed and glowing as if just back from a holiday by the sea.

The ivy on the demesne wall was greener than he'd never seen it. The trees glistened. The air was washed clean. The sky was an innocent duck-egg blue. Butlershill was as pretty as any village in the world.

Guard Keegan was nowhere to be seen. Four men usually slept in the dormitory room. But there were only three suitcases there. Gone. He had slipped away. He wasn't going to give them the satisfaction of a bureaucratic mauling. He had disappeared.

The boy racked his brains trying to understand why Keegan had done what he'd done. And how could he not want Paula Cartwright? Maybe the desperate soaking circus opened his eyes. He saw the reality of things. A burst spirit and the drink forced him to the edge of a world he finally knew wasn't for him. An existence that promised magic but gave you rain. Amazing. Magnificent. Truly a trapped gorilla. But now he'd escaped.

They knew so little about him. Brothers? Sisters? Parents still alive? Men were transferred to Butlershill and eventually they were moved on. They left behind them only tree rings in his soul.

They never saw Keegan again.

O'Keefe

When guard O'keefe first arrived his father was pleased.

'The great thing about him,' he said, 'is he doesn't drink.' He'd been stationed in Limerick but when the Troubles really got going along the Border, he was posted to Butlershill. IRA men from the South kept coming up to Cavan and Monaghan to blow up Customs and Excise posts in the Six Counties. If they could get a potshot at a policeman or a British soldier, so much the better. Their prime aim was to cause economic chaos. They lived in hiding among Republican sympathisers before crossing over into Fermanagh, Armagh, Tyrone to carry out their plans.

Butlershill, a station with a sergeant and two men, had been transformed into a busy frontline outpost with ten men at least, along with constant visits from Irish troops on reconnaissance.

The new Garda, excited at first at the prospect of chasing IRA men, soon realised that their only function was patrolling byroads and keeping alert for strangers with strange accents. Endless night-duty was a real penance.

'Yes,' said his father, 'he's a Pioneer. Doesn't touch a drop.'

Pioneers had taken the pledge never to taste alcohol. When he first arrived, O'Keefe wore civvies. Displayed on the lapel of his jacket was a

111

Pioneer pin. Josiah was his name but he told everyone his friends called him Josh.

He drove a black Model T Ford, which looked like a big box camera with wheels and was fifty years out of date. A pony tub-trap was as modern and more comfortable. He didn't care that it wasn't a flash Zephyr Zodiac like Jim Reilly's or a speedy V8 like Rinty Maguire's. He had the air of someone supremely satisfied in his own company.

O'Keefe was just about five foot nine inches — the minimum height for a Garda. At first he had been turned down because he was half an inch short of requirement. But so determined was he to prove them wrong, he did months of neck-stretching exercises and hanging from the branches of trees, before appealing the decision. He told Headquarters that the night before he did the original medical, he had had to sleep in the back of a car, resulting in him being 'kinked up' and not at his natural height. With the intercession of the local bishop, he persuaded them to measure him again.

Barefoot, standing against the stick in the Depot Hospital, when the guillotine dropped on his head, he was bang on the mark, to the amazement of the administrative staff who remembered him from the previous time and had him marked down as a troublemaker. His decent examination marks, his new height, a Diocesan push and he was over the line.

He had bested them.

The day he arrived, the boy helped him carry his belongings into the station dormitory. His father had arranged for him to sleep there with three other men. There was a hurling stick tied to his suitcase when he lifted it out from the back seat of the Model T.

'Do you play football, Guard O'Keefe?'

'I excel at all codes.'

'I'll tell the team about you. We need new players.'

'Are you the Sergeant's son?'

He had crinkly, thick yellow hair. His face had the look of a horse. Or a big sheep. His features appeared flattened. As if he had a nylon stocking dragged over his head. He walked with an urgent swagger.

After his mother got a glimpse of him she dubbed him 'Dallamullog', an Irish word for deception, delusion, hoodwink. It could be self-delusion or to hoodwink someone else.

'God help us, he looks like he's wearing a mask.'

She had a knack for nicknames. The steward in the demesne she called 'Thunder', because of his massive belly. It stuck. Occasionally even Lady Sarah referred to him as such. It was simpler than his real name — ex-Major Swithin Pokely.

* * *

O'Keefe's stout leather suitcase had been meticulously packed with freshly laundered shirts, ties, socks, vests, a pair of brown shoes and a pair of sandals. He had casual clothes and his uniform on separate hangers. When he hung

113

up his greatcoat, he meticulously picked a stray bit of cotton from the collar. When he fingered the lapel the boy noticed there was a tiny effigy of the Child of Prague on the inside. O'Keefe's mother must have sewn it there.

'Is there a railway station here, boyo?' he asked.

'It closed a few years ago. We got fourteen other stations though.'

'How do you mean?'

'In the chapel. Stations of the Cross.'

He grinned, then chuckled.

'Begob, you got me there all right.'

His suitcase had a label with the letters J.O'K. He sat on the iron bed and combed his thick yellow hair.

'Our body is the suitcase. Our brain is the contents. What do you think?'

'I'm not paid to think, boyo. Just to obey orders.'

He turned and looked out at the demesne wall, the rolling hills, the endless trees.

'I must have done something terrible in another life to be sent to a place the like of this.'

'What do you fear most?'

'You're a rare tulip, aren't you, boyo? All these questions.'

Picking at his comb, cleaning it, he flicked a bit of fluff from his fingers into the empty fireplace.

'Are you not afraid of getting shot? Up here along the Border.'

'The only thing I fear at all, I'll be honest with you, is a dream I keep dreaming. The woman who taught us when we were kids was a terrible cruel oul rip. I end up marrying her. Then I wake up.'

'In what way was she an oul rip?'

'I haven't time to be gasbagging with you. I have to introduce meself to your oul fellah.'

His hurley stick was leaning against the end of the bed. He picked it up and took a smooth swing at an imaginary ball.

'My wrist work is renowned.'

Everything he did was precise and everything he said was full of himself.

The dormitory was just a biggish room. It was never meant to sleep four men. Hooks were screwed into the walls from which they could hang their clothes. A long deep wooden shelf had been put up for personal effects. Flashlamps, cufflinks, shirt collars, shirt studs, playing cards, newspapers. Sometimes the men hid a copy of the *News of the World* under a *Sunday Independent*. His father didn't approve of England's gutter press. The *News of the World* was considered to be an occasion of sin.

'Ah, the new man.'

His father had come in. He and O'Keefe shook hands.

'You're very welcome. You've got a Model T Ford. I haven't seen one in a long time.'

'It's never gone out of fashion, Sergeant. If you know about mechanics.'

'I prefer the motorbike. Have you ever ridden one with a sidecar?'

This was another one of his father's extraordinary statements. From O'Keefe's blank look, it was obvious he had never ridden a motorbike with a sidecar and he wasn't prepared to show the slightest interest in anyone who had.

'What time do you want me to report for duty, Sarge?'

His father didn't like his sideways smile, his offhand tone bordering on the cynical.

'When my generation joined the Force, we did it to build a country. It's up to you younger ones to secure it. I'll see you at parade tomorrow morning. Nine a.m. Not a minute sooner nor a minute later.'

He said the same thing to all new men.

O'Keefe stared at him from under his blond eyebrows. The sideways smile reappeared.

The boy left them to it and went round to married quarters. His mother, the poker in her hand, was sitting by the range, staring into the fire.

'A penny for them.'

'I was just thinking, darlin'. If only I could win the Sweep-stake. Or pick the winner of the Grand National. I knew a man backed Tipperary Tim. I had a shilling each way on Cottage Rake. If you haven't got cash, you aren't free. Women aren't free anyway. Most of the men aren't that free either. Well, is Dallamullog settling in?'

'I don't know how he and Daddy are going to get on.'

She poked the lazy fire. Sparks briefly leapt up, a whisper of smoke sprouted, a blue-green flame came reluctantly to life. She kept staring at it. As if it might bring her good news. Behind them on the hill a straggle of hunters followed their baying hounds. The hill had never been tilled. The grass and rushes were scraws, the hedges impenetrable blackthorn and briar. A herd of cattle, frightened by the intrusion of dogs and men, retreated to the very top of the hill. They watched in a concerned clump, their heads stiffly erect, and when man and dog had all wriggled away through a gap down by the river, they stumbled back out into the middle of the field and with bovine apprehension stared after them. In the range, the wind blew a continuous sound like a cuckoo with one note.

'Did you get beaten much at school? It's just something Dallamullog said.'

'No child got beaten whose family had a bigger income than the teacher. No one dared touch us. Except Dada.'

★ ★ ★

On his very first Sunday in the village, O'Keefe lined out with the local team. During the week he'd met Stumps Gargan, the captain, Rinty Maguire, the club treasurer, and Jim Reilly, the club chairman, in Reilly's pub and convinced them that, though hurley was his game, he was a talented footballer and had played at senior level, unlike Butlershill who were only junior.

'If you can play as well as you can talk, you'll be just what's wanted,' Jim Reilly said.

Football affairs and other private matters were discussed in the bar backroom. It was a tiny space with a small square table and three forms against the walls. There was also a tall bar stool which Reilly sat on when holding court. In the aged and smoke-stained tongue-and-groove ceiling was a perfectly round hole and on the wooden floor directly beneath, a semicircle of burn marks on an old piece of lino. It was all that remained from a time when the room had a pot-bellied stove.

Sometimes his father used the room when meeting his Royal Ulster Constabulary equivalent from across the Border. They met late at night, slipping in the back door and out again on completion of their police business. Only Jim Reilly knew of these affairs of State.

'I've a preference for playing in the half-forwards,' O'Keefe said. 'Taking frees is my speciality.'

Reilly looked at him with a side of his mouth and one eyebrow raised. Rinty Maguire grinned into his glass of brandy. Neither of them spoke. Stumps Gargan was the best free-taker in that part of Cavan and they weren't prepared to concede that any polisman, especially one from Offaly, could hold a candle to him. Stumps had an honest open face. If someone came along better, he'd happily stand aside. The team had never won the Championship. Maybe O'Keefe could be the one to get them to the promised land. For Stumps, football was the metaphor for a life seldom lived.

The boy stood in the door listening to them. Reilly gave him a wink and he went and pulled a pint of stout. He let it settle until it wore a neck of froth smoother than a frog's belly. It made a pleasant thud on the small table when he placed it down in front of O'Keefe.

'I don't touch alcohol,' O'Keefe said, pointing at his Pioneer pin. 'Are youse blind? I remain to be convinced it's in any way conducive to a sporting life.'

The men looked at one another. O'Keefe, with his crinkly yellow hair and cunning sheep face, was as full of himself as a botfly on a horse's rump.

'Oh, sorry, I thought that was just for show,' Reilly said.

'Where's the game being played?'

Rinty Maguire told him it was in Belturbet and he'd give him a lift.

'I have my own car.'

Rinty laughed.

'The Model T yoke? You'd run faster pushing a pram.'

'Whatever you drive, I'll race you to Belturbet on Sunday.'

'You're on.'

'What do you drive?'

'A Ford V8.'

'Begar. You must be a smuggler or something.'

They laughed. But didn't comment. Maguire was the biggest smuggler along the Border. A mixture of rapparee, Dick Turpin and Robin Hood, he was the first name in every Customs and Excise notebook. Catching him with a load of razor blades, pigs, lengths of steel, apples, whiskey, cattle, flour, tea, sugar, butter or any one of a dozen other commodities was their dream. He even smuggled manure, bagged or natural. Their nightmare was his Ford V8. They drove Anglias or Prefects — only a few evolutionary steps beyond O'Keefe's Model T. Maguire was uncatchable. Even his pickup truck was faster.

A political border was as good as a gold mine. The only thing not worth smuggling, it was said, was dandruff. Everything else had a profit on one side or the other. The British-imposed Border guaranteed spite. A hatred bred in the bone. It stopped the free flow of relationships. It knotted souls, gnarled faces, twisted money. For a smuggler, twisted money was value plus. The Border land of Fermanagh and Cavan was a Spanish Main of opportunity and adventure. Rinty Maguire, as far as Customs were concerned, may as well have had a patch over one eye and a skull and crossbones flying from the roof. He was, however, a peaceful man operating on charm and with a smile and twinkle no misfortune could quench.

Life in Butlershill and its Northern counterpart, Butlers-town, was tight and controlled. Rome and Westminster ruled. People were so confined they might as well have been living in barrels. The staves couldn't be broken. The Free State was ruled from the confession box. The Six Counties from the barrel of a gun.

Night was a third jurisdiction. Rinty could drive in the dark. If he had to drive in daylight he usually found someone else to do it for him.

Smuggling and football were an escape from pulpit strictures. For the more serious-minded, there was the IRA.

'There's a snag about the game,' Jim Reilly said. 'Father Gaynor doesn't want us to play it. It clashes with Holy Hour. It's the Feast of the Assumption or something.'

Holy Hour was sixty minutes of guaranteed purgatorial boredom for the benefit of old ladies fearing death, and a handful of dragooned children. You went to Mass in the morning, Holy Hour after dinner, Evening Benediction after tea. It was a whole day spent beseeching God to beat the Devil out of Ireland and stop the Russians coming in.

To play a game of football on such a day was to challenge Father Gaynor's authority and tantamount to welcoming Satan and Joe Stalin into the parish.

'We'll tell him we'll come back and do the Benediction. The game is in the Championship. We can't not turn up.'

'Will he accept that?' O'Keefe asked.

'When they were rebuilding the chapel, I smuggled bags of nails, cement and an ojus pile of slates for him. Let him rant away to blazes.'

'Good enough so.'

Rinty drank the spare pint.

★　★　★

The boy walked home with O'Keefe. He was wearing white socks and sandals and a green and yellow summer shirt with short sleeves. It looked American.

'What does ojus mean?' O'Keefe asked him.

'It's a corruption of the Irish — 'o deas' meaning 'Oh, good'. Some people say it's from 'Oh, Jesus'.'

121

'Huh. Have you a girlfriend?'

'No.'

'Time you had a bit of a howlt, isn't it?'

As he strutted along, his sandals slapped the road and dislodged pebbles. There was only one stretch of tarred road. From outside the village up to the chapel.

'What's the women like round here?'

'The best of them are in Liverpool or Birmingham. Have you a girlfriend?'

'Getting them is no problem. Getting rid of them is.'

He rubbed his hands together vigorously as if looking forward to something.

'There's bound to be a dance somewhere on Sunday night. Do you want to come?'

He didn't answer him. He was ashamed. His father wouldn't let him go to a dance. He didn't like him listening to Radio Luxemburg. He didn't like him putting Brylcreem in his hair. He'd never tasted alcohol — despite helping Jim Reilly in the pub. The only time his parents ever went to the cinema was to see *The Robe* and *Quo Vadis*. The only pictures on the walls were religious and a copy of a photograph of Buda and one of Pest in Hungary. His father found them in the drawer of a wardrobe he'd bought at an auction. Their furniture was basic without style or taste and was little different from the furniture in most other houses.

'What's the point of buying anything better when we have to move eventually? When we have our own home, when we retire, then we'll have the best,' his mother said. He doubted it. The things around you shaped you.

He and O'Keefe went past the spring well by the Methodist chapel and up the slight hill to home.

'This hill is haunted.'

'What?' O'Keefe said, with a jerk of his head.

'At night sometimes there's a light. Like a carriage lamp with a candle burning inside. It floats over the ground about four foot up, and comes straight down the dead middle of the road. It stops then. For a few seconds. Then it veers off up that gap there.'

'Jesus,' O'Keefe said. 'Did you see it?'

'I was coming from the village one night with the milk. My blood froze, I'm not coddin' you.'

'What is it? Was someone murdered?'

'The gatehouse into the demesne — an old woman used live in it. When she ran out of sugar or tea, she'd come down the road to the Widow's house there, to borrow some. They say it was the light she carried. This stretch of the road always feels spooky. Can you feel it?'

'Jesus protect us,' O'Keefe said. 'This place would put the wind up you.'

He shivered and rubbed his hands together and when they reached the Garda Station went quickly into the dormitory.

The boy went round to married quarters. His mother was in her bedroom, sitting before the dressing table. Her bedroom suite was definitely the best thing they owned. The bed, the wardrobe and the dressing table were all of a kind — polished veneer. The dressing table had side drawers, a main drawer, hinged wing mirrors and the main mirror.

Stripped to her big black bra, she had been examining her breasts.

'I thought I felt lumps. But I don't think so. Don't look so worried, darling.'

She brushed her hair. On the back of the brush were hand-painted red roses.

He told her if anything ever happened to her, if she ever died, he'd die too. She laughed.

'It's going to happen one day.'

She moved one of the mirrors so it reflected the sky, a dim slash visible over the big hill at the back of the house.

'The sky seems so small here. The hills block it out. And the trees in the wood. Even the birds find it hard. I saw a grey crow this morning. It had to flap its wings so hard in the dead air.'

'I scared Dallamullog. I told him about the light.'

'You shouldn't have. Let him settle in first. He'll discover it for himself. If there's such a thing at all.'

Looking at her, sitting semi-naked, he wondered how he could get a girl and look at her in any other but a respectful way. How did you commit sin? How did you act the animal? The more you saw, the more the mystery. His mother didn't really believe in the supernatural. She'd never seen the light. Like he had. But she'd had a beloved sister who died young and who appeared to her in her dreams. What were dreams but another reality? The possibility of spirits made a hard life understandable. There just had to be something afterwards.

He looked out the window. In the little field between them and the creamery a big stone stuck out of the earth. It looked like an animal come up for air. Evening was falling on it. It was like a seal floating on a bed of clay. Maybe it too was dreaming. A sculptor could release stone soul.

'Poor Dallamullog. I bet he's a bit of a Holy Joe at the back of all his fancy footwork.'

His father would never admit the possibility of ghosts. He was terrified of them. He rarely swore. But when he first told him about the light, he said angrily, 'There's no such damn thing, have bloody sense, man.'

His father had to pin down the world as lived. Bicycles had to have lights at night. Cars had to have a licence. Donkeys had to have their hooves pared and shod. Men could not drink in a public house on a Sunday evening unless they lived more than three miles away. The three-card-trick was illegal. Robbery was a crime. Murder was a mortal sin in the eyes of the State and the Church. He had no time for anything else. He couldn't serve a summons on fairies, ghosts, banshees or IRA men. Because he couldn't catch them.

'The dead and buried don't move until the Last Day.'

★ ★ ★

Word spread quickly, as it always did when a new Guard arrived. Women found plenty of excuses to go to the village and walk slowly past the Garda Station hoping he might be outside taking a breather, reading the rain gauge or fixing a bicycle puncture.

The day of the match, every single woman left in the place turned up. Young and old. Girls for whom time was running out. Those who couldn't face the reality of a marriage like their mother's eventually emigrated. England was full of Irishmen. For those women still at home, a new man in the parish could be their saviour.

The team met up outside Reilly's. O'Keefe pulled up in his Model T. Everyone looked at it and hid their amusement.

O'Keefe had washed it for the occasion. Pools of light gathered on its shiny black surface. The spokes glistened. The inside smelled of polish. The grille at the front was spotless. The big round headlights gave it a human appearance.

Rinty Maguire, his laughing head stuck out the driver's window, pulled up alongside in his dusty V8.

'Are you ready, Guard?'

'All set,' O'Keefe replied.

'Rightio. First man on the Diamond in Belturbet. I'll give you a start. I won't follow until you've gone out over the railway bridge and I'll count to ten.'

'Anyone coming with me?'

None of the players moved. 'Boyo?'

He got in beside O'Keefe. On the back seat were his togs, socks and dubbined boots with laundered laces.

O'Keefe wore brown trousers with reddish lines and a yellow jumper. His thick wavy hair was as yellow as a sheaf of corn. His features were blunt and pale. Lips full, nostrils wide, cheekbones tough, eyes sleepy and piercing. He put his sandal down hard on the accelerator and sped between the thick green hedges. They shook, creaked, rattled like a horse-drawn hearse. Instead of going out on to the main Cavan-Fermanagh road, they shot into a farmyard and came to a stop behind a shed where a barking collie was chained.

O'Keefe sat still and didn't speak. It was obvious he was going to pretend he'd gotten to Belturbet before Rinty. Sure enough they heard the V8 shoot by and screech left on to the wide tarred road.

After a short while they drove out of the yard.

'He needn't think he's going to make a fool outa me.'

When they arrived at the football field, Maguire dismissed him with a laugh.

'We landed in the Diamond, you were nowhere to be seen, so we come on down here,' O'Keefe lied.

'Tell that to the Marines,' Rinty said. 'They'll believe you. I won't.'

'You didn't have the pleasure of passing me on the road anyway.'

O'Keefe, football boots in hand, socks and togs under his arm, strutted on to the field. By a blackthorn hedge, Stumps Gargan introduced him to the team.

'Don't worry,' Red Connolly said to him, 'you couldn't be any worse than the other fucken Guards we've had playin'.'

O'Keefe secured a net on his head to keep his

hair in place. Then he folded down the top of his togs so it looked like he was wearing a white rope round his waist.

The rest of the team exchanged looks. But they didn't say anything. This Guard might actually be good. Any man with such an opinion of himself had to be half decent.

The game commenced. Butlershill were awarded a fourteen-yard free. Right in front of the posts. Stumps, the regular free-taker, went to take the kick. O'Keefe baulked him. Stumps, his face a calm map of hard-earned experience — it was early in the game anyway — left him to it.

'I earned it,' O'Keefe pronounced. 'It was me that was fouled.'

They'd only been playing a few minutes and already his gleaming white togs were caked in cow dung. He'd been knocked over twice.

'Begod,' Red Connolly said to him, 'you'll catch the flu. You're lyin' more times than you're standin'.'

The referee placed the ball for the free, and O'Keefe stepped back and composed himself. Hairnet perfectly in place, hands out from his sides, fingers spread, he ran up to the ball and somehow managed to kick it about ten yards wide.

The supporters hooted and cheered. A Garda making a fool of himself was as good as a tonic. The moment would ignite memory for ever. A woman shouted, 'You should have put the hairnet over your foot.' Everyone laughed.

For the rest of the game he utterly failed to redeem himself.

The Sergeant, in mufti, was at the match. Standing alone, arms folded, he guffawed every time O'Keefe made a fool of himself.

After the game he was scathing. 'What an amadaun. A disgrace to the Force. You played well, though, I have to hand it to you.'

He didn't like his father watching him play. Every time he got the ball he could see him on the sideline going stiff with nerves. His father had ridden to the match on his bicycle. A good deal of his sub-district was on the way, so as well as observing his terrain, it kept him fit and whetted his appetite. Business and pleasure. When he arrived home the table would be laid, the tea wet and ready to be devoured; a big plate of salad, boiled ham, boiled eggs, home-baked bread and afterwards an apple pie. He'd then sit reading the *Sunday Independent*. World affairs gave him endless entertainment and pause for thought. Disputes over wills he liked best. Families fighting over poverty-stricken land. He'd been called to many's a home where brothers and sisters were at war over wet acres or thatched shacks. The repressed feelings often erupted in murder.

'What is world war but disputes over territory?! If we could take it with us I could understand. But the damn land buries us. Good God.'

Invariably he'd end up rolling the newspaper into a baton with which he'd swipe at flies. He usually missed first time. Inevitably they'd return to their assigned place of death, when he would hit them with force enough to knock a man.

129

Little black bodies lay on the tablecloth like bloodied bits of eyelash.

'Ah-hah, yah beggar. Gotcha!'

After the match the team hurried to get dressed. They had promised the priest they'd attend Benediction. The boy walked down the town with O'Keefe to the Model T, which was parked up a side street.

'Are you going to Benediction?'

'I'm going to a dance tonight. Why don't you come with me?'

'I wouldn't be let.'

'Come on, boyo, grow up. I'll show you how to get a girl.'

'How?'

'Pick a big fat one and ask her to dance. Then take her home in the car. She'll be pleased as Punch.'

'I haven't got a car.'

'Or ask a good-looking one. Tell them you're a solicitor. If it's a foxtrot, shift them round the floor quick as you can. Women love speed. Then ask her would she like to be driven home.'

'I still haven't got a car.'

Rinty Maguire stopped beside them.

'Don't get upset about it, Josh. You were too speedy for them. It's stickin' out a mile you're a born footballer. They didn't give you enough of the ball.'

Rinty smiled broadly and talked softly. He knew how to butter people up. O'Keefe was pleased with the flattery.

'Once they get the hang of my style . . . you know. It was a bit vi-sie ver-sie today.'

Rinty's eyes glinted bright as the sun hitting the Model T.

'Oh, that's it. By the way, this yoke's giving a spot of bother. The carburettor. Someone towld me you were good with engines. Would you like to take her for a test spin some time?'

O'Keefe's eyes sparkled. Lips pouted, he closed one eye and nodded acceptance. On the way home he didn't speak much. He had to prod words out of him.

'Why did you wear a hairnet? That's what women do. When they've had their hair permed. Or wearing curlers.'

'The sleeker you are, the quicker you are.'

Passing a lake, he veered into a gap and they sat in silence looking out at the boggy water. O'Keefe leaned against the door, deep in thought, his arms folded. They'd wound down the windows. A flock of swans came over. Their wings whanged the air and their outstretched webbed feet ripped the water when landing.

'That teacher you dream about, in what way was she cruel?'

'I have no intention of telling you, boyo.'

'Why not? I won't tell anyone.'

'You think there's a separate sun up there shining just for you.'

'Doesn't everyone think that?'

O'Keefe looked at him. His eyes were fuzzy warm. Dreamy.

'Every year at school we'd be examined by a woman doctor. The girls would be sent out of the room and she'd line us up round the walls. Twenty-four of us. She'd go from one to the next, putting her hand down your trousers and feeling your mickey. The big bone-spavined mare of a dirty oul rip of a teacher would do the same thing. She'd go from one to the next, hand down your pants. What authority had she? The doctor never said a thing to her. They were in it together. We were only seven or eight.'

The swans floated before them, bumping the choppy water. Each one had a mate.

School was the lie of the land. The truth never faced. A daily terror from which there was no escape. His own primary school teacher in Butlershill was a battering red-faced drunk, who kept girls back after hours on the pretence of giving them extra tuition. It was said that some years before, a certain boy who hated school was punched so hard about the head, on the way home he developed a splitting headache. Next day he died. The ruling cockroaches scuttled about barely disturbed and soon all was forgotten.

'Did you become a Guard from an urge for revenge? Justice?'

'What other employment is there?'

They reversed out of the gap and drove home along a road crude with potholes and danger- ously sinking stretches. A road through the no man's land of Border country. The fields on either side were marshy and covered in rush, dock and ragwort. The few cattle on the land stared after them, intrigued by the sight of O'Keefe's rattling Model T.

★ ★ ★

Rinty Maguire called to the Garda Station from time to time. He'd beep the horn until O'Keefe came out. They'd lift the bonnet of the V8 and lean in looking at the engine. Relaxed as farmers hanging over a gate. Occasionally O'Keefe would put on a glove and feel around in the mechanical entrails.

The boy often turned the engine over at their command. The big, smooth V8 was a thorough-bred mare compared to the awkward, boxy foal that was the Model T.

When Rinty wasn't laughing, he was winking. O'Keefe always looked serious.

'You're by far the best man ever come about this country. For engines and the like. If you ever want to take a quick trip to Dublin, Josh, just let me know, and I'll give you a loan of her. How are you gettin' on with the Sergeant, Josh?'

'Oh, no bother. I know the law as well as any of them.'

★   ★   ★

One afternoon a tubby tough woman came round to married quarters looking for O'Keefe. His mother answered the door.

'Guard O'Keefe wouldn't be round here. He's probably out on duty. Is it a legal matter? There should be someone in the day room.'

The woman was in her thirties, broad-shouldered, with curly short black hair and a weather-leathered face plain as a pounder. She wore a yellow frock and green knee-length knitted stockings. Stout flabs of flesh flopped over her kneecaps. She said she'd met O'Keefe at a dance.

'It's a private mattur. He brung me home from a dance last night week a month ago and sez for me to talaphone him. He took advantage of me in the back of his oul jallopy.'

'God bless us and save us,' his mother said, her fingers up to her mouth in shock, 'he didn't, did he?'

'He dropped the hand from the word go, missus, I'll be straight wid yah.'

His mother, though horrified, was also amused. Her eyes twinkled in her concerned face. She liked drama. Especially if she was on its periphery. The arrests and summonses for local crime rarely spilled round to married quarters and were anyway too tedious to set the blood racing. This strange woman was different.

'Are you intending to press charges of some kind?'

'I'll be hanest wid yah, missus. I worked in England a lock a years and was never trated the like a that.'

'What did you work at over there, dear?'

The woman looked at her, realising she was encountering innocence. She cocked her head backwards, checking she was seeing and hearing properly.

'I was in the hotel trade. Heavin' coal and emptying piss-pots. I may as well be straight with yah, missus, in Birmingham if yah dropped the duds for any man, he put ten bob in your tobacco pouch.'

His mother, shocked, turned and looked at her son. The poor creature was no saint but she was

134

brutally honest. His mother was no hypocrite.

'Would half a crown be any good to you, dear?'

'It wouldn't be bad to me.'

He went into the kitchen and in a secret compartment of his mother's purse found a half-crown.

'The blessin's of God on you, missus. And on your fine son there. He's the image of yah. If you see yer man and his oul car, tell him bejesus I'll be dug out of him when I catch him.'

She stomped along the concrete path, her fists clenched and swinging, her shoulders rolling.

He sat with his mother, the passing minutes flavoured with the strange woman and O'Keefe. When his father came in for dinner, his mother adopted a holy and sentimental tone as if worried about the woman's sinful life. His father had little sympathy for the woman but blamed O'Keefe.

'He's a know-all. He was supposed to be on duty at a Border checkpoint yesterday evening and when I went out there, he was nowhere to be seen. He turned up eventually. He said a woman came down from her house needing help with her sick husband. As far as I could ascertain, the woman's husband died two years ago. That Model T is only a trap for poor trollops who know no better. He's a know-all. Contradicted me when I questioned him on the larceny and unauthorised taking of pedal bicycles. 'Sergeant,' he says, 'soon bicycles will be a thing of the past.' As the Scotsman says, I have me doots about that buck.'

135

For his father, a new year, a new decade, a new moon, was of no consequence. Bicycles would continue to be stolen, he'd have to search for them and women would continue to be codded by the likes of O'Keefe. Tying the wind in knots was an easier task than pinning down a stolen bike. His notebooks were full of the bare details of bicycle theft.

'See there, you have to record the frame number. The make. People don't realise there's 132 different models. A Raleigh is RH. A Rudge — RU. A Claud Butler — CB. You then have to enter L or G for lady's or gent's. It's a minefield. Then there's all the other business I have to keep an eye on. Weights and measures. Cruelty to animals. Children absconding. Drunks. The worst crime to my mind, bar murder, is a drunk man in possession of a stolen bike. At night.'

The law was a thousand traps and he had to know each one by year and Act of Parliament.

The boy and his mother often laughed behind his back. His exasperation at the idiocy of the world reminded them of Laurel and Hardy. Though he looked nothing like them.

On the wall above the kitchen table was an electric clock. It had a light-green plastic surround with the legend 'Coruba Jamaica Rum'. It had been given to his father one Christmas by a publican who was emigrating with his family to New Zealand. Twelve thousand miles away. When they moved to Butlershill they took the clock with them. His father had made a tiny shelf for it and got an electrician to connect it. When his father was promoted to sergeant and they were moved, his native town was only thirty miles away but it might as well have been twelve thousand. He had been cut off from his roots. His father told him he'd get over it. Every item in married quarters was temporary or a permanent reminder of an unquantifiable loss. Coruba Jamaica Rum . . .

O'Keefe burst into the kitchen. He wore his uniform raincoat and cap, the strap in place under his chin. The weather had suddenly turned wet and windy.

'I believe you had a visit from a certain woman. I'm sorry by the way for bustin' in like this. But. Do you think I'd let the like of her into my car? I danced with her, okay. Then she clung round me like midges round a dog. I want you to know that, Sarge.'

His father didn't like being called 'Sarge'.

'Calm down, man. Your personal life is of no concern to me. Provided you don't bring the Force into disrepute. I'd advise you to go out to the checkpoint immediately. You're due there in five minutes.'

O'Keefe's face was wet and the shoulders of his raincoat soaking.

'You expect me to go out in that downpour, Sarge? You wouldn't put a dog out in weather like this.'

'Fortunately, you're not a dog. There's an Army patrol due there shortly. I'd get going if I were you. That's my solid advice.'

His mother, concerned at the tension between them, stood frozen by the dresser, a washed and still suddy soup bowl in one hand, the dishcloth in the other. O'Keefe reminded him of a statue in the chapel on Good Friday. The big creaking raincoat, cap and black shiny strap were like a cloak. His nose, lips, ears, cheekbones looked hooded. Dallamullog. One side of his face had a lopsided grin. The other was blank as a rasher. His eyes were darting blue.

'Betcha that one came in here slandering me. If she had any money I'd sue her. My car isn't for the likes of her. If you ever want a lift to a football match, Sarge, or if you ever want a lift into town, missus, you only have to request.'

His raincoat rustling he bundled himself out the door and was gone.

They sat for a moment in silence. He and his mother wondered what to say. The rain battered at the window, big drops jerking down the pane.

His father picked up the newspaper. But they could tell he wasn't reading it.

'Don't you know damn well he had her in the car. Poor creature, God help her. She's been to Headquarters in Monaghan complaining. It's gone all over the Division. 'He dropt the hand,' she says.' He let out a deep guffaw, pleased O'Keefe was being made to look foolish.

His mother laughed. The rain dwindled to a stop.

A few days later, O'Keefe was BO for the day. Undaunted by the scandal, bored, he'd come out for a breather and suggested pucking the ball between them. On the lawn in front of the Station, the boy stood in a makeshift goal as O'Keefe took shots at him with his hurley stick and ball. O'Keefe had given him a stick of his own with which he tried to defend the goal. He managed to save some shots but quite a few ripped into the thick hedge which separated the Station from the house next door, which was rented by a company director and his wife, Mr and Mrs Gregg.

'What really happened with that woman?'

'She didn't get in the car to say her prayers, did she?'

With a swivel of his shoulders and wristy snap, O'Keefe hit the ball past him so fast he barely saw it. Like a cannonball, it tore through the hedge and shattered the window in the house next door. Mrs Gregg, a baby in her arms, came running out to see what had happened. The baby had been in a pram by the window and was covered in glass. Luckily his eyes had been closed in sleep.

'If the goalie had been any good he'd have stopped it.'

Mrs Gregg was gentle and pretty as a small pink rose. She and her husband were from Belfast. They walked the roads on Sundays pushing a big pram. Every now and then they'd stop to admire and smell the wild flowers along the way. Her husband was a huge man with a belly as big as today and tomorrow. He weighed about eighteen stones. He walked very erect. Sometimes you'd see him in the garden at the back of the house looking up at the sky. There were evenings when the sinking sun plastered the sky in sensational rose and russet. Mrs Gregg called him 'Hubby'. 'Hubby' ran a firm that made shoes.

O'Keefe said he'd replace the pane of glass immediately.

'Is the ball within in the room? Can I have it back?'

They found it under a sofa. The room had a carpet, a plush new suite of furniture with velvet cushions, a big polished gramophone, a television with doors and copies of Renaissance paintings on the walls. There were antimacassars on the armchairs. Beside the gramophone was a stack of records. The one on the top was a Kathleen Ferrier. An antique bookcase was neatly packed with literature. Lots of Dickens and Shakespeare, the British Encyclopaedia and law books.

He hurried round to the shed at the back of married quarters and fought his way in past a forest of buckets, brooms, brushes, mops, goose wings, lengths of wood, an old Primus stove, a roll of worn lino. Luckily he didn't have to penetrate the deeper chaos of discarded bicycle wheels, gardening equipment, damaged saucepans, lengths of wood, paint cans, chairs with legs missing. Underneath a pile of newspapers he found a crude wooden crate. This was one of his father's toolboxes. He rumbled through it until he discovered the chisel and hammer and a measuring tape. As he was about to emerge, a bucket of sawdust fell on his head. Why it was there he didn't know. Other than his father couldn't bear to throw anything away. Even sawdust.

When O'Keefe saw him he didn't say anything for a moment. 'Since I saw you a minute or two ago, you've developed a severe case of dandruff.' He helped O'Keefe remove the broken glass, the old putty and the holding nails from the frame. Then they measured up for a new pane. His father's tape measure was frayed along the edges and some of the numbers on the first few feet were invisible from use. He'd found it in the Garda Station he was posted to in 1923. Drumshanbo in County Leitrim.

O'Keefe, though BO, risked leaving the day room empty and set off for the hardware shop in Cavan in the Model T. He went along with him. His father was in Dublin having another barium meal test. Any little ache and he insisted on going to Dublin to have it 'looked at'. All the other men were on duty out along the Border. No one would know O'Keefe had deserted his post. However, if an inspector or the Chief happened to call and found the place empty, he'd be for the high jump. On the other hand, he was afraid 'Hubby' might sue for loss and damages and endangering the life of the baby. He wanted to repair the damage before he returned home from work.

In the hardware shop the glass was carefully wrapped in thick brown paper and tied with string. The assistant also gave them a lump of putty oiled with linseed. O'Keefe on the way back to the car bought sweets and two ice creams. He put the glass down on the floor, leaning against the driver's door. It would be safe there. He didn't want to risk it slipping from the shiny leather seat in the back.

He drove along belting out 'I Need Your Love Tonight'.

'Do you think will the Russians invade Ireland?' he asked, hoping to stop O'Keefe's raucous singing.

'If they do we'll give them a Céad Mile Fáilte.'

They travelled through weather-beaten drumlins scored with thick hedges, the land pocked with dog rushes. The hills were never ploughed. They were too steep. Cattle standing sideways on looked in danger of toppling over. Gaps in the hedges were blocked with old brass bed-heads or flattened-out tar barrels. The land looked woebegone, indestructible but somehow modern compared to the Model T. A collie tore out a farm gate and pursued them along the dusty road, trying to bite the rear right tyre.

'The only gospel is the gap in between.'

'I don't understand.'

'They can say what they like to you, give you all sort of bulsh, but when you see a lassie across a dance floor, that flash is all that counts.'

'How do you cross that bridge?'

'That's it, boyo. How do you get your hands on the electric?'

'But are you not claimed from then on?'

'That's the one good thing about this job. You can always put in for a transfer.'

They came up the hill towards the One Tree Cross. A great oak tree at an intersection of roads marked the spot where in 1649 Eoghan Roe O'Neill took the final salute of his troops as he lay dying from the poison in his military boots, secreted there by the perfidious English.

Swinging round the sharp bend, as they headed left for Butlershill, the rotational forces forced the driver's door open. Saving himself from falling out, O'Keefe hadn't time to grab the pane of glass. He abruptly braked, causing the car to shoot across the road and dunt into the opposite grassy bank. Leaping out they ran back to the parcel lying in the road. O'Keefe handled it gently, hoping for the best. Before he even undid the limp string, it was obvious the glass was smashed to smithereens. He stood in silence, crinkling the damage with his fingers.

'Isn't that unfortunate?'

'It could have been worse. You could have fallen out.'

'I didn't. But the pane of glass did. The story of my life.'

'Ah well, the putty is okay.'

O'Keefe looked at him.

'I can never tell, boyo, if you're the full shilling or laughing at everyone.'

The driver's door was hinged to a jamb in the middle of the car. The slot for the handle catch had worn down with use and age.

'What are you going to do?'

'We'll have to go back to the hardware.'

Keeping the brown paper and string, he tossed the broken pane into the ditch. Giant hogweed grew from the hedges and massive thistles disputed the ground with the oak tree. In the distance, near the edge of a wood, was the dilapidated remains of a hunting lodge on what was once a private estate. Archduke Franz Ferdinand had been a visitor.

'He was assassinated in 1914.'

'Who by — Patrick Pearse?'

He couldn't tell if O'Keefe was serious or not.

They headed back to the shop. Already they'd been away for over an hour and by the time they got back to town and purchased another pane and drove home, the Station would have been two hours at least without a Barrack Orderly. If his father found out, he'd have to report it to Divisional Headquarters. O'Keefe could be in serious trouble.

Shoe to the floor, he hunched over the steering wheel in silence, willing the car onwards. But the engine could only give about thirty miles an hour. His anxious face was a moody cloud, as if he had pulled a cloth over his emotions and his features. He sucked a Fox's Mint.

Near a cemetery, they slowed down and had to stop when they came across a group of men dragging a dead donkey into the side of the road. There was a man on each leg and a boy waddling with effort as he lifted its head by the lugs. They were dragging it into a gap. Death undignified, its old limbs were wide apart, revealing the soft underparts and the pinky-pale skin round the groin.

He let the window down.

'Ignore them,' O'Keefe said.

He didn't.

'What happened?'

'The oul brute was ailin' this long while. He couldn't have picked a more inconvainyent spot for to go and die.'

Its hooves, unpared, were grotesquely long and unshod. Lying on the grassy verge was a britchin held together with wire, a collar stuffed with straw, blinkers, rope reins and a stout ash plant.

Under the land were the countless skeletons of beasts. In the cemetery on a nearby hill were the headstoned skeletons of man.

A butty barrel of a fellow, with hairy weather-blackened arms, dropped the donkey's leg he was holding, came over and stuck his head in the window. He stared across at O'Keefe.

'You're the go-boy inturfaired with me daughter, are yah? This is the jallopy okay, this yoke, yah hoor-master yah.'

'What the hell are you talking about?'

'Yah know full well. You tried to get up on me daughter.'

'I'd get up on that ass first.'

The man jumped clear as O'Keefe, laughing, accelerated away.

Having delivered his verbal skelp, his humour improved immeasurably. He started singing again: 'There you goin' bab-ee, here am I . . . '

The woman who had called to married quarters looking for him was a tinker and the men with the donkey were tinkers. They lived by their wits in a hard world, misfortune and the law stalking their way. The Garda Síochána were suspicious of anyone without a permanent address.

The shopman in the hardware was surprised by their reappearance. O'Keefe was too ashamed to tell him why.

'She wants another one. Just to be on the safe side.'

On the journey back to Butlershill, O'Keefe entrusted him with the new pane. Wrapped as before, it sat secure on his lap.

'I don't mind things going wrong if they can be put right. You might break a cup. Next time use a ponger. If someone insults you, say you're sorry to them. That cuts it all short. It puts them feeling guilty.'

'You didn't say sorry to the tinker man.'

'Just because some galoot holds out a noose doesn't mean you have to put your head in it.'

A ponger was a tin mug. From porringer. Like ojus, the sound of ponger was the local sound of Cavan. Pawnjurr. It exploded from the lips as pungent as manure flung from a graip. They had their own ponger. His father drank cold water from it. He'd dip it into the bucket, drink deep, then, with wristy vigour beyond necessity, shake the remaining drops into the basin by the window. Sometimes his mother buffed it with a cloth until it shun as near silver as she could get it. Cheerfully it reflected the weather outside. Especially if the sun was out. Mostly it hung dull on its hook. It was their only barometer.

'Never worry over spilt blood. Back home, I never seen me father cry in his life. Or me mother. They were as well matched as two stones.'

'Why did they call you Josiah, Josh?'

'After some oul uncle who'd run away to join the British Army.'

As they drove slowly by the One Tree he gripped the steering wheel tight and gurgled softly in his throat. The sound of a sheep.

'You can tell everyone you met three donkeys today. Two in 'assassinated' and the dead one on the road.'

'You're so sharp, boyo, you'll cut yourself.'

When they got back to the Garda Station, Rinty Maguire was waiting for him beside his V8.

'He's in there,' he said ominously, emphasising the direction with a crafty nod of the head. 'I happened to be in Dublin and met him in the street. And gave him a lift home. His appointment was cancelled. The surgeon was hit on the head be a golf ball.'

They could see his father in his private office inside the front door. When he saw them, he sprang up and came out, his face cold but his manner deliberately calm.

'Ah, O'Keefe, good, let's have a bit of a chinwag, will we?'

'No bother, Sarge.'

His father knew well the Force's disciplinary procedures. To have mentioned private police matters in front of Rinty Maguire, or any member of the public, would have been a violation of regulations. He wasn't about to provide O'Keefe with a bolthole. The facts of why he deserted his post and its consequences were not for Maguire's ears.

'He'd a never known you were gone missing at all, only for me meeting him in O'Connell Street. My fault entirely. I want to see you anyway as a matter of fact, Josh. Go aisy on him now, Sergeant, don't put him into the black hole or anythin'. We need him on Sunday.' He laughed, in good spirits, rubbing his hands together. Nothing cowed him. Locals said he could knock a bit of jizz out of Hell itself. He sagged comfortably into his big car and sedately drove away.

They followed his father into the day room.

'You thundering jackass, O'Keefe. Going off and leaving the place deserted? The phone ringing like mad and no one to answer it? And you — go you round to Mammy. You're surplus in here.'

'Sorry, Daddy, but . . . this pane of glass.'

His father's eyes were cold as marbles. O'Keefe, a sideways twist on his lips, didn't utter a word. As if tempting his father to lose control.

'Guard O'Keefe broke next door's window with a hurley ball. We went to get a new pane. It fell out at the One Tree Cross and we had to go back and get another one. And we were held up by a dead donkey.'

He looked at them as if they were a pair of hopeless clowns. It was also a suspicious look. O'Keefe broke his silence.

'You can make a song and dance out of it if you have to, Sarge, but what the boyo says is about the height of it.'

The *Garda Síochána Code* was over seven hundred pages long. The pages were screwed in between two hard covers. His father plonked it down on the table, the noise heavy with importance. Opening it on a well-thumbed Chapter 6, his index finger dropped like a stone until it landed on 6.4 — Offences reserved for Commissioner's decision. He read aloud:

''I(e) . . . all offences of desertion of post as station orderly . . . 'You're in the soup, O'Keefe. Regulations, 1926 as amended 1942 — 'dismissal; forced to resign; reduction in pay; a fine;

148

transfer; reprimand; caution'. I'll have to report you. It can't be hidden. Not with your friend Rinty Maguire knowing. He'll spread it all over the place like chaff in a wind. I pity you.'

O'Keefe looked animated for the first time. Surprised.

'Pity? Declare to God, Sarge, I didn't shoot anyone.'

He stopped smiling cynically and removed his cap. His hair was wet with perspiration.

'There's also the matter of immorality. '(d) Offences relating to immorality or association with undesirable characters' — that woman who called looking for you. Just before you got back here, her father telephoned, complaining on her behalf. He said there was a tribe of them would swear you debauched her in the back of your Model T. He also said you ran over and killed his donkey and didn't stop at the scene of the accident. An hour ago. He wants compensation.'

'That's a total lie, Daddy.'

'You're not supposed to be in here at all. Give that pane of glass to next door and go round to Mum.'

'Before he goes anywhere, Sarge. You've discussed my business in front of him. He's not a member of the Force, is he? My rights have been violated. I can drag you through it as much as you can drag me. I skipped off fast as I could to replace the neighbour's glass. I wasn't swinging the lead. I was only doing the decent thing. Why don't we forget it? I didn't kill anyone's donkey. What goes on in me car has nothing to do with anyone bar meself and the woman in question.

Immorality is a religious word. It's best left in the confession box. Am I right or am I wrong, Sarge?'

His father, rummaging through a shelf of dusty forms, didn't say anything until he found what he was looking for — Form D.1. He sat down at the table and stared at O'Keefe, forcing him to look away. He didn't bandy words with any of the men where religion was concerned. That was against regulations. O'Keefe was trying to blackmail him.

'My son, it seems, is a witness to at least some of the events in question. I don't think you have a leg to stand on in regard to the outcome of an inquiry. I personally can't charge you with anything. That duty will be carried out by the district inspector or superintendent. The question of immorality doesn't interest me. Leaving the Station unattended, however, offends me very much. It's tantamount to desertion. I'm proud of this uniform. Before you were even born, we stuck it out and gave body and blood to our new-won country.'

'And you have the medal to prove it.'

'Don't interfere. Go you round to Mum.'

He didn't move. His father was angry. He rarely alluded to the Scott Medal he won for bravery. It was banked away in his soul, where to reveal it would be to betray it. To boast was to tempt the gods. The actual medal was in a big black box under his bed, along with legal documents, personal records, a box camera, a photo album and holy oils from a shrine in Walsingham, England.

'Guard O'Keefe in his own way is . . .' He ran out of words.

'Is . . . is . . . what?' his father said.

'Is . . . is . . . what?' O'Keefe repeated.

They looked at him as they would at a criminal under interrogation. They couldn't help it. They had trained eyes.

'My solid advice to you is go round to married quarters and help Mum. She's cleaning down cobwebs today.'

He went round next door instead. Mrs Gregg, though she was washing clothes, wore a smart tweed skirt, a white blouse, high heels and a pearl necklace. The black range in the kitchen was spotless. No marks from boiled-over milk on it. No frazzled bits of food or dried spit. Her pink lipstick gave her mouth a rosy pout. As he laboriously fitted the new pane of glass, she danced in and out to him and to her baby back asleep in its pram. Her permed hair was short and black and wavy.

'What are you thinking of doing when you finish school?'

'England. Maybe. I suppose.'

'Someone said you might become a priest.'

'I've never been sinned against. Or sinned. Alas.'

'You'll get plenty of both in England.'

They laughed. She proffered a plate of choco-late biscuits to his puttied hand. His linseed fingers. They didn't speak for a while. The baby gurgled. A bubble of milk cornered its mouth.

'Bobby Wobby bwok a puddy, didn't you, darlin'?'

'Why do mothers talk like that to their babies?'

'To make the words cuddly.'

Neat as a wren she darted into the kitchen and poured hot water from a kettle into a white aluminium basin.

'You'll have freedom in England. I wanted to be an actress. My parents insisted I go to university. After Cyril and I got married I joined an amateur group. Second-rate shouters in melodramas. Awarding themselves prizes.'

A flock of crows, their scattered caws audible, flew low across the fields at the back of the house.

'It's like living in a Van Goff painting,' she said.

Van Goff — he'd just about heard of him.

'Crows are scraps of black searching for night.'

'Gogh is gh not ff by the way.'

'Right, yes, thanks, Mrs Gregg. Van Gogh.'

Pert and cheerful in her sunlit cage, she didn't notice the bars. The cage was her own.

The Board of Works in Dublin owned the married quarters. There was no incentive to improve it. The Board of Works, according to his father, only employed builders who used sea sand because it was cheap and painters who watered the paint so that rooms glistened with condensation. In winter the green walls froze.

Guard O'Keefe came in without knocking. He glanced about, wrinkled up his forehead in surprise and said, 'Where's herself?' A dart of his tongue and a quick leer sparked his face.

Mrs Gregg was in the kitchen rubbing a shirt with a big lump of carbolic against the wooden flutes of a washing board.

'Hello, missus, sorry about all this, nearly done now, sorry for the excitement, accidents happen.'

He turned to him, winked and gyrated his hips.

'As long as you don't make a habit of it,' she answered. She slurped the shirt round in fresh water, then hurried out and down the back garden, the shirt and other items dripping all the way.

O'Keefe stared after her, then beckoned urgently with his head.

'Do you see what I see?' He had his foot in the door, keeping it open, so they could see out the kitchen window.

Scraping putty from his fingers with a knife, he went to see what it was catching O'Keefe's attention.

She was pegging the shirt on the clothesline. Very large and white, a breeze giving it form, it hung like a skinned carcass in a butcher's window. He always imagined his soul that colour. A bulky suety emptiness within him, nearer to death than life. O'Keefe's mind was in the here and now. The far end of the line was hung with dainty underwear.

'The whole lot begod,' he chuckled. 'Hah?'

Each article was red as a rose in rain. The brassiere was tiny compared to his mother's. The knickers were as a hanky to a towel compared to his mother's bloomers. The suspender belt was just like an advert in the *News of the World*. They reminded him of doll's clothes. Now that he thought about it, her house was as neat as a doll's house in a shop window at Christmas.

' 'Up stepped Johnny with his camera, it was a nice snap-shot, he took the bloomin' lot . . .' '
O'Keefe sang quietly.

'How come you're here?'

'Your old fellah sent me round to formally apologise. She's related to some bigwig in the county council.'

His face a mask, still as a gundog, O'Keefe stared down the garden. He hadn't been in the house five seconds when he spotted the unmentionables. The boy had been replacing the windowpane for at least an hour and hadn't noticed. He'd spotted a crow flying past the window, a spud in its beak tilting him down. But he hadn't seen anything else.

'Wise up, boyo, it's all around us.'

As she finished shaking out and hanging a big pair of long johns and a massive woollen vest, she turned towards them. O'Keefe held his hand up as if saluting her. Despite his mask of a face, when she came in she gave him a look that said she knew what he'd been gawking at.

'Soon every house will have a washing machine. Carbolic soap will be a thing of the past. Your smalls will be easy handling then. Do you not think so, Mrs Gregg? Hah?'

Ignoring him, she stood over the pram looking at the baby. O'Keefe winked behind her back.

Red. Not the red of debtor's ink, blood, haws, not the rusty Red Brae in rain. Secret silken red sweet-papers for candy flesh.

The bar of carbolic soap by the kitchen window was the colour of dead skin. Pared bunions. It too reminded him of his soul.

The pegged shirt, long johns and vest, pumped up by the wind, billowed in dull slow motion. The reds danced as if teasing the breeze.

'You've done a good job.'

'Thank you, Mrs Gregg.'

★ ★ ★

He went back to married quarters. His mother had the tin bath in the kitchen and was washing clothes. The village mothers seemed to do the same chores at the same time every week. She was kneeling on newspaper and scrubbing hard at a washboard. Water had slopped on to the lino and the newspaper. Pots of water steamed on the range. The pile of clothes, the furniture, the walls were utterly drab compared to next door. Over the mantelpiece the picture of the Sacred Heart was cheap and melodramatic. On the top of the sewing machine was a copy of the *Manual of Criminal Investigation*, Dublin Garda Síochána Headquarters 1946. His mother was kneeling with her back to him. He opened Chapter V. Sexual Crime. The forensic exactitude of the language in contrast to the desperate lives involved was always riveting. Exciting even.

'The handywoman or ignorant person usually makes use of crude substitutes, such as knitting needles, pieces of stick, wooden skewers . . . Sea tangle tents, which have the appearance of . . . '

Hearing his father coming in, he quickly put it back on the sewing machine. His father tossed a booklet down beside it. It was an index of the publications banned in the State. They were

155

known as dirty books. Hundreds of them. Sex. O'Keefe was right. It was all around. Fresh air was free, football was free, anything else was under lock and key. Out of wedlock was a death sentence. Yet passions constantly boiled over. Pregnant girls went to England or into homes run by nuns. Death by other means.

His father stood over his mother, watching her scrub a uniform shirt collar. He rarely sat in the kitchen except at mealtimes. And for a short time after eating when he read the newspaper. He relaxed out in the open. Digging in the garden, patrolling the countryside, cutting turf. Domesticity never interested him. Rooms were too small and full of bits of furniture and knick-knacks waiting to be knocked over.

'Good. You're hard at it,' he said to his mother. 'What have you done about O'Keefe?'

'I'll leave him to stew in his own grease for a while. His nibs here has complicated things.'

'How is your stomach now?'

'Funnily enough I don't feel it now. Thanks be to God.'

'You're a hypochondriac, man. How many times have I told you? Have a titter of wit.'

On the range was a boiled potato left over from the previous day's dinner. His father picked it up and peeled the skin, using his thumbnail. He saw him looking.

'What? Before your ancestors were evicted they used their thumbnails. There were no glasses to drink from either. They used eggshells. They were happy. Blast that old hag and all belonging to her.'

'Ah for God's sake will you have sense, man. That's all history.'

The hag in question was a Mrs Gerrard who evicted all his people on 13 March 1846.

'She ended up the oldest, ugliest, richest hag in Ireland with not one to attend her funeral.'

He gouged the soft potato open and rammed in a ball of country butter with finger and thumb.

'Use a knife — please!' his mother shouted. 'We're not in 1846.'

His father grinned boyishly at her annoyance, then, carefully taking a bite, gently chewed as if tasting potato for the first time. His mother sighed and plunged another shirt into the bath.

When his grandparents were alive, 1846 was within living memory.

'The truth of the matter is the situation has been compromised by you being with him. Any inquiry and as sure as sixpence he'd want you as a witness. Now do you see?'

'You've saved O'Keefe's bacon,' his mother said.

'The same O'Keefe, mark my words, if we give him enough rope he'll hang himself. That's my solemn opinion. I bet my bottom dollar.'

'Mrs Gregg's house is full of books.'

His father opened the range and was about to throw in the potato skin, when he stopped.

'Will I give this to the hens?'

His mother kneaded the shirt up and down in the water.

Someone knocked on the door. His mother, groaning, got up from her knees. His father followed her out. He followed his father. All three of them crammed into the narrow hallway and saw a woman in her late forties staring at them. She wore a fur coat, a cloche hat, sensible shoes and thick stockings. She had a bicycle pump in her hand.

'I'm looking for Guard O'Keefe. Someone told me to come round here. He asked me to a dance in Cavan but he never turned up for me. He was seen there. I'd just like to know what happened.'

'Is he not in the day room? What's your name?' his father asked bluntly.

'Mrs McEntee. Eileen. I'm widowed.'

'Sorry to hear that,' his mother said.

Her face was well painted and powdered. Her eyes were rimmed with mascara. She wore one plain earring. She noticed him looking. Gently pulling her earlobe she said, 'I lost it on the way here. Coming down the Red Brae.'

Her face was long, her lips thin, her damson eyes lovely. The fur coat and cloche hat were not items ordinarily worn round Butlershill. She looked proud and sad.

Women in trouble, in pain, hurt him. It was something he inherited with his mother's tears.

His father looked perplexed. You could tell he was angry with O'Keefe. Where the hell was he now?

'Go round to the day room and see if he's there. Tell him a Mrs McEntee is of a mind to have a word with him urgently.'

O'Keefe wasn't in the day room. He called his name but on getting no answer decided to go into the dormitory. His legs stuck out from under a bed.

'A Mrs McEntee wants you, Josh.'

'Sssh, I'm not here. Tell her I've been called out to the Border.'

'But you're BO.'

'Tell her any bloody thing you like but I'm not here.'

'Did you have her in the Model T?'

'She's no spring chicken.'

'Did you . . . like . . . drop the hand?'

He sat down on the same bed and wondered if he were ever fortunate enough to be with a girl, and they were mutually affectionate and she fully consenting, confirmed in writing, would he even then dare . . . drop the hand? It was clearly a practice fraught with terrible risk. There was O'Keefe, a grown man, a policeman, cowering under the bed, two women, at least, hunting him.

He went back to married quarters. The woman was with his parents in the kitchen, the bicycle pump still in her hand.

'No, Daddy, he's not in the day room.' Strictly speaking he hadn't told a lie. He was in the dormitory under a bed.

His father pursed his lips for a moment and raised an eyebrow. He knew O'Keefe wasn't far away. He decided to carry on with the conversation he'd been having with the woman.

'What make of bicycle have you, Mrs McEntee?'

'A Raleigh. My husband, RIP, bought it for me.'

'RIP,' his mother echoed.

'A Raleigh? A sturdy machine. It'll last you a lot longer than your husband did. God rest him.'

There was a silence then. His mother looked into the suddy bath. Bubbles she believed were a sign of money. Her hands were raw red from scrubbing. His father looked up at the clock. Coruba Jamaica Rum. The woman smiled weakly and nodded, stood up and left. He followed her out to the gate. She slotted the pump back on her bicycle.

'As soon as I see him I'll tell him, Mrs McEntee.'

She rode away without a word.

His father decided not to initiate a charge against O'Keefe.

'You banjaxed the whole thing.'

★ ★ ★

Next day Jim Reilly asked him would he come down and do an evening behind the bar. The money was always welcome and the change of atmosphere. Chisholm Flood and his brother, Squealer, were there. Rinty Maguire came in. A stranger rushed in, sunk a bottle of stout at a gulp, then hurried out. Chisholm was drinking heavily and telling them about the time he drove a herd of cattle across the whole of Texas.

'Took me two days. I could hardly see with the snow.'

'You're some man,' Rinty said, winking behind his back.

A few men who had been cutting wood in the

demesne arrived, their tongues hanging out for a drink. They were hardy-looking fellows with big fists. One of them took a newspaper, the *Irish Catholic*, out of his back pocket and opened it on the counter.

'There's an ojus article in here about Joe Stalin. The Rooshin Komminist. He hid a blade in his moustache. If you said boo to him he'd slit your windpipe.'

The men gathered round and looked at Stalin's photograph. Even Squealer took a squint.

Chisholm didn't move. He raised his pint and said solemnly, 'Poor old Joe. He wasn't the worst of them.'

Rinty Maguire laughed aloud. All the men did. Chisholm's humourless features were set in ice. It was best to ignore him.

'Tell O'Keefe I want him, will you? The V8 is giving trouble. I wonder could he drive it to Dublin for me.'

The door opened and 'The Pig' came in. The local teacher. To every child he ever taught he was known as The Pig. He was wearing a dark-blue suit, shirt and red tie. His thick ridgy hair was oily and carefully combed. He was stockily built with a drinker's blotchy red face. He saw him behind the bar.

'Hah. It's you, is it?'

From behind the bar he could smell the familiar sweaty dreggy animal smell. The men visibly straightened up, tense. He had mauled most of them. One of them said, 'Ah, hello, sir.'

On his way home from a funeral he had

161

popped in for a quick drink. He went from one to the other shaking hands, ingratiating himself and asking what they were having. On him.

'No hard feelings, lads, bygones are bygones.'

They were grinning, shy boys again. He had beaten them all, most days of the nine years they spent in school.

He called across the bar, 'Give each man his pleasure, boyo.'

Chisholm, almost without looking, swung his hand back and hit The Pig flush in the face. Blood instantly pumped as if a vein had burst. He staggered back against the door, holding his nose with one hand, groping for the handle with the other. Squealer jumped from his stool and hit him a punch so hard in the ribs you could hear bones cracking.

'Mary Kate, for tha', eek,' he shouted incoherently.

The boy rushed round from behind the bar and opened the door. O'Keefe, in uniform, was passing. The Pig fell at his feet.

'What the hell's going on?'

'He got hit. The teacher. Rinty Maguire wants you to drive to Dublin.'

'Tell him I'll be in touch.' Without interest, O'Keefe watched the teacher crawling across the footpath to his car. He understood what had happened and why.

The men in silence huddled over their drinks. Over the years the fear beaten into them had soured to hatred. Mary Kate was a niece of Chisholm and Squealer's. She had been made pregnant and committed suicide.

162

Violence could erupt quicker than lightning. Chisholm's hand had flashed backwards with perfect accuracy faster than the eye could see. The blood had burst from The Pig's nose in a perfect arch. Red. When he opened the door to allow him escape, he had to restrain himself from adding to the blows. Soul destroyer. An animal that had ruined the peace of children. And was still doing it.

'Eek,' Squealer said, pleased. 'Bo-boned him.'

'You certainly did that,' Rinty said dubiously. 'So long as he doesn't take the two of you up the steps.'

One of the woodcutters, unannounced, started singing a thumping song. Head back, voice raucous and oiled, every so often he pounded the counter to emphasise the emotion of the words.

In market or fair you'll find us there
Possessed of manly pride . . . (Thump).

Jim Reilly had a new dog, Waddy. A black and white beagle, kept in a shed out the back. Somehow it had gotten out and into the bar and was sniffing the blood on the floor.

He pulled a few pints, took the money, whistled the dog into the back kitchen. It hadn't licked the blood. Taking hold of a hank of flesh on the back of his neck, he coaxed him down the back steps to the shed.

Rinty, whom he hadn't noticed slipping out of the bar, was in the yard. The V8 was there, the boot open and Rinty was handing out boxes to a stranger. Bat-like, he could flit through the dark

163

barely seen. And always had a chuckle and a wink ready to reassure. The boxes probably contained razor blades. They looked too small for butter.

'You saw nothin', boyo.'

★ ★ ★

After cleaning up and washing the glasses, stacking two crates of empty bottles out the back and rolling two empty Guinness barrels out the front, he went home.

The village was deadly quiet. There wasn't a light on in any window and the moon and stars were shut away behind blackness. A tethered goat on the green, sensing his presence megilled — a plaintive bleat dwindling to a belch. She wanted company. She was always on the green, a long rope around her neck securing her to the village pump.

Passing the forge, a light flashed on and off. It was O'Keefe sitting inside his Model T. He was on duty. He was supposed to patrol round the village green, stroll up to the railway bridge, walk back to the Methodist chapel, on past the Garda Station to check the main gate into Lady Sarah's demesne, then to the Mill Dam (a thatched house with two yew trees), then back again and out the road to Lady Sarah's rear gate. This beat only killed about fifteen minutes. The slow night hours were purgatorial. He was being punished. But his father was in bed. So every now and then O'Keefe sat into the car for a quick snooze.

He called out, 'I'll walk up with you, boyo.'

There was a street light outside the Methodist chapel. But the bulb had gone again. It never seemed to work for long. Even when they replaced the bulb it only lasted a few nights.

'It's a spooky spot this,' O'Keefe said. They saw something in the distance. A pinpoint of light sharpened by the surrounding darkness. They stopped and stood in against the demesne wall.

'It could be that ghost lamp thing I saw one time. It looks like it. You better say a prayer, Josh.' He enjoyed frightening him.

O'Keefe fumbled at the lapel of his overcoat. On the reverse of it was the tiny pewter statue of the Child of Prague in its tin reliquary with a red plastic window. 'Child of Grace have mercy on me,' he whimpered.

Up against midnight his cockiness had disappeared. The brilliant pinpoint grew as it approached. They couldn't hear footsteps or the ticking of bicycle wheels or hooves. It wasn't low enough to the ground to be a cat's eyes. Whatever it was it was much nearer now. It had to be a lamp of some kind. A lantern maybe. A breeze trembled the trees in the demesne and above them there still wasn't a single star to be seen. The night was blacker than the Earl of Hell's waistcoat. Maybe it was a candle cupped in a hand. It moved steadily in the dead centre of the road. It was only a few yards away now.

'Shine your flashlamp, Josh,' he whispered.

The beam of light isolated a woman's profile, as pale as if O'Keefe had thrown a bucket of whitewash on her. It was Mrs McEntee, the

165

widow, slowly freewheeling down the hill on the bicycle bought for her by her dead husband. The flashlamp had chiselled her out from the darkness. The light hitting her hadn't startled her. As if she were locked away inside her head. O'Keefe walked quickly onwards.

'She put the heart crossways in me. What the hell has her out at this hour?'

'Maybe she can't face her half-empty bed.'

Outside the Station they stopped. A pheasant honked from up in the trees and the moon at last squinted through a rip in the clouds. O'Keefe's face was as pale as the woman's had been. A startled sheep-face.

'Maybe she knows you're on night-duty and she's out looking for you. Did you take advantage of her?'

'As if I'd tell you.'

'I was only asking.'

'If you must know, I had the hand up the back of her corset yoke. I snagged a nail on a hook thingamajig. I drew blood. Looka.' He shone the flashlamp on his left index finger. The end was wrapped in a white strip of bandage.

'Do you intend suing her?'

'Jesus, boyo, you're some headcase.'

He opened the gate and headed round to married quarters. O'Keefe called after him in a loud whisper. 'Rinty wants me to drive the V8 to Dublin tomorrow. Do you want to come for the spin?'

'Okay.'

Before he went inside, he paused. He could hear O'Keefe's footsteps slapping along the road.

Like the sound of an otter crossing stubble. In the night the dead were alive and the living were dead. Next door in Mrs Gregg's, the baby cried out for a brief moment. As if surprised in a dream.

He liked O'Keefe. Despite his superior exterior he was quite innocent.

★ ★ ★

Next morning his father said he could go to Dublin. He needed to get new books from a shop in Nassau Street. *David Copperfield* and a book of Ovid poems. Reluctantly his father gave him the money.

'Where all this education is leading to God only knows.'

'Knowledge doesn't weigh him down,' his mother said.

'A bleddy good job because by now he'd be flat as a pancake.'

His mother spooned porridge into their bowls, holding the saucepan tipped at an angle away from her so the steam didn't cloud her face. No day started without gruel. His father had a boiled egg as well. He sliced the top off with a knife. It was the neatest thing he did. If she ever asked him to open a bag of sugar or take the wrapper off a new pound of butter or untwine a parcel at Christmas, his cack-handed ripping and grunting always annoyed her as much as it made her laugh.

'Honestly! You'd swear you were trying to break into the Bank of England.'

'The way they've sealed the damn thing you'd

167

swear it was the Bank of England.'

They warned him against doing anything foolish in Dublin with O'Keefe. 'I hold out no hopes for that clig,' his father said.

'At least he doesn't drink.'

On the way to Dublin, O'Keefe sped through the countryside and took each bend as fast as he could. The V8 was luxurious compared to the Model T, the leather seat comfortable, the air smelling of brandy, smoke and polish, the engine powerful.

'It's some passion-wagon, boyo, hah?'

'I hadn't realised corsets were so dangerous. You could have been killed.'

O'Keefe laughed. 'She bolted on me anyway. I had no intention of going to a dance with her. There's more holes in a plank than one.'

They passed a tower on a hill the other side of Kells. It looked like a lighthouse without a sea. 'It's a class of a white elephant,' O'Keefe said. 'Some oul Englishman built it. They say he was lonely in the head.' It was a funny expression. But that's exactly where loneliness lay.

At school he sometimes missed home and yet he wanted to be away in the world as far as he could go. Lonely for what? The scraw hill behind the Garda Station? A shadow on a wall? The frozen barrel of water out the back and a winter wagtail pecking at the ice? His mother contemplating her swollen feet as she soaked them in the white enamel basin every Saturday night? Looking at them as if they didn't belong to her. 'Honest to God, where have the years gone?' Maybe.

There was only one other car on the road. And that was way behind them.

'Did I tell you I'm studying for the sergeant's exam? Janey Mack, if your oul fellah could get it I'm sure I can, hah? There'll be three stripes on my arm before long, you'll see.'

Studying O'Keefe in profile as he drove along, he noticed his ears were long and pointy. 'Have you anyone belonging to you from Mars?'

'Hah?'

'Did your mother know anyone woolly with four legs?'

'You're vexed, boyo, because I insulted your father, aren't you, hah, hah?'

He laughed, accelerated and beeped the horn for pleasure. The car took a bend shrieking in protest.

They arrived at a garage in a suburb of the city. A young boy wearing a man's cap, his face streaked with grease and wiping his hands on a balled-up newspaper, nodded to them and opened wide a big double-door. O'Keefe reversed the V8 inside. He told the boy they'd be back in a couple of hours.

'The carburettor and check the exhaust as well.'

'Me father knows,' the lad answered. 'Rinty was on to him.'

O'Keefe didn't hang around the oily garage. He was wearing new brown shoes, a white shirt and brown tie and his good brown tweed jacket. He smelled of Old Spice and his thick wavy hair glistened with Brylcreem. He walked quickly through the streets as if he was on important business. He wanted to post a letter in the GPO in O'Connell Street. 'It's to a lassie in the last place I was. I'm pretending I'm stationed in Dublin.'

'How do you get all these women running after you?'

'A filly can always tell a good stallion.' The streets were flanked with red-brick houses and small front gardens with roses and honeysuckle. Wisps of blue smoke came out of some of the chimneys. He could smell turf and black pudding. Dublin was a homely capital.

Every good-looking girl they saw, O'Keefe gurgled in his throat and audibly sucked air through his teeth. 'I wouldn't mind saying a decade of the Rosary with her, would you?'

They went to the GPO, then walked across O'Connell Bridge, stopping to look down on the Liffey. It was the colour of porter slops at the end of a night's drinking. They looked along the river to the quays, the Customs House and out to sea. 'The best view in Ireland,' O'Keefe said. 'Fifty thousand a year can't be wrong.'

In Nassau Street they got the books he wanted. He'd try to read them for pleasure as well. When they got back to the garage the boy's father was there. 'All ready,' he said, slapping the roof of the car as if dismissing a cow from a byre. 'There wasn't much wrong with it,' the boy said. His father looked at him.

They headed home, O'Keefe driving much more sedately than before. Soon they had left the red-brick houses behind and were out in the country. 'She's handling lovely now. That man and his son are Ford experts. What did you think of Dublin?'

'Ojus. The girls too.'

'When you were buying them books I chatted a lassie, did you not see me? She's agreed to meet me next week at a dance.'

'I saw you okay. The one with the hump and the wooden leg?'

'No use being jealous, boyo. I told her I was a detective.'

'What's sea tangle tents?'

'What? Sea tangle tents? Ah, Janey Mack, you've been reading your oul fellah's *Manual of Criminal Investigation*. You'd get more thrills in the *News of the World*.'

He could feel his face going red. O'Keefe was spot on. He felt ashamed. 'Do you know or don't you?' he asked truculently. 'You don't, do you?'

'Sea tangle tents are twists of brown paper, like you'd light a pipe with. There's strings attached to them. You shove them up inside the woman, you know how that's done, don't you? After a time up there, they swell and then you pull them out. And that brings on what's called an abortion.'

The road was practically empty of cars. There was a black Prefect away in front of them, an Anglia way behind. He wanted to appear sophisticated but at O'Keefe's definition all he could think to say was, 'Holy God.'

When they arrived back in Butlershill they pulled up outside the Garda Station. There was a car parked there and very soon another car drew up behind them. O'Keefe in cheerful mood

171

dropped him off but before he could drive away two men stood in front of the car and another man rapped the window. Customs men. They had followed them the whole way to Dublin and back. His father came out. He and the Customs exchanged nods. 'You amadaun,' he said quietly to O'Keefe. 'He used you. Rinty.'

One of the men, small and fat with a moustache, went to the rear of the V8. 'The boot was loaded with razor blades and butter on the way there and five thousand French letters. Let's see what you have now.'

French letters? O'Keefe was stunned. French letters? The Devil's currency. Five thousand?

In the boot they found musical instruments. Three fiddles, a piano accordion, a banjo, twelve flutes and a set of bagpipes. O'Keefe was astonished. Musical instruments? He started breathing heavily, his face a blank. Dallamullog. This time he had hoodwinked himself. Why had he not put two and two together?

'Did you not think to look?' his father asked him, genuinely bemused. O'Keefe, in a daze, walked into the Station followed by his father and the Customs men carrying the instruments. They looked like a ceilidh band. 'Go you round to married quarters. You clig. Always where you shouldn't be.'

His father's rebuke made him angry. He felt humbled and sad for O'Keefe. They'd throw the book at him. He'd be cashiered straightaway.

His mother was worried. 'What if they charge you as well? French letters? Dear God in Heaven guide and protect us.'

'Maybe they were for Protestants. And English people.'

'They were in me hat. Land of saints and scholars how are you?! We're a leaking boat. Sin pouring in through every crack. You'll have to go to Confessions immediately.'

'I did nothing wrong, Mum. I didn't know they were there.'

'I know, I know.' She stopped wringing the end of her apron and laughed, shimmering, as if being tickled.

'Poor Dallamullog. That's the best yet.'

★ ★ ★

Next morning, top brass from Customs and Excise arrived dressed in uniforms and caps with gold braid. Shortly after, Chief Superintendent Barry — The Bully — and an inspector pulled up in a squad car, driven by a detective from Monaghan. They all cramped into the day room where his father seated them on a form and chairs. The boy stood beside O'Keefe, who was in full uniform. They were looking with loathing and amusement at O'Keefe. The Bully and the head Customs man were grunting like farmyard animals ready to charge. O'Keefe turned his head away from them and stared into the empty fireplace.

The musical instruments were on the table in a higgledy-piggledy pile. Innocent dead abstracts robbed of content. How could they be the subject of crime? He looked at O'Keefe. He stood like a sheep surrounded by dogs. The detective picked up the bagpipes. He said they were a 1933 Hutchinson set worth a small fortune when repaired. The flutes he said were black-ash flutes as good as new when worked on and very expensive. One of the fiddles, he declared, would fetch a hundred pounds. He examined an ornate bow inlaid with tortoise shell. 'They take the keys from an old piano when they need ivory.' He held up the banjo by the neck. Like it was a frozen goose. 'This could be worth five thousand pounds.'

The Bully rumped about on his creaking chair. 'What we have here is a full-blown conspiracy to defraud the Exchequer and Inland Revenue. He picks them up cheap round the South, takes them North, has them done up, then sells them down here. He declares nothing. On either side of the Border. These instruments are the very soul of the country,' he thundered at O'Keefe. Scowling at him, he all the time scratched at the inside of his knee. It made a sound like a dog tearing at a door.

The head Customs man spoke. 'I think we may discount your son. It is obvious he was an unwitting accomplice.' His father dismissed him towards the door with the back of his hand.

He shot out, glad to escape, and banged the main station door shut but opened it quietly again and stepped back in so he could hang about in the hallway listening to the proceedings. He didn't like leaving O'Keefe on his own. He heard the *Garda Síochána Code* being slapped down on the table and a thumb and knuckles scratching angrily through it. In a hubbub of voices, he made out the words 'cashiered', 'sacked', 'kicked out', 'disgraced', 'thundering jackass'. Then everything went quiet.

Eventually he clearly heard his father speaking. 'O'Keefe was used by Maguire, that's solid enough, isn't it? He was soft-soaped from the start. Told what a great footballer he was and so on. He is by nature too cocky for his own good. On the one hand he's a sober, non-smoking, quiet kind of an individual but on the other, he has this wild streak inside. A know-all. He doesn't stop to think. He's a class of a hothead. To my mind he had no idea what was in the boot of that car. Going or coming. It looks bad a member of the Force being nabbed in this fashion. That's a sure thing. But I think, sir, had he known he was being taken advantage, he wouldn't be in this position. He's a class of a hothead. But one thing about him — he's a Pioneer.' With tremendous emphasis, he added, 'Never touches a drop.'

In the pause that followed, he could hear The Bully rumping on the creaking chair. Certainly a teetotal policeman was a gift. That had to be weighed in O'Keefe's favour. They well knew a policeman's lot was very often not a sober one. Bully Barry had raided many's the outpost and found the men half-scuttered on the way to oblivion.

One of the Customs picked up a flute and blew a note. It was a forlorn sound more like a bleat than a bird. 'What about that tinker's daughter business? He was a laughing stock all over the Division.' He assumed it was the

175

inspector talking. The accent was deadpan Midlands. There was a silence and then someone laughed. When The Bully laughed as well, all the others joined in. When they stopped laughing, for a while no one spoke a word.

'What about those French letters?'

'We scuttled them. Dirty dogs. The enactment of lechery without consequence.' It was the voice of the head Customs man.

★　★　★

Three days later, O'Keefe was shifted. Transferred way up further along the Border to the top of Donegal.

'He can cool his heels up there,' his father said with relish. In the dormitory the boy watched him pack his things and helped him by carrying out his greatcoat and hurling stick.

'Goodbye, Josh.'

'A spooky place, this. I won't be crying over it.' He got into the Model T and drove away.

Fleming

His father announced there was a new man coming. He had a wife and two children — twins — and they were going to be living in the last thatched house in the village. All the other houses had slated roofs. Two of them even had television aerials — pointing across the Border towards Belfast. The entire area was now electrified. And most of the roads were tarred. Farmers were buying Davy Brown tractors on hire purchase and getting rid of their faithful horses. There were now ten families with motorcars. His mother was pleased the new arrival had a wife. She'd be company.

'I could do with a friend.'

His mother had the dinner ready for one o'clock. Friday was a fish day. They were eating whiting boiled in milk and served with mashed potato.

They heard a commotion outside. A car horn beeped. Doors slammed. 'That'll be them, the new man,' his father said. 'Go out and ask them in for a cup of tea.' Married quarters and the Garda Station were part of the same low structure. A concrete path circled the building front, back and sideways. It was a squat glorified bungalow with the Garda Síochána insignia on the wall above the front door. He met the new man coming round the corner, carrying a bulging shopping bag.

'Young fellah, your dad's in, is he? Ned Fleming.'

They shook hands.

'Are you on your own?'

'No, she's coming.'

He was older than his father, slightly stooped and had a thick moustache. Two fingers on the hand he shook were nicotine yellow. The moustache under his nose was yellow and black. The uniform hung limply on his thin frame. He had such a thick scraw of grey hair his cap sat high on his head, the peak aiming at the sky. It gave him a jaunty look despite his age. He must have been about sixty. A baby cried. He turned to look and before anyone came into view, said, 'The wife.'

He knew when she came round the corner, carrying two babies, that he would never forget her. That moment. She was so much taller than her husband, so much younger, so beautiful, he couldn't believe she was his wife. Her fair hair was bundled up, a clasp in the shape of a bunch of blue flowers unable to keep some of it out of her eyes. Her face was round and full, the skin milky pale. A silver chain with a crucifix dangled round her creamy neck. She wore a brown suit — jacket and skirt. The skirt was short as if she'd grown out of it. The hem was just above her knees. Her legs were long and strong and bare. She wore flat shoes. He held his hand out to her but immediately felt silly. In the crook of each arm, balanced against her hips, were her two babies, neat and white as bags of sugar. She looked about twenty-seven. Her husband had to be twice her age. She smiled at him and, feeling lucky, he happily smiled back.

When they went into the kitchen he could soon smell Johnson's baby powder, milk, wet nappies and fish. His mother took her down to her bedroom to help her change the babies and feed them. When she'd indicated she breastfed them and didn't need a bottle to be heated, his mother, glancing at him sanctimoniously, her arms spread wide, gently whooshed her out of the kitchen as if she were a big dairy cow.

His father was looking at Fleming, trying to weigh the situation up. He too was wondering — how could this be? She was such a stunner. Ned Fleming just didn't look anywhere near her match. How did it happen? His father started talking about police matters.

'You'll find this place busy enough, Ned. What with the Border and one thing and another. What was that I heard about you in Galway? I'd like to hear it from your own lips.'

'You know it all, Sergeant,' he said, sticking a Sweet Afton between his lips and patting his pockets for a match. His father handed him the tongs. He retrieved a glowing coal from the range and held it up to the cigarette and puffed it to life. He quickly held his cigarette packet out. 'Sorry, Sergeant, do you smoke?'

'In moderation.'

Fleming put the packet back in his tunic breast-pocket. 'I summonsed a local politician. Man dear, I might as well have sat me bare arse on a wasps' nest. They even made representations to the clergy. I wouldn't back down. He

179

only got fined. Drunk as a monkey behind the wheel. The old woman he knocked down is still in hospital. They got rid of me and so here we are.'

'If you don't mind me asking, where's your wife from?'

'She's a Mayo woman. I met her at the Galway races.'

His mother came in carrying one of the babies — the boy. Mrs Fleming had the girl. His mother placed the boy in his arms.

'Careful now, Danny. Keep your hand under his head. Gently. I'll rustle up some food. You must be famished, poor creature.'

'We are that, missus,' Fleming said.

'I wasn't talking to you,' his mother said. They laughed.

Her teeth were perfect. She had a dreamy air about her to do with her Milky Way eyes. He couldn't stop looking at her. She was golden ripe and full as a goose egg.

'I have an appetite and a half,' she said in a kind of an apologetic tone. She smiled at him holding the baby.

'It'll not be long 'til you have one of your own,' Fleming said.

His father laughed. His mother gave a doubtful smile.

His mother could always manage to come up with food at a moment's notice. She gave the remnants of the fish and the last of the mashed potatoes to Fleming and for his wife quickly made an omelette on the old iron pan with the long handle. She loved babies. She looked from one twin to the other with longing and pity. She'd never have another one of her own.

'It's a wonderful world for children. And then they grow up.'

'It makes you think, right enough,' Fleming said, as he picked at his teeth with a curved fishbone. Whiting didn't have as many bones as herring or pike, which was about the only thing you could say in its favour.

His father didn't like conversation taking a doomy turn. You signed up for life the way you signed up for the Force. No use complaining. Get on with it. 'The Man above has it all worked out. That's all we know.'

'They've got another child,' his mother said. 'A three-year-old. He's down in the village.'

'When we got off the bus and he saw all the kids on the green, we couldn't rein him in.' Fleming smiled and nodded as he spoke.

His mother poured tea and sliced a currant cake she'd baked the night before. It took away Friday misery. His father poured the tea from his cup on to his saucer, to cool it, then sloshed it back in the cup. His mother turned her eyes up in disgust.

'All marriages end in failure,' Mrs Fleming said.

They waited for her as if she hadn't finished the sentence. But she didn't add anything. His parents seemed to be trying to think of something to say but didn't have enough information. What did she mean? The baby held in the crook of her arm, she awkwardly buttered a cut of the cake with her free hand.

'Do you mean we all die in the end, is that

what you mean?' his mother asked anxiously.

'That's right, something like that.'

'How long have you been married?' his father asked bluntly.

'That's a good question,' Fleming replied.

'Be the hokey,' his father said, implying there were serious issues at stake even if he didn't know what they were.

'All marriages begin in failure. Maybe that's what I meant.'

'Now you're talking,' Fleming said, the words muffled, preoccupied as he was with picking at a back tooth with the fishbone.

His father stood up and announced that duty called. He wasn't prepared for a discussion bordering on faith and morals with a couple he knew little about and who were dubious enough to warrant suspicion and further enquiry. Not after an enjoyable dinner. Other people's marriages might begin or end in failure but not his. All dinners cooked in his marriage were a gift. His stomach was judge. Why upset the judge? He'd had enough of barium meal tests.

The Flemings went round to the day room to get the key to their rented accommodation, the landlord having left it in that morning. He watched them walk away towards the village, Fleming carrying the bag of baby stuff, she carrying the twins. Her head was last to disappear when they went down the hill.

He remembered, from Christian Doctrine, the definition of supernatural and preternatural. A preternatural gift was one to which a particular creature has no right but may be enjoyed as a natural right by some higher creature. Fleming's wife was a gift. What had he done to deserve it?

★ ★ ★

Helping Reilly in the pub some days later, the customers in the bar discussed the previous night's explosion along the Border. A Customs post had been blown up by the IRA.

'Serves them right,' a stubby man with the nickname 'Butt' said, 'blow them the fuck out of it.'

From behind the bar he reminded Butt that Jim Reilly didn't allow swearing on the premises.

'Fuckem and double-fuckem. Fuckem from a height. And fuck you too, you fucken little fucker.'

He finished his pint with a high elbow flourish and barged out the door. A few guffaws and a derisive cheer followed him. In Butlershill, use of the four-letter word was epic poetry. A regular, PeePee Brady, said, 'Don't mind him, boyo, he had a load of pigs seized last week.' 'PeePee' was from his Christian names, Peter Patrick.

An old man sitting alone, nursing his pint, shook his head and said with quiet conviction, 'I heard tell he got a legacy from Amerikaw. She's got everything she wants. I seen her in Morgan's in Clinis yesterday and she bought a whole clatter of bran' new saucepans. When he kicks the bucket, she'll have the crock a gold to herself, now do you see?' He had a curious way of pronouncing place names. Clinis was Clones, a nearby town.

'What's he talkin' about?' PeePee asked.

'The new Guard and his wife. Have you not clapped eyes on her yet?' The speaker, Plucker McCabe, had a red and blue nose from a lifetime drinking spirits. It was said the thumb-sized bags under his eyes were full of brandy.

Simon 'Blackpuss' Hall, the Flemings' land-lord, came in. He was a rangy, loose-limbed man, always in wellingtons, black trousers, a collarless shirt, a waistcoat, a black hat, and always busy. His trousers were held up by braces and a thick belt with a buckle big enough to shoe an ass. He had a rectangular moustache which despite his age was black as soot. An abstemious man, he ordered a glass of red lemonade.

'Me throat's parched with dust. I've been at the hay all day. Then I had to go and bring a new double bed for Mrs Fleming, from Cavan. Big as a boxing ring.'

'Yah didn't try the gloves on with her, did yah?' PeePee said from under his fingers, which were always up on his lips. As if he was unsure whether to let the words out or not.

The men laughed. Blackpuss, unmarried, was well known for trying it on with women even though he was in his seventies. 'If I got in with her, I wouldn't have gloves on. Or anything else either.' The men laughed again. He had a good-sized farm and gave some of them an occasional day's work.

From behind the bar he could see a long silver spoon sticking out of Blackpuss's pocket. Like a magpie, Blackpuss couldn't help taking anything sparkling. His father said an arsonist, a poisoner, a kleptomaniac couldn't be cured. It was from the Greek and meant stealing madness. He probably filched the spoon when he was in Cavan getting the bed for Mrs Fleming.

'On the way home, boyo, she wants you to call in on her.'

'Me? I won't be going home until nearly midnight.'

'Doesn't matter. She wants you to do something for her.'

The men looked at him, grinning. He felt embarrassed.

'What does she want?'

'Probably try out the springs with her,' Plucker said.

The men laughing, he went out the back of the bar and into the room where Jim Reilly held meetings. Reilly was there with a number of people discussing a drag hunt which the local hound club were running on the coming Sunday. Reilly looked up at him.

'I have to go now,' he announced bluntly, 'in a minute.' He knew he was blushing.

'Your ears are red; we were just mentionin' you,' a hunter called 'Wire' McGurn said, pleased to see him. 'We wonder could you lay the scent for us? There'll be a dead fox and aniseed in a sack and all you have to do is drag it over the course before the race. Three mile around Kilifana lake, finishing in McCaffrey's gap. We need a fit lad the like a-yah.'

McGurn was a thin, bent, elderly man, as rooted in his country as a briar in a hedge. He'd do it for them but he couldn't wait to get out and up the village to Mrs Fleming's house.

The night was warm, the Milky Way spangled across the sky. Like the Finn River under moonlight dancing with silver eels. Just above the wooded hills a bright planet hung alone.

He knocked on the door. Mrs Fleming, barefooted, bare-legged and wearing a nightie that didn't pass below her knees, answered. Her fair hair tumbled round her shoulders.

'Ah, good lad, will you do something for me?'

The hallway was blocked with a bicycle and an old bed, and he crushed something underfoot: an apple. In the kitchen nothing seemed in place. Dirty dinner dishes were still on the table. There was a bread crust and eggshells on the floor. Chairs were in the middle of the room in no particular order. A plastic child's spoon with a lump of rice still in it sat on top of the range. There were unwashed nappies in a basin over by the window. He could smell urine.

'Your father's put Ned on a week of rising patrols. He went off without the sangwidges I made up for him. And his flask of Ovaltine. Will you take them to him? He needs to eat reglar on account of his ulcer.'

The skimpy nightie just about prevented her mighty breasts escaping.

'Where is he — your husband?'

'Ned. He's out be Annie's Bridge. You'll find him there. Borrow my bike. It's got a dynamo.'

His mouth was as dry as the crust lying on the floor. There was nowhere for his eyes to rest except on her bosom or her face. He tried staring at the floor but felt like an idiot.

'An ulcer?' He couldn't think of anything else to say. There was a narrow stairs leading from the bedrooms down into the kitchen. A young boy, dragging a white aluminium piss-pot, came down the stairs, bumping along on his bottom from one step to the next.

'Go back to bed, Oliver.'

'Bum-bum poo-poo, Mammy,' he protested. The back door was open to the night. The boy went out, put the pot down on the concrete step but instead of sitting on it, he did his business on the step itself. A perfect brown coil steamed in the amber light. An upturned cone pointing at the stars.

'Go to bed now, Oliver,' she said casually. He clunked the pot down over it, hiding it. 'Ba-bat there. Goat.'

He went back up the stairs. Just before he disappeared, he stared down suspiciously at him through the rails.

''Night, Oliver.'

He shot out of sight. She got up and closed the back door but didn't do anything about clearing the step.

'He thinks the corncrake is a goat.'

Along the swampy river the corncrakes spent the summer. Their grating call was their worst enemy. People wanted to kill them for keeping them awake all night.

She lit a cigarette. 'Smoke?'

'No thanks, Mrs Fleming.'

'My name is Apricot.'

She smiled with tremendous woebegone innocence. He half thought he was dreaming. He

187

didn't care her house was a mess.

'Why are you called Apricot?'

'My mother.' She shrugged and blew a whirl of smoke from the corner of her lips. 'Apricot O'Neill. We were kings in another country.'

'Which country was that?'

'Tyrone. But Cromwell shooed us out of it.' She pronounced Cromwell 'Crumell'.

People claimed the past as though it were only a short while ago. At college the teacher said history was a pot forever boiling.

'Ah, there it is,' she said, taking up an off-white dressing gown from the back of a chair. She put it on and tucked it round her. She was like a Greek statue come to life. Which statue he hadn't a clue. But she was standing there in front of him, a living, smoking marble goddess.

'You're going to be a big help to me, that's great. Off you go now. Ned will be hungry.'

'What do you . . . think of But . . . Butlershill, Apricot? Now that you've been . . . here a while, Apricot.' His tongue acted like it was glued to the roof of his mouth.

'I don't go out much. So.' She shrugged and twitched her lips. She picked a fleck of tobacco from her long pink tongue.

He now noticed the twins, asleep in a pram under the stairs. He got her bicycle and fought his way out the hallway past the old bed with its burst wire mesh spring, whilst trying not to walk on the upturned bucket of apples. Her house was an untidy Garden of Eden with a second-best bed.

As he rode off, a corncrake rattled the dark as

188

if complaining, 'It's you disturbs me. Crake. Crake-crake.'

It was late, after midnight. The dynamo, low down on the right fork, gave him just about enough light but he knew the road well enough. The air was warm and perfumed with new-mown hay, woodbine, wild roses, bluebells, the damp grassy fields. Descending the hills at speed almost burst his lungs with pleasure. He was never happier, never so puzzled. He was going to ask Guard Fleming how it was he got to marry Apricot O'Neill. He went up a laneway rutted with potholes. The hedges were so thick, out-growing fuchsia and honeysuckle whipped his face. Going past a gateway he could smell the cattle standing there. Rancid grassy belchers with big eyes glinting moonlight. Apricot eyes. Riding by a lake, he stopped to listen and look up at the stars. Ursa Major was tilted like a plough going up a drumlin. A duck quacked suspiciously from the water, 'I know you're there. We can see you. Quack-quack.'

He rode onwards and from the top of a hill saw the Finn River snaking through the dark land. Like the Milky Way across the heavens. One was the reflection of the other.

He wasn't far from Annie's Bridge. Men jumped out at him from the hedges and shone lights into his face. Headlights were switched on. A jeep. It was the Irish Army. A tall officer, middle-aged, stood before him. 'And where are you going without a bell on your bike?'

'I have a bell on my bike.' He rang it. 'Except it isn't my bike. I'm looking for Guard Fleming.

I have sandwiches for him and a drink.'

'His wife isn't with you, is she?' His men laughed. They were all around him and the jeep light was now partly blocked by their bodies. The officer was a captain, confident in his power and authority. He and his men had obviously seen Mrs Fleming or had heard about her.

'Where is Guard Fleming? I need to be going.'

The Captain, staring into him, didn't answer for a while. 'You're the college boy. I saw you going round to married quarters one day with your mother. Fleming's down on the bridge.'

They stood to one side. The jeep light turned off, it took him a few seconds to get used to the dark again. They stood in a clump, their rifles at the ready. But for the veneer of technology, democracy and clothes, they might as well have been a bunch of cavemen with clubs.

Since he had ridden up the laneway he had crossed the Border twice. He wondered why anyone would want to fight over such a squelchy territory. Yet under starlight it was a treasure island, worth every song ever written about it.

He bumped down the lane, which had become rougher and bumpier the closer he got to the bridge. He could just about see the dark shape of Fleming standing alone by the parapet.

'Guard Fleming?'

'Oh be the holy, you knocked the heart crossways in me.'

'Sandwiches and Ovaltine?'

'Me belly was thinking me throat was cut.'

On the parapet he fumbled open the old newspaper wrapping and ate hungrily.

'Grand. Grand now. Do you want a bite?'

'No thanks, Guard Fleming. The soldiers stopped me.'

'The place is crawling with them tonight. On both sides.'

The river gently slapped the stones beneath them and purred through the reeds. In its flowing moonlight nighty and the swampy fields under their deep dark eiderdown of blue, the Border land seemed happily asleep.

'Well, what are they saying about me?'

'Who?'

'The people round about.'

Even in the dark, Fleming appeared old. Unlike his father, there was no sense of dynamism from him at all. It was hard to imagine why he was still serving. Perhaps he'd been sent to Butlershill so his father could persuade him to retire. The night lay in dark patches in the slack folds of his uniform raincoat.

'They wonder how you managed to marry your wife.'

He chuckled and threw something down into the river. A crust perhaps. He pointed a matchstick with his thumbnail then sucked at the end to soften it so he could get it in between his back teeth.

'Uhm, agh, well,' he grunted, as he poked around in his mouth, 'ahm, it happened. Do you study the stars at school?'

A curlew shot from the water and soared away, its cry curving across the sky in the shape of its beak.

'We do. Atlas holds up the heavens.'

'Oh. You do the Classics, do you? Do you know about Pandora?'

'She opened the jar and let out Old Age and Madness. And Corruption. Passion.'

'Better looking than Helen of Troy. And as lazy as she was beautiful.'

He wondered was he referring to his wife. He was pleased he knew about the Greeks. He was softly spoken. Intelligent. Gentle.

'Why are you on duty here tonight?'

'Tonight I'm the eyes of the State. So it can sleep in peace. I was married before, did your father tell you?'

'No. No. What happened? Is she . . . she must be dead, is she?'

'Dead. A long time ago now.'

He leaned across the parapet, looking down into the water. They both did. He didn't want to ask him how she died in case the memory caused him pain. They could see a slither of eels flowing darkly through the water. Sometimes they twisted over so their bellies shone silver. A big pike leaped amongst them, the splash visible in the moonlight. Fleming leaned his head right back.

'It reminds me of our old hayshed and its rusty corrugated iron roof. Full of holes. And the light coming through.'

'Maybe there's wee green men up there looking down on us. Wondering why we don't come to them. It's a time-space world,' he added, quoting his physics teacher.

Fleming's silence for a while matched the immense silence of the night. Then he said,

'Well, as the woman said, if you have the time I have the space.'

'What happened?'

'I had a motorbike. I made me own sidecar. We were married two year. I got an old chassis, did it up good as new. A friend got me sheets of plywood. I made a neat door, the whole shebang. A plastic windscreen. A roof. I made it comfortable for her with duck-feather cushions. She liked seeing different places round about. We travelled to the Cliffs of Moher one day. I went for a bit of a walk. She stayed in the sidecar having a cigarette. When I came back, the whole thing was alight. She was burnt to death. Trapped. I mustn't have heard her screams above the roaring of the ocean and the wind. She was wearing a summer frock. It caught fire. That and the cushion. Desperate. Desperate to the wide world.'

★ ★ ★

Later on when he rode home — the soldiers were no longer in the laneway — he could think of nothing, see nothing but the image of the sidecar burning. Hear nothing but Ned Fleming's first wife screaming. Imagine nothing but his awful pain. He couldn't marry again until years later when he met Apricot O'Neill. Only her beauty could cancel out the past.

His emotions switching around, he didn't return her bicycle. He couldn't face her knowing what he now knew. Besides, it was too late.

When he reached home, his mother was sitting

193

up waiting for him. She was darning one of his father's woollen socks. She had the ponger in the sock, right up at the heel, stretching the hole there, the better to darn over it. She'd washed her hair and had a towel round her head. Her face was pale, her eyes wide with delight at seeing him.

'I thought something had happened you. Where were you?'

'Mrs Fleming asked me to bring sandwiches to Ned. At Annie's Bridge. Know something, Mum, he's a very nice man. He's intelligent too. I can see why she would marry him. He's a caring person. That's what I think.'

'And you know what I think? I think she's another man's leavings.'

'What do you mean?'

'He married her because no one else would have her. She has another man's child. That boy isn't Fleming's. So Bessy Darcy told me.'

Bessy Darcy was the priest's housekeeper. Her wagging tongue could dish out scandal like a farmer spreading dung.

'That's a horrible thing to say about her. In that way. Another man's leavings. Ned's first wife died. Did Daddy tell you that?'

'He did. And I prayed for her. And him. Poor man. I never liked motorbikes.'

His father had borrowed a car one day and they drove to the seaside. Even though he couldn't drive properly. His mother was happy to sit in the car and stare out at the sea. Women were like that. Men had to be doing; women had to be thinking.

He'd return the bicycle next morning and he'd ask her was she another man's leavings. Not in those words. But he'd try and find out. Another man's leavings. He hated the phrase. It was demeaning, without charity, loaded with moral disapproval and a warning to others not to have sex outside marriage. It was also a slur on the man who would dare marry such a woman. They didn't need rope to hang you. They could do it in words.

★ ★ ★

In the morning he put a good dollop of his father's Brylcreem in his hair and, though he hadn't started shaving, sprinkled his aftershave all over his face, neck, ears and hands.

When his father saw him he said, 'Good God, man, you smell like the inside of a hoor's handbag. Where are you going?'

'I'm returning Mrs Fleming's bike.'

'I'll do that. I have to see Ned.'

'She wants me to help get rid of an old bed as well.'

It was clear his father didn't want him going near her. He was trying to baulk him. But he went out the door, jumped on the bike and rode down to her house.

Simon Hall was with her. Blackpuss. She was wearing a smart skirt and matching jacket and brown shoes. Her sheaf of hair was pinned back behind her ears. She wasn't wearing make-up. Her face was buttercup, her eyes big as half-crowns. Her body was such a configuration of curves her clothes couldn't disguise it. She was as tall as Blackpuss, who stood close to her, his face only inches from her as he talked.

'Where's himself?'

'He's still in bed. He was on duty all night. Do you want him?'

'No, no, not at all. Let sleeping dogs lie. The young fellah here can help me with the bed.'

He put his hand out and gave a friendly pat to her hip. Then, before she could object, he stood back so she couldn't take offence.

She looked across to the boy, smiled and raised her eyes. He wondered could she smell his aftershave.

Blackpuss went towards her again and in a confidential voice said, 'That shed down the garden — we'll carry it out and put it in there. It might come in handy to block a gap.' Farmers used bed springs and bed-heads to stop cattle escaping through holes in the hedges. 'If that's okay with you, missus; you're the boss.'

This time he pawed her rump. She stood stock-still as if challenging him. But he broke away quickly and went out into the hallway. She blew exasperated air through her lips.

'You smell awful nice.'

'So . . . so do you, Apricot.'

The boy, Oliver, was out on the back step bashing a clock with a big boot obviously belonging to Ned. 'Get that end, boyo, and we'll dump her for the time being. Mind the step. And the cawdee.' Cawdee was a young person.

The shed was quite a big one, backing on to the creamery river. They slung the spring up

196

against an old wardrobe and a number of drawers that had belonged to a dressing table. There was a mildewed mattress in there as well. Black-puss adjusted his hat and rested his hands on the buckle of his belt.

'She's some pussycat, what? Huh?'

When they came out, he looked across the river at the big hilly field sweeping down to the swampy bottom.

'There's a hill needs reseeding,' he said, plucking at his moustache.

His small eyes took in everything in sight, near and far.

The previous summer he'd helped him save hay. He liked Blackpuss. He was free and easy in his opinions and didn't care a rap for man nor beast. 'When we're shoving up the daisies who'll give a rap for us?'

During the war he was caught stealing the iron railings that ran along the demesne drive up to Lady Sarah's mansion. He was taking the iron across the Border and selling it for Britain's war effort against the Germans. It was a black mark against his character for which he was still held at arm's length by his Protestant neighbours.

He wished he'd go away and leave him to talk with Apricot. They went back inside the house. Blackpuss stood close to her as he reported on the bed manoeuvres. As if it was an affair of State.

'We put it in a safe place out of the way of your young lad. Say hello to Ned for me.'

For a moment he thought he was going to kiss her. But almost without her knowing, he landed his hand on her thigh. She stood still. She was used to pawing. He left and they watched him ride away on an ancient Raleigh bike that looked as if it weighed a ton.

'You were such a good lad last night, going to Ned with the sangwidges.'

From upstairs they heard a snore. She laughed.

'He'll sleep 'til the cows come home.'

Her boy came and clung to her legs, his arms right round them. As if reading his thoughts, he'd gotten between him and his mother. The kitchen was tidier but not by much. There was a pot of cabbage soaking in cold water down by the leg of the table and the sweepings of the floor lay scattered in front of the range. The white aluminium chamber pot was on the table with eggs in it.

'Your husband told me he was married before.'

'Yes, he told me he'd told you.'

'How did you and he end up together?'

'We're together but I hope it's not the end.'

He felt easy in her presence because he knew, for now anyway, he hadn't the guts or the cheek or whatever it took for a man to put his hand on a woman. Unlike Blackpuss.

He sat at the table. She sat by the range. The boy went upstairs. Probably to waken his father. Though it seemed it wasn't his father. According to the gossips.

Her hands were on her knees, rubbing them through her nylon stockings. Her sleeves went up her arms, revealing her slender wrists. She

198

fingered her earlobes. Her ears were perfect too. Putting her hand up the edge of her skirt she tugged her petticoat down. She sat demure as a nun.

'I was never one for me books. At school. I got a job in a hotel and then I come home to look after Mammy. After Daddy died. I met a boy me own age. This is all what you want to hear, isn't it? People should mind their own business. I'm not saying you. You look a bit like him. A lot like him, God's honest truth. We couldn't keep our paws off each other. You know the way it is.'

'I don't.'

She looked at him as if checking he was serious. She smiled; she could see he was.

'I fell for him anyways and got with a baby. As soon as I told him, he wanted me to go to England for an operation. I near hardly knew what he was talkin' about. Me mother wouldn't hear of the like. Then, like a cut cat, he run away. To Manchester, leaving me in the lurch. I hadn't judged him rightly. I begged his family for his address but they didn't have it or wouldn't give it. I cried me eyes out. I haven't seen him from then 'til now.'

She picked up the poker from beside the range and prodded at the fire with not much enthusiasm. Her tragedy made her more lovely in his eyes.

'It was the talk of the country, I needn't tell you. The priest and the nuns started comin' round. They'd take me in and have the babby offa me. Mammy wouldn't let them. I didn't know what to do. He was born in our own house. The midwife said a decade of the Rosary as she was deliverin' it. In case the Devil was lurking about. When I wheeled him out for the first time in the pram, didn't the priest tell me to have some shame and not be seen showing off my sin around the town. My best friend, Maggie Wilson, never spoke to me again. Hardly a soul round the place had the guts.

'And then, what do you think? Didn't this oul eegit of an auctioneer businessman start comin' round after me. Every time he saw me he come over pawin' and scrapin'. 'I don't mind,' he says, 'about the babby. I'll take the two of ye on.' Holy Mother of Smokes, he was the quare oul cod. He promised me the wealth of the world.

'Then didn't I meet Ned at the Galway races. He was on duty. Fellahs were walking after me. They thought I was someone. Then when they heard me speaking they knew I was the same as themselves and didn't they start bumpin' me and pawin' at me and beggin' to take me out. One big bostoon of a horseyman had me by the wrist. Ned stepped in and told him to let me go. That's how I met Ned. He looked after me from then on. The priest, when he heard we were transferred to here, told me to pass me son off as me young brother. That Mammy couldn't look after on account of her health. I was another man's leavin's, he says, plain as you like, right into me face.'

She plonked the poker back into its bucket with a clatter. Her accent was sing-song Mayo and rough at the edges. Her beauty was such she could barely understand it. It was a burden to her, giving her a sad air and a fatalistic delivery. He couldn't take his eyes off her. Her face and stature were firmer than his dreams. She was out of his reach, though he could have stretched out and touched her. She stood up with her back to the range, her hands on her hips and looked down at him. He got to his feet. She smiled to him like a young girl.

'Off you go now,' she said, like a woman. He did as bid, like a boy.

As he was going, her son came down the stairs singing 'How much is that doggie in the window?' He had a sweet voice.

He heard Fleming calling, 'Apricot, can you come up here a minute? Like a good girl.'

Next door lived a man who played the button accordion. The strains of 'She Moves Through The Fair' wafted out the open window, then changed into 'Smoke Gets In Your Eyes.'

★ ★ ★

His father came down the hill on his bicycle. He was going for a swim. He went along with him. At the lake his father stripped naked and stood facing the water, enjoying the sun warming his strong body. The lake was surrounded by meadows and whin-bush hills. There wasn't anyone else around. Locals were afraid of the water. They never learned to swim. The mothers were all superstitious and dreaded every lake in the county. Of which there were hundreds.

His father was brazen in his nakedness. When he pulled on his old red flannel trunks, he splashed his head and made the sign of the cross. He had a big brown mole near his shoulder blade.

He joined his hands as if in prayer and, standing where he was in the shallows, did a spectacular belly-flop. He came up flicking his head like a wet dog shaking itself, then plunged about like a whale, enjoying the turfy freshness and the bracing temperature.

He watched for a bit and then joined him. He didn't have togs so had to get in naked. It was like swimming in Guinness, the water was so brown and black.

'Man oh man, isn't this grand?' his father shouted.

The muddy bottom was a mixture of soil, sand and big stones. You had to be careful of crigging your toes.

A goods train whistled as it entered a deep cutting on the other side of the lake hill. They stood up and listened. They could hear the wagon couplings and wheels rumbling and then saw the engine emerge, steam whooshing, smoke streaming, the sun flashing on the coal tender. It was like a picture in a book.

'Pigs and cattle from Leitrim and Belturbet, and barrels of stout for Clones, Monaghan and Dundalk,' his father said. He plunged down again and, turning over, floated on his back. By now his flannel trunks barely covered his pubic hair.

That train rattling in the velvet distance he knew he'd never forget. He'd never forget first seeing Apricot O'Neill. He'd never forget standing with his father in the lake, the sun shining on them, the water glinting, the train ripping through the cutting to emerge as if from a dream.

Over in the long reeds he noticed what looked like two lumps of wood. Pikes basking.

When they finished splashing about and rubbing themselves down — it was so much better than a tin bath — they came out on to the grass. His father had a skimpy towel but he walked about naked, letting the sun and breeze dry him. He had to do the same. His father had the towel gripped in his hand and wouldn't let it go.

'Isn't it great to be alive?'

He was a bit ashamed walking about naked with him. His father was proud of his body, his strength, his chiselled face and piercing clear blue eyes. He'd had a haircut. Ned Fleming had done it with a scissors, comb and cut-throat razor.

'Bedads,' he had heard him saying to his mother, 'he's good for something anyway.'

They ran over and back through the soft long grass. Not a soul about; it was a kind of paradise. His father stopped and towelled at his head. Then he threw the towel to him.

'You spent a bit of time with Mrs Fleming.'

'I did. What do you think of her?'

'She's no better than she should be. And no worse than she is.'

They dressed and headed up the field for the gap through which they'd come.

'Have you no sympathy for her? Her delicate situation?'

'Don't talk to me, man. Something similar happened to us before I left home. My brother, Jack, met an older woman. He was only nineteen. She landed him in it. Young fellahs are no match at all for older women. They had to get married. A baby. It couldn't have happened at a worse time. He was just ready to take over with the digging and the hay, the milking, helping my father. Your grandfather, God rest him. Lo and behold didn't they tough it out and went to live in the town, only a few miles away. Oh, she was a brazen one. They had nothing. Hardly a penny to their name. 1920 it was. The shame. They went to Glasgow. It was worse there than at home. They couldn't get enough work to buy a loaf of bread. They had to come back with their tails between their legs. I had joined up by then. When I'd come home on holiday, I'd sneak into the town and give him a few bob.'

'Why did you have to sneak in?'

'Granny. My mother. She was very bitter about it. Just when they could have done with help, he goes off and does that. Caught like a rat in a sack. A woman who should have known better. I often wonder did she do it on purpose, to trap him. Every Christmas Eve, Granny — my mother — lit a candle in the window for each member of the family. A candle for Peg, Eileen, Maggie. A candle for Julia. A candle for Helen. Sarah. Susan. A candle for Petey. A candle for me. But never a candle for Jack. It was heartbreaking. They were living with their baby in one room in the town with hardly a stick of furniture. He got bits of work cutting turf or ploughing for someone. I was next in age to him. I whispered to Petey one night I was leaving home next morning for Dublin. 1923. 'You're welcome to the place,' I says. I didn't want it.'

'What happened Jack?'

'They went to England. To Oxford. He got work in a car factory there and, thanks be to God, they survived. He was a great skilled worker of course, Jack was. Marvellous in the month of August to see him wield a scythe. They have their own house now and everything. They had another child, but, God help us this day, didn't she get killed running across the street. The cross some people have to bear!'

They walked along the dusty road, his father stony silent.

'I'd bring them eggs, a bag of turf. A shilling.'

He was still back in the past.

'What did Uncle Jack look like? Was he tall or small?'

'He was the very spit of yourself,' he answered, swinging his leg over the bar of his bike and riding away, leaving him to walk home. The Parthian shot was a warning. Keep your passions under control or you'll end up like him in more ways than one.

★ ★ ★

The sun, high in the sky, blazed like a ruck on fire. As well as rain, the Border fields loved their share of heat. Now the dew had been burned away, farmers circled their fields turning hay with forks, flicking the swathes over, fluffing

205

them up so the warm air went through them. In the ragwort football field a bullock rumped against a goalpost, then turned about and rubbed its neck up and down against it. Two Red Admirals, giddy with life, flitted over a hedge. A Devil's Needle landed on the road in front of him. It had a long slim body, long legs, big eyes, gorgeous blue and white wings.

When he got back into the village, Apricot was coming out of Tully's shop with a bag of groceries. Steadying herself, she got on her bicycle and rode home. She was an amazing sight. She wasn't wearing her jacket. Her skirt was well up her thighs and her white blouse had ridden up her back. Her legs were bare. The children ran after her. Jim Reilly stood watching from the pub doorway. The blacksmith, a hessian sack for an apron, a big hammer in his hand, looked up from shoeing a horse. Even the horse lifted its head. Her legs were so long she had to pedal with her knees close together to stop them hitting the handlebars. The bike was too small for her. She overflowed. 'Grace Kelly on a bicycle,' Jim Reilly said.

★ ★ ★

The following Sunday they asked him again to lay the scent for another drag hunt. He put on his football boots and an old pair of trousers tucked into his socks. The sack containing the scent — as usual a dead fox and aniseed — stunk. The neck of the sack was tied with a rope, the other end of which he had in his hand.

He dragged it behind him over the three-mile course. He had to get a move on because the hounds needed a fresh scent. They were let out fifteen minutes after he started running.

The course was round by a different lake, which for the most part was surrounded by flat fields. However, there was a big hill riddled with briar, rushes, ragwort, dock and thistle and some blackthorn clumps which always managed to snag the drag bag. When he reached the top of this hill, almost out of breath he slowed down.

Away across the lake he could see another hill packed with the spectators. He headed for them and to the winning gap. The gap was between two fields. First dog through the gap was the winner. It should have been a straightforward business sorting out the best hound. But dog owners skulked as near the gap as they could get and called quietly or whistled softly to their dog to entice them through. For some reason a dog who was away ahead quite often wouldn't come through into the winning field. They'd remain sniffing about and waiting for the others to catch up.

The hound men didn't like drag hunts. They preferred the real thing. Hounds liked to kill. A fox. A hare. Dogs knew there was nothing at the end of a drag but a pat on the head or a bit of bread. That's why they wouldn't come through the gap. Fights often broke out among the owners. His father always made sure there was a member on duty. That was why, across the water, he could see the sun glint on Guard Fleming's silver buttons. Whenever he saw Fleming now he couldn't help thinking of the sidecar burning on the Cliffs of Moher.

As he ran down the final hill, two men burst out from behind a clump of whin and ran with him. They were tough-looking. He was alarmed. One of them had a lump on his forehead.

'You're okay, gauson, we'll trot with you to the end. You're annoyin' your one. Apricot. She towl a friend you were only dry-ridin' her. Billser here — she gave him the eye a Tuesday.'

'Right,' said Billser, 'so lave her alone.'

They grinned at him. He had no idea who they were.

He heard a great cheer and a deluge of barking and knew the beagles had been let loose. He ran as fast as he could to the finish. He soon left the two behind. Like dogs, they were out for the kill.

All of a lather, he ran through the gap and up the hill to Guard Fleming. He didn't mention anything to him about the two men. But he'd definitely speak to Apricot.

As the dogs neared the finish, the owners and supporters crowded towards the gap. Men acting as stewards tried to keep them at a distance. Someone whistled and quickly received a whack on the ear. The blow was swift and powerful enough to land the man on his bottom in the long grass. He was wearing his Sunday suit and for a moment it looked as if he had just sat down for a rest.

Two dogs were way out in front. The owners, crouching low, tiptoed along the hedge towards the gap. People shouted at them to get back. One of them was a tall man from a neighbouring parish. The other was Atty Brady, a stocky local. Ned Fleming, true policeman, watched dispassionately the passions boiling. He held his arms outstretched at one point. His uniform hanging slackly on his thin frame gave him, for that moment, the disembodied appearance of a scarecrow.

The leading pair — the brown and the white — having led all the way, came bounding up to the gap but, instead of coming through, stopped when they noticed the crowd on the hill. As if they knew what was expected of them, seemingly out of spite, they went off the scent, cocked a leg and drank eagerly from a pool of water. The watching crowd hardly dared breathe. The pursuing pack was rapidly gaining ground. But the two would not come through. The brown one was owned by the big stranger. The white was Brady's. Someone, quiet as could be, coaxed them with a clicking tongue. The brown cocked its head and shot through the gap, when it was immediately grabbed by its owner, who slipped a length of binder twine round its neck. The crowd shouted, cheered, swept forward. First prize was a cup and a fiver. Brady's dog was now caught in the pell-mell of the rest of the field and didn't even gain second place.

The summer field became a torrent of men and dogs and flailing fists. Guard Fleming tried to placate Atty Brady, who was trying to punch the winning owner, claiming his dog had won illegally.

'My lad, Leggykelly Buck, was done out of it. Be a cunning call.'

Still holding his dog with one hand, the stranger backed up the hill in front of Brady, not letting him gain the upper ground. He calmly hit him a few good blows on the chin and would have knocked him out but for Fleming intervening. The field, as if transformed in a dream, was a seething, surging tangle of limbs, vibrant faces and desperate roars. Fights ignited all over the place. Like whins catching fire.

The grass, velvety in the sun, was mashed by boots, shoes, wellies; rolled over by tossed bodies; torn out in lumps to wipe bloody faces; pawed to mud by dozens of confused dogs.

Someone accidentally hit Guard Fleming and drew blood from his nose. Blood pumped on to his shirt and uniform jacket. As if he was being pelted with haws. Someone shouted, 'Hit him again, he's no relation.'

Jim Reilly staunched the blood with a rag and took him away in his car.

The stranger prevailed. Holding the silver cup aloft, he brazened his way out of the field in determined triumph. He had come down with his dog from Drung and had beaten the locals at their own game.

A woman — his wife — scolded Atty Brady. 'Bad and all as you are, couldn't you have got the upper ground of him itself?' Three hundred and sixty four days of the year Atty was as peaceful a man as existed.

The boy retrieved his bike and headed for the village. It had been a wondrous dogfight. But the blows were struck by men. He'd felt demeaned by the 'dry-ridin'' remark. That's what one cow did to another, denoting she needed the bull. The Billser fellow was a bull. Not him. He was only a boy. He was in the way and if you were in the way you got trampled on.

He sat with Apricot in her kitchen and she smiled as he told her what happened at the drag hunt. Told her about Billser. It was always the same. Men hung outside her house like tom cats crying at night for the mog within. His mother had been to visit and had invited her for tea that evening. So she'd see him later. On his way out she told him Ned was having a rest upstairs.

'Poor Ned. A punch on the nose wouldn't upset Ned. Sure he's been attacked several times.'

He went home. His mother had the kitchen spotless and though it was a sunny day there was a roaring fire in the range. 'I'm a salamander, no mistake.' She hated an empty fireplace. Heat was generous; cold was mean.

He brought in her white blouse which she'd washed, starched, ironed and hung on the privet hedge to dry. Her best brown skirt hung over the back of a chair. Her suede high heels were placed neatly on a sheet of newspaper on top of the sewing machine. Her stockings looped the line under the mantelpiece. The line was a length of hairy twine nailed up by his father. She'd been reading the *Sacred Heart Messenger*. It lay on the table, the page held open by a spoon.

'There is a God no matter what they say anyway,' she said quietly, as if speaking her thoughts.

'No doubt, Mum. But does He mean us any good?'

'Good has to be earned. God loves a trier.'

His father came in from patrolling round the district on his bike. In a lather of sweat, he stripped off his shirt and vest. His mother had a towel ready. They took it in turns to rub down his back. Hands on the edge of the sewing machine, he bent over and with the strong smell of perspiration might have been a horse.

'A bit lower. That's it. Good.'

They exchanged looks and his mother turned her eyes to the ceiling.

'If I had a nosebag, I'd hang it round your ears.'

She handed him a glass of barley water.

'I stopped a lorryload of men. They said they were a football team. I sent them packing.'

'Guard Fleming had his nose punched at the drag hunt.'

'That'll learn him.'

'They're coming to tea this evening. So make sure you're here.'

He finished off the barley water and picking up a fresh vest and shirt went down to his room. He hated the inconvenience of visitors. All the small talk and false manners and the waste of time, when he could be reading the paper or down the garden moulding the spuds. Or just sitting in the kitchen watching his wife, the gentle way she did everything, her ease in the world, something he never had and never would. They were years married. He wasn't used to her yet.

★ ★ ★

212

Apricot arrived first. She had the twins in the pram and parked them over by the window. Her son Oliver came in with a tin drum hanging round his neck. He was in brown sandals and neat pleated pants and a blue shirt with a bow tie. He hated the clothes but he loved the drum and every now and then whacked it with tiny drumsticks. When he did, the twins twitched their legs and arms. Apricot, barelegged, wore a white summer frock. She had her hair tumbling round her shoulders.

His father came into the kitchen in his good grey flannel trousers and shirt. He had dragged a wet comb through his hair.

His mother had the table packed with homemade bread, pies and cakes she'd baked, eggs, salad, beetroot, fresh scallions from the garden, milk, cream. She had her best crockery on display and silver cutlery. Most of it had been her mother's. They were the only items she had to shore her life against misfortune. A knife and fork were from the convent she boarded at on the shores of Lough Conn. There weren't many days when she didn't think of that place. The German, French, Scottish nuns. Her friends, her sisters, her favourite and dear dead sister Aloysius, who promised she'd come back from the dead and speak to her.

'Has she come back yet, Mum?'

'No, not yet.'

The boy startled them all by banging on his drum. The Sergeant stared at him.

'Bedad, any more of that and you'll have to have your tea down with the hens.'

The boy froze, looked as if he was going to cry, then, removing the drum, sat still as a plump cushion.

His mother told Apricot about her family and how well off they had been. Occasionally she liked to boast. To remind the world she came from good stock. As she spoke she fussed about, serving, pouring, stirring, cutting bread.

'And what happened to you?' Apricot asked.

'Oh, well, I met the Sergeant, for a start.'

They laughed. His father smiled. He didn't believe in laughing and chewing at the same time. The *Reader's Digest* said laughter was the best medicine. But as far as he was concerned not while eating. The best medicine whilst eating was mastication.

The door opened and Ned Fleming came in. He had a bandage across his nose and the rings under his eyes looked dark. He looked comic. Wistful. Not well. Yellow-looking.

'Why me?' he said with a shrug. Apricot laughed.

'Sit down, Ned,' said his father. 'You'll be better in the shake of a lamb's tail. An unfortunate occurrence, nothing more.'

Fleming lit a cigarette and snuggled it through his moustache into his mouth.

'It was a woman hit me. Mrs Brady. She caught me accidentally. The ring on her finger did the damage.'

'She's a bit of a targer, the same woman. Especially with drink taken.'

'I've been at it a long time now, Sergeant. Same as yourself. We've put in more than enough years for the full pension. I just had a good look in the mirror. I've decided I'm retiring.'

They looked at him, genuinely stunned. His father, pinning a scallion to the plate like it was alive, and cutting it with a knife, turned to him.

'You're not serious, man, what? Retiring?'

'Yes, Sergeant, yes. I've put up with insults, assaults, the reprimands of scoundrels, attacks, the deepest personal tragedy . . . I got over them all. But for some reason, this is the last straw.' He pointed to his nose. 'I look like something you'd see in a cartoon.'

They laughed. Even the boy joined in and was about to batter his drum but, looking at the stern man who threatened him with hens, thought better of it.

'I've enjoyed my time too, the best comrades you could ever meet, don't get me wrong, Sergeant, but me two brothers outside London are getting me a job in a factory. I'll do a few years there and then we'll move back over to the West.'

'And what'll your wife do, and the children, in England?' his mother asked in a fluster of concern.

'They'll stay here. I'll be home on holidays. Then, after a few short years, like I say, we'll go home.' Home was Mayo.

Apricot O'Neill nibbled at crumbs. She smiled happily and hopelessly. She shrugged. Her life had always been decided by others.

Ned in England; she'd be alone. He filled instantly with the thoughts of a thief. He dismissed them for the dishonourable fantasies of a fool. He'd be away at college most of the time.

'I will help you all I can, Mrs Fleming.'

They looked at him. Admiring his shining innocence.

'' 'Pon my word,' said Fleming, 'it's well for the parents has such a son.'

His mother dispensed apple pie with a silver cake slice.

'What sort of work will your brothers get you in the factory, Ned?' his father asked.

'An electrical factory. They make bulbs.'

His father looked suitably impressed. In the modern world an endless supply of bulbs was a necessity. He glanced up at the bulb hanging above the table. His mother was glad she'd cleaned it that morning.

'You could have told me, Ned,' Apricot said quietly, like a child.

Simon 'Blackpuss' Hall, without as much as knocking, came in.

'Don't get up, don't stir, I'm only here for a second. Evening, Sergeant. Hello, missus — fresh and well you're looking. What happened, Ned, did a galloping turkey kick you? Mrs Fleming . . .'

'You'll have a cup of tea, Mr Hall?' his mother said.

'You will, Simon, sit down, man.'

'No, no, Sergeant, thanks all the same.'

He was wearing a dark Sunday suit, the jacket double-breasted, and a white shirt and black tie. His black moustache was brushed and shiny. His eyes were old but lively. They danced from face to face all the time.

He cupped his hand into Apricot's waist and raised it so he was almost touching her breast. She was in her chair at the table and couldn't move. He had her pinned. Speaking softly into her ear as if imparting a most precious message, he said, 'That busted bed, I'll collect it out of the shed in the morning; there's another tenant looking for something like it. Sorry to interrupt now; they said in the day room to come on round. So I did. So I'm gone. Goodbye now.'

As he withdrew his hand he spirited the silver cake slice from the table into his pocket. The boy and his mother and Apricot noticed. His father and Ned didn't. The decorative handle stuck out of Blackpuss's suit pocket.

He opened the kitchen door for him and, as he went past, deftly removed the knife. Without fuss he placed it back on the table.

'He's a grand old character,' his father commented.

'He is, he is,' Fleming agreed.

His mother and Apricot laughed. Men were such eegits.

'Sherlock Holmes and Watson were only in the ha'penny place compared to these two,' his mother said. She and Apricot laughed even louder. The two policemen had no idea why.

Apricot held her hand out and his mother slapped it for fun. The twins in the pram gurgled, belched and emptied into their nappies, like badly bunged drains suddenly unblocking.

The boy, Oliver, went over and looked at them. 'Jesus, Mammy, that's a cat-melojun stink.' He hit his drum a few wallops and went outside.

217

Word quickly spread round the village that Fleming had retired and gone to England to do heavy work in a light factory. Apricot cooked dinners every day for four of the Guards. It brought in money and their presence round the place kept the tom cats away. The Billser buck began calling to the house. He soon got a black eye for his troubles and came no more.

Summer ended; he returned to college. Autumn half-term came and went. Winter gripped the rivers, lakes and hills. He couldn't wait for Christmas and when it came he heard that Ned was home. He met him outside the house one evening. He looked tired. Yellow-coloured. He told him he'd read they were building a telescope in an American desert that would be able to see a bee's wings beating on Mars. It was going to put all man's other achievements in the ha'penny place.

'We'll see the meaning of the world then, I'm telling you, boyo, we'll see it all then.'

When he related this to his mother, she became tearful and said Apricot had told her that Ned wasn't well. He had been suffering from cancer even before he went to England. He never complained. There was no hope for him.

The new year came and the day after Little Christmas, the seventh of January, he died. He heard Apricot tell his mother that he left money enough for her.

''You'll be no pauper anyway to get another

man to look after you.' Them was his last words. I don't want another man. I've had enough of men. I'd never get one as good as Ned anyways, would I?'

His mother helped other local women make tea and sandwiches for all the sympathisers crowding into the house.

'Sorry for your trouble, Mrs Fleming,' a neighbour said.

'Ah sure, death's no trouble at all. It's life gets me into trouble.' Someone dropped a plate. It broke clean in two.

Apricot sat beside the pram, gently rocking the twins to sleep. She smiled shyly to everyone and was calm and strong.

He was in the house when Mr Tully came with the coffin. He asked him to lift the body in as he didn't have his helper with him. Ned in his illness had shrunk to very little. He was as light as a feather.

As they were screwing down the lid, the boy, Oliver, came into the room.

'What's in the box?' he asked.

'Ned,' replied Apricot. 'Your stepfather.'

When she led him out of the bedroom, Tully said quietly, 'Poor wee bastard doesn't know yet.'

The funeral was away over the far end of Mayo. Apricot and Oliver and the twins followed the hearse in Jim Reilly's car. His father went with them.

★ ★ ★

Blackpuss came round to married quarters and asked him to lend a hand with a little job he had to do.

They went down to Apricot's house and from the shed at the back, lugged out the mildewed mattress. Blackpuss poured petrol on it and set it alight. An angry reek of damp smoke snarled upwards.

'Say nawthin', cawdee. Everyone will think it was the mattress Ned died on. I don't want to burn it. That's near enough good as new. I want to let the house again, straightaway, if I can.'

'But what about Apricot?'

'Take my word, we'll not see that one again.'

Walking home, when he looked back he could see wisps of smoke rising above the houses. It made him feel lonely for Apricot. He thought of Ned too. The smoke was a fake symbol of his spirit rising heavenwards.

Late that night his father returned from the funeral. They could tell he'd been drinking, something he didn't do often. They could smell the porter, he burped and to convince them he was completely sober, spoke slowly, making sure he didn't slur his words. His mother hated drunk men.

'Well, how did it go?' she asked.

'They treated us decent, I'll say that for them. There was any amount of his friends he'd served with over the years. I knew some of them. It was a good turnout now. The local TD was there, oh bedad he was. Fleming was no daw, let me tell you.'

'What about Apricot? When is she coming back?'

He pursed his lips and wiped them slowly with the back of his hand.

'As the Scotsman says, I have me doots she'll ever darken this part of the country again.'

Dempsey

The Priest, father Gaynor, started calling round to married quarters most days of the week. Even first thing in the morning he'd be sitting in the kitchen by the fire, breviary in hand, lower lip trembling. He was a law unto himself. Forever fighting with the bishop, other clergy and the local Church of Ireland vicar, the Reverend Dr Maddock.

His mother had to do extra fussing about, tending him, making tea, chatting to him, telling him about her family. He liked that they had been well-off middle-class merchants with plenty of money to dispense on good causes like priests and nuns. They had a big shop business and a bakery and all the children were educated privately — the girls boarding in a convent, the boys in the best school in the county.

His father wasn't pleased. The peace of the house was upset. He couldn't come into the kitchen barefooted, tucking in his shirt, buckling his belt or in his pyjamas when he'd wash and shave by the back window. He couldn't shout at the radio when de Valera was making a speech and one evening he couldn't listen to a heavyweight boxing match because Father Gaynor was sitting by the fire, lip trembling, encased in a truculent mood forbidding mundane pleasures.

The priest had no interest in talking about

222

peasants. His father's family therefore was rarely discussed. They'd been shown the road in the Famine. But sixty-six years later the Congested District Board split up the big estates and they were able to move back to where they'd come from originally. They loaded up the mule and cart with their few chattels and the very straw from the cabin roof and by the grace of God arrived back on the same sod from which they had been cruelly evicted. Thirty acres they were given. Seven times more than the rough acres on which they'd been existing before Friday, 13 March 1846. The government had built a stone house for each family — two up and two down. His father remembered that when they arrived, led by his mother — 'your granny' — they went into the house and sank to their knees weeping for joy and thanking God for delivering them out of bondage. The year was 1912.

'Ten years later, the British left Ireland.'

'Well, most of it.'

As his father told the priest the story, he tightened his face against emotion and to distract himself crossed his legs and swung his right foot up and down as he spoke.

'A mule?' Father Gaynor said. It was his only comment.

His father was vexed. The mule remark was socially loaded. They weren't dirt poor, able only to afford a donkey, nor were they well off enough to own a horse. His father, without saying a word, abruptly left. In the hallway, they heard him pull a pair of dungarees up over his uniform trousers. The dungarees were old, worn and instead of a button one of the straps was secured in place by a nail. They could hear him grunting and when the nail fell out, clearly heard it hitting the tiles.

'Bad cess to it.'

Eventually he appeared in the vegetable garden, transformed, as if the shovel he wielded was a magic staff. He moved through the potato drills, moulding them, flicking the clay over the just-sprouting spuds with wristy strength, firmly patting down the sides. He was smooth, calm, his back turned on the world of crime and whatever was going on in the kitchen. He wasn't interested in the domestic blather of priests and housewives. Every place he'd ever served, the local curate had a cosy bolthole where he was guaranteed pious servitude and endless tea and cake. The priest was a good listener, the wife warm and kind. It was like marriage was supposed to be.

Father Gaynor closed his breviary on his index finger.

'You know, I shouldn't be called 'Father' Gaynor at all. I'm a Doctor of Divinity. My correct title is Dr Gaynor.'

'You don't say?' his mother said. 'Well, from now on, we'll call you nothing but Doctor.'

He opened his breviary again and, lip trembling, murmured theology as if there was a fly in his throat.

'I'm not a Maynooth man. I studied at Salamanca. In Spain. My forte is history. I specialise in local history.'

'Is that right, Dr Gaynor? Aren't you the genius?'

The boy went out and down the garden to his father.

'He says he wants to be called 'Doctor'. He's a Doctor of Divinity.'

'Is that so?'

A white butterfly landed on a newly planted cabbage. His father took a swing at it with the shovel, practically mashing the cabbage. The butterfly flitted away, wheeled zanily and, without his father being aware, landed on his hat.

'The beggars. The damage they cause.'

Seeing a caterpillar upside down under a leaf, he squeezed the life out of it. There was a lifetime of wipe stains down the side of his dungarees.

'He only wants to be called Doctor because the Protestant man is a Doctor — Dr Maddock. He's a priest. Maddock a vicar. But they want to be called Doctor. No one is satisfied with what they are. Everyone wants to be something else.'

His father was happy in his vegetable garden. On his bike. Walking in the woods. Occasionally mulling a bottle of stout by the fire. He never wanted to rule the world.

'But if God grants me a murder before I retire, I won't say no.'

The butterfly left his hat and landed on the warm roof of the nearby corrugated shed.

When he went back into the kitchen, Guard Dempsey was there. A tall chunk of a man, he was drinking a mug of tea and eating a hunk of bread and jam like any schoolboy. The priest was still stuck in his breviary, churning the words in his throat, lower lip trembling angrily.

Dempsey, a bachelor, was laughing with his mother. He had come to Butlershill from Kerry to do penance for crashing the only squad car they had down there and for not taking the job seriously. Every time you saw him he was laughing or making other people laugh.

'Ah now, missus, I'd say you have another kitten in the sack.'

'Go 'long with you, man, at my age? I'll never see forty again.'

'If I'm any judge, you'd still snap a trap.'

She tenderly rubbed her stomach. 'How on earth did you guess?'

They laughed. She enjoyed the banter. The priest was looking at them. It seemed as if he'd taken her words seriously.

The boy sat over by the dresser, listening to them, trying to concentrate on the book he was reading. When he complained to his mother about the lack of decent books in the house, she joined the Companion Book Club, London. They posted out a book every month. It cost her money but she was stung by his criticism. He felt terrible about hurting her sense of pride. He embraced her and kissed her forehead and apologised.

'We do everything for you. It's not much compared to your friends at school. But I can't be running up to Dublin every time you want to read a novel.'

The hens paid for them. She saved up the egg money and sent a postal order to 8 Long Acre, London, WC 99.

The first book to arrive was *Afternoon of an Autocrat* by Norah Lofts. It was a snobbish yarn concerning one Sir Charles Augustus Shelmadine, who mysteriously died on page thirty-six. The book he now had in his hand was the second to arrive: *The Guns of Navarone* by Alistair MacLean. Guard Dempsey said he'd read it.

'It's good the way the first paragraph ties up with the last.'

He hadn't reached the last page yet but he turned to it. He could immediately see what Dempsey meant. The first paragraph had a character striking a match in the dark, by scratching it across the rusted metal of a corrugated-iron shed. It is observed by Mallory. In the last paragraph Mallory, again in the dark, watches as the great fortress of Navarone is blown sky high.

He closed the book, smiled and nodded to Dempsey, who was now looking at the *Irish Independent* which lay open on the table.

'There's a bit here about your man, the playwright. Sean O'Casey. They say he's one of the greatest ever.'

Father Gaynor snapped his breviary shut and grabbed the newspaper in both hands.

'O'Casey is like a dirty old crow who flies over a beautiful country and whenever he sees a bit of dirt and dung, lands down and wallows in it.'

'Not being a farmer or a crow, I wouldn't know much about that, Father.'

'He wants to be called Doctor now,' his mother said, 'Dr Gaynor.'

'Go on?' Dempsey said. 'I've got a shockin'

sore toe, could you take a look at it, Doc?'

His mother bit her lip to stop herself laughing.

'If I were you, Guard, I'd think it about time I went back on duty.'

'If? If a duck could ride a bicycle, it wouldn't need a bell.'

Dempsey went out and his mother, fiercely chewing her lower lip and pretending to cough, poured the priest yet another cup of tea.

'Ah you will, Dr Gaynor, you'll have the last drop.'

'No, thanks. I'll bid adieu. A new arrival? Sometimes we can't see the wood for the trees.'

He was a medium man to look at. Not tall, not young — he was in his fifties — not fat, not thin, his long face the colour of lard, his dark hair turning to snow. His opinions were fierce. He had been appointed by God. Smiling his sideways smile he went humbly out the door.

At last they had the kitchen to themselves.

'A new arrival? Is he serious? What does he mean?'

'Heaven alone knows. He's an intelligent man anyhow. And a wonderfully saintly man. We must always respect our priests.'

His mother was concerned education would make him anti-clerical. Or turn him into a Communist.

'Take that old thing down and get rid of it.'

The swan-necked tilley lamp still hung high above the table. The arrival of electricity had consigned it to cobwebbed oblivion. When he lifted it off its nail, the base left a perfect round stain on the wall. In the shed, instead of flinging it on top of all the other junk, he put it up in a space in the rafters. A limbo for once vital household objects. There was a Primus stove there, a wet battery for a wireless, a smoothing iron and a ceramic hot-water bottle. They weren't dumped. They were to hand in case civilisation took an uppercut from the atom bomb.

When his father was vexed he stayed vexed. Anytime the priest parked his car out in the middle of the village street, he threatened to summons him unless it was moved in. The priest was God but he was Caesar.

★ ★ ★

Father Gaynor's housekeeper was in her thirties and an odd mixture of stern matron and handsome wench with her big bosom and plump apple-red cheeks. Most housekeepers were elderly. Bessy Darcy wasn't. You couldn't quite understand why she was with him. Why wasn't she married? She went to the dances in local parish halls and fairly flung herself round the floor with a succession of partners. At one dance a cattle-dealer, 'Jobber' Magee, slapped her on the back, saying, 'Ah-hah, a fine Mullingar heifer.'

The following Sunday at Mass, Father Gaynor threatened to ban dances entirely. He would not stand anyone insulting 'my Bessy'. He castigated the parishioners for their crudity, bad manners and ignorance. 'Particularly one beast, who shall be nameless.' Everyone knew he meant Jobber Magee.

Sometimes in the evening, the housekeeper, 'my Bessy', visited married quarters. His mother often asked him to leave the kitchen when she arrived.

'We want to have a good chinwag.'

So eager were they to talk and laugh and swoon righteously, they'd forget sometimes he was still present. When Bessy smiled she showed gaps in her teeth. One time when she came in, there was a bit of straw on the back of her coat. He'd seen her another night up against Conlon's gate with a stranger.

He overheard her one evening, in an excited stage whisper, confiding to his mother that some few days previously, Father Gaynor had been ill in bed with a fever, and when she went in to him with a bowl of soup, he hauled her down and dived on top of her.

'What it was, you see, he had such a high temperature he was raving and didn't know what he was doing, so he didn't.'

'Oh that's what it was,' his mother agreed. 'Poor Father Gaynor. Did he, in his sick distress, manage to take rough advantage, Bessy?'

'Lord have mercy on us, but he nearly had the berassywee torn off me, so he had.'

'Blessed Jesus, you don't say?'

'Next day he didn't remember a thing about it.'

'No? Ah, he's such a good man. A saint, a walking saint.'

Listening to them was better than anything the Companion Book Club had so far come up with.

If on weekday mornings there was no altar boy

230

to serve at eight o'clock Mass, Bessy, in her official capacity as housekeeper, stood in. As no female was allowed on the altar, Father Gaynor, far from the eyes of Rome, donated a pair of his trousers for such an occasion and, thus accoutred, Bessy participated on the sacred side of the rails. She filled the trousers to bursting. One old man who went to Mass every day said, 'Her rump is enough to tempt the Good Thief down from his cross.'

The trousers hung on the back of the sacristy door when she wasn't wearing them.

★ ★ ★

The boy was sitting in the kitchen with his mother, asking her silly questions to do with the five senses.

'What's your favourite sight?'

'The first daffodil of spring.'

'What's your favourite sound?'

'The sound of the bus bringing you home.'

Guard Dempsey came in and told him he was 'a-wanting' in the parochial house. Father Gaynor had phoned the Station. Could he go immediately?

He borrowed his father's bike and rode up the hilly mile. The country was raw drumlin, covered with rock and whin on one side, a cutaway turf bog of scraw, reeds, willow and hazel bush on the other. Treacherous water, the colour of porter, glinted just below the overgrown surface. Bawling calves and a herd of goats ran to get a better look at him. He could whiff the goats. A rough hairy odour that tasted like their milk.

The priest was waiting for him in his study. A picture of the Pope hung above the mantelpiece and a statue of Blessed Martin de Porres stood in a window. A shelf was lined with theological tomes. On a table, covered with a red cloth edged with tassels, was a tray with a bottle of whiskey and a bottle of red lemonade.

'Why do you want to see me, Father? Doctor?'

Bessy bustled in. She wore black high heels, a floral frock, a blouse and cardigan. He could smell her perfume. She was fairly raddled with lipstick.

'I'm off now, Father Jim, so I am. I won't be that long.'

She banged the outside door after her.

'You see the liars women are? 'I won't be THAT long.' That's the clue. She'll be ages.'

'Where is she going?'

'Who knows. Out and about. Women go out and about, do you not know that?'

He was looking hard at him.

'Your mother sends away for books.'

He took one from a shelf and launched it on to the table. He stared at him, then at the book, then back at him.

'Hymp. Hah. Hah-hah. Hymp.'

The sounds were challenging but he didn't know what they meant. The priest impatiently gestured with his hand that he should pick it up. He opened it. Four-hundred pages. *Via Dolorosa* by A North Country Curate. *Via Dolorosa* was the Way of the Cross. The road of grief. The road of suffering. The road Christ walked to Calvary.

It wasn't from the Companion Book Club anyway.

'Hah. Hymp. That's a book.'

His lower lip trembled and he munched his mouth in and out angrily.

Flicking the pages the boy glimpsed the name of a character — Henri St Pierre. The same kind of cod name as Sir Charles Augustus Shelmadine.

'It doesn't leave this room.'

'A North Country Curate. Who is it? Why doesn't he give his name?'

'That would be telling. Wouldn't it? This is north country, isn't it?'

He had a strange look in his eyes and moved his head from side to side as if strutting. He snatched the book from his hands and put it back on the shelf.

He was implying he was the author. He was the North Country Curate. He had written *Via Dolorosa*.

'You're the North Country Curate? That's amazing. I'd like to read it.'

'Oh yes. They think I'm an ignoramus like themselves. They see me rubbing a headstone and they think I'm mad. Hymp. Hah.'

He had been walking with his mother near the graveyard one day and they had seen the priest down on his knees rubbing the lettering of an old headstone with a dock leaf.

'I suppose it keeps him sane,' she had said.

The boy looked at him now. 'I'm . . . impressed.'

'Don't be so impudent. Your father is a mere detective for Dublin. I'm a detective for God.'

'There may be something in that. I'd better go.'

'I'm not finished with you yet. I haven't even started. Your mother is going to have a happy event. I want to make a cot for it. I can carpenter. I want you to come with me to the sawmill. I need timber. I have a measuring tape. Your mother is a fine person.'

The banter between Dempsey and his mother — the priest had definitely taken it for real. How could he be so deluded? He had studied in Salamanca. He was a theologian. He was an historian. He had written a book.

'Don't tell your parents. I want to surprise them.'

★ ★ ★

They drove to the sawmill which was out in the countryside. Stacks of timber stood higgledly-piggledy on the narrow road at the front and all around a corrugated building. In a spacious shed a circular saw spun like a Jenny-whizzer. Sawdust spattered the earthen floor. The mill was Protestant-owned. They were attended with courtesy but without the usual ceremony of fawning respect for a priest. The proprietor was a big man with sandy hair and fine dust on his overalls and in his eyebrows and on his forehead.

When the lengths of timber were cut and loaded into the car boot and on to the back seat, the priest paid the bill.

'Thanks, Padre. We appreciate your custom.'

He didn't like being called Padre. On the way home he muttered blackly about that part of the district being a nest of bigots.

He was angry because the people in the mill were outside his control.

'My mother isn't pregnant.' He wasn't listening.

'I'll drop you outside the Garda Station.'

'Carpenter isn't a verb.'

'You're an impudent pup. Get out, go on. Thanks.'

At tea when he told his parents what the priest was up to, they laughed.

'Let him make the cot,' his father said. 'Never come between a fool and his folly.'

'Honestly,' said his mother, 'for all his intelligence he's such an innocent.'

His father, elbow on the table, gently chewed at the side of his index finger. Some kind of mood had hit him.

'A penny for them,' his mother said.

'Oh, I heard there a minute ago, on the grapevine, Headquarters are going to close us down. As soon as the Troubles are over. We won't be needed. They'll move us someplace else. They'll throw us away like the spring in a busted clock.'

It was always plain to see how much he cared for the job and how little they regarded him.

'The machine doesn't care for the cog.'

His mother rested her hand on his father's hand. At the same time he put his hand on his father's shoulder. One day, soon, he would take that dark-blue tunic off and never put it on again. He'd rip off a silver button for a souvenir.

'I'll hang on until you've finished your schooling, then they can do what they like with me. I'll retire.'

Away at college, the boy never stopped worrying about them worrying about him. His mother sent a letter every fortnight. To please her, his father added a few lines at the end: 'We're thinking about you. Work hard. Cavan lost again. Don't let it upset you. Daddy.' Another one was: 'Did you see where all them soccer players got killed? RIP. Never go up in an aeroplane unless you have one leg on the ground.'

★　★　★

After tea he told them he was going for a spin. He had a mad idea to seek out Bessy Darcy and talk to her, be near her. Maybe by some miracle she'd dive on top of him. He'd go up to the parochial house and scout around to see had she returned.

Father Gaynor had already started making the cot. A window was open. He could hear banging, sawing, hammering, muttering. Bessy usually left her bicycle round at the gable end. It wasn't there. He walked down the hill to the old school. To live again the suffering days he spent there.

Closed for a half-holiday and without children milling about, it looked weird as an empty prison. A squat brick bungalow construction, it stood on top of a rocky drumlin. The playground was a scrap of flat rock and grass at the bottom of the slope. Behind was a wood. Playground and school were enclosed inside a three-foot wall. At the back, a hygienic distance away, were the lavatories. Cubicles with round holes in wooden benches high over a cesspit. You were never allowed to hang about there. The big fat lady teacher kept a beady eye, making sure nothing immoral occurred. An iron gate gave access to the back of the cesspit. The greatest sin that could be committed was to unbolt the gate and go in and look up at the girls' bums. There was a ledge at the back of the pit on which men could walk when emptying the stinking mess. Cleaned out once a year during the summer holiday, it was a job only the tinkers would undertake. Where they dumped it all no one knew or dared ask.

As he stood at the back of the school, looking towards the lavatories, he remembered Maggie Kane, a classmate, kissing him. Surprised at herself, she had fled into the school and, before anyone could inform on her, told the teacher it was he who had kissed her. It was the first time a girl had kissed him.

He thought he heard voices. Hurrying back round to the other side of the school he squatted down behind a water barrel. In a recess between the toilet block and the perimeter wall, he saw Guard Dempsey and Bessy the priest's house-keeper. It was definitely her. Dempsey had her up against the wall and was thrusting at her with his pelvis. She was thrusting back at him. Like they were having some kind of fight. Their clothes were intact. Dempsey was in mufti. They stopped the dunting and kissed. Then he put his hand right up under her frock. Her thigh was visible above her stocking top. In the falling dusk, her pale flesh was startling. Dempsey had taken a tight grip. She forced his hand away. They kissed like they were dying of hunger. He lifted her up and sat her on the wall. She must have been at least twelve stone. Dempsey was strong. So was she. She launched herself off the wall, her arms around his neck, her mighty legs tightly round his waist. They tumbled laughing to the ground. Dempsey rolled her over and got on top of her. It was amazing. It was like a wrestling match. He fled in case they caught him spying.

'Where did you go?' His mother asked.

'Oh just, you know, round and about.'

'See anything interesting?'

'Nothing unusual.'

How could he be such a fool to think he could cope with a woman like Bessy Darcy? Dive on top of him? He'd be killed stone dead.

★   ★   ★

Every morning when the priest came to the house, his parents never mentioned they knew he was making a cot for a baby that was never going to come. They were reluctant to interfere with his dreams. He was the priest. He was chosen by God. He knew what he was doing. He probably only wanted to show them how grateful he was for their daily hospitality. And anyway, the cot could always be given to some other household.

His father said he'd probably fall out with them soon anyway. He'd fallen out with other families. He'd befriend some housewife, daily call on her, praise her to the skies and then after a few months take umbrage over something trivial and never go back near her house again.

'Leave him be.'

His mother became discontented. She would love to have had more children. The as yet invisible cot became a symbol of her quiet regrets.

'I just wish he wouldn't interfere in that way.'

'Don't worry, Mum. Bring him to his eyesight the day he brings the cot here.'

'I wonder should I mention it to Bessy.'

'Maybe mention it to Guard Dempsey.'

'Dempsey? Why him?'

'Right, right.'

He'd love to have told her about what he'd seen behind the school. He had to tell someone.

Cleaning glasses for Jim Reilly in the pub, he told him.

'Honest to God. They ended up down on the ground.'

'Then what happened?'

'I was afraid to watch. In case they caught me. I left.'

'I'd say you missed the best part of the show. Oh now, the same Dempsey wouldn't be one bit afraid to throw a saddle on yon mare.'

Reilly had a laconic way with words.

'He was in here a while back and told me he coorted her firm and strong. He said he coorted her one night up agin a barbed-wire fence.'

★ ★ ★

On the Sunday, the priest gave a sermon based on Chapter I of the Gospel of St Mark. He spoke

239

about Elizabeth, stricken with years, becoming pregnant, to the amazement of Zacharias. He ended the sermon saying, 'Blessed are the ways of the Lord. Miracles do happen. They can even happen today, even here in Butlershill.'

On the way home his mother was furious. But when later in the day Father Gaynor called to the house, she didn't say anything to him. She made the tea and sliced a currant cake and put out a dish of country butter and homemade vegetable marrow jam. His father joined them.

So did Guard Dempsey. It was obvious from the moment he eased his big frame in the door that the priest wasn't pleased to see him. Dempsey's tunic was open and his whistle chain dangled out of the breast pocket. His jet-black hair was neatly parted, combed and creamed.

'Is Bessy not with you, Father?'

'What's it to you if she is or not?'

'I find her pleasant going, that's all.'

'Pleasant going? She's not a horse.'

Dempsey laughed.

'I suppose you heard, Dr Gaynor, they're going to close us down. When the Troubles end.' His mother was trying to get them on to what she thought was a safe subject. She hated even a hint of tension. Whenever his father was in a mood, she'd sit still, looking at the floor, her face pale.

The boy was over in his usual corner by the dresser, finishing *The Guns of Navarone*. 'If the Troubles end. Which I doubt.'

The priest turned to him, his face a briar patch.

240

'No one's asked you. Keep your nose out.'

Dempsey laughed.

'It's a serious comment. Besides, the boy is in his own kitchen.'

'He's always snooping about. He's impudent. I saw him walking up round the school recently. Why? The school is closed at the moment.'

He must have spotted him from the open window. He wanted to say — did you see anything else? Dempsey looked at him, his face blank but his eyes sharp.

He lowered his head into *The Guns of Navarone*.

'There's nothing to stop anyone going where they like as long as they're not breaking the law.' Dempsey was smiling as he said it, but he must have been on edge too: he was tapping his knee against the leg of the table.

The priest turned to his father.

'You must feel bad, Sergeant — no murder to end your days.' He cackled dryly.

'Well, in the early days I solved three cases. The last the famous McDonald murder. I'll have to be satisfied with that.'

'That was a family squabble that just blew up, wasn't it? It wasn't premeditated. I wouldn't call the like of that murder. A murder is someone setting out, purposely, to take someone's life.' He scowled angrily to stop his father contradicting him.

His father bit into a lush cut of buttery cake. He chewed it round his mouth, enjoying every crumb of it. Then he spoke.

He was wearing flannel trousers, a white shirt

241

and tie and a jacket his sister sent him from New Jersey. His hair was recently cut short. He looked like an FBI man in a movie.

'Have you ever heard anyone confess a premeditated mortal sin?'

His mother looked shocked. Dempsey twisted his mouth to one side. The priest didn't answer. His lip trembled. He closed the breviary.

'Explain yourself, Sergeant.'

'A mortal sin, to my mind, is something done to purposely fly in the face of God. I doubt you heard many such in your lifetime. Most sins are venial. They certainly aren't done to spite God. To my mind. You spend your days listening to schoolchildren telling you about the sweets they stole. Or old women confessing getting into a bad temper with the pains in their legs. Or girls confessing that a man put his hand up their dress. As if they could stop them. I saw the jury bring in a guilty verdict to a murder charge. Have you ever heard anyone tell you they purposely flew in the face of God? Armed with full previous knowledge of the risk involved?'

The silence was such they could hear the phone ringing in the day room. The sound had to travel through a wall, across a small bedroom, through the even smaller joke of a sitting room, across the hallway and into the heart of married quarters. The kitchen.

'Are you saying, Sergeant, the two of you have wasted your lives?'

'I am, Dempsey. Make sure you don't waste yours.'

He read the last page of the novel and tossed it

on to the sewing machine. The great guns of Navarone had blown up. His mother twisted her wedding ring. His father, legs crossed, swung his foot up and down. Dempsey blew on a button of his tunic, then shone it with his hankie. The priest was frozen in stony temper. The phone stopped ringing.

His father for the most part had read only law books and spent a lifetime dealing with ordinary people day to day. Yet he had raised a theological hare.

'My lips are sealed. The silence of the confessional is golden.'

It didn't sound that convincing. He hooked his index finger inside his white collar and eased it away from his Adam's apple. His life was based on mystery and believing in miracles. Things which couldn't be seen. Even his carpentry was ridiculous. He was making a crib for a baby that didn't exist. In his father's life, you either had a light on your bike or you manifestly didn't.

His father had been angered by the priest's remark. 'Armed with full previous knowledge of the risk involved.' That was a quote from the citation given with the Scott Medal for bravery. It was apt when defining a mortal sin. He was proud of his father for pulling that one out of his hat. He'd won the Scott Medal in 1932. He had arrested two armed Irregulars in County Leitrim whilst unarmed himself.

On his father's behalf, emotionally wild and woolly, and to his subsequent eternal shame, the boy jumped up and verbally attacked the priest.

'What brave act have you ever done? You bully

the parishioners from the safety of your pulpit every Sunday morning. Daddy's one of the bravest men in Ireland. Do you want me to show you his medal? And now they're closing the Station and just throwing him aside. How dare you?!'

His mother grabbed his wrists, terrified he was going to strike the priest.

'Jesus, Mary and Joseph,' she said desperately.

His father, without standing up, calmly reached out and getting hold of the bottom of his jacket yanked him down on to a chair.

Dempsey started laughing. 'Ah now, that's the best yet.'

His limbs had turned to jelly. He had intended saying lots more and couldn't understand why he hadn't.

'There's no need for any of that. Calm down,' his father said.

Looking into his hard stare, he knew his explosion had very little to do with defending his bravery or honour or whatever. He just flipped. Probably out of frustration. He wasn't sure.

'Apologise to Dr Gaynor, go on,' his mother appealed desperately.

'No, no, leave him be.' The priest turned to him. 'I'll tell you what I do. I bury the dead.' He spoke very simply and with stung feeling.

'Of course you do, Dr Gaynor,' his mother said. 'You're a great man entirely.'

Dempsey laughed. 'Ah now, it's as good as a concert.'

He felt truculent. His temper slurped through his veins. He knew he wasn't going to button his lip. He also felt tearful.

'When I went up to the school . . . you must have been snooping too. Peeping out the window. Did you see who else was up there? I wasn't the only one. Yes.'

Dempsey no longer laughed. The priest stood up.

'Who else was there?'

'My lips are sealed. My silence is golden.'

The words were glib imitation. He wished he'd shut his mouth. The atmosphere had chilled. His father looked at the priest and then at Dempsey. At the slightest hint, he could go all inquisitorial. He'd pin you to the spot and wouldn't let up until you told him what he wanted to know.

They heard someone outside. The situation was saved by the abrupt arrival of Bessy Darcy. She bustled in, all elbows, arms and bosom. The kitchen shrunk like a crowd had arrived.

'If anyone else comes in,' his father observed, 'the village will think there's a funeral.'

She wore a white frock with buttons down the front and a blue cardigan which hung open on either side of her amazing uplifted mother-hen breasts. Her black hair, in curls, looked newly permed. A slash of lipstick on her mouth wouldn't have looked out of place on the back of a sheep. She wore her black high heels, no stockings. Energy bounced from her round the tiny kitchen. It shook off her like a dog coming out of water.

'Oh, Father Jim,' she said, swiping the dandruff from his shoulders, 'I told you where the clothes brush was, so I did.'

'Guard Dempsey here says you're pleasant going. What do you think he meant?' He sounded peevish, diminished.

'Howya, Guard? How's she cuttin'?' She said it so casually, you couldn't imagine she'd lain under him at the back of the school.

'Like a mowing machine,' Dempsey answered her, pretending to be carefree and normal.

Turning around she hit the corner of the table with her rump. A dash of milk splurged from the jug. His mother grabbed a cloth from the clothesline over the range.

Bessy noticed him sitting back in his corner retreat.

'His nibs here as usual. Spotting everything like a hawk on a telegraph pole.'

She didn't give a rap for man nor beast. Her big face beamed like a giant smile painted on a doll. He wondered was she married to Father Gaynor in all but name . . . Who was to know? But then what about Dempsey and the other men she met at dances?

She took his mother's hand and squeezed it affectionately between her two hands.

'It's wonderful news about the baby. When is the stork arriving? Father Jim told me all about it.'

People believed in things that hadn't happened and never would. No one was immune to the outlandish. The only science he came across was in the physics lab at school. The country was run like a tatty magic show. No end of mumbo-jumbo and hands delving into tall hats and under black cloth and producing white pigeons

246

as if from nowhere. The people gave themselves up to three-card-trick men.

'My mother isn't pregnant. He's making a crib but there'll never be a baby to go into it. Not in this house anyway. Put the man out of his fantasy, will you, Mum? Dad?'

Out of shock and respect for the priest and his seriously trembling lip, no one spoke.

He sat back in his corner again. His father decided the best policy was to change the subject entirely. He commented on the announcement that women were to be recruited into the Gardaí.

'I can't see them being able to stop a fight at a football match, can you, Father Gaynor?'

'I'll have it finished soon. The crib.'

Bessy's shoes had dainty straps. They were fastened into place across her insteps. The two tiny buttons were black and yellow like a blackbird's eye. The straps were nearly hidden in her pouting flesh.

★ ★ ★

Next day, having again being summonsed by the priest to attend him in the parochial house, he was walking up to the chapel when he met the Church of Ireland vicar, the Reverend Dr Maddock, coming the other way, pushing a bicycle. The front wheel had a puncture. He was wearing a top hat and some kind of bat-black clerical apron or cassock. He wore gaiters which seemed to be made of cotton. They had black buttons up the sides.

His father claimed the garb was a political

247

statement. He was trying to pretend Catholic Ireland was Anglican England and the present a previous century.

His bicycle was as ancient as himself.

'Can I help you, Dr Maddock?'

'Thank you, no. A thorn. I'll repair it when I get home.'

His face had shrunken with age but his false teeth had stayed the same. They clomped loosely in his mouth when he spoke.

'Wait a moment. You're . . . I know you, don't I?'

'I'm on my way up to see Dr Gaynor.'

'I've just been turned away from his door. Silly chap. I read something he wrote about Traducianism. I wanted to challenge him. Civilised debate. Said he was busy making a crib. Christmas isn't for ages.'

'No, it's for my mother. He thinks she's pregnant. But she can't have any more children.'

'Oh. He says he's written a book. He has brains. We know that. Oh yes. To spend one's life up a theological cul-de-sac, eh? You're a boarder in a seminary, I believe. What do you intend doing?'

'I'm searching for a certain . . . je ne sais quoi. Could be a record player. A magic pair of football boots. A girl. Maybe go to England. Everyone else seems to. Get a job on a building site.'

'It would be such a shame to waste your artistic gifts.'

He was so flabbergasted he couldn't think of anything to say for a moment.

248

'Ah . . . Have you not yet forgiven my little prank?'

' 'The one to whom little is forgiven, loves little.' Luke, Chapter 7.'

Without further comment he pushed slowly away with his ladies' bike.

The pointed remark referred to an incident years before. Without his parents knowing, one Sunday he accompanied a Protestant friend, Sammy Henderson, to Bible class. Lots of children attended and they all played together afterwards. The class ended, they piled outside. When Dr. Maddock emerged, the first thing he saw was the outline of a man drawn on the side of his dusty Morris Minor.

'Who did this?' he enquired crossly.

'I did,' said an innocent young girl, 'but Sammy's friend put on the cock and balls.'

As he walked along, he wondered why the priest wanted to see him. Maybe he'd ask him to interpret the quote from Luke. He vaguely remembered the chapter from Christian Doctrine studies. It was about the prostitute who washed the feet of Jesus with her tears and dried them with her hair. Some woman. No, he wouldn't mention it. He'd look it up later. It had something to do with the more sins you had forgiven, the more you loved the person who forgave you. He felt himself a bit of a hopeless case: he had no interesting sins at all. In the distance he could see the chapel high on Killoughter hill and the wall of the nearby cemetery. Because of the rock, most coffins never got anywhere near six foot by two. He sat on the grassy verge of the road and lay his head back on a clump of fern. The sun was high and warm. His history teacher said the relationship between Ireland and England was sadomasochistic. They had punished us for centuries, yet we couldn't wait to go there.

The goats and calves came to the fence. He introduced himself. Said hello. Told them to escape. All that awaited them was a butcher's knife. They seemed to understand. Towards the far hedge there was a cow and other cows were trying to ride her. The sign she needed the bull.

A horse and cart came clopping along the road. Old Pat Dolan, sitting on the floor by the horse's rump, was driving the cans of cream from the creamery to Ballyhaise. There it would be turned into butter. He hopped up on the back. The cart wheels had rubber tyres. The going was soft and jingly-jangly. Pat looked up towards the cemetery and the yew tree by its gate.

'The Lord have mercy on the dead,' he muttered.

Near the chapel he hopped down. Pat hadn't noticed him.

Father Gaynor's study had become a carpenter's shop. There were lengths of wood everywhere — leaning against the furniture, on the table, on the floor, behind the door. There was a pile of sawdust and shavings swept roughly into a corner.

In the middle of it all, a crib was taking shape. The corners were stout struts connected top and bottom with thick rails. The four sides were wooden bars, giving a cage effect. Already it looked big enough to hold a bull calf.

Father Gaynor was in his shirt sleeves and minus his dog collar. He raked his greying hair with his fingers. He cleaned his glasses with a corner of his shirt sticking out over his trousers.

Maybe he was going to loan him *Via Dolorosa*.

'It's all snug double-joints.'

'Pardon? *Via Dolorosa?*'

'What? Are you some sort of amadaun?'

'Possibly.'

'I want you to go and get paint. The shop at the Finn Bridge.'

That was across the Border. Things were cheaper there.

'But first of all I want you to see Bessy. She's up in her room. Don't be impudent. Go on. Knock first.'

He went up the carpeted stairs. On the landing a door was open. He could see a prie-dieu and a cassock lying on a single iron bed and a white chamber pot under the bed. There was a picture of a town in Spain. He could make out the name. Salamanca.

He knocked on the door opposite. A key turned. Bessy opened up.

'Why do you lock it?'

'Anytime Father Jim takes his collar off. We have rules. You're impident. Here's the money for the paint. Snooping is a mortal sin, so it is. You'll go to Hell when you die. What did you say to Guard Dempsey? What did you say you saw? You saw nothin'. You're impident, so you are. You'll go to Hell for all eternity, so you will.'

She stood with her back to the door and spoke in a loud whisper. She wore slippers and a tight skirt in which she bulged. Her cardigan bulged too. The buttons of her suspender belt pressed against the skirt. It was great being alone with her. Her face wasn't all that good-looking. Her nose looked like a thumb of cream on top of a currant bun. It didn't matter. Energy hopped off her. Her lush lips didn't need lipstick.

'Your lush lips don't need lipstick.'

'If that's dirty talk, you can stop now. I'll tell Father Jim. You're very impident, so you are. I'll tell your mother.'

The bed was a brass double. On a small mantelpiece there was a statue of the Blessed Virgin, open hands appealing to the world, a snake underfoot.

'I saw you and Dempsey. By accident. Resisting curiosity, the demands of decency insisted I didn't stay long enough to applaud.'

She closed her fist as if she was going to hit him.

'The sooner you go back to school, the better.'

'You've been seen going into Lady Sarah's demesne at night.'

'How could they and it supposed to be night?'

'And the two of you were at the pictures in the Luxor in Clones.'

She wrung her hands together and he thought she was going to cry.

'People is evil. God help me. People are quare and horrid. What am I going to do at all?'

'Where are you from, Bessy? Have you a family?'

'I've none at all belonging to me. God's truth.

252

I only want to be good, so I do. Men have pestered me all me life.'

She was a big country girl, rough-spoken, alone, living with a priest. She loved dancing. She was a magnet, electric. He stepped towards her. He had his hand held out to touch her but at the last moment went out the door. The priest was flesh and blood too. For the first time he felt sorry for him. How could he stop himself? Because he was ordained in Spain he could attend plays without asking the bishop's permission and sometimes if he was running late he'd absolve all the children of their sins collectively. But there was no rule you wouldn't break for a woman wild as Bessy. She'd churn any man's emotions.

★ ★ ★

On the way to the Border shop he met Dempsey. He was standing in a hedge along a road a short distance from the Six Counties. In his full uniform he looked powerfully built. His face was big but the features fine and suntanned. He looked like he was sculpted from sandstone.

His blue eyes danced with devilment. His eyebrows were black as tar.

'Don't cause me trouble, boyo, that's all I'm saying.'

'You're going out with her, aren't you? Jim Reilly said you courted her up against a barbed-wire fence.'

Dempsey laughed.

'I'm not coddin', you're the funniest lad I ever met in me life. You're so innocent people can't

253

stop laughing at you, do you not know that?'

'You threw a saddle on her, didn't you?'

Dempsey put his hands on his knees and laughed so loud a dog barked from a house half a mile away.

'Betcha you'll go to university and grow a beard. You'll know everything and damn-all at the same time. Let me tell you about Bessy. Before she teamed up with Father Jim, she'd been in England. For the best part of nine months. Do you know what I'm saying? The nuns took it off her. The priest took her in. Now do you know?'

A cattle lorry came along the road from the North. Dempsey stepped right in front of it, big hand held aloft.

He went on to the Finn Bridge shop to get the green paint. He was in Fermanagh. A gentle backwater of flat land mostly, cut in two by a river that twice became a lake as it flowed across the border from the South and, though going geographically North, back into the political South again. The woman in the shop was a Protestant. She was thin, world-weary eyes, friendly.

'How are things in Butlershill? Anything exciting happening?'

'There's nothing happening in the world that isn't happening in Butlershill.'

'I wish I could say the same for this godforsaken spot.'

'Do you think I should grow a beard?'

'No.'

A tin of green paint was cheaper in

254

Fermanagh. Butter made in Cavan was cheaper in Fermanagh than in Cavan. Cigarettes were dearer in Fermanagh. Tea was cheaper in the North. Sugar cheaper in the South. A mug of tea was political. When the skullduggers made the Border they didn't mean it to be ironic.

★ ★ ★

When he got back to the parochial house, Father Gaynor was sitting in his study, sunk on a sofa, surrounded by the chaos of his woodwork. By his feet was a hammer, pliers, a handsaw, an awl, loose nails strewn about. They were the tools of a crucifixion in a Renaissance painting. He was still without his collar. *Via Dolorosa* still stood in dusty silence on its shelf.

'Give the change to my Bessy. She's upstairs. Go on. Knock.'

When he went up, she didn't open the door and he thought he heard her sobbing. Perturbed, he went home.

His father was in his small office round the corner from the day room. He had a letter giving notice that the county health inspector intended to carry out rodent disinfestation at the chapel burial ground and that a sign — 'these lands are poisoned' — would be erected.

'I'm sure the tenants won't object. RIP.'

He pinned the letter into the Miscellaneous Record book.

His father let him turn the pages. There was a list of people licensed to own bulls, stallions, boars. There were eighteen people licensed to

255

sweep chimneys. There were sixty passport renewals issued. There was even a list of people who felled trees. Each one had a date, address, the number of trees to be felled, the type of tree, where growing and a notice number. The Garda Síochána had their finger on the very heartbeat of the community. Nothing escaped them.

'He's leaving. He's put in for a transfer.'

'Who?'

'Dempsey.'

'You're coddin'? Why?'

'You tell me.'

The news was a surprise, a shock even. He'd spoken with him earlier on and he'd never mentioned a thing. People were as cute as rats. He hated the idea of Dempsey going. He hated the idea of anyone going. He had lost all the friends of his childhood. You were supposed to put down roots. Friends were the roots.

'He's been skating on trouble all his life. I spoke to the Sergeant he last served under. There was never any problems with him as a policeman. But he got into terrible tangles with other men's wives. He's done fifteen years in the Force and he's been shifted to five different stations. He has pull as well. That's why he gets his way. Give me a drunk any day of the week. You can deal with the like of that. He's one of a family of fifteen brothers and sisters.'

'He's going out with Bessy Darcy, isn't he?'

'That's what I'm saying. The priest isn't pleased at all.'

They could hear the Angelus bell ringing from its rocky perch a mile away across the hills, the rocks, the whins, the bog water, over the goats and calves, the pigs in their cluttered sheds, in the lark- and pigeon-laden sky. Six o'clock.

★ ★ ★

That night in married quarters he and his mother sat by the range listening to a corncrake in the tiny field between the Station and the creamery. You never heard two corncrakes. Just the male seeking a partner.

'Take care but she isn't pregnant.'

'The corncrake?'

'Bessy. Why else was she crying?'

His mother never sat down without having something in hand to work at. She was sewing buttons on a shirt. She wore thick grey stockings, an old skirt, an older blue cardigan, a blouse. She hardly ever spent money on clothes for herself. She had the one overcoat which must have been fifteen years old. Her hair was clipped back behind her ears. She look tired. The kitchen was spotless but it was impossible to make it look good. The table was a collapsible one which was surplus to requirements in a previous station. The armchair was frayed; his father had a habit of hitting the armrests with his fists when he heard Dev or Lemass on the wireless. The sewing machine was brightly polished but a Singer sewing machine never looked modern. The dresser was the dresser; it wouldn't sell at an auction. The Board of Works bottle-green walls were a headache. The big picture of the Sacred Heart, with the small red lamp burning in front

257

of it, was pious and scary.

'You must look forward, one day, to owning your own home.'

'It'll be wonderful, please God. Mama had a set of Chippendale chairs the like of which you'd never see. We had a sitting room bigger than this kitchen and my bedroom put together.'

'That small, eh?'

She chuckled.

'Go along with you, laughing at your poor old mother.'

'How did the fall from grace occur? Precisely.'

'Precisely? Drink and politics. The old chap followed both instead of his business. Even when we had to move to Dublin, he didn't stop. We were in Moore Street one evening. We heard a fellow saying to another, 'Come on, we'll go and listen to that oul eegit; he's on his soapbox again.' We stood in a doorway. He was preaching under a street lamp about the lack of money in the country. 'If the government are short of money,' he says, 'let them print some. Print as much as is wanted.''

'Did you think you were getting out of poverty when you married Dad?'

'I married him because he was a good man. And he loved me. And still does. What more can a person want?'

'If a person loves you, does that mean darning socks, sewing shirts, making porridge every day?'

'Not if you want a selfish life.'

'Home Duties'. His mother and the other women in the village, the men too, believed that Hell existed and if you were sent there you

258

burned for all Eternity. Father Gaynor told them it was true and so did his bishop and so did the government in Dublin.

'Do you really believe in Hell, Mum?'

'I don't think about it. I get on with things. Now don't annoy me, I have to get these damn buttons sewn on his shirt.'

His father came in, duty done for the day. She boiled milk for him and gave him a ginger biscuit. Sitting on his own at the table, staring at the wall, he drank the milk from a pint glass. There was a knock on the door.

'Good Heavenly Father, who can that be at this hour?'

It was only half past nine. Bessy came in like a blast of wind. Her white raincoat was unbuttoned and crumpled as if she'd been lying on it. Her permed hair stuck up in places. There was mud on the high heels of her shoes.

'Sorry for callin' and it so late.'

'I'm off to bed now,' his father said, gulping down the last of the milk and hanging his cap on the back of the door. 'I'll leave ye to it. Oíche mhaith.'

As soon as he went out the door, Betty sat in close to his mother. There was a track of green paint on the back of her coat.

His mother stopped sewing.

'Is anything the matter, Bessy? You look hot and bothered.'

'Is it any wonder? I was out and I come in and didn't he still have the collar off him. The poor man is in a horrid state with the making of that blasted crib. He has it painted now, so he has.

259

God forgive me but didn't he grab me round the knees and tried to straddle me. I said an Act of Contrition and fought him off as best as I could. In the circumstances.'

She stopped abruptly and leaned in even closer to his mother. Their faces were inches apart.

'Blessed Jesus, Bessy, and his Holy Mother, were you able to break his clutches?'

'He's been working too hard and then doing the painting; he's out of his mind with the worry of it all, so he is, he doesn't know what he's doing, God help him. The smell of yon paint would put your head astray, so it would. It'll be dry be morning and he wants help getting it down here, so he does. He's only a weak poor creature to look at him, but with the Devil in possession, he's horrid hard to dislodge. Satan, it's all Satan. Poor Father Jim.'

'But he didn't manage to stain his character, did he, Bessy? Is that what you're saying? There was no mortal sin committed, was there? Tell the truth now, Bessy.'

'No, God no, there was no mortal sin, thanks to be God. But he come horrid close, so he did.'

His mother, eyes wide with holy horror, started sewing again.

'Poor Dr Gaynor. He's a saint the way he's tempted. You're great the way you fight him, Bessy.'

'I've fought bigger beasts nor Father Jim. I'm not going to take it lying down, so I'm not.'

Listening to them he often wondered were they speaking in libidinous code or shorthand.

Their lives were fiction. Crucifiction.

From down the hallway they heard the noise of his father beating the bedroom floor with his boot. He got up and went out.

'Jesus this night,' Bessy shrieked, 'was he here all the time? The impident ting.'

His father wanted to know what was going on. Why weren't they going to bed? Wasting electricity talking to that one.

'If you ask me, she's the reason Dempsey's put in for a transfer. Of course she is. I wouldn't be one bit surprised if she was with child. Why else is the priest making the crib?'

'Did you mention it to Dempsey?'

'I did. He denied any such thing.'

'Who else could it be?'

'With the help of God we'll never have to find out.'

He was propped up on a pillow, the *Sacred Heart Messenger* in one hand, his massive boot in the other. His rosary beads looped the iron bed-head. He dropped the boot on the floor. His uniform trousers, neatly folded over, seams together, he had placed under the mattress. He called it bed-ironing. The attached galluses hung down. He'd used the biblical expression 'with child'. Pregnant was too racy a word — a touch sinful. His bedroom was small and barren and cold even in summer. His parents . . . himself — they each slept alone.

He went back up to the kitchen. Surely if she was pregnant she'd have told his mother? She was still sitting in close to her and had her skirt pulled up her thigh to show her a ladder in her

261

stocking. She was a full churn of milky-white flesh. The force of her body a mystery to her strange innocence. Her cheeks were red with the excitement of talking. She was a big eating apple.

'Did you meet Guard Dempsey tonight, Bessy, by any chance? There's mud on your shoes, by the way.' He affected a casual tone.

'Oh, butter wouldn't melt in his mouth. What is it to do with you? I don't like talkin' in front of him, missus. Go to bed, you impident ting, you're a Komminist.' Communist was about the worst thing you could call a person. There was a special place in Hell for Communists and Catholics who got married in a registry office. His mother winced at the accusation. Frightened at the very idea.

'He's not, Bessy. Don't say that word.'

'He's saying I went into the wood after Dempsey, that's what he's saying. Maybe I went into the wood to get wood. Maybe I went in to pick flowers.'

'At night?'

'Declare to God but you're askin' for a toe up the hole. And Father Jim wants to see you urgent tomorrow, so he does. Time I was goin' home. God bless.'

She went awkwardly out the door as if the gap wasn't big enough for her. She yanked at the knob and bumped into the frame and banged the door behind her hard enough to knock the woodworm unconscious.

★   ★   ★

262

Next morning Dempsey handed his father Form D.19 — his application for transfer out of the Division. His reasons were numerous: on the grounds of ill-health, exile from Kerry, the disagreeable climate of Cavan/Monaghan, betrothal — he was marrying a lady from Killarney who refused to move anywhere near the Border — and the severe ill-health of his mother, who desperately needed to see him regularly.

His reasons were purposely derisory. Especially the 'exile from Kerry' one.

His father was disgusted. The younger generation laughed at Authority.

However, he wouldn't stand in Dempsey's way. He was wary of Dempsey because of his political pull in the Phoenix Park and a cousin who was a 'money-handler' — an accountant. His father never had any pull. Everything he attained was achieved by his own efforts. After he joined the Force it became clear to his superiors he had talent. Soon he was in plainclothes investigating murders. Then de Valera came to power and he was put back in uniform and sent to Cavan.

Gardaí were not allowed to 'express or manifest political opinions'. But he heard an old-timer say that the country was run by Dev and the Archbishop of Dublin.

'We're a go-ahead country. You can go to England and when you die you can go to Hell.'

★ ★ ★

As ordered by the priest, he walked up to the parochial house to help him with the crib. He

263

wondered had Dempsey told Bessy he was leaving.

The exceptional weather, so early in the year, was beautiful. The fields and trees glistened. The hedges were full of fresh blackthorn and briar. The road was warm. It was the only tarred stretch in this part of the parish. The goats and calves and cows didn't come to greet him. The field was empty. They too were probably on the way to England. Where they would be welcomed with a basin and a butcher's knife.

He could hear in the distance the priest shouting and Guard Dempsey laughing. When he got to them they were lifting the crib on to the roof of the priest's car. The crib, painted cabbage green, was heavy. It now had a tongued-and-grooved floor. The car didn't have a roof-rack. He glimpsed Bessy peeping from an upstairs window. The priest had a length of binder twine which he tied to the crib and then brought through one window of the car and out the other and back through the crib again. This he did a number of times. Dempsey made to tie it off.

'Leave it. I know knots. Stop it. Let go, man.'

'Did you study knots in Salamanca as well?'

'Get out of my way. Let go.'

'If it all comes undone it'll be your fault so.'

The priest was bawling, Dempsey chuckling.

The crib was broad, the roof of the Ford Anglia narrow, and the knots in the binder twine slack.

'The knots are slack, Father. Doctor.'

'When I want your advice, I'll ask for it. Don't

be impudent. Shut up. Bessy!'

She didn't answer the call. The priest sent him in to get more twine. Bessy knew where it was, but she wasn't in the kitchen when he went in, so he came out again without it. Dempsey went in. Father Gaynor shouted at him.

'Not you. Come back. Bessy — the ball of twine!' He had his thumb on a knot and was trying to make it tighter. They heard Dempsey laughing.

'Go back in quick and tell Bessy I want her out here. She's upstairs in her room. The ball of twine — I had an idea we'd need it.'

He went into the hallway and hearing a noise looked into the back kitchen. Dempsey had Bessy up against a fireplace. His hand round the back of her knee, he had her leg raised. Her hands were on his shoulders.

'I hate to interrupt your tango lesson but Father Gaynor wants the ball of twine.'

Dempsey laughed. 'We're only messing.'

He was amazed at Dempsey horsing about in such close proximity to Father Gaynor. He was amazed at Bessy letting him.

'What's going on in there? Bessy. Come out here.'

She blew her lips derisively.

The twine was inside an old meat-safe. It was the kind of string used to tie parcels. It didn't look strong enough for the job but there was plenty of it. When they went outside, Father Gaynor grabbed it, doubled it and tied one end to the fender.

'What the hell are you doing?' Dempsey asked.

The priest didn't answer. He roughly balled the twine and threw it under the car, intending it should come out at the front. It didn't.

'Reach under for it, you that's young. Go on. Don't be impudent. Quick.'

He got down on the ground and scrambled about until he managed to grab it. Dempsey and Bessy were laughing. When Bessy laughed, she revealed the gaps in her teeth. It gave her an impish look, a touch sinister. Dempsey was dressed in his best casual clothes. A Donegal tweed jacket, smart green trousers and stout new shoes. Father Gaynor was wearing his good clerical suit. His petulant lower lip trembled constantly, as if he was the most vexed man in the world. Looping the twine round the bumper, he drew it up over the car bonnet, through the crib, then down the back, where he tied it off on the fender again.

He wondered would they be able to get it into married quarters. It looked too big for a normal door. Perched on the roof and with all the crude binder twine and string, it looked precarious indeed. It also just didn't seem suitable for a kitchen. Perfect for a pregnant sow maybe — but a baby? Anyway, there was no baby. It was bizarre. The four of them got into the car.

'Put your hands out and grip the string for extra safety. Don't be impudent.' Dempsey and Bessy howled laughing.

The hills were very steep. There was a real danger the crib might topple into the ditch. A man on a bicycle hopped off when he saw them coming. He looked amazed as they went past. It was the Reverend Dr Maddock. In his gaiters and top hat and leaning back for safety in the hedge, he might have been an abandoned scarecrow.

'The oul bigot. How well he had to see us.'

'He's a very nice man. And very intelligent. He has a number of degrees from Trinity College Dublin. But for lack of ambition they say he could have ended up Archbishop of Canterbury.'

'He'd have been well suited. Canterbury is the home of imbecilic heretics. You're an impudent pup. Shut your mouth and keep it shut.'

'Leave the lad alone,' Dempsey said, laughing.

'And you, I don't care who you are, leave my Bessy alone.' At this they fell silent.

He couldn't, for long, keep his glib tongue quiet.

'You know the way the Pope is really the Pope when he speaks *ex cathedra?* A priest is really a priest when he wears his collar, isn't that right, Father Gaynor? Is he a man or a priest when he takes it off? When he's in bed, say.'

'You need a toe up the hole, askin' Father Jim queskens like that, so you do. You were told shut your gob, so you were.'

'Here, any more of this and I'm getting out of the car,' Dempsey said very seriously. But then he laughed.

'What are you laughing all the time for, Dempsey? In or out of my collar, I don't trust a man who hee-haws constantly.'

The car lurched to the side and only for Dempsey staying the crib with his hand, it would have slipped off the roof like a rider whose saddle girth had snapped.

'Jazus' sake, Father Jim, aisy on the axsellerator.'

Somehow they reached the Garda Station. His parents came out to greet them as they carried the crib around to married quarters.

'Well, be the Lord Harry,' said his father, 'put a roof on it and it would make a powerful henhouse.'

'Hello, Bessy,' said his mother, 'are you well?'

'Why wouldn't I be?'

The door into married quarters was three foot wide. The crib was four by four by four. The priest pulled, yanked and tried to force it, his face red as a turkey cock from effort and anger. All he succeeded in doing was getting a streak of green paint on his jacket.

'Take it apart, maybe, then reassemble it inside.'

Apart from his father, they all rounded on him, but without much conviction. Except for Bessy.

'That suggestchin is null and void. Yah impident ting. Shut your gob or it'll be shut for you. He's a Komminist.'

'Now, now, none of that,' his father commanded. 'It's been put together so well, it would destroy it to take it apart. It can't be got in unless we petition the Board of Works to knock down the walls. The plain truth is, I think you've done a bit of a cockle-doodle-dandy, Father Gaynor. Measurement-wise.' Dempsey laughed, his foot banging off the ground as he did so.

'Come in let ye,' said his mother, wiping her hands on her apron, 'and we'll have a cup of tea anyway.'

As they sat in the kitchen it was plain to see

the priest had been brought to his eyesight. Stunned, he looked hopelessly about, acknowledging, if only to himself, there was no space for the crib even if they had managed to get it in. Cutting himself off from his self-made predicament, he started reading his breviary. As if a guillotine had come down on his emotions.

'Poor Dr Gaynor, he has the patience of a saint.'

'Which saint would that be, Mammy? St Joseph? Take the crib back up to the parochial house. It might come in useful one day.'

In silence, they tried to work out the meaning of what he'd said. He wasn't quite sure himself but he knew he'd put a cat among the pigeons. He had implied that Bessy might have a baby some day. If so, to whom? The priest? It would never be allowed to get that far. Bessy would be sent to England. Guard Dempsey? He was leaving and Bessy would never see him again.

'You know Guard Dempsey is leaving, Bessy, do you?'

'What?' She was startled.

'I'm leaving, we're all leaving, once we've drunk this tea. Thanks, missus, it's a grand drop.' Dempsey tried to look casual. But he looked daggers at the boy.

'Oh come on, let's have no more huggermugger. He's applied for a transfer. In a few weeks he'll be gone. Isn't that right, Dad?'

Bessy jumped up and thumped Dempsey on the shoulder.

'Is this true? Begod, if it is I'll be dug out of you.'

Dempsey got to his feet and his father got between them. His mother grabbed the good china jug and put it up on the mantelpiece out of the way.

Dempsey was looking hard now. And he wasn't laughing. He could handle her. He was bigger than her, heavier than her. What could she do to him? Her prominent bosom made her look vulnerable.

She exploded in rage and sobs. Her face and teeth, her whole body, were torn with emotion. She took a swipe at Dempsey and, though his father was in the way, managed to clatter him on the side of the face. Dempsey grabbed her arm and they swung out of each other. The armchair was upended.

'Yah bollickin' bowsy,' she roared at him. 'I knew damn well you were no good.'

'Come on, Bessy, I was going to tell you. I'll write to you.'

Father Gaynor slammed his breviary down on top of the range.

'How dare you lay a hand on my Bessy. Let her go, let her go. You're behaving like an animal.'

He grabbed the sweeping brush and hit Dempsey on the small of the back.

'Take that collar off and you'll not do that again. I'll split your head open.' Dempsey made a lunge but his father and mother jumped between them, terrified most terrible sacrilege was about to be committed in married quarters.

'He's taken his collar off far too many times, God forgive him,' Bessy shouted.

His mother turned to her son.

'Now you see what you've started?'

'The little fecker, I'll swing for him. I don't care if he is your only son, so I don't.' She was screaming now and trying to get at Dempsey. Tears were raining out of her eyes. Her perm went completely limp. Like it had been punctured. Or melted like an ice-cream cone in the sun. She threw the teapot at no one in particular. It smashed into the glass in the dresser door but somehow the glass didn't shatter. Tea splashed all over the lino as the teapot, minus the lid, shot in under the range.

'Bessy, enough is enough,' Father Gaynor appealed. 'You'll be looked after no matter what, you know that. You're the best housekeeper in the diocese. Your dinners are better than you'd get in the Gresham Hotel. The bishop himself knows that. Come on, let us, in the Name of the Holy Father, go home now. No more of this excessive display, no matter how understandable. I'm telling you, Dempsey, your suffering has only begun. From now on your life is a *Via Dolorosa* I wouldn't wish on my worst enemy. God will not be mocked. Come on, Bessy, like a good woman.' They'd never heard him speak with such authority and concern. In his good clerical suit (despite the green paint), his greying hair parted neatly in the centre, his yeasty face newly shaven, he looked both vulnerable and intimidating.

Bessy didn't budge. She was still steaming, casting about for something else to throw at someone. She wore a red frock with buttons the whole way down the front.

His mother examined the sweeping brush.

'You've broken the handle, Dr Gaynor,' she said simply. He looked pleased. 'You must have a powerful back, Guard Dempsey,' she added. Dempsey looked pleased. Bessy, breathing heavily, knocked his father aside with her bosom.

'You can't trust any man, I don't care who he is, saint or sinner. You were going to sneak off and leave me in the lurch.' She stuck her face right in Dempsey's. 'You're an animal.'

'So are you,' said Dempsey.

'By the way,' said his mother, trying to distract them, 'the Companion Book Club have sent you another book. It's there on the sewing machine.'

'It's not *Via Dolorosa* by any chance, is it? The book Father Gaynor wrote. That's the one I really want to read.'

'You'd be safer reading your catechism, yah impident ting.'

He ripped apart the book's cardboard packaging.

Mary Anne by Daphne du Maurier.

'If you believe that, you'd believe anything,' Dempsey said. He was laughing again.

'What?' his father asked.

'*Via Dolorosa* by A North Country Curate. Your man there goes round pretending he's the author.'

'What the hell would you know about it?' Father Gaynor said, lip trembling.

'Not much, I've never read it. But we had it at home. The man who wrote it was a relation of me mother's. He was a parish priest in

Lancashire in England. So stop telling fibs, Father.'

He laughed and, when no one was looking at him, hurried out the door. Bessy chased after him.

'Come back here, yah hoor-master,' she shouted.

He was very surprised that Guard Dempsey knew about *Via Dolorosa*. He wasn't surprised Father Gaynor hadn't written it. In a world of make-believe, you needed fantasy.

He read the first sentence of *Mary Anne*.

'*Years later, when she had gone and was no longer part of their lives, the thing they remembered about her was her smile.*'

He doubted Daphne du Maurier imagined a big-bosomed smiler with gappy teeth.

★ ★ ★

Father Gaynor never came to the house again. He'd fallen out with them. The crib sat on the lawn for a few days until he and his father carried it round the back and put it in the hen run.

Guard Dempsey was transferred. And not that long after, Father Gaynor was sent to Birmingham. On missionary work, it was said. His housekeeper went with him.

One night when they said the Rosary, to the trimmings at the end his mother added one of her own.

'Dear God, please preserve Dr Gaynor. He's such a saintly man. At the back of it all. And his housekeeper of course.'

Quigley

His mother sent him down to Tully's. It was Good Friday but they sold necessities up to noon. The pub side of the shop was shut all day. Tully was behind the grocery counter. He hooked his thumbs inside his braces and pulled them forward to let them go with a slap.

'That's a hardy one.'

'The sun's out anyway.'

'All light and no heat.'

'A box of matches and a tin of baking powder, Mr Tully, please.'

'Have you a girlfriend yet?'

'No. But I hope to rectify the situation.'

'You'll rectify feck-all away at college. When I was your age, I had plenty wild oats. But I never sowed them.'

Tully had never married. Out the big window the village green was overgrown with weeds and rough grass. The sun scattered glassy light and the pump, with its cow-tail handle, seemed to have an icicle snot hanging from its nose.

The door opened and a middle-aged man, Kit Clarke, came in. He lived with his wife and daughter in a badly thatched cottage at the back of the village. His legs were congenitally bowed. People joked he'd have made a great jockey. He wore a cap and looked rusty and dusty from hanging over the ashes all winter.

'Has the *Celt* come in yet?'

'No, Kit,' Tully flatly answered, 'sure today is Good Friday.'

Most locals only read the weekly paper. Kit glanced at the floor, moved his false teeth in and out with his tongue and abruptly left.

They watched him cross the street but he didn't head up home, making instead for a lane leading to Tully's farmyard.

'Have you done any Stations of the Cross yet?'

'I did. And a bar of Aero, please, Mr Tully.'

'Right, gauson.'

There was no Mass on Good Friday. Everyone did the Stations of the Cross, then went outside the chapel for a few moments of contemplative relaxation, then back in for another round. He did it to please his mother but also in case there really was a Purgatory. You got ten years' plenary indulgence for every round. It meant if you were sent to Purgatory when you died, you had ten years less to do. Purgatory was the same as Hell. You suffered the fire but you were released eventually. He did three Stations. That was thirty years off.

Putting the matches in one pocket of his jacket, the tin of baking powder in the other, out of curiosity he crossed over to the farmyard gate. But he couldn't see Kit anywhere.

The normally muddy yard was a thick pudge of frozen hoof prints and iced-over puddles. At the far end was a hayshed and barn. He ripped the paper from the chocolate and, leaning over the gate, munched contentedly. He didn't want his mother finding out he'd wasted money. Especially since he was supposed to have given up sweets for Lent.

A chaffinch landed on the side of a puddle and head cocked sideways, puzzled, looked at the ice. Prettier than a sparrow, duller than a bullfinch. *Fringilla*, the Latin word. Mass was in Latin. Nearly everything else in English. His mother could sing *Silent Night* in German: *Stille Nacht, Heilige Nacht.* The nuns taught her. His father could sing like a bird. A big black one. *Corvus.* Latin for raven. Another term and college would be over. Something to look forward to. But what? He didn't know.

He decided to go into the barn. Sit in there for a few minutes, finish the last bit of Aero, daydream.

He climbed over the gate, crossed the frozen ground and pushed open the barn door. Kit Clarke, pale neck stretched, was hanging from a rope. His ashen face, because of the crude knot in the noose, tilted horribly to one side. His hands were in his pockets. He'd thrown the rope over a beam and stood on a sack of corn. When he stepped off, he must have knocked the sack over with his heels. It had just happened — the corn was still spilling on to the floor. Eyes bulging, twisting slightly on the rope, he appeared more alive than dead. It was a ghastly sight. A nightmare. More real than the Stations of the Cross. A shoe dropped off. It had a hole in the sole. His bottom dentures appeared between his lips. Maybe they'd been shoved out by his choking tongue.

Terrified, he ran across the frozen yard. Tully wasn't in the shop.

'Help, help. Kit Clarke has hanged himself.'

276

There wasn't a soul about. He ran like mad to fetch his father. And still shouting through the empty village, 'Help, help. Kit's dead. Kit's hung himself.'

The BO in the day room was Guard Quigley. His father was in his office. The two of them marched quickly down the hill, hardly speaking, waiting to see for themselves. Quigley had come to the village some time before. He had a wife and two boys and three girls. The eldest daughter was the same age as himself. So far he'd only managed to say hello to her.

Tully was now outside the barn, rubbing his hands against the cold and the shock.

'Holy God, Sergeant, it's a terror.' Making the sign of the cross, he stepped aside.

They stood in the doorway, staring.

The dentures still stuck out. The face had taken on a darker, dumber, agonised look. His clothes were shabby — the dark trousers old and stained, the belt around his waist a thick length of frayed leather and elastic. A silver watch chain ran from a hole in his jacket lapel into the breast pocket. A football medal hung from the chain. His bowed legs belittled him. The bag of corn had more life in it.

'What are we going to do, Sergeant, what are we going to do?' Tully asked, still rubbing his hands.

'Have you phoned for the doctor? Go on and do it. Quick.'

'I'll take the weight, Sergeant, you undo the rope,' Quigley said. 'He's as dead as a maggot.'

His father looked up at the roof.

'He just threw it over the beam. Then looped the two ends round his neck, crude as you like.'

'Do you see the Devil's signpost?' Quigley observed sardonically. 'Pointing to Hell, hah?'

'It's not the first suicide I've attended. It's the nerves in the neck does it. When the sawbones confirms death, we'll inform the family.'

Out of horror and respect, his father spoke and moved quietly. He twirled a barrel across the floor on its rim, then stood up on it. Guard Quigley stuck his head through the bowed legs and, gripping round the knees, raised the body up high enough for the noose to be unknotted. The corpse wasn't heavy but neither was Quigley. He was tall and thin and pale as the corpse. Shortly after joining the Force he'd had TB. Somehow he was cured and allowed to stay on. In view of what he'd said about the Devil's signpost, the boy was surprised he lifted the body the way he did. When the rope was freed, the head flopped to the side. Quigley, under the weight, staggered comically. His father grabbed the collar of the dead man's shirt and steadied them. They lay the body on the ground, the head resting on the sack of corn.

His father, taking a white handkerchief from his pocket, knelt down on one knee, the hankie protecting his trousers from the earth floor. Quigley bowed his head.

He watched them from the door. His father believed in God. His faith was as important to him as the *Garda Code*. They prayed for the dead man. Suicide. That he might only be in Purgatory. Not the other place.

'Blessed Virgin Mary, you who saw your own dearly beloved Son taken down from the Cross, please intercede on behalf of poor Kit, a man never done a bit of harm to anyone in his life. Amen.'

'Amen,' Quigley agreed.

'Amen.'

In a shed next door a cow mooed. A cat came in. Seeing Kit's shoe she went over and sniffed at it without much interest.

'Go home and tell Mum what's happened. Tell her delay the dinner.'

Dinner was always at one o'clock precisely. Not today.

He wondered why Kit had killed himself and why so casually? It had to be more than the non-appearance of the newspaper. Had the collective suffering of Good Friday got the better of him? Deep down he must have been in some kind of mental pain.

★   ★   ★

He went round the back of the village just to pass the house. Mrs Clarke, a thin peck of a woman, stood outside, letting the sneaky sun shine on her. Even at a distance he could see the hair on her face, on her upper lip. He was tempted to tell her the bad news. He smiled and waggled his fingers but she didn't respond. She was looking towards the village. Her roof needed rethatching. Weeds grew through the straw and tufts of the straw were missing — rotted out by years of wind and rain.

He sat with his mother in married quarters, their hands held out to the fire. They wondered would Kit be buried in consecrated ground. Maybe they'd bury him in the cordoned-off spot with the unbaptised babies. The babies went to Limbo. There was no fire there. Just lonely darkness. For ever. They never got out. A suicide could be in Purgatory for a million years. Burning. Such exquisite torture could work on a spirit, not on a body. Kit's body was just a battered old suitcase. The spirit had fled out the roof of the barn. Angels would nab it up in space somewhere and fly it off to be judged by St Peter.

'Hanged yourself, Mr Clarke, just because the *Anglo-Celt* hadn't come out? Off with you to Purgatory. A million years. See you then.'

The graveyard high on the hill was more rock than clay. They had to cart in loads of clay to get depth. No one got six foot. Babies got two foot. Just about deep enough to stop foxes getting at them.

He was afraid he'd see poor Kit in his dreams. Twisting slowly at the end of the rope.

'Nonsense. Kit never did anything to you. You only dream of people who made you afraid when they were alive.' His mother spoke the words with certainty.

She stuck a fork into a slice of bread and held it close to the flames. He'd smear it with butter and blackcurrant jam. She told him about a dream she'd had the night before. A recurring dream. Her family had lost everything. Because her father's life was immersed in alcohol and politics. They had to scrabble about until her brothers managed to get a house in Dublin. She thought of becoming a nurse but couldn't afford the uniform. Black shoes, black stockings. She couldn't even afford to go to England. She met a nun who had taught her in the convent. They were disappointed with her. She'd done nothing of use. She had wasted her capabilities. Her education. Her life was therefore a waste.

'Surely you can see that, Lizzie?' the nun chanted to her.

'But it's only a dream, Mum.'

'Yes. But it happened. Uncle Paddy got a corner shop going. I worked for him. One morning, by chance, Sister Mary Joseph walked in. I was mortified. The very next day I met Daddy for the first time.'

It was confusing the way his parents called each other Mammy and Daddy. Sometimes she called him 'O'Hay'. They rarely referred to each other by Christian name. As if in front of anyone else it was an intimacy too close to embarrassment. If his mother raised her voice, his father would say, 'Big Bertha, Big Bertha.' Big Bertha was a massive gun in the First World War. In a marriage, a couple could live very closely as strangers.

'Where was your mother when all this was going on? The shop. The nun.'

'Dead. She was putting flowers into a vase. We found her sitting at the table with a rose in her mouth like she'd been doing the flamenco. It was comical. She must have been arranging the flowers and, preoccupied, put the rose between her teeth for a second. A heart attack. The nuns despised men. They reminded them of their fathers.'

'Maybe I better start dressing like you. Be a wolf in sheep's clothing.'

She laughed. 'You're getting more like him every day.'

It seemed a bit of a waste to end up being your own father. A reflection in his mirror. Sitting down to breakfast with yourself across the table. Not much fun in that.

The fire struggled. There wasn't a good pull in the chimney — too cold a day, no wind. Smoke came out through every crack in the old Board of Works range. His mother hated a smoky kitchen. She sighed in despair.

'Maybe Sister Mary Joseph was right.'

He stood behind her and put his arms around her. He kissed her head. Even then, he knew if in years to come he dreamt of her, it would be a symbol of one thing only — happiness.

★ ★ ★

His father didn't come home until teatime. He washed his hands and his face. His mother shot a spout of hot water from the kettle into the basin. He stood for a good while looking out the back window into the freezing gloom, the big white towel with a blue striped edge bundled in one hand. He dabbed at his face even though his face was dry.

'Sit down, man, can't you?'

He took off his tunic and boots. He'd had to

deal with the doctor, the coroner, the Superintendent from Cavan town, the priest, the vicar, the undertaker — Tully; he'd had to inform Mrs Clarke and her daughter, who was twenty. The daughter roared the house down and ripped the apron she was wearing. The Clarkes were destitute and without Kit would be even worse.

His father, looking puzzled, silently chewed on a crust of bread.

'The worst thing about it — I still feel his warm flesh on my hands. It'll be like that for ages. The dead never say goodbye. And to add to it, the rope's disappeared.'

'What do you mean, O'Hay?'

'The rope he hanged himself with. It's gone. Tully came and asked me where it was. You didn't notice anything, did you?'

'No, Daddy.'

'Tomorrow morning go out to Quigley's and ask him did he see anything, will you? He's not on duty tomorrow and I haven't time. I have to write the whole business up.'

It was an ill wind. He'd see Quigley's daughter. Rita was her name. She went to St Louis's convent in Cavan. She was supposed to be the brainiest girl there. He knew where they lived — outside the village in a rented house. Quigley was always trying to improve it. They had a big family, they needed space and Quigley had greyhounds. He was building a shed. Mrs Quigley had turkeys.

Just across the road from them was a car mechanic's workshop. It was a low corrugated structure standing on a bit of waste ground. The corrugated sheets were painted grey. It looked like what it once was — a Gospel hall. Bits of engines, old tyres and assorted mechanical bits and pieces lay all around. Nettles and dock grew up through a lot of it. The owner, Colm McDaid, was tall, heavily built, jet-black hair, strong arms, a big brown laughing face with a horse of a mouth and a scar down one cheek. When he came outside for air, he'd lean against the door-jamb rubbing his oily hands with a dirty cloth. Not long after Quigley arrived in Butlershill, he summonsed McDaid for driving without tax and insurance. McDaid hated him.

★ ★ ★

When next morning he got to Quigley's, his wife was out on the road with another woman who gripped a hessian sack. Mrs Quigley had a turkey cock which she controlled with a length of string tied to one of its legs. The woman took a hen turkey out of the sack. She wanted the cock to tread her hen.

'I heard tell you'd got the best cock in the country.'

McDaid in his shed heard her.

'You haven't seen mine, missus,' he called out.

Mrs Quigley had a square piece of leather which she fitted on to the hen's back. This was to stop the cock clawing and hurting the hen when he jumped on her back. It was held in place by straps and a buckle. It was a peculiar refinement that had much to do with morals and concern for the weaker sex. She looked with disapproval at the cock when it clambered on to the leather and gripped the hen's comb in his beak. With its grey claws, fierce red wattles and angry eyes, it had the same kind of energy as a mating bull.

Ferociously pecking the hen and tramping all over her, it kept slipping off the leather. Normally it got a purchase on the hen's feathers. It made angry sounds as if cursing at having to hammer a job on a hen whilst standing on a ridiculous piece of shiny leather. The hen, as if to get the ordeal over, sat as still as possible on the dusty road. Eventually the transaction was completed.

'You'll get great poults from that fellah,' Mrs Quigley said. 'I give him Aurofac-A every day.'

A preacher had come along the road and stood watching the extraordinary sight. He was a middle-aged man wearing neat black trousers and a black jacket. His grey-reddish hair, short on the sides, on top was carefully parted in the middle. He had the well-scrubbed look of the Puritan wanderer. The heels of his shiny boots were worn down from walking. His trouser legs were a bit short — they hung about his ankles. His jacket sleeves were on the short side too. He tried to smile but his religious face couldn't quite carry it. He clutched a thick Bible to his chest.

McDaid, standing in the doorway of his workshop, wiping his hands, was enjoying the two women and their turkeys. The preacher went over to him.

'I have a message for you, sir,' he said with great seriousness.

'Who from?' McDaid asked.

'From the Lord.'

'It mustn't be very important if he sent it with a hoor the like of you.'

The women laughed. McDaid stuck his tongue out at Mrs Quigley and, grinning, went back inside. The preacher wandered on.

McDaid had danced with Mrs Quigley at a crossroads ceilidh and made Guard Quigley jealous by doing so. McDaid had swung her off her feet in the 'Walls Of Limerick' and between moves in the 'Siege Of Ennis' had his arm around her waist. At the end of the dance he playfully slapped her on the bum. It was shortly afterwards Quigley summonsed him.

Guard Quigley was working out the back of the house, mixing lime and water. There were white splashes on his face and on the old uniform trousers he was wearing. The trouser bottoms were tucked into his socks. His ankles were thin as his arms. He had a longish chin, which curved upwards. He seemed to smile all the time, like he knew something you didn't. Two greyhounds lay stretched on the ground watching him. He looked a bit like a greyhound himself — light on his feet with hungry, restless eyes.

'Guard Quigley, Daddy wants to know did you see the rope?'

'What rope?'

'The rope Kit Clarke hanged himself with. It belongs to Mr Tully. He's looking for it.'

'You know why, don't you? The tinkers will buy it. A rope hanged a man is considered lucky.

They'll cut it into small lengths and sell them as lucky charms. To gullpins.'

'Have you any idea what happened to it, who has it or where it might be? I mean, who would steal such a rope?'

'I didn't steal it. I borrowed it. It's there behind you.'

The rope was thrown in a wheelbarrow. He wasn't the slightest bit concerned about taking it and not telling anybody.

'Why do you want it?'

'See that guttering up there — the bit coming away at the end? I have to put a ladder up. I was going to tie it off with the rope for safety. One end round a top rung, the other through the window and secure it to the bed. No use going up a ladder unless it's dead safe. Do you not think so?'

'I see what you mean. I'll tell Daddy.'

'Take it with you. Give it to Tully. How well he missed it. He's as mean as a church mouse.'

'It is his. And Kit Clarke using it to jump out of the world has made it no ordinary rope.'

He could see Mrs Quigley looking at them through the kitchen window. She was ironing clothes, her hand moving quickly over and back. She was as pretty as a finch in a cage. A plump finch.

'You don't want to take them two dogs as well, do you?'

'Why?'

'Because they couldn't catch a cold never mind a hare. I'm taking them to Longford next week and if they don't put up a show they're not

287

coming home. I'll let them out to hell in some field or other. Costs a fortune feeding the brutes. Useless.'

All the time he was crumbling lumps of lime into a bucket and stirring with a stick. The lime, after quarrying, was burnt in a kiln, thus rendering it malleable. At college one of the priests said that's what happened to the souls in Purgatory. Your sins were the hard rock which fire destroyed, your soul becoming white in the process and then, when mixed with holy water, used by the Angels to brightly wash the walls of Heaven.

The rope was a long one, hairy with age and the colour of rust. The kind of rope used to ratchet up cocks on to a hay-shifter. Or to drag a bullock out of a drain. He put his arm through the coils. Quigley showed no concern whatever at its loss. He dipped a goosewing in the bucket of whitewash and splattered it along the back wall of the house.

Mrs Quigley cheerily waved goodbye. The turkey cock, after the surreal exertions of creativity forced on him by his silly owner, wallowed in a dusty hole at the front of the house. It made a threatening gobbledy noise as he walked past. With its wattles, flushed comb, beak, mad eyes, it looked like a creature from a bad dream. It began making peep-peep noises.

Easter Saturday. A day dead as a tomb. McDaid looked out at him from the door of his shed. He'd noticed the rope. His big black beady eyes peered at it. He'd been an IRA man years before. It was then he got the scar on his face. A bullet. He had political connections. He was dangerous because of that and because of his great strength. He'd beaten up plenty of people — at football matches, in the pub, at political rallies. He didn't like Guard Quigley or any policeman. He liked women. But he treated them near as roughly as he treated men. He liked Mrs Quigley.

'Quigley's supposed to be catching thieves. He's the biggest one of the lot.'

'Hope you don't mind if I reserve my opinion on the matter until the evidence is of such quality even your cat wouldn't disagree.'

McDaid's mouth hung open and his tongue, speechless for once, was stuffed down behind his big lower lip. It gave him the look of a sinister buffoon.

Along the road to the village he couldn't believe his luck. He met Rita Quigley, strolling towards him with a bunch of daffodils. Her hair was up loosely on her head in thick blonde hanks and wisps. She wore a light cornflower-blue dress which had three buttons at the neck. Her legs were bare. She wore tight ankle boots made of fine leather and decorated with black buttons. They must have come from America; she had an aunt living in Boston. She got her looks from her mother — full lips, dainty nose, big eyes. The high sky above was spring blue. So were her eyes. She was as tall as her father. She had powdered her face a little and had used a blue lipstick. And perfume. She was older than he was and, like him, was studying for the Leaving Cert. She rode her bicycle to St Louis's convent in Cavan every day, a distance of eight miles.

'Where are you going with the flowers?'

'They're for home. Mum loves daffodils. I picked them in the wood. Where are you going with the rope?'

'This is the rope Kit Clarke hanged himself with. I'm returning it to Mr Tully. He owns it. But I was thinking — tomorrow is Easter Sunday . . . why don't you and me return it to the barn where it was before Kit put it round his neck? We could maybe sanctify the place.'

A spark of alarm flashed in her eyes. She didn't know what he meant. Neither did he. But he was talking to her.

'What do you mean? How . . . sanctify?'

'I don't know. But we could think of something.'

In his mind he thought of it as a circus rope. Old Kit had used it to climb out of his world of pain. Or to walk across it into Heaven like a high-wire artist.

'How come you have it?'

'Your dad borrowed it by mistake.'

Her eyes flashed again. Maybe she sensed her father was light-fingered.

The wind tucked her dress between her legs. He knew so little about women. He wasn't even sure whether it was a dress or a frock. It looked like a shift with short sleeves. She held the daffodils to her nose, whilst she thought of something to say.

'They don't have much of a perfume,' she said, smiling.

'Except when they are decaying.'

She held the flowers down by her side as she

290

scrutinised him. Standing there on the dusty road, high hedges on either side, he was powerless. If only she used the force she had, in some way. He thought of all the Gardaí who had liaisons with various women. It barely cost them a thought. How did they do it? He felt, as she looked at him, such an honest look, he felt as if the day was about to explode in his head and destroy his chances. All he wanted to do was kiss her. She was a bare three feet away. He couldn't cross the gap.

'I have to go.' She moved past him. He could smell her freshness. Everything had its own smell. The living and the dead. He was doomed. She turned around.

'Okay. I'll meet you so.'

He tried his best not to gush thanks.

'It is Easter,' she added. 'It would be nice to pray for Kit.'

That immediately worried him. But he covered it up. As he walked away, lugging the rope, he wondered what kind of person she really was. Very bright anyway. Guard Quigley liked to boast of her triumphs in exams. She was sure to get a scholarship to university. The sciences, languages, history — she was good at them all. What she said about praying for Kit could be a problem. Prayer could get in the way of kissing her. He'd have to think up something.

★   ★   ★

When he walked into the Station with the rope, his father wasn't surprised that Quigley had taken it. They had served together in the early days over in the West of Ireland. Quigley was a dandyish fellow in those days, dancing through life and always involved in some moneymaking scheme or other. He very nearly came a cropper when he and a local farmer bred a greyhound and, discovering it to be swift, doctored its appearance with dye. They eventually entered it in a race under a different name and at a good price with the bookies. It was a wet night in Longford and the dye ran. Quigley claimed he'd only done it for a laugh. Like he'd survived his TB crisis, he somehow survived his dyeing.

When he'd been transferred to Butlershill, his father wasn't pleased. Quigley had little interest in crime and when he summonsed someone it was usually out of spite. He refused to do nights. He'd get his wife to go into the Station and report him sick. Next day he'd appear with a sheepish grin and a sardonic look in his eyes. It was a clever mixture of apology and the suggestion that nights were for fools. Patrol the Border? For why? The IRA had guns. The B Specials had guns. The Gardaí had batons. And if you managed to hit someone, you'd spend the rest of the week filling in a report about it.

'No, Sergeant, you and me know nights are a waste of time. The Border'll be there long after we're gone.'

His father had a degree of sympathy for the point of view but duty was duty. Along the Border most crime was carried out after midnight. And as for Gardaí not being armed, didn't he arrest two armed Irregulars with his bare hands? And

292

he had the medal to prove it.

But every time the boy or his mother mentioned the medal, which wasn't often, his father went quiet. It reminded him of how long ago it was, and how worthless it was to him now. He had only a few more years to go — if that. They were closing the Station down. Who'd ever remember the murder case he solved? He was there when the judge put on the black cap.

'The poor man, we said a prayer for him the morning he was hanged.'

Whenever that case was brought up, it usually ended with his mother defending his father and rounding on him.

'Why are you always on the side of the guilty?'

'Because they're guilty, Mum.'

His mother was worried in case he went down the wrong tracks and disgraced them. His father was resolute. Life would take its course and the law was there to help it on its way.

★ ★ ★

By the Saturday evening the entire neighbourhood had heard about Quigley taking the rope. The Chief Superintendent, when it was reported to him, hurried over from Monaghan to consult with his father. He came blasting into the kitchen in a hurricane of passion.

'Theft. Blatant. I'll see to it he's cashiered. I've had enough. Can anyone say he actually earned his salary all these years? No, Sergeant, don't argue. Give them enough rope and they'll always end up hanging themselves.'

'He has a wife and five children,' his mother said.

'No, missus, it's not a charitable institution we're running. Where is the rope now, by the way?'

'I have it, Chief Superintendent Barry. Guard Quigley gave it to me. Mr Tully wants me to return it tomorrow. He's away this evening preparing another corpse.'

The Bully Barry looked at him.

'Sitting in the corner there, I never noticed him. Talk about cute.'

'Tully is the undertaker as well, sir,' his father said. 'He often uses the self-same rope to lower coffins.'

'Guard Quigley readily returned the rope and Mr Tully may not want charges preferred, Chief Superintendent Barry. Mr Tully is superstitious. He may not want a legal wrangle over the rope used in a suicide. Mrs Quigley does all her shopping in Tully's. In the circumstances it may be construed that Guard Quigley and Mr Tully are on friendly terms. The paragraphs on page thirty-four of the *Code* are worth rereading in this regard.'

He'd just made up the bit about page thirty-four. He'd no idea what it said. He guessed the Chief didn't know either.

He regularly thumbed through the *Garda Síochána Code* just for the hell of it. His father had underlined most of it and had written in new legal additions along the length of the pages. In puce pencil. His father knew reams of it by heart. He was looking at him sceptically,

294

knowing he was bluffing about page thirty-four.

He had no problem confronting Chief Superintendent Barry, the man at the head of the entire Cavan/Monaghan Division. Would he be as brave with Quigley's eldest daughter?

The Bully looked baulked. He sat down, but, getting a prod from the broken spring in the armchair, immediately shot up again. He was in mufti — a dark suit and a hat which he hadn't removed, even to acknowledge his mother. She'd take it as a slight.

'If you want my solemn advice, sir, let sleeping dogs lie. My wife is right — he has a big family. My son is right too. The Quigley custom is valuable to Tully. In a small place like this, every penny counts.'

There was a part of his father that liked Quigley. They'd known each other in the bygone days. There weren't many old-timers left. He wasn't much in the way of seeking out crime but, compared to the new generation, he'd been in at the birth of the Force. And he had mouths to feed, including a couple of useless greyhounds. He hadn't a hope of winning the English Derby, which was his pipe dream. His wife was a good person, who kept a good home, dressed well, looked after her children well and every time you met her she had a smile on her face. She came from a good family too. She had an uncle a parish priest. For his father that was the clincher.

The Bully's face was getting redder by the minute. He wasn't saying anything but such were his outraged feelings he looked as if he was about to explode. It seemed as if Quigley was going to get off the hook. Again.

'By Jesus, Sergeant, this is the last time. I want you, personally, to fix the useless so-and-so. Understand? I won't rest until we rid the Force of him and anyone else like him. Understand that?'

It was amazing how much power he had. It danced in his eyes. His fists were clenched all the time, like he wanted to punch the person he was talking about or somebody else who happened to be in the room. His father knew well the rages. His fists were clenched too.

He pointed twice at his father with a big blunt finger.

'You. You, I'm holding personally responsible. I want him out of my Division.'

He turned and stared at the boy sitting in the corner. His parents stared as well. He tried to look humble in their gaze.

'You can be too clever for your own good, do you not know that? Sitting there smirking. I hope Cavan are walloped in the first round of the Championship.'

The Bully turned to his mother.

'Happy Easter, missus.'

He went out the door like a bull through a gap. His spiteful words about Cavan were astonishing. When he first took over the Division, he promised he'd see to it that Monaghan were going to win the All-Ireland final for the first time in history. He had all the men who were good footballers transferred there. But every year the result was the same — they were well beaten. Usually by Cavan.

When he'd safely gone, his father laughed.

'By the Lord Harry, you seem to be able to get under his skin.'

'Me?'

'Yes,' his mother said, 'you have an arrogant streak. So did Lucifer. And look what happened to him. The brightest of all the Angels and yet he ended up in Hell.'

He couldn't help laughing.

'It's not funny,' his father said. 'Where is the rope now?'

He pulled the rope out from under his chair. He held the coils in both hands. Snake coils. Coffin dropper. Person swinger. Bell ringer. His mother shivered and made the sign of the cross.

'Oh get rid of it from in here, darling.'

'Don't worry, Mum. I'm taking it back tomorrow.'

He didn't tell them Rita Quigley was going to be with him. He hoped she wasn't going to go back on her word. He racked his brains trying to work out what his strategy should be. How was he going to get his lips on hers? Supposing she ran home and told her mother, who would then most certainly tell his mother? His copybook would be well and truly blotted. It would get back to the priests at college. Everyone would know about it. They lived in a country where a kiss could send you to Hell or England.

★　★　★

Easter Sunday, every man, woman and child went to Mass. You had to go to Communion at

297

least once a year. Easter Sunday was your last chance. He saw her there. Up in the choir. He could hear her singing. The priest made incisions in the big Paschal candle and inserted incense. He wore a white chasuble. The altar was ablaze with candles and flowers. Everyone wore their best clothes. Suits, frocks, cardigans, white blouses, best shoes. Even if the children came from poor homes, their heroic mothers had them done up bright as bubbles in the sun.

His father wore his full uniform. Even the greatcoat. His boots were shiny black and the night before, he'd asked him to shine his buttons. He collected them, a few at a time, on the button-stick, shook Brasso out on a cloth and buffed them up until their brilliance was incontrovertible.

'Good boy yourself — they'd pass a commissioner's inspection.'

The brass button-stick, Brasso tin and cloth were kept in the side drawer of the sewing machine.

He saw Mrs Quigley turn her head at the same moment McDaid, who was sitting in a pew on the other side of the chapel, happened to look in her direction. For a second their eyes locked. McDaid was wearing an expensive tweed suit and waistcoat. It couldn't be denied — he cleaned up well. The scar on his face looked deeper.

Mrs Quigley wore a lemon-yellow suit. The skirt was tight, the jacket well cut and she had a white blouse with an expansive bow collar. On her head was a dainty hat and veil, the same colour as the suit. The whole rig-out must have come from America. You wouldn't get the like in Belfast, never mind Dublin.

The choir at the end of Mass sang the hymn 'Tantum Ergo Sacramentum'. Rita Quigley sang the first few lines, then the rest of the choir joined her.

As everybody shuffled out at the end, he hung back so as to coincide with them coming down from the gallery. His luck was in: at the holy-water font he bumped right into her. There were too many people around to say anything but he gave her such a wide-eyed look, she knew what he meant. She nodded slightly and blinked her eyes. He went home with his parents, certain she'd be there. After dinner. He'd just have to hang about the village until she turned up. They hadn't mentioned a precise time but nothing happened in Butlershill until dinner was over.

★　★　★

He sauntered down the hill with the rope. He felt a bit foolish carrying it. One old lady blessed herself. An old bent man hobbled after him and asked him to rub the end of the rope on his back.

'Any luck is good luck, even the Devil's luck. Thanks, sonny.'

He'd put his father's Brylcreem on his hair and dabbed a spot of aftershave on his face. As he went out the door, his father had kicked up a fuss.

'Where the hell do you think you're going? I

don't want you touching my hair lotion.'

'It's Brylcreem, actually. Lotion is a liquid substance.'

'What? Mum, this fellah is going out like he's all dolled up for a dance.'

His mother came rushing into the hallway.

'Leave him alone, O'Hay. Off you go now.'

His father's face was blank and pale with unexplained and unexpected anger. He kept the jar of Brylcreem in a small white cabinet with a mirror secured to the door, that he had since 1925. It was hung up on a nail in the hallway.

He knew from reading, confirmed by feeling, all about Oedipus. Fathers and sons came to a crossroads and that was all there was to it.

He was done up like a Teddy boy and he had the rope and he was going to meet Rita Quigley.

She was outside Tully's shop, half sitting on her bicycle, waiting for him. Smoking. Striped tight trousers. A loose jumper. The snug ankle boots with the black buttons. The aunt in America was as good as a legacy. He had to say something . . . and quick.

'This is the rope.'

'Couldn't be anything else, could it?'

'We'll leave it in the barn where Kit found it. Then we'll tell Mr Tully.'

'McDaid shouted at Daddy this morning, accusing him of stealing it.'

There was worry in her eyes. It was plain she loved her father. Parents could be disastrous but we still loved them.

She left her bike outside Tully's and they walked across the street and down the narrow alley to the farmyard. It was a sunny day and the frozen path to the barn had melted, helped by all the footprints to and from the barn door. He looked about — no one had seen them going into the yard. As he pushed the door open she looked apprehensive.

'What are you going to do?'

'Haven't a clue.' He hadn't. But he was thinking hard.

'I have my rosary beads.' She paused by the door.

She was deadly serious. If she got them out it would be a disaster.

'Let's get inside first of all.'

They went inside. There was a donkey tied to an iron ring on the far wall.

'Hello, Neddy,' she said cheerfully.

'Why are donkeys always Neddy?'

'After King Edward. He was very stubborn.'

'Yeah?'

'Do you know *A Midsummer Night's Dream*?'

'I haven't read that one.'

'There's a man in it who turns into a donkey. Nick Bottom.'

The donkey turned and looked at them. The bag of corn Kit Clarke had stood on had been moved. There were still a few ears of corn on the spot. The boy had the rope on his arm. For a moment he felt he had turned into a donkey. She was looking at him, waiting for him to say something or do something. The cigarette in her hand was down by her side.

'You said something about sanctifying the place.'

She put the cigarette between her lips. Her jumper sleeve went up her arm revealing her slender wrist. Her upper lip was shaped like a bow. He'd read in the News of the World that that was a plus point in women. There was something about bosoms as well and something about three gaps between the legs. As far as he could tell she was all pluses.

'First of all . . . I've written a poem about you. Well, I haven't written it — it's in my head.'

She took another drag on the cigarette.

'Go on then.' She raised her eyebrows and her smile was twisted. He hadn't written a poem and there was nothing in his head. But there was such a thing as making words up on the spur of the moment. The donkey was looking at him again. A she-ass. She didn't believe him either.

'It's called 'You'.

> Marshmallow sweet sixteen
> All the dogs ever been
> All the cats got the cream
> Never seen what I've seen
> You.'

She was still as an icicle. But her cynical smile faded. He didn't know where it had come from but it definitely changed the atmosphere between them. For the better. It pushed them towards conspiracy.

'It's quite silly. Is it supposed to be? I quite like it.'

He felt great. Confident. Could it be that easy? But then the thought struck him that maybe she wanted him to do something risky.

'This is the place a man died. Easter is the time when a Man died and rose again. This rope . . . this rope . . . You know the cincture the priest ties round his waist? This rope is like that cord. Longer of course. The cincture is a symbol of . . . '

'Of holy purity.' He almost jumped out of his skin. That was the last subject he wanted to discuss.

'Right. Yeah. Well . . . I think we should tie it round our waists. No, no, wait a minute. That would be using it in a positive way. Not the way poor Kit used it.'

He dropped the rope on the ground, loosened it and grabbed hold of the jumbled coils. She wasn't convinced but he felt sure she was interested in some way or other. He had no idea what he wanted to do with the rope apart from tying it round their waists so they'd be in some way closer.

'You mean I tie one end round me and you tie the other end round you?' She stood on her cigarette butt and squirmed it out. Then reached for a rope end. She was definitely calmer than he was. Practical.

'No, no, not exactly, we start in the middle of the rope. We stand together, face to face like, then circle ourselves with it. Put our left hands down by our sides . . . like this . . . '

He was standing right in to her, he felt her breasts on his chest, closer than he'd ever been to a girl.

' . . . I put the rope round my waist with my

right hand . . . then put it round my back and you take it with your right hand . . . go on — take it. And so on until we are coiled together.'

She gave him a look that had raised eyebrows and a doubting smile.

'Why don't we just make a big noose and put it round our waists? And pull it tight. Like this, look.'

She quickly, deftly made a noose and dropped it over the two of them, then tightened it round their waists. It wasn't what he had in mind. But what did he have in mind? They were so close to each other their cheeks were touching. It was no longer a game.

'Now what?' she said.

'Maybe say a prayer for Kit. I'm sure you could think of one.'

That definitely reassured her. He was convinced she had been about to run away. She was religious — he had to keep that side of it going. The prayer was a good idea. They were in the noose, tight as two birds in a nest. He could hardly believe it. He'd have to do something drastic. She was staring at him, waiting.

'Kit's desperate hands himself did slay. That's from *Venus and Adonis*.'

'I haven't read that either.' She was a bloody brainbox. A Shakespeare poem that wasn't on the syllabus.

His cheek was right beside her cheek. He could smell her hair. She was fresh as a daisy woken by the dew. No paint on her face, no lipstick. His whole body was tied to hers. She was tall. It was weird being tied to someone you hardly knew.

'God hath given you one face and you didn't have to make yourself another. That's *Hamlet*.'

'I know.'

What, he wondered, what on earth was she really thinking? This was some stunt he'd come up with. But so far he was getting away with it. The donkey shifted its feet a few inches. The shoeless hooves were unpared and pointy as winklepickers.

Her hands touched his hands.

'What now?'

'Well . . . maybe . . . we should kiss? I don't know, what do you think? A kiss is holy. Jesus was betrayed by a kiss. We kiss old Kit goodbye. Sort of.'

Her eyes flashed alarm. He was pretending to be casual, as if tied together with rope, in Tully's barn, was the most natural thing in the world.

'I'm not sure,' she said. 'I've never kissed anyone before. Properly.'

'No? Neither have I. Properly.'

This had to be it.

He reached his hand round on to the back of her head. She turned her mouth to him. They both closed their eyes. He knew about pushing tongues into mouths but he didn't want to risk it straightaway. He'd brushed his teeth twice before leaving the house in case he got lucky. He was so tight to her their hearts were beating like scurrying dogs. Her lips were hard and hot. She opened her eyes when she felt him pressing into her. They heard voices out in the yard. He felt sick.

The door was pushed in and his father and Tully appeared.

Nothing could shock his father. He'd seen it all before. But this he'd never seen.

Neither had Tully. He looked at them as if they'd been captured, taken to the barn and bound up.

'Who tied youse?' he said, his face a maze of wonder. 'Was it the IRA?'

'What the hell's going on?' his father shouted. 'What are you up to? Why are you roped together? Is this some kind of dirty work? Upon my soul, if it is you're in for it.'

He'd got Rita Quigley into this and by the look on her face he was going to have to get her out. For a few seconds he riddled his brain for suitable words. The white cat came into the barn and straightaway leaped up on to the bag of corn and sat comfortably down.

'We are dedicating the rope to Kit Clarke's memory and remaking the moment of his desperation. The donkey has played a vital part. It's a bit like the stable in Bethlehem. Minus the cattle and sheep.'

'That donkey isn't even supposed to be in here,' Tully said, going to it and giving it a slap on the rump. 'Oul Cawley must have put it in after he left the pub last night.' Cawley was a tinker, always stealing fodder or lodging for his beast.

His father's face was getting tighter and paler.

'Take that rope off and get going. I don't know what you were up to but I have me doubts it was very much to do with Kit Clarke.'

She undid the noose. She looked desperate and lovely.

'I want that rope to lower a coffin tomorrow morning,' Tully said, beginning to wind the rope round his elbow and between his thumb and index finger.

'Did he talk you into this? You are supposed to be an intelligent girl.' His father looked angry and suspicious. It was a stock police face. One of three. A smiling, carefree look to get a criminal off guard. Angry and suspicious when he didn't know what had gone on but feared the worst. A downright roar of rage when he caught someone red-handed.

Rita stood right in front of him and spoke with curt emphasis.

'I was a willing participant in our Pascal rite, Sergeant. Danny is to be praised for his noble intentions, not castigated. Happy Easter to you both.' She went out the door, Tully beaming after her, singularly impressed.

'Begod, Sergeant, I wouldn't mind being tied up with her meself, hah?'

Outside he had to hurry after her. She pushed her bicycle nearly as fast as if she were riding it, heading out the road home. He practically had to run to keep up with her.

'I'm sorry, Rita, I didn't know they were going to turn up, did I?'

'I'm mortified.'

'Are you afraid my father will tell yours?'

'No, Danny. Just as well they came in. You were aroused. I felt it. That's why I'm mortified.'

'Why mortified? You mean you subdued your

passion? In the religious sense? Without passion the world couldn't turn, could it? No engine goes without fire. Same with people. You're a box of matches waiting to strike.'

She looked shocked at his audacity but then laughed, then she went serious.

'I'm going to tell you something. I've resolved to enter the religious life. I wanted to tell you that back there. I'm going to be a nun.' She stopped walking quickly. Then stopped altogether.

Such was the glowing, visionary look on her face he knew she wasn't making it up. He was shocked now. This was the girl for him. He'd never been so excited in his life as he was in the barn. You could hang, you could live — it was all the same to the Devil's signpost. A nun?

'A nun? Why? You're joking. Tell me you're joking.'

'Someone has to pray for this wicked world. Marriage holds no appeal for me. As soon as I've done my Leaving Cert I'm off to the novitiate. I've already been accepted. The world is dangerous and needs prayer.'

'Are you saying I'm dangerous?'

'That's exactly what I'm saying, Danny.' She laughed. Then looked sad for him. He knew by that look there was no hope.

'You're going to live a life all covered up in big black habits and veils, cut off from the river in your own body? Are you crazy?'

'No, I am not. You mustn't be angry. I'll pray for you.' She smiled — the kind of smile flashed for a dying man. She hopped on her bicycle and rode away.

He stood in the road. From the top of a nearby ash, a scald crow swooped down over him as close as he'd ever seen a crow come to a human being. Its caw was an angry cackle of shrieks and dog growls. Inside the demesne that ran right along one side of the village, dozens of crows' nests made the trees look like high racks, full of abandoned hats. Light clouds scudded across the blue sky. A sharp wind knifed through the leaves. It had turned cold. He went home.

He lay on his bed for about ten seconds. He went down the garden and stared at the hills. He ignored a rat in the hen run. He brought in a few sticks for the fire. He ignored his mother. He lay on the bed again. He got up and went back to the kitchen. He had discovered the perfect girl and lost her the same day. The pain was indescribable. If his father and Tully hadn't discovered them, what would have happened? He'd never know now. Did she really want to be a nun? The country was full of them. All flapping about like pints of porter on legs.

* * *

At tea his parents looked at him but didn't speak. It was his mood that now coloured the evening. They were afraid of him. That wasn't good but that's the way it was. They were afraid he might do something bad. Do what Kit Clarke had done. They chewed in silence. He was playing with crumbs. One of the glass doors in the dresser didn't shut properly. It suddenly swung open in ghostly fashion.

'Jesus, Mary and Joseph and the ass,' his mother said, trying to be both reverent and amusing at the same time.

'Tully came looking for the rope,' his father said. 'That's why we went looking for you. We got the shock of our lives finding the two of you tied up. Now, knowing you, I'd say you dreamt the whole thing up. On the spur of the moment. Am I right? By the Lord Harry, I take my hat off to you. It was the best caper ever I seen. You were as tight to her as the label on a bottle.'

His father, grinning, gave him a playful punch on the shoulder. He was probably proud of him getting a girl like Rita Quigley to fall for his great rope trick. Or he was trying to cheer him up? Give him heart? Whatever — the trick failed. In his soul he had gone from millionaire to pauper in minutes. He was confused. A nun? Was she making it up?

'I can understand you feeling dejected. Rita is a special girl. But it's well known she is dedicating her life to God.'

'How was it I didn't know?'

His mother had been talking to her mother. The mothers of the parish knew everything. And they kept a good deal of it to themselves.

The evening had closed in around the Garda Station. His mother drew the curtains and switched on the light. It was always a moment he dreaded. The drabness of the walls, the furniture, the lino, was clearly revealed. The bulb was caked with fly dung and grease and the lampshade was dusty. The ceiling was cracked and stained by smoke and steam. The wooden chairs they sat on were basic government issue. They had ink stains on them. They'd come to married quarters from various day rooms. The curtains trembled every now and then — the windows weren't draught-proof. He couldn't blame his parents. They were waiting for Paradise. The day when they'd have their own home.

He made his mind up. He was going to go out to Quigley's tomorrow. Maybe he could come up with something. He had no idea what.

★　★　★

Easter Monday. When he got to McDaid's shed, Guard Quigley was outside it, looking about him as if searching for something amongst the abandoned bits and pieces of broken cars, building equipment and an upturned farm cart minus its wheels. Nettles and grass grew through most of it. The shed was shut. McDaid was gone to the races in Fairyhouse.

Quigley, as usual, had his dark trousers tucked into his socks. He was wearing shoes, a clean white shirt and a green gansey. He always looked neat except in uniform. His thin physique didn't suit uniform. He was rubbing his chin with thumb and fingers as he stared at something lying in the grass.

'Guard Quigley.'

'That's a brave day.'

A day was brave because it had dared being fine in a climate usually unforgiving. Horrid days in winter were naturally expected and accepted.

But in spring and summer horrid days were like the first gulp of tea when you'd forgotten to put in the sugar.

'Anyone at home?'

'The missus is in town with the children. But Rita's about.'

He was rooting about with his foot. Stamping the grass and weeds so he could better see a part of a car or something lying half under the upturned cart.

'Give's a hand with this, will you?'

They shifted the cart, revealing an iron frame, an indeterminate contraption, of what former use he had no idea. Quigley, however, was intrigued. He left him to it and, crossing the road, went up the short path to the house. Rita was outside, sitting by the door, reading a book. She smiled when she saw him coming, then gave a quizzical look, wondering what he wanted. A geometry book, she had it opened on Theorem 30. She must be doing Honours Maths, he thought.

'What do you think the meaning of life is?'

'We may not know until we wake up and find ourselves dead,' she replied immediately.

'Okay. Well, what do you think the meaning of this life is? Here on Earth. Do you think it's a generous thing to cut yourself off in a convent? Live in a religious hive like a swarm of black bees buzzing around a reverend mother all day and night. What do you think will be going on in your body? I mean . . . behind all that. Under all that. Do you not want children? Every woman wants that.'

'No they don't. Your own mother has a sister

who is a nun, hasn't she? So has my mother. Sacrifice is a noble thing. We must save our own soul as we see fit.'

'Oh come on, I'll never see you again.'

She looked at him, moved on his account, but also as if she had to tread carefully. His stomach was sick, like he was tumbling from a great height.

Barefoot, in a white dress, the sun shining on her. Hair up in a straggle of ends held in place by a blue ribbon. On a chair outside an ordinary house in the middle of nowhere. Maybe this moment was going to haunt him for the rest of his life. Easter would soon be over, he'd be back at college . . . might never clap eyes on her again.

'We better say goodbye.'

'No, Rita.'

'Yes, Danny.'

'Not say goodbye. Kiss goodbye. That would have meaning.'

She got to her feet and placed the book down on the chair.

'Okay.'

Surprised, he followed her into the porch. She stood against the wall. She looked very serious. Demure. He copied an embrace he'd seen in the cinema. He held her to him with his right arm and put his left over her left shoulder. She put her arms round him and held him surprisingly tight. He felt her entire form pressing against him — the soft, the smooth, the firm. He kissed her lips and she put her tongue in his mouth and kissed him warm and hard. Definitely she put her tongue in his mouth first. They called it

French kissing. Kissing like she was not only saying goodbye to him but saying farewell to the world. Then she disengaged. Her lips were red and wet. She licked them.

'I will pray for you, Danny, every day.'

She went in and closed the door. Jesus. That was quick. Once they made their mind up, a plough horse couldn't shift them.

When he came outside, he saw Guard Quigley stumble round the corner of the house, carrying something. At McDaid's shed, the cart was back in its original position. The weeds and grass which they had trampled had been restored to as normal as possible. He sauntered home — what use hurrying? He wanted to work out his feelings. You could meet someone but what could you do if they didn't meet you?

There were primroses on the grassy bank of the road and on the other side a tongue of water gurgled out of a field into the open gully. Ivy clung to the trees. New briars sprung beside long vicious old ones. Hogweed stood tall everywhere. All along the way, the hedges were full of holly trees. In the snapping wind everything fluttered. Especially his heart. You could be sailing along nicely, then suddenly get buffeted aside like a boat in the middle of a lake.

There was a small lake lying at the foot of a wide whin-, rush-and fern-infested hill. Two tern left the water and sped together skywards. They dived, flattened out at the last moment, soared again and one chased the other, desperately trying to catch up. Long-winged feathery darts of white and black, they skirmished so fast the eye lost them against the light. Twisting, turning, zig-zagging crazily, they were yet suddenly able to slow down and fly incredibly slowly. Like they were walking nonchalantly on air.

★   ★   ★

When he got to the village, a flock of children were playing football on the green with a sock-ball — scrunched-up newspaper and corks stuck down a sock and sewed up to resemble the expensive real thing. Laughing happily as they ran around and through one another, they were as exhilarating as the tern.

Jim Reilly was outside the pub. He called him over and asked him to lend a hand in the bar that evening.

A house-proud woman was attaching a striped cloth to her front door. A kind of deckchair material. It was meant to protect the paintwork from the sun. What sun? It was a status symbol in a country that was all symbol and little substance. Two small girls watched her. One said to the other, 'It's a door frock.'

When he got home, his father was in his office. He was still writing reports about Kit Clarke's suicide.

'He's being buried tomorrow. They delayed it so his brother could get home from Sunderland. There's a wake in the house tonight.'

'Are you going?'

'No. But I'm sure you will.'

'Have you ever had your heart broken by a girl?'

His father looked up from the report he was

writing, studied his face for a while, then smiled.

'No, never. Why? Has Rita Quigley broken yours?' He laughed, a kind of guffaw.

The boy leaned against a map of the district pinned to the wall. His father laughing upset him. Was he so hard, he couldn't understand another's pain?

'What's funny?'

'Believe you me, you'll get over it.'

'She's going to be a nun.'

This time he laughed outright.

'Be the hokey,' he said, 'that's a good one. Look here, have a titter of wit. Up to not that long ago the father was an alcoholic. She wants to avoid married life as a result. The convents are full of poor girls like that.'

'Guard Quigley was an alcoholic?'

'Yes, yes. When he had TB he was given bottles of stout. That was all they had before penicillin. He grew too fond of it. Them days I saw many's the fine fellow die. You'd see the family burning the mattress the day after. You don't know you're alive, boyo. This country was hanging by its fingernails.'

He went round to married quarters. His mother was down on her knees washing the lino. He hated himself for letting her do it. For not doing it himself.

'Someone has to do it. If I don't, who will?'

She had varicose veins and a touch of arthritis. He tried to think of one thing he'd ever done for her. Maybe bring in wood for the fire, collect the eggs, go down to the village for the messages.

'Rita Quigley is going to be a nun. Maybe men

316

and women don't get on enough of the time to make their children want to copy them.'

'There's no end to people getting married, is there? Every creature wants a partner of some kind or other. What can we do, darlin'? It's God's will.' She started soaking meal in preparation for the next morning's porridge. She put her hand down into a sack and when she withdrew it he could see the oaten dust on her wedding ring.

'You make porridge every single day of your life, Mum.'

'I do. But I don't have to eat it. I hate it as a matter of fact.'

'Married quarters — it's as good as a jail sentence.'

'Stop it. Daddy and I have beaten a path through the jungle and we're not going to leave it now. We'll see how you get on. I hope we'll see. And not be pushing up the daisies.'

★ ★ ★

He walked up to the graveyard hoping to see Kit's grave being dug. He was surprised to see a large crowd there. For a moment he thought they were burying Kit. But it was an Easter commemoration for an IRA volunteer killed during the War of Independence. People crowded round a memorial cross and a well-dressed middle-aged man was standing on a chair making a speech. He quoted from Patrick Pearse at the grave of O'Donovan Rossa: 'The fools, the fools, they have left us our Fenian dead and while

Ireland holds these graves, Ireland unfree shall never be at peace.' The listeners applauded and girls cheered.

Away in the blue distance were the mountains and below them in the valley Lady Sarah's demesne and outside her walls the Orange hall. Over to the left was the primary school he'd attended and behind it Shannow Wood. Further off, down low like a lark's nest, was the village itself.

A plainclothes detective from Cavan stood one side of the cemetery gate. Everyone knew who he was. Even when he dressed up as a monk or stuck on a beard and pretended to be a school inspector.

As the crowd departed, carefully picking their way round graves, he was surprised to see McDaid amongst them. He was in his best tweed suit and on familiar terms with the orator. As he passed the detective he said loudly, so everyone could hear him, 'Where were you when we had to fight the Black and Tans?' Turning to the memorial cross he pointed and said, 'That man was a man. Only twenty-two.' He clenched his big fist as if ready to defend himself should the detective try to arrest him. The detective grinned and, after McDaid had gone, wrote something in his notebook.

He followed the crowd back to the village. There was about a hundred of them, mostly young men and women. The dead hero's elderly family took it slowly. The hills were steep and the village a mile away. The main bunch were in celebratory mood, talking loudly and laughing.

One tall youth with black hair and twinkling eyes, wearing a good suit and a white mac which hung open, linked two girls. They wore berets and clung out of his arms and laughed at everything he said. Without warning or introduction he started singing. 'Ireland, Mother Ireland.' He sang with a swagger, his head moving proudly as he let rip with the words, giving them a sentimental authority to outdo John McCormack. The dusty road, the shuffling shoes, the tall hedges on either side, the little fields, the clump of people, was a prosaic setting but exciting, even sensational. As if he and the two girls had burst through reality to fly in a romantic oxygen far above ordinary.

> Oh land of love and beauty
> To you our hearts are wed
> To you in lowly duty
> We ever bow the head . . .

They were about the same age. How the hell did he do it? Two women and he didn't even have one. The girls were loving every minute of it, loving everything about him. They were attractive, lively, in tight skirts and jackets, black stockings and high heels. One had blonde hair, the other black. They looked up at his face all the time, as if he were a film star. Some kind of hero. They didn't seem to have a care and they didn't care that they were passing the Garda Station and his father was out looking at them . . . looking at him. He dropped out. Ever a coward. A rebel heart but an overruling head.

'They're making for the pub.' His father was contemptuous. But then he added, 'God help them.' He couldn't bear the thought of young people risking their lives in a useless Border campaign against impossible odds.

'This country, any country, isn't worth the shedding of one drop of blood.'

★ ★ ★

The pub that evening was packed. The young man and the two girls weren't there but everyone else seemed to be, including McDaid. Chisholm Flood and his brother, Squealer, sat on high stools by the bar. Chisholm was telling someone he'd shoot them and Squealer was squealing into his pint. A woman sang 'Come back, Paddy Reilly, to Ballyjamesduff.' She had a decent voice but no one was listening to her. It was possible she didn't even know she was singing; she was dribbling from the mouth. A span of Guinness spittle. Jenkins, a house painter, in for what he thought was going to be a quiet drink, looked about him in awe.

'The lunatics are all in tonight. And they've taken over the asylum,' he said.

Jim Reilly, flat out, pulled pints as fast as he could. The settling glasses of black stout and their white collars stood packed along the bar like a regiment of priests. Curate was an apt name for a barman. A drunk claimed to have won twenty pounds on the winner of the Grand National. He gave a slurred commentary on the race every few minutes, ending at the last fence, barely audible, his head slumped on his chest. McDaid hit him a rap with his knuckles on the top of his head, silencing him for good.

'I'll bate any man in Ireland, bare knuckles,' McDaid shouted, 'any man or woman.'

'Would you bate me?' Chisholm challenged him.

'I'd bate you with a woman's glove, and the Squealer along with you.'

'Fuck yah and double fuck yah, fuck yah from a height, I'll shoot yah.'

'Here, here, none of that, that's enough, no bad language, it's not necessary, and you'll not shoot nobody in here, youse are not at home now, quit it now I'm telling youse.' Reilly's voice was nearly hoarse with rising indignation. 'Come on, boyo, collect them empties.'

'Eek. Agh. Eekek. Squee. Agh. Eek.'

Carrying empty glasses, fingers stuck haphazardly in each one, he paused in front of Squealer and said, 'I agree with every word you said.' People laughed.

McDaid turned on him.

'You're only a peeler's brat and don't you forget it. We know what you're after — Rita Quigley's knickers. She doesn't wear any. She didn't last night anyway.' He laughed and a good many others laughed with him. 'And neither does her mother.' He laughed again. But this time no one joined in. Guard Quigley had come in. He was in uniform, on duty, and there to clear the pub — it was long after closing time. Drinkers turned their backs, pretending they hadn't seen him. Others gulped what was left of their pints and dived out the back door, inflating the moment to the ritual of escape, even though they weren't being pursued.

'Now you see, now you see,' Reilly said, 'the Guards is here, home to hell the lot of youse, the Guards is here.'

'I'll give you five minutes to clear the premises,' Quigley said quietly. 'Any man found on after that will be summonsed.' 'Found on', shorthand for 'found on licensed premises after hours', was part of the country's linguistic soul. Like 'God willing' or 'Not a bad day'.

Quigley looked peculiarly out of place in the packed pub. Pale and thin, a shadow in uniform too big for him, compared to the raw-faced blocks of weather-hardened drinking men before him.

As Quigley retreated out the door, McDaid shouted after him, 'Away and hang yourself with that rope. Were you practising to take over from Pierrepoint?' He snorted down his nose, pleased with himself, drunkenly truculent. He appeared as if he was going to finish his pint peacefully but instead made for the door, taking the half-full glass with him.

'Danny, g'out there and see what's going on.'

He finished wiping down the bar, flung the sopping cloth in the basin of scummy water and went out.

McDaid was nowhere to be seen. Quigley was lying on the ground. He helped him to his feet and into Reilly's house, which adjoined the pub.

'He hit me and when I was down he threw the contents of his glass into my face.' He wiped his face with his hand. Drops of porter ran down his forehead. He looked even paler than normal. McDaid hitting him was no triumph. Quigley was a weak man, someone who had been ill for a large part of his life. McDaid was a brute, an experienced brawler, who saw every day as a fist fight and who always appeared to be vexed.

'He took my cap as well.'

It was a serious charge for a policeman to lose his cap or let it be stolen by a corner-boy.

'I'll go and get Daddy, will I?'

'No, don't. He has enough on his plate. I'll be all right.'

'He'll arrest McDaid.'

'There wasn't any witnesses. And if there was they'd deny seeing anything. I'm not liked, boyo, I know that. Even your dad doesn't like me. A policeman doesn't have to be liked.'

He was going to protest on behalf of his father but decided Quigley's self-assessment was probably accurate. Birth or life had given him a crafty look and a sardonic smile. A grinning greyhound look. It didn't help. Yet he wasn't bad-looking. Sickly but intelligent and even a kind of charm. He sat on the stairs in Reilly's hallway, breathing deeply, pulling himself together, his blue shirt soaking.

'Rita likes you. But she's promised herself to God.'

He was hoping he'd see her at Kit's funeral the next day. Then he had a thought.

'Do you want me to walk home with you?'

'Not at all. You're a good lad. No point in me going back in there. They'll have cleared away by now. It's not the first time a thug has thrown porter into my face. I played for the county, you know. Bet your dad didn't tell you that. The TB put a stop to football. I was lucky though. The Force kept me on. We'll always be grateful for that.'

He sounded slightly maudlin. He wondered, was he a malingerer? Whatever, he was a man dealt a poor hand of cards.

Capless, Quigley headed up the street to the Station. Maybe he wasn't much of a Garda but how many men had produced a girl like Rita?

He went back in to Reilly. Quigley was right — the pub was empty. The tables and floor were littered with cigarette butts and splattered with spilt drink. He helped swab it all away and Reilly gave him half a crown.

He remembered it was Kit's wake. He'd hardly known the man but finding his body had linked him in his mind, probably for ever. The dumb agony on his wrinkled face, the false teeth protruding, the hanging corpse slowly twisting in Tully's barn. The shoe dropped off. That life could so quickly disappear . . .

As he walked round the back of the village and up the muddy path to the house, it was immediately obvious that the wake was a subdued affair on account of the circumstances. Normally a wake had a certain levity despite the presence of the corpse. When he went in the open door, he could only see five people. The wife, the daughter, the brother from Sunderland and two neighbours. The daughter, when she saw him, started crying into her shawl. The mother,

324

thin as a sweeping brush, sitting by an open fire, told him to help himself to a cup of tea. The tea things were on the table along with a plate of sandwiches. The coffin was in the corner, Kit lying in it, his lips caved in. They must have removed his false teeth. Some people bought false teeth second-hand.

'You're good to come anyway,' said the daughter. She was a buxom girl with a thick lower lip and the blackest eyebrows he'd ever seen. Her lower lip gave her a sullen appearance. Her eyes made up for it. Though red from weeping, they danced with life. Her overall vibrant air wasn't overcome by the sight of her dead father or the hardened mud floor or the tattered thatch visible above the rafters.

'Let them remember,' said the mother, addressing the room, 'Jesus was born in a stable.'

The brother from Sunderland was wearing a black suit and brown boots. He looked a slightly livelier version of the corpse.

'Howaya? I'm tired but I had to make the effort. I'm on nights. Over there they work the twenty-four hours. The food mightn't agree with you. But if you could get the right landlady you'd have the shirt washed as well. A fellah I know from Enniskillen, he got to be cock-lodger from day one. That's the ticket. Are you a working man?'

'No. I'm still at college.'

'Oh. You'll be all spit and polish then. What persuasion are you?'

He wasn't sure if he meant religious persuasion.

'He's the one found Kit,' the wife said. 'He's the Sergeant's son.'

The daughter handed him a cup. He had half hoped Rita would be there. He was full of half hopes. Nailed above the fireplace, a clock shaped like an Alpine chalet struck eleven. It had two pendulums.

'The old wall-wagger,' the brother from Sunderland said, 'the old wall-wagger. Kit's problem was his heart wasn't in it. Never from the word go.' Before the boy could ask him what he meant, he said, 'I met Stanley Matthews over there. I'm Richie, I says to him.'

'Really? What did he say?'

''Good evening, Richie.''

A wart on his left cheekbone had a long black hair. He gently pulled at the hair as he contemplated what to say next. He didn't add anything further about Stanley Matthews.

'I'm Danny.'

When he announced he was going home, they protested and the daughter, almost shrieking, cried, 'No, no, Danny, sure it's early yet, stay a while, stay a while longer, can't you?'

Her clothes were flimsy but she cheered them up with a cloth rose and a string of pearls. Taking her fingers in his, he bowed and kissed the back of her hand.

'Delighted to meet you, Miss Clarke. Though the circumstance is tragic.'

She looked alarmed, then smiled to her mother.

Richie, surprised at the gesture, suspicious, pulled gently at the hairy wart.

326

He turned to Mrs Clarke and said, 'I'm sorry for your trouble, Mrs Clarke. Goodnight.'

She clutched the top of her blouse with one hand as if there were buttons missing. Maybe she was cold. As she'd been sitting in the shadows he hadn't noticed her moustache. But now that she stood close to him he couldn't help looking at it, though he tried not to.

'Don't worry, we'll be all right. He didn't mean to do it. People think one thing but it's the other way about. It's always the other way about.'

They both looked over at the coffin. Rifling desperately through the rest of his funeral clichés, he came up with, 'Well, he's at peace now, Mrs Clarke.'

On the way home he thought of her remark about things always being the other way about. That was life in a nutshell. Things were usually the other way about, or, if not, if only they were.

★ ★ ★

Next day a good crowd attended the funeral, which he hadn't expected considering there were so few at the wake. Kit wasn't buried in the Catholic graveyard — it turned out he had been a Protestant who had married a Catholic. Tully was the undertaker but didn't attend. The coffin was walked the whole way from the house. Someone whispered that they couldn't afford the hearse. Tully gave them the coffin out of decency and the fact that Kit committed suicide in his barn. A relay of men shouldered the coffin. Richie, the brother from Sunderland, carried it all the way

327

without being relieved. When they got to the Protestant church, more people were waiting for them, clustered outside the gates. Amongst them was McDaid. Most of the mourners were Catholics. But when the coffin was carried into the churchyard, apart from his wife and daughter, none of them followed. They weren't allowed. To go to a Protestant service of any kind, even a wedding, without special dispensation from a bishop, was to commit a mortal sin. McDaid was the only one who went in. He wouldn't take orders from Rome as he hadn't in the past from London. The dangerous blaggard had guts. The Church of Ireland was the Church of London. The Catholic Church was the Church of Dublin. One God — a million enemies. Disobey either and you'd be a parish leper.

When the boy followed McDaid, a couple of old ladies who knew him, scandalised, whispered and nodded in his direction.

He was concerned, scared even. His parents would be told. Rita would find out. He'd be an apostate in that part of her that wanted to be a nun. He looked round to the gates to check she wasn't there. She wasn't. Behind the crowd, now blocking the road, were the scabby hills rising away up to the Catholic graveyard on its fort of rock, adorned only with a lone yew tree.

The sparse cortège wound its way round to the back of the church. Beside a freshly dug grave, the carriers awkwardly put down their burden. The earth smelled good. Like when his father turned over the first clump of spring in the vegetable garden. Mrs Clarke and her daughter, in thin black clothes, clung to each other. Richie had an unlit cigarette in his lips.

There was a rope beside the grave. He realised it was the rope Kit had used to hang himself. It was to lower his coffin into his grave. There was no undertaker and it seemed there was to be no vicar either. The family and mourners stood wondering how to proceed. He realised why they were round the back of the church. Kit's grave was separate from the main part of the cemetery. He wasn't going to be allowed burial beside the righteous — 'Safe in the arms of Jesus' — and those whose headstones declared they had died gloriously at the Somme.

'We can't stand here all day,' McDaid said. He and another man, an agnostic Presbyterian, got hold of the rope and arranged it in two strands under the coffin. As they were about to lower it, the vicar came out from a side door. He hadn't seen him before. He was either a visiting parson or a new appointment. He wore ordinary clerical black. The only concession to ceremony was a black stole round his neck. He didn't even have a Bible.

'Well, lower the coffin,' he ordered a reluctant gravedigger who stood nearby.

McDaid on one side of the grave and the rebel Presbyterian on the other took up the strands of rope — a strand in each hand — and with effort lowered the coffin six foot under. This graveyard had a deep bed of clay. The rope was pulled clear. The gravedigger looked to the vicar. He didn't respond.

'Is that it?' McDaid asked.

'The Office for the Burial of the Dead is not used for any that die unbaptised, or excommunicate, or have laid violent hands upon themselves. It would be scandalous so to do.'

Kit's wife and daughter clung even tighter to each other. They looked shattered. They'd probably been up all night sitting by the corpse.

The vicar, a youngish man, had a scrubbed, bloodless face.

Richie, taking the cigarette from his lips, fumbled it back into his packet of Sweet Afton. He didn't seem concerned at the stern words.

The vicar spoke again.

'O death, where is thy sting? O grave, where is thy victory? The sting of death is sin, and the strength of sin is the law. Be ye steadfast, beloved brethren, always abounding in the work of the Lord. Amen.'

This really was the churlish priest. He wished he had the courage of Laertes . . . I tell thee, churlish priest, a ministering angel shall old Kit be when thou liest howling.

'You're all the same, doesn't matter the cut of your jib,' McDaid snarled. 'Kit was one of the best. He made hay for me many's the summer.' He scooped up two big handfuls of clay and stone and lobbed them into the grave. It rumbled on the coffin lid like someone was down there beating a roll on a drum. The vicar slipped back into the church through the side door.

Richie took out his cigarette again and a lighter. 'He loved that song . . . what's this it was? The day before I went to England, he threw the record into Kilifana lake.'

It was a strange elegy. Each person threw down a handful of soil. *Kyrie eleison. Domine dirige nos.*

'Don't worry, we'll be okay now,' the daughter said to her mother, embracing her again.

'People can say what they like,' the mother replied, 'but it's the other way about.'

★ ★ ★

Walking home he saw a hare bounding gracefully across a hill. A grey crow flew above, weighing it up for danger or food. He thought of the poor grasp people had on life. Your fingers could slip at any time. Inside a person the loneliness could be immense. The planet itself, Earth, was a billion years from explanation.

He came across his father along the road. He was standing stiffly by his bicycle, cycling clips on, tunic cloth belt buckled as per regulation, white chevron of three bars mounted on blue cloth on the upper part of the right sleeve, looking up at one of the oak trees just inside the wall of the demesne. He had no idea what he was doing there. It looked odd. He was probably, purposely, waiting for him — he'd have heard already that he'd gone in to the Protestant funeral. When he saw the uniform in the distance, the big boots, he filled with anger. It was impossible to escape him.

'Just the very man. You're a good climber, aren't you?'

'Why? What's up?'

'What's up indeed. Quigley's cap. That bowsie McDaid flung it up there last night. See it? It's all round the Division. The Chief was on the phone. A laughing stock. See can you get it, will you?'

'McDaid was the only one to go in to Kit's funeral.'

'You went in, didn't you? You'll have to go to Confessions.'

He didn't reply. He was fuming. Gripping the ivy, he clambered up the wall and, standing on top, managed to get on to a branch of the oak. As a boy he'd climbed most of the trees in the demesne. The oak bark reminded him of elephant skin. Poxed with lichen and moss. Because of the crows' nests right at the top of the tree, the branches were spattered with droppings. Quigley's cap was caught securely on a twig as if carefully placed there. He shouted down, 'Is Guard Quigley okay? McDaid beat him up, did he tell you?'

'It wasn't much of a victory. McDaid is a brute. Poor Quigley isn't in the full of his health. I'm trying to persuade him to retire.'

'Is Mrs Quigley having an affair with McDaid?'

'What? None of that talk. Good God. Who said that?'

'I heard someone whispering it at the funeral.'

'Corner-boys. Disgusting. Mrs Quigley is a good woman. She does all the flowers for the chapel. She washes the priest's vestments. Give that branch a shake.'

He hadn't answered the question. Mrs Quigley

was never about the village much. None of the women were. They spent their lives inside.

He climbed higher, enjoying it, good at it, keeping his feet in close to the trunk, looking down on his father looking up, his tense face, penetrating eyes, his soul fretting and sweating about Hell and Headquarters. The hare, the crows, monkeys in the jungle — they didn't want to control your thoughts. Go to Confession because you went to Kit's funeral? The vicar with the sour face ... Man was supposed to be in advance of all others because he had come down out of the trees.

His foot disturbed a piece of rotten bark. The most amazing insect crawled out. It had, compared to the rest of it, a massive pair of antlers. He shouted down, 'There's a what-do-you-call it? A stag beetle. It's amazing. Big black antlers on it. Must be a male. It's fantastic.'

'Don't touch it. Come on, give that branch a shake. We haven't got all day. And if you want my solid opinion — any girl would let you tie her up with a rope that just hanged a man, good God Almighty, man, have sense. What the hell were you up to at all?'

'Juggling with reality. I was tied up as well don't forget.'

He shook the branch as hard as he could. The cap bobbled about and seemed set to free itself but didn't. He could see his father raking his bottom lip with his top teeth. It was a habit he had when on edge. He shook the branch again. Crows wheeled above, cawing madly at being disturbed. Their grey beaks looked as if they

were made of steel. He had to be careful — he
didn't want to knock the stag beetle off the
branch. It hadn't moved. Maybe it was in shock.
He worried about his footing. He was so high
up, the boughs weren't that strong. He clung
with one hand to a branch above his head.
Leaning out as much as he safely could, he
shook for all he was worth but the cap wouldn't
free itself.

With a fatal sound like the crack of a pistol,
the branch he stood on snapped. To save himself,
he grabbed the branch he had been shaking. It
broke under his weight. As he plummeted, his
feet hit a strong bough further down, breaking
his fall, and in a split second he managed to
hang on to another branch. He had saved
himself — just. His wrists seemed strung out like
chewing gum. He was shaken to his roots as if
the tree had taken revenge.

His father's terrified voice shouted upwards,
'Are you all right? Jesus protect us.'

His ribs hurt, his feet hurt more.

'Take your time, rest for a bit. You did the trick
anyway. The cap's down. Good boy, you're a
topper.'

Painfully he inched downwards. When he
reached the top of the wall, breathing heavily, his
father lifted him clear. He could barely stand.
His father had his arms around him, holding him
up. He hadn't been this close to him since
boyhood. The smell was familiar — Palmolive
soap and perspiration.

'I hope I didn't kill the stag beetle.'

'Have a styme of sense. Stag beetle, me arse.

334

You could have been killed. There's only one thing for it — can you manage to get on the bar of the bike?'

He managed. His father got on and steadied himself before pushing off. His boots pounded the pedals and sometimes his big hard knees knocked the boy's dangling legs. Every jolt of the road hit him in the ribs. His father had given him Quigley's cap to wear as an easy means of carrying it. It smelled of Palmolive soap, sweat, Jeyes Fluid and ink. The gear lever on the bar of the bike dug into him. He was in agony. The bits of him not shaken by the fall were rattled by the untarred pot-holed road.

When they got home he was carried into his mother's bedroom, his mother wailing like a banshee. Her bed was the most comfortable, the room good enough not to be ashamed of if they had to call the doctor.

'Will you stop keening, woman? He was shaken to his spine, he'll be right as rain in a couple of days.'

'Blessed Jesus, sending him up a tree, have you taken leave of your senses, man?'

Quigley's cap sat on the end of the bed. The Garda badge had a decorative S tangled by its tail in a superior G.

'Agh, for God's sake, he'll be better before he's twice married. Won't you, boyo?'

He groaned — exaggerating somewhat.

'Danny darling, Danny darling. Will we call the doctor?'

'We'll wait 'til morning. He hasn't anything broken. Have you? Stop wailing, woman, I told you, for God's sake. Save it for when one of us is dead.'

Though his ribs hurt he couldn't help laughing. They bent over him, holding him, feeling him, his father's big hard hand on his forehead. Above the bed was a picture of Pope Pius XI. A smooth stout Italian wearing a skull cap and a cape edged with ermine. It was an Apostolic Blessing on the occasion of his parents' marriage. The writing stated they had humbly prostrated themselves at the feet of his Holiness, imploring his Blessing.

'Try and get forty winks,' his father said.

★ ★ ★

Butlershill was supposed to be in the middle of nowhere. Yet news spread faster than Fleet Street. Nothing modern could match wagging tongues. Neighbours began arriving at married quarters enquiring after him. Jim Reilly brought six bottles of stout in a brown paper bag.

'I'm a Pioneer, I don't drink, you know that, Jim.'

'About time you started. It's a great pain-deadener.'

Most of the policemen came in and a new man, Guard Driscoll, stuck a copy of the *News of the World* under his pillow when his mother wasn't looking.

He was astounded when Chisholm Flood's face appeared. He stood in the doorway staring at the furniture. When he saw the commode by the bed, he nodded at it, winked, by way of acknowledging the comfort of such an invention. He had a moustache of porter on his unshaven lip.

'Thank you for coming, Chisholm. I'm okay.'

He wore a torn open-necked shirt, brown shiny boots, green trousers and a cap backwards on his head. A slick of hair was stuck dead centre of his forehead. Greased by his fingers tugging at it all day.

'Get up the fuck outa that or I'll shoot yah. I'll shoot yah where you're lyin'.'

'Why, Chisholm?'

'Doesn't matter. I'll shoot yah.'

People were the only medicine and they came in a variety of bottles.

'Take one of them bottles, Chisholm.'

'I thought begod you were never goin' to ask.' He stuck a bottle in each pocket and went off.

He sunk into the softness of his mother's bed and fell asleep. Later he felt her hand on his face.

'Danny darling, how are you? There's someone to see you.'

'Oh, I've seen enough, Mum.'

'I'll tell her to go so, will I? Miss Quigley.'

He shot up on to the pillows and barely felt the pain. His mother stood aside as Rita stepped in. He was relieved he had agreed to wear his father's pyjama top. Normally he slept in his vest.

'Have you time, Rita, to have a cup of tea?'

'No thanks. I have to be going soon. Oh, okay, I will have a cup, thank you.'

That meant his mother had to leave them alone for a few minutes. High heels, nylons, a

337

tight skirt and a short coat. She had a white beret on her head. She was clutching something.

'You're a bottle of medicine I'd drink any day.'

'No double-talk, Danny. Or I'll go immediately. Is that understood?'

'Sit down.' He patted the side of the bed.

'No, no, certainly not, what do you take me for?' If her scolding tone really was the measure of her thoughts, he had no chance whatsoever.

'I wrote another verse. You know — 'You'.' She smiled her usual disapproving amused smile. When she smiled, her teeth came on parade like the sun was shining on them.

He had never been alone in a room with a girl. He was in bed and she was as near as damn it. He had to think quick.

No one ever saw the gleam
No one knows what I mean
No one ever dreamt the dream
Lived the reality of what I've seen
You.

Still as a statue, all starched and stern and smelling of perfume, she weighed his words — probably for sin. How was he going to entice her to sit on the bed? She bit her lip.

'Hm . . . what can I say?'

'Say what you think.'

'I have a present for you. We're so grateful to you for being kind to Daddy last night and for climbing the tree to rescue his cap. And getting nearly killed.'

She handed him what looked suspiciously like

338

a prayer book. He undid the press-stud on the overlapping cover.

Saint John's SUNDAY MISSAL.
And Every Day Prayerbook.
C. Goodliffe
Neale Ltd. 15, Booth Street, Birmingham 21.

SUNDAY MISSAL was in red. There was a black and white sketch of the Blessed Virgin holding a chalice and round her head the words 'Ecclesia Sancta'. On the opposite page was a full picture, in colour, of Christ on the cross with two women in blue purity and a man in brown.

He didn't know whether to laugh or cry. She was looking at him, her eyes wide open, as if she had presented him with a gift beyond price. She was deadly serious about being a nun.

'You didn't come to Kit's funeral.'

'I consulted with the priest and he advised not to in the circumstances.'

'Kit brought us together.'

'We are not together.'

His mother came in with the tea. He could tell she was pleased that Rita wasn't sitting on the bed. She put the tray with cups and saucers, spoons, teapot, jug of milk, bowl of sugar, two side-plates and a packet of Nice biscuits on the dressing table.

'Will I get you a chair, Rita? I will.'

'No, no, it's not necessary,' she answered firmly. 'I'll be going soon.' His mother turned the light on and went out, smiling and bowing to her.

'Can I say something? Are your mother and McDaid friends?'

'There's nothing wrong with being friends. That's all they are,' she answered defensively, 'as far as I know.' The last bit had an enigmatic slant to it. She looked at the tea things but didn't move to pour the tea. Her legs were wide enough apart to stretch her tight skirt and her bosom filled her coat. She licked her lips. 'I pray for McDaid like I pray for Mammy. But we must save our own souls first. And that's what I'm doing.'

'You know when we kissed goodbye . . . what we did with our tongues, was that not a sin? A mortal one.'

'It was. I can't wait for Saturday. To go to Confessions.'

'Yeah? There's no chance, I suppose, of you not going away to be a nun?'

She shook her head emphatically and smiled.

'Well, we better say goodbye again. I mean . . . you're going to Confessions on Saturday. One sin, two sins . . . not much difference is there, Rita?'

'There most certainly is. Please pray for me, Danny. I will certainly pray for you. I'd better go now.'

'What about the tea? Not to mention the biscuits. Let's dunk a biscuit together.' No chance and her words confirmed it.

'I will apologise to your mother. On the way out. Goodbye.'

'Don't say it. Kiss it. Like before.'

'Certainly not. How could you?'

She looked shocked, angry. Her beauty was stern, her teeth icicles. That was the last he'd ever see of her. But she came to the bed and sat down on the very edge, her back to him. She was so close he could hear her breathing. He felt nervous, desperate. She turned her head. She was only inches away. He couldn't believe it. Up close her face was so big. Her eyes swam with feelings. Her skin was creamy, silky. He noticed a perfect round chickenpox mark on the edge of her right eyebrow. A few seconds passed. He was scared. Next second, their tongues were delving like bees in a flower, kissing deep and burning. He felt she was swallowing him, she was that good a kisser. He put his hand up her skirt. He gripped something. Her suspender. She trapped his hand against the inside of her thigh, pressing her hand on his, angry with him, yet she was shaking, her whole body electric. Nothing was warmer than flesh. Maybe molten lava.

'That's . . . that's it. Stop it now. Goodbye.' He clung to her and they kissed again even deeper than before. Then she struggled away from him and, flustered, went to the door, tugging her skirt down. Just in time — he heard his mother coming from the kitchen. He was red-faced and flustered too.

'Are you going, Rita? And you never had the tea?'

'Rita gave me a lovely present.' He held up the prayer book.

'Ah well now, aren't you the generous thing? I'll see you out, dear.' His mother gave him a narrow-eyed glance as she went, not convinced by his beatific look.

He lay back on the pillows. His ribs hurt, no doubt about that, but his thoughts hurt most of all. His sense of loss. Saints were always depicted as being pretty. They drove you demented. And the *News of the World* was an old issue — he'd read it at college. He opened it again at the story of the policeman's wife running away with the vicar. He realised nothing happened in the world that hadn't already happened in Butlershill.

He got up and his mother gave him his dinner which she'd kept on a plate in the oven, a saucepan lid over it. Floury potatoes, cabbage, turnip, carrots, two big chops and gravy. Then a glass of milk.

'Nothing wrong with your appetite, thank God.'

'I don't know what I'm going to do. When I finish college. But one thing, I hope I have money one day. Cos I want to . . . buy you things. Furniture. A brand spanking new overcoat. Pearls. A purse jammed with fivers. A car. Yeah. A car. A Zephyr Zodiac. Like Jim Reilly's. A V8. No, a Wolseley like Lady Sarah Butler-Coote's. Yeah. She saw me up the tree. She was walking along and saw what I was up to. You're as much a lady as she is. Yeah, a Wolseley. So you can drive over to Mayo, on your own, and see all the places you loved.'

'Go 'long out of that, darling. I'm fine, don't worry about me. God is good. Your health is your wealth.'

She laughed, looking at him, tickled pink at his hopes for her because she didn't think for a moment they'd ever amount to anything. She called him a dreamer. Someone who'd love to spend his life sliding down moonbeams.

'Ah, Danny, you're a concert.' She had tears of laughter in her eyes which she wiped with the corner of her apron.

When his father came in, he said Quigley had gone on sick leave, claiming that McDaid had injured his back.

'The missus came in and gave me a doctor's certificate. And yet when I rode past the house he was out the back building a wall.'

'If you ask me,' his mother said, 'Guard Quigley is a man who likes sliding down moonbeams.'

'Bit like me, is he, Mum?'

She laughed and stirred up the warm water in the washing-up basin with her hand. She never removed her wedding ring. The gold was faded.

'Did you mention McDaid to her, the rumours?'

'Bedad I did. She came into my office with the cert. She's a presentable woman, we all know that. 'He grabbed me one night,' she says. McDaid. 'What could I do in his powerful grip? Every woman he meets he tries to grab her bits.' I'll leave it up to yourself what she meant.'

His mother looked scandalised but excited too. 'If she's not careful, Quigley might take the lash to her. No wonder he hates McDaid.'

'He's bought a new greyhound. The man's an eejit. A tinker sold him a pup, telling him he's a near relation of a winner at White City. That's in England. Mother and daughter. Saint and sinner.'

'And I'm madly in love with the saint.'

They looked at him like he'd come in the window on a moonbeam. In the silence he heard the low purr of the electric clock. Coruba Jamaica Rum. They were afraid to speak.

Eventually his father got up and after jingling the coins in his pocket said, 'I feared the worst when I saw that rope business. You're some chancer. All the same, I have to take my hat off to you. The poor girl.'

'McDaid — he's not all that bad. He says what he thinks. He does what he wants. He's not cowed by the craw-thumpers.'

'McDaid, for your information, used to hang around Kit Clarke's wife. That'll give you some idea. Anyone's fair game to him. A wife of his own, a farm as well as his mechanic business and he's still not satisfied. He's one of them hardchaws that couldn't settle down after the Treaty in '22. Most of them went to America. Keep away from him. He'll not do you a good turn if he can do you a bad one. He's got a relation a bishop. The same bishop got more than one sergeant promoted to inspector even though Headquarters didn't want it. McDaid is a law unto himself. Keep well away from him. Get the padareens.'

He went to the sewing machine and from the narrow drawer untangled the rosaries.

They knelt down and, leaning on chairs, prayed. A night-time ritual, an article of faith, unvarying, inevitable, soporific. Each evening of their lives. His father in strange pietistic mode, kneeling erect, shoulders back, head up towards the Sacred Heart picture, his voice loud and precise, trying his best to storm the gates of Heaven.

'And tonight we say a prayer, thanking you, Lord, for saving Danny, when he nearly fell out of that blo . . . that tree. And we pray for his intentions that he may live a life of purity in the bosom of his country and his God. We implore Thee, Lord, to grant us this favour.'

'Your intentions, not mine.'

'Doesn't matter.'

He was a holy version of Chisholm. He wouldn't shoot you — he'd pray for you. Whether you liked it or not.

He was sorry for saying anything, because the mood became heavy and they'd go off to their beds annoyed. His father never let anything upset his sleep but his mother would fret all night.

When he stood up he was stiff and his ribs hurt and he wondered would he be able to return to college in a few days' time and what was the point of it all if he never saw Rita again? He even wished Kit Clarke hadn't hanged himself. And then he'd never have got entangled with her in the first place.

★ ★ ★

When he began to feel better, he took a walk out towards McDaid's shed. He wanted to, somehow, have a conversation with him. Maybe learn something from him. How, for instance, could you forget a girl you were crazy about? He had lain in bed for days reading *As You Like It*. In

345

his head was the line: 'Men have died from time to time and worms have eaten them, but not for love.' Did Shakespeare mean that?

The worms were knocking at Kit's coffin. And he couldn't get out of his head the image of him hanging in the barn. The body slowly twisting in the air. And he wondered about the stag beetle up the tree.

When he came round a corner of the road, nearing McDaid's, he heard voices and then saw something happening in front of the shed. It was a struggle of some kind. He thought for a moment it was Mrs Quigley mating her turkey cock with someone's hen. A little closer and he realised it was Guard Quigley, Mrs Quigley and McDaid. She was between the two of them, trying to keep them apart.

When they saw him approaching, they stopped shouting but Quigley and McDaid had each a hold of Mrs Quigley and were pulling her. McDaid was in his working clothes. Quigley was in old uniform trousers, an open-necked shirt and woollen vest, and his trouser bottoms were tucked into his socks. His boots were dainty compared to his father's, the black leather finer. McDaid was so much bigger than him. Mrs Quigley appeared calm. She went with each pull she got and when McDaid's grasp on her slipped, she and Quigley tottered backwards and nearly fell over.

By now he was right up beside them.

'What's going on? Stop it, please. Mr McDaid.'

'Shut the fuck up. Clear off before you're killed.'

Quigley, gamely hanging on to his wife, looked

346

ashamed. He was breathing heavily. His wife had a smile on her face. She looked a bit ashamed too but not much.

'If you don't stop it, I'm going to get my father.'

'Do,' Quigley said.

'You needn't bother,' Mrs Quigley said, 'it's only a tiff.'

A lorry came along the road and separated them for the moment. As soon as it had passed, the two men grabbed her again. This time McDaid had her about the waist. She kicked her legs a little by way of protest. McDaid looked like a big bear with a victim clutched to its chest. Quigley caught hold of her arm. Hens and turkeys, hearing the commotion, had come down to see were they being called to a feeding. They were led by the turkey cock. It struck him then — McDaid was like a big turkey. A fierce red neck and wild eyes and his greasy black hair sticking up. He looked frightening because all the time, as well as the anger, he had a cynical smile. Like he knew what he was doing, knew his power.

'Go 'way home, you,' McDaid said to him, 'I'm telling you for the last time. This has nawthin' to do with you or your oul fellah.'

'You're not a man; you're an animal. This is complete chaos,' he shouted at McDaid.

McDaid let her go. She stepped away from him. McDaid's hairy arms were oily and he had a dirty rag bandage round an elbow. He looked at Mrs Quigley like she'd betrayed him. Abruptly, he went back into his workshop and

347

pulled the wooden doors shut.

'You came at the right time,' Quigley said. Then he got hold of his wife and shoved her up the pathway to the house. She gave a kind of a lurch but went willingly enough. He watched them disappear in the front door and heard the door bang hard. Of the three involved, Quigley was the one with dignity. He knew he was up against powers greater than himself but he fought bravely for what he considered his own. The wife was a smallish woman with generous curves and a warm personality. When McDaid had her round the waist and she was thrashing her legs in the air, she looked wild and enticing.

★ ★ ★

The road he walked was potholed and splattered with stale cowpats and fresh horse buns. The crows were hard at it building in the trees, and the fields were full of smaller birds in shrieking flurries criss-crossing, hedge-hopping or station-ary on branches, singing.

When he got back to the village, someone was warbling in Reilly's pub, the voice saturated with porter.

> Only for a day
> Only for a week
> Only for forever
> We'll be one . . .

He peeped in the window. It was Kit's brother, Richie. He was on his own. Behind the bar, Jim

Reilly, his two hands spread on the bar, stiffly watched him.

> I'll be in your heart
> And you will be in mine
> When life is bread and water
> I'll turn it into wine . . .

It must have been the song old Kit loved and threw into the lake.

When he got home, he told his parents what he'd seen. McDaid and Quigley fighting over Mrs Quigley like she was a rag doll.

'Divine Jesus,' his mother said. 'This country's obsessed with sex. One half trying to do it, the other half making sure they don't.'

They knew about a young priest in a neighbouring parish who, armed with a blackthorn stick and a flashlamp after dances in the parochial hall, went along the hedges and ditches looking for courting couples. A cow with a calf had charged him in the dark and knocked him into a river.

'If the Church isn't careful, the population will die out.'

'It's dying out anyways,' his father said, 'all the young taking the boat.'

His father was troubled by this. What sort of country had they fought for? What sort of country had they built? His father was a pious man but deep down he had subversive thoughts which he chased away by contemplating the Suffering on the Cross.

He went to his room and got out his biology

notes. The teacher was generous with rare words if he ran an errand for him — fetch twenty Player's or post a letter or place a bet. McDaid's scarred face was red and threatening like an animal trying to frighten you away by looks alone. A lizard, a turkey cock . . . He found the word for it. Aposematic. He was beginning to look forward to getting back to college. His ribs still hurt but the doctor wouldn't bind them; they weren't broken. He was told to rest for another week and then go back.

★　★　★

He was in bed one night reading a few back-numbers of *The Dandy* and *Beano* and listening to the men in the day room talking and laughing with soldiers who were on their way to patrol the Border. He heard the phone ringing and the muffled voice of his father answering it. It must have been a serious call because everything went quiet. He imagined his father giving a backward slash of his arm to silence them.

A few minutes later he came into married quarters, said something to his mother and then came down into his bedroom.

'You'll have to go out to Quigley's. He took something belonging to McDaid — a contraption for making cement blocks. McDaid saw him taking it. It's out in the old quarry. Quigley has it out there.'

'So?'

'McDaid's reported him to the Chief. They are going to turn up in the morning early and catch him red-handed. One of the men in Divisional Headquarters has just given us the tip-off.'

'But it's midnight.'

'I want to go to bed. You that's fit and able, go on. Take my bicycle. But don't change gear. I don't want you snapping the cable again.'

He wanted to protest but deep down he was pleased. He might see Rita. The last time he met her at her house, the first time they kissed, he thought he saw Quigley going round by the gable end lugging something heavy. That was probably it, the contraption for block-making.

He couldn't relax riding his father's bike in case he broke the gears. He slowly went along in second. It was pitch-black but sometimes the moon appeared as if from behind a high hedge. There was light only in two of the village houses and the only sound was the mudguard rattling and the wind whooshing the trees.

McDaid's shed was in darkness. So was Quigley's house. He rapped hard on the front door. The greyhounds started yelping and the turkey cock did its high-pitched peep-peep. A light came on upstairs and Mrs Quigley stuck her head out the window. In the halo of light behind her, he could see she had her open-necked nightdress clutched protectively in one hand.

'Who is it?'

'It's me — Danny.'

'At this hour? Rita isn't here. She's on retreat. In the convent she's entering. She'll be back tomorrow. Today.'

'No, no, Daddy sent me. Guard Quigley has something belonging to McDaid for making blocks. In the quarry. McDaid has told the Chief Superintendent and he's coming out first thing in the morning to catch him red-handed. Someone in Monaghan phoned with the tip-off.'

'Holy Jesus. Hold on.'

She withdrew into the room.

A retreat was a few days isolated in prayer with like-minded contemporaries. She'd be discussing her vocation with the reverend mother and a father confessor. Praying, singing hymns, going to Mass. Rita. It was enough to make him weep.

He could hear coughing. Quigley poked his head out.

'Tell your father I only borrowed the blinkin' thing. The block-maker. I'm building a shed for the greyhounds. I'll return it in the morning.'

'I think you should return it now. The morning might be too late.'

'I'll go out to the quarry at daybreak. I know the Chief — he won't get over from Headquarters until after nine at the earliest. Thank you, boyo, very kind. Careful going home now.'

Rita. Rita. Rita. Why? He could understand someone cutting themselves off from the world. But when you saw the sallow faces of nuns they reminded him of blocked rivers. Would the convent know the force within her? Would her hands turn white and bloodless from being joined and held up for hours to God?

★ ★ ★

When he told his mother what Quigley said, she blessed herself.

'He's a thundering jackass, that's what he is.' The expression was one of his father's. 'Does he not realise The Bully Barry hates him? They'll cashier him if they can, as sure as there's cotton in Cork.' That was another one of his father's.

The quarry was out the Cootehill road. He got up early and walked to it. He went into a field alongside and climbed up until he was right at the top of the rock face. He had a clear view down into the open space where lorries came for loads of stone. The quarry summit was covered with whin and grass. He hunkered down and waited. It was after seven o'clock. He could see the block-maker. It was standing near a pile of sand. A number of cement blocks sat in a row where they had been set out to dry. At half past eight a car came along the road, turned into a lane and the two occupants got out and walked back. There was a workman's hut over at the side, near the quarry entrance. The two men went in behind the hut. McDaid and Chief Superintendent Barry.

At nine o'clock Quigley rode up on his bike. He pedalled right into the quarry and dismounting, leaned down on the saddle, looking calmly around him. Then he ambled over to the block-maker and dragged it nearer the pile of sand. He put it down on its side and started covering it up with the sand, hiding it. He kicked the sand over it as best he could with his feet. Why hadn't he brought a shovel? Probably all part of the nonchalant way he looked at the world. He seemed completely relaxed, without the slightest suspicion he was under observation.

He thought of Rita. That was her father down there. He would have loved to have been able to help him. Why hadn't he got up out of bed when he was warned? Taken the damn thing back to McDaid's and dumped it where he found it? Maybe he and the wife had been in each other's arms and outside events could not impinge. Sleep . . . Tomorrow . . . Sort it all out in the morning . . .

Quigley stopped kicking at the sand, undid his flies and urinated. His legs wide apart, hands on his hips, he observed his own flow, a man at ease with himself.

It was then The Bully, in full uniform, strode out from behind the hut, followed by McDaid. Caught the way he was, it put Quigley immediately at a psychological disadvantage. Even from the top of the quarry he could see him crumble before their eyes. The Bully pointed at the block mould.

'Is that your property, Quigley?'

'No, sir.'

'Did you have permission to take it?'

'As much permission as he had to try and take my wife.'

It was a good answer but legally useless.

'You know the law as well as I do.'

'It's only an old yoke he probably forgot he had. It was thrown out the side of his shed. I had no intention of keeping it. Even less intention than your friend had of keeping my wife.'

Everyone knew McDaid and the Chief were

old political friends. Quigley's remark was an attempt to muddy the waters and an implied threat — if he was charged, he'd endeavour to entangle the two of them in a conspiracy against him.

From the top of the quarry the boy clearly saw The Bully's face redden.

'Don't try and bandy words with me. Your hatred for Mr McDaid is well attested. It cuts both ways, Quigley. You stole the rope as well.'

'I did no such thing. I borrowed it.'

'You can explain the difference to the judge.'

'You've got no children, have you, Chief? Neither has your friend.'

As a sympathy ploy, if that was what it was, it only served to antagonise. The Bully stabbed near Quigley's chest with his index finger. 'Why were you trying to hide it under the sand?' He turned to McDaid, who was grinning all the time. 'Remove the evidence.'

McDaid bent down and taking hold of the block-maker, powerfully swung it up on one shoulder. They walked out of the quarry and on up the road to their car.

Quigley shouted up to him.

'You can come down now, boyo.'

'How did you know I was here?'

'I noticed you. Crouching behind the whins like a big hare.'

He scrambled down the adjoining field and came into the quarry through a hole in the hedge. Quigley had taken up his bike from the ground and was leaning on the saddle. He coughed and spat out with not much emphasis. Then he lit a cigarette. McDaid and The Bully sped past without looking in. The block-maker stuck out of the boot.

'If only you'd come out last night, Guard Quigley.'

'Sure I know.'

'When I saw the two of them arriving before you did, I should have hightailed it to warn you.'

'It can't be helped, boyo, it can't be helped now.' He wore his dainty black boots and bicycle clips. He put his fingers through his hair, pushing the greying quiff backwards.

'I've always taken her as she comes,' he said.

'Who?'

'Life.' He smiled weakly. 'The great thing is Rita going into the convent. Away from this wicked world. I won't ever have to worry about her again. I don't care about me. I'll survive. I survived TB, didn't I?'

He wheeled his bike out to the road and pedalled away.

The quarry face was about fifty yards back from the road. It had been sledgehammered, dynamited, picked at for generations. From the top down to the base, the stratified rock told the story of the area. A good deal of it was weeping red. Right round the edges, whin was taking possession. Whin and blackthorn, grass, dock, ragwort, thistle and nettle. One day the whole quarry would be forgotten as the adjoining fields crept closer. What was life to a force that could smother rock?

He ambled away slowly, stopping to think from time to time, picking the first young bluebells for his mother, the first primroses, daffodils, forget-me-nots. Rita Quigley, I will forget you not. Will remember you in knots. His mother was pleased with the bouquet.

★ ★ ★

As he went by the day-room window, Quigley was standing to attention in front of the Chief. His father was there too, making notes.

Quigley was being suspended from duty. Pending criminal charges. At the very least there would be a sworn inquiry conducted by the state solicitor. The proceedings held in the Phoenix Park before the Commissioner himself. Witnesses would be summonsed to appear, if necessary.

At tea that evening his father said they were throwing the book at him.

'He's as good as hanged. This time the Chief has his teeth in the back of his neck and he won't let go 'til there's blood.'

'It's not fair.'

'You keep out of it.'

'But what about the wife and children?' His mother looked on the verge of tears.

'He'll be cashiered. Let go in disgrace. No pension, no gratuity. Not a penny. They'll even take back his bicycle clips. Oh that's a fact.' His father was in awe of the bureaucratic machinery. It was the next best thing to a judge putting on the black cap. He got out his *Garda Síochána Code* and, on Quigley's behalf, studied the disciplinary procedures just to see was there any way he could trip up The Bully or The Bully trip him. On the hard front cover of the *Code*, the 735 pages of which were bolted together by its two long brass bolts and nuts, was the underlined word 'Confidential'. On the inside page it said:

As approved by THE MINISTER FOR JUSTICE.

His father, rigid with intensity of purpose, his finger isolating various points, read and reread Chapter 6. He didn't go to bed until midnight.

★ ★ ★

Quigley remained in the Station until dawn, writing out a statement.

His dilemma was clear. Resign without a penny. Dismissed without a penny. Or be sacked as a penniless criminal after a public trial. Could he bear to have his name and all the details published in the local paper? He feared it might even ruin Rita's chance of entering the nunnery. He hoped he might be able to get some legal leeway by proving The Bully Barry and McDaid were friends and were acting maliciously against him because he had summonsed McDaid for having no insurance and car tax. But according to the *Code* he could get into even deeper trouble by attempting to take the Chief Superintendent's good name. Chapter 15.1, page 105, stated that he exposed himself to the possibility of severe penalties should any charge

358

or allegation prove to be groundless or vexatious. There was also the matter of his greyhounds. On page 41 of the *Code*, 6.12, it expressly forbade a member owning greyhounds to race or train them for a coursing or race meeting. Everyone knew Quigley entered his dogs in Longford and Clones as often as his hopes rose above reason.

Then there was the rope business. That would definitely be dragged up at the inquiry. Pinching a rope that had just been used in a suicide would make him a somewhat sinister laughing stock throughout the country. However innocent the circumstances. The Dublin papers would latch on to it, never mind the *Anglo-Celt*.

The whole district was exercised by the possible outcome. Most of the women were on Quigley's side because of his wife and children. The men in Reilly's pub drank deep at the satisfying thought of him being dismissed. It would definitely be good riddance to bad rubbish. When the fit took him, he was a stickler for bicycles without lights, dangerous driving, after-hours drinking.

That was the contradiction of being a good policeman. The better you were at the job, the less people liked you. But if you didn't summons anyone, no one had respect for you.

★　★　★

Mrs Quigley came to married quarters in a distraught state. She and her children were going to end up on the side of the road. Quigley had precious little savings — any money he had disappeared on his useless greyhounds. Recently one of them took the fits just before a race and escaped out into the local town.

It was after dark when she came. She was ashamed to be seen in public. She'd come the back way through Lady Sarah's demesne knowing she wouldn't meet anyone. Her eyes were red from weeping and his mother did her best to shed a few tears to show sympathy.

He sat in the corner as usual, shadowed between the wall and the end of the dresser. It was as good as a confession box.

'It was my own fault. I should never have let McDaid near me. What on earth was I thinking? God has punished me. Not that I did anything. He tried to grab my bits and then Jim saw us. I'll be blunt: years of marriage wear you down. Jim never sits still like a Christian. Always on the go with his ideas. I told him not to build a shed for them damn dogs. My big worry is Rita. She's taking it badly.'

'How do you mean, 'badly'?'

'She loves her father. She's so worried about him. And I don't know what happened between her and your son. She's not the same since.'

'In what way?' His mother looked alarmed.

'Oh, she's not pregnant or anything. I think he tried to take God from her.' His mother's body jerked with horror. Her black hair clipped back to her ears, her face seemed massive with shock.

'What do you . . . how do you mean?'

'He tried to stop her being a nun. That's what I'm saying.'

'How could he do that?'

'He told her she had to choose between him and God.'

'I never said any such thing.'

Mrs Quigley, who had her back to him, leaped up out of the armchair.

'Mother of Jesus,' she shouted, 'you there all the time. That's it, you see. He butts in to everything going. He helped Jim find that block-maker thing as well. Outside McDaid's. Jim wants him to appear as a witness, so he does.'

'I am happy to do so. Rita — do you think if she was the prize in a fight between me and that Man there,' he indicated the picture of the Sacred Heart above the mantelpiece, 'I'd have a chance of winning?'

They stared in awe at the picture. Over the years it had creased in the middle and no longer fitted neatly in the frame. The glass was greasy from steam and the Saviour's long hair looked greasy too. The little red devotional oil lamp burning in front of it flickered and went out. Mrs Quigley, alarmed, as if it was an omen, blessed herself.

'It just needs refilling,' his mother said.

'I'd like to see Rita again, Mrs Quigley.'

'Well, you can't, so you can't. So you can't.'

She went to the door and, her lip quivering, seemed about to cry.

'What am I going to do?' she said simply.

In a skirt over her nightdress, a cardigan and shawl, stout black shoes, legs bare, her hair loose and straggly, tossed by the wind on her way through the wood, she looked like a dumpy pigeon blown off course.

'Counting Rita, I have five children to feed, so I have. We owe rent on the house as well. I told him not to be putting work into it when it wasn't our own.'

His mother went out with her and they stood in the black night talking at the gate. The wind dunted through the trees and the clouds were so deeply banked above them, there wasn't a sign of moon or stars. A motorbike sped up from the village, the engine making a deep-throated gargle like a corn-crake stuck on one note, all the way up and down the long drumlin road towards Cavan town. The shaft of advancing light put him in mind of a knight charging through the dark with a jousting lance.

He got the paraffin can and tundish and refilled the Sacred Heart lamp. His mother always kept a half-crown under it, for a rainy day. The red globe was dusty, the paint peeling and the wick nearly burnt out. He turned the little cog up as much as he could. He folded a page of newspaper into a thin taper and, taking a light from the still-burning fire, lit the wick, put the globe back into its prongy holder and placed the lamp back up on the mantelpiece, on top of the half-crown. The whiff of paraffin was thick enough to taste. He returned the can and tundish to the shed at the back of the house. Tundish was an English word that had become with use uniquely Irish.

His ribs still hurt when he took a deep breath. His mother came back in.

'I'm going to go back to college on Monday.'

362

'What did you do to Rita that you upset her so much?'

'Nothing. I put my hand up her skirt.'

'What? My God. Up there is private property.'

'I didn't steal anything.'

'It's a mortal sin. That girl is every bit as intelligent as you are. More so in fact. Why demean her? You're as bad as McDaid.'

'I wanted to . . . I wanted to be able to say I done it. I couldn't help it. I didn't want her shutting herself away in a convent without knowing a man's hand on her flesh.'

'You're not a man. You're still only a teenager. A man and a woman have to meet on equal terms.'

'Was that you and Dad?'

'None of your business. I think so.'

His father came in, the fresh air on his face, the night all over his uniform. He stood looking at them, full of vigour, eyes brighter than his silver buttons.

'Will you have the usual?' his mother said.

'Bedad I will.'

He struggled out of his greatcoat.

'Help me with this.'

He got up and helped him by pulling the end of the sleeves. He was hopeless as an abandoned horse trying to shake off bridle and britchin at the end of the day. He even had to take his cap and hang it up. It was his father's way of convincing himself that he was loved by the only two people he cared for.

His mother put a pint glass of hot milk and two digestive biscuits on the table. His father sat down and, one hand tentatively touching the glass, the other holding a biscuit, became for a few moments a priest partaking in a ritual of grace.

'What were you talking about?'

'Oh, this and that,' his mother answered. 'We had Mrs Quigley.'

'I know that. I called out to the house. He's come to a decision. He's coming to tell us tomorrow. Chief Superintendent Barry will be here. I think he's realised the jig is up.'

'Who? The Chief?'

'No. Quigley. He's at the end of his tether. He says you wrote a poem for his daughter.'

'I didn't write it. I made it up.'

'Whatever you did, it's upset her anyway.'

'She's far too sensitive for her own good,' his mother said.

'That rope business would upset anyone.' He munched the biscuit, then softened it in his mouth with a gulp of the hot milk; they could no longer hear his champing.

'Out with the poem until we see. Come on, let's hear it.'

> Marshmallow sweet sixteen
> All the dogs ever been
> All the cats got the cream
> Never seen what I've seen
> You.

They looked at each other, utterly perplexed.

'There's another verse.'

'Let's have it,' his mother said, giving an amused look at his father who, stunned, searched hard for meaning.

No one ever saw the gleam
No one knows what I mean
No one ever dreamt the dream
Lived the reality of what I've seen
You.

They waited for his father's verdict. He swished the remaining milk around in the glass.

'If you want my solid opinion — it's smutty. Seen what? It's full of innuendo. If that was published they'd ban it. The cat's got the cream? At least you didn't bring the rope into it. The one good thing — you haven't written it down, have you? Take my advice: don't. What do you think, Mum?'

'Well, it's not Shakespeare.'

'But on the other hand — what would I know?'

'The *Garda Code* — you're the best there is. The *Garda Guide* — there's no one to beat you. Poetry — you're the bottom of the barrel, Dad.'

His father drank the last of the milk and pushed back from the table, scraping the chair along the lino. He stood with his back to the range.

'We learned 'The Deserted Village' at school. The master was Tom Morrissey. He played the fiddle at weddings as well. He was walking the classroom one day, over and back, jingling the coins in his pocket. Lost in thought. Without realising, he spoke out. 'I'd destroy him with kicks,' he says. You wouldn't know what winter scholars were, would you? Big fellahs who only came to school after the harvest. We went to

365

school barefoot. No, I don't suppose I'd know much about poetry.'

He had hurt him. It always astonished how close and raw was his father's history. Ireland, an ancient country, had no past. The past was only yesterday.

The three of them silent, washed in the sallow electric light, isolated amongst the few sticks of furniture, impaled on their thoughts, miles from Dublin or Belfast, forgotten by London and Rome, let the last of the day drain away down the outside gullet with the falling rain. He hoped Mrs Quigley wouldn't get soaked on the way home.

When his parents went to bed he turned on the wireless. He twiddled the knobs and in the cackling ether just about heard Buddy Holly singing. 'You go your way . . . ' Yeah, sing to the end of time. But Time was singing us . . . we're just notes in a big bird's throat.

★ ★ ★

They were all up early in the morning. His father was in good spirits. The Bully Barry and an Inspector were coming and Quigley had to appear before them. He'd be told the final details of the forthcoming inquiry. The where and when.

While his father washed and shaved, they polished his boots and brushed his uniform and snared the buttons on to the button-stick and buffed them up brilliantly. Then he wiped the peak of his cap until it shone black as a magpie's neck. His mother got the breakfast together as

366

she polished the boots. A big boot on one hand, she paused to juggle with cups and saucers. His father couldn't wait for the cut and thrust of the legal bloodletting. He hoped Quigley was going to put up a fight.

'We rowed together in Carrick-on-Shannon Boat Club. Must have been 1930. He wasn't bad either. As a policeman, he was always just too tricky for his own good. This time I'm afraid he's crossed the line. He's going to get the boot and no mistake. If he'd just hung on for another few years he could have retired on a full pension. He'd have beaten them.'

At five minutes to eleven, the Chief and Inspector pulled up at the gates. In full uniform, they bustled into the Station, bristling with importance.

Half an hour later, Quigley still hadn't arrived. The Bully was beginning to raise his voice and hammer the table.

'By holy, if he isn't here at half past, he's had it.'

'He's had it anyway, sir, hasn't he?' His father was enjoying the tension. Enjoying that The Bully was annoyed. The Bully wanted to personally tear Quigley apart. Probably rerun the Civil War into the bargain.

The boy was outside the day room, listening. Ready to flee if any of them came out. The tension was such he could almost feel it out in the hallway.

'I think, Sergeant, you better go and find him,' the Inspector said, 'see what he's up to. He wouldn't have done harm to himself, would he?'

'He wouldn't have the bloody guts,' The Bully said, thumping the table.

Afraid, he left the hallway and went outside. He wondered should he go to Quigley's house and see what was going on. He was about to get a bike when he saw him coming up the hill.

He was in mufti — brown shoes, smart grey trousers, shirt and tie and a tweed jacket. His hair was newly cut. He looked smart. But pale. And the furrows in his brow were deep. He had his usual dandy smile at the corner of the mouth and looked at him from under his eyebrows. It was a look both charming and crooked.

'Well, boyo.'

'They're waiting on you, Guard Quigley.'

'Is that a fact?' There was a big hessian sack on the back of his bike. He removed the string holding it on. It didn't look heavy enough to be potatoes or turf. But it was stuffed full of something. Maybe he was going to try and bribe the Chief. But what with? Lugging the sack in one hand, he went inside.

He heard the voices.

'You're late, Quigley.' A silence followed. Desperate to see what was going on, he nipped out and stood one side of the day-room window, peeping in. The Chief sat at the table, flanked by the Inspector and his father.

'What have you to say for yourself?' the Inspector asked, in a voice both blustering and reasonable. Authoritative — that was the word.

Quigley didn't reply. They were politically poles apart; he hated them and they hated him.

He opened the hessian sack, which was

leaning against his leg. He pulled his uniform tunic out of the sack and threw it on the table. Then he threw a pair of trousers on top of it.

'Do you think I'm going to give you and your kangaroo court the pleasure of torturing me before sacking me?' He flung his cap on the table. The Bully, nervous, moved his mouth and head and had his fists up on the table but didn't say a word.

'And if I didn't go, you'd get a judge to do your dirty work in the District Court. And I'd be sacked anyway.' He delved his hand into the sack and tugging out his greatcoat, threw it over The Bully's head. The Inspector jumped up and removed it. The Bully adjusted his cap, which had slipped over his eyes.

It was plain his father was enjoying the way things were developing. Chief Superintendent Barry was being humiliated and didn't dare say anything to Quigley in case he had a gun in the sack. Quigley next dumped his waterproof coat and pull-ups on the table.

'If you think you can walk out of the Force just like that, let me remind you, you have a number of people with outstanding summonses against their names.'

'You can shove the summonses up where the monkey shoved the nuts,' Quigley replied with a dry chuckle.

The Bully risked saying something. 'Have you taken leave of your senses, man?'

Quigley delved his hand into the sack and emerged with a pair of handcuffs. He flung them at The Bully's chest.

The Inspector sprung to his feet. He knew what was coming next — a truncheon and whistle and chain. There was no knowing what he'd do with them.

'You wouldn't be wearing that Sam Browne belt only Dev gave it to you. You wanted to shoot at any man wearing that there uniform in 1925 and then spent the rest of your life pretending to be a model citizen. You're nothing but a hypocrite.'

He reached deep down into the sack and retrieved his truncheon. He held it threateningly in his fist for a moment, then flung it with full power at The Bully's head, missing him by inches. It hit the telephone on the wall, smashing the receiver from its cradle. The pieces fell to the floor.

He made for the door but realising he hadn't emptied the sack, peered into it. There was only his whistle and chain left. He dangled them, then twirled them like a sling. The Bully and the Inspector dived under the table.

'Stop him, Sergeant, he's your responsibility,' the Inspector shouted.

Quigley gave a derisive guffaw and threw the whistle and chain on to the table, which by now looked like a table in a jumble sale. He went out the door. The Bully and the Inspector popped their heads up. But almost immediately Quigley came back in. Bending down he removed his bicycle clips. He tossed them across the room with a disdainful flick of his wrist.

'If you don't die roaring, there's no justice in Heaven.'

The Bully looked stunned. He'd forgotten how men hated him. The red rage drained from his face, leaving a normal close-shave pale and blue. His sour eyes blinked as if searching for insight.

The boy left the window and quickly went round to the front. Quigley came out, pale and trembling with confused emotions. He had put himself out of a job and his family out of a home.

'Tell your mammy we'll be out of here, day after tomorrow.'

All the time he had been flinging his uniform and equipment across the day room, his father hadn't moved. He sat still as a statue, only moving his eyes. Enjoying himself immensely.

At the end of the Rosary that night, he declared it was the most moving exit of a Garda he'd ever witnessed.

'The guts of the man was unbelievable. I never thought he'd show such spirit. The Bully was terrified.'

'But what did he achieve? He only made himself a buffoon.'

'He stood no chance at all. Wife and family put out on the road? Without a red cent? Evicted you might say. Is there no morality left? What do you say, Mum?'

'The only thing I can say for them is a prayer.'

★ ★ ★

His father went to see them next morning. Quigley told him his wife had a relation in Kerry

371

who could put them up for a short while and, with a bit of luck, get him a job in the Forestry.

'Incidentally, the block-maker thing is dumped back in the weeds and long grass outside McDaid's shed.'

'How does McDaid get away with it all the time?'

'Give him enough rope and sooner or later he'll hang himself, so to speak.'

'What about Rita? She's only a few months from finishing her exams. How can she move the whole way down to Kerry?'

'Quigley mentioned that very point. There's a good school down there. She'll attend it.'

'Did you see Rita?'

'Yes, she and the mother came in from the chapel. They'd been praying. You could tell both of them had been crying. Faces all red and weepy. Rita went straight upstairs.'

'Crying? Praying? I wonder why. Exactly.'

'Why do you think? Life gone wrong. Why else?'

⋆　⋆　⋆

Tully was hired to shift them. A car would take the wife and children; the furniture, clothes, tools, greyhounds and the turkey cock would go on the back of Tully's lorry. Richie Clarke, Kit's brother, was now working for Tully. After Kit's funeral he hadn't wanted to go back to Sunderland. Tully gave him a job.

Mrs Quigley sold her hens and two ducks to his mother, who out of charity paid well for

372

them. She emptied every vase and purse she had and made his father cough up a few pounds as well. She even took the half-crown from under the Sacred Heart lamp.

On the morning they moved, they waited outside the Garda Station to see them going, to shout goodbye. Mrs Quigley and the children were in the car driven by Tully himself. They waved as they went, the children smiling, delighted they were going for a spin. A while later, the lorry, driven by Richie, came slowly up the hill, laden with the guts of a lifetime. On the very top were two wardrobes and a bicycle. The load looked secure enough. It was tied together by a rope going over and back the top of the load several times. The same rope old Kit used to hang himself. The greyhounds' snouts stuck out between the crate slats.

Rita was in the cab, sitting between Richie and her father. She must have noticed him standing on the side of the road. But she never looked out.

Sullivan

His life as a college boy was over. He had sat the exams and passed them. He was a loose cannon now and a clean slate. He was ready for anything, yet hoping for something that would show him the way. It was tremendous to be at home with his parents, to be able to sleep late, go to bed late, wander round the roads, walk through the demesne, sit in the kitchen with his mother, cycle with his father round the sub-district, play football for the team, put off for tomorrow the question he had to answer: what was he going to do?

He even went up to the chapel to pray for Divine guidance. Sat there on his own in the middle of the day with not another soul about. The chapel smelled of Cardinal polish and candle grease. It was a frightening atmosphere not because of the tabernacle containing the actual body of Christ who died for our sins but because of the memory of all the coffins that had rested before the altar awaiting burial in the adjoining cemetery. As an altar boy he had served at funeral Masses umpteen times. 'Eternal rest grant unto them, O Lord: and let perpetual light shine upon them . . . ' '*Dies irae! Dies illa. Solvet saeclum in favilla . . .* '

He hoped some perpetual light would shine on him. He believed somehow it would. It was a relief to step back into the light of day. Tinged with sadness because he knew childhood had gone up in smoke. What was he going to do? He still hadn't a clue.

Deep down he knew he had to become a man like his father. A complete person like his mother. They had met and his existence was the proof that one and one made three.

He discovered a nest of bees at the bottom of the hen run. He sat on an upturned bucket listening to the never-ceasing intense buzzing. Except it was a bizz not a buzz. The high-pitched bizzing reminding him of a choir tuning up. A high note energetically held for ages. If he moved at all, a bee would shoot close, inspecting him for danger.

The new Garda, Tim Sullivan, came across him one evening.

'That's some racket, boyo. Take care you don't get stung.'

'If you leave them alone, they'll leave you alone.'

Sullivan was only a few years older than himself. Tall, decent-looking, fair hair, a delicate pale face, an easy-going nature — nothing troubled him. He was stationed in Cavan town but came daily out to Butlershill in the squad car. Anyone who drove a car had an advantage with women. A Garda squad car — what could be safer? Sullivan had no problems meeting girls.

He had driven out from town in the squad car with a parcel for the boy's mother. When he went into the kitchen his mother, excited, apprehensive, was holding a long dress in front of her, one hand pinning it to her chest, the other hand smoothing it out against the length of her body, right down to the floor. The dress was black satin, narrow and had straps. The wrapping paper, string and box were on the table.

'What do you think?'

'What's it for?'

'The Dress Dance. All the important people will be there. The Chief, the judges, barristers . . . Daddy is hiring a dress suit with a dickie bow. He's got out those shoes from the wardrobe. He wants you to polish them up for him.'

The black, light-leather shoes were found in the bottom drawer of a wardrobe his father bought years before at an auction.

'How much are the tickets?'

'Seven shillings and sixpence. Dress is optional but we're going to make a night of it.'

The two tickets were on the mantelpiece, leaning against the Sacred Heart picture. The Garda insignia was embossed in gold, the details proudly printed in shiny black.

Cavan Town Hall
Annual Garda Divisional Dance
Gala Night
Dancing 8 to midnight
Music Peggy Dell Orchestra
Proceeds in aid of Garda Benevolent Fund

They made the kitchen look dull.

'If the dance is as good as the tickets, Mum, it'll be some night.'

'I love Peggy Dell. Do you remember that

night in Turners Hill? When you were only a little boy?'

'I do, I do.'

'I may have to shorten these straps. I hate a strap slipping down all the time. I went to many's the ball in the old days. At home. Before it all fell apart. I know how to wear a formal dress.'

If her feet matched her dancing eyes, she was going to have a whale of a time.

'I was at a dinner dance and a ship's captain asked me on to the floor. He was Portuguese. He was old enough to be my father. It was a quickstep. He was panting like a cracked bellows by the time it finished. Such fun.'

'Where was that?'

'Ah now, where do you think? Ballina. A world of ships sailed up the Moy in those days.'

Any time she mentioned her native town, her eyes went dreamy. She hung the dress on a hanger from the corner of the mantelpiece whilst she got out her sewing box. The round box had been a cake tin.

'Did you hire the dress or did you buy it, Mum?'

'I bought it in Vera Brady's. Daddy gave me the money. Vera has some great bargains. If only I had the cash. Anyone buys an overcoat gets a free hat along with it.'

★　★　★

Next day Guard Sullivan came into married quarters with another parcel from town. This

377

time it was the hired dress suit for his father, who refused to try it on.

'I gave them the measurements and that's all there is about it. My legs aren't going to grow any longer in the next few days, are they? And if they do, I'll wear a pair of wellingtons.'

There was less than a week to go before the dance. His mother's step lightened, her inner gaiety shone. He watched her stirring the porridge. The mundane ritual of saucepan, grey gruel and wooden spoon, took on a different meaning. Under the lightness of her touch, the spoon had a happy rhythm whopping round the pot. She floated on air. She had something exciting to look forward to, something out of the ordinary. Ordinary was standard. As if issued from the Board of Works. At least once a day she went to her bedroom to look at the dress. He could hear her singing. 'I'll be in your heart . . . ' She had a fine voice. She sang in church but only as part of the congregation, not part of the choir. It was as if her life was so tied to his father's there was no time for her extrovert nature to assert itself. His father loved her being cheerful but often his days were heavy with the toil of trying to solve petty crime, when, judging his mood, she'd retreat into her shell.

★　★　★

That week, he got an insight into how his father operated. He involved him in little ways in the running of the Station. Giving him the experience of police work, hoping it might

378

influence him in the choice of a career. Months had gone by and he still had no idea what it was he wanted to do. His father would put up with him rattling round the house only for so long. He had the feeling his father wanted to be alone with his mother. It was inevitable. Three into two didn't go.

'You have no trade or calling whatsoever.'

'It's no crime, is it?'

'It soon could be. A man without money grows desperate. What are you going to do — rob a bank?'

He was with him in his office, killing time, when a man came to see him.

'Before you say anything do you object to my son being here?'

'Not at all, Sergeant.'

'Remind me of your name again, like a good man.'

'Tamper Conlon. Me Christian name's Payther. But they do call me Tamper.'

'I presume 'Payther' is Peter, no?'

'Ssh, Danny! That's immaterial for the moment. How can I help you, Tamper?'

'Tamper is an unusual nom de plume. What's the derivation?'

'Wha'?'

'Danny, if you're not going to be sensible, just leave us to it.'

'I beg your pardon, Sherlock. I do apologise . . . Tamper.'

Tamper was an unmarried, middle-aged farm labourer living on his own in a cottage outside the village. He had an egg-shaped face, not much of a chin, plumpish cheeks, narrow head. His sparse hair was slicked down and parted in the middle. He looked more like a faded bank clerk than an agricultural worker. The corner of his mouth was juicy with tobacco.

'I keep a ten-bob note under the clock on the mantelpiece. Always do that, so I do. It's me money for groceries or maybe to go to the pictures in Cavan. I get a lift in and out with someone. I put it there of a Saturday evening. Of a Sunday I go to first Mass. The last couple of Sundays when I get home the ten-bob note is missing.'

He came to an abrupt halt as if he'd just revealed a crime so sensational he couldn't continue with the horror of it.

'Have you got a cat?'

His father stared, angry at him asking such a stupid question.

Tamper stroked his almost invisible chin as if the question was worthy of consideration.

'A cat . . . burglar.'

His father stopped taking notes and narrowed his eyes.

'Sorry, Daddy.'

'Tell me, Tamper, do you lock the door after you?'

'I do, Sergeant. I locks the doer and lave the kay under a stone.'

'Why do you not take the key with you?'

'I get the odd hole in me pocket and I don't want to lose it. I always know where it is — it's under the stone.'

'Whoever it is, is letting himself in, taking the

380

money and then putting the key back under the stone. Someone has seen you doing that; he knows the key is there. Do you suspect anyone? Have you any idea at all who it could be?'

'If I did sure I'd clatter him quick as look at him.'

'We mustn't take the law into our own hands, Tamper. Clattering a suspect is a policeman's job.'

His father's expression was tinged with regret. He was beginning to realise that even if his son applied to join the Force, the interviewing panel would never accept him. He couldn't be serious for five minutes.

Tamper peeled a few strands of plug tobacco and with thumb and penknife put them in his mouth.

'I heard tell you're going away to be a jockey. I heard that, more luck to you.'

Neither he nor his father commented. A jockey? The only horse he ever sat on was Chisholm Flood's plough horse and apart from not falling off he showed no aptitude whatever for an equestrian career. Tobacco juice oozed from Tamper's lips. You could smell the pungent flavour.

'Is there anyone living nearby who you think might be capable of sneaking into your house and taking your money? Think now. It could be a young person, it could be a bachelor fellow like yourself, it could be a woman maybe. It could be a neighbour. It could be anyone.'

Chewing his tobacco cud, Tamper stared at the floor, then turned his head into his shoulder,

381

his face contorted with thought.

'The only one round about is Pat Reilly. He does call to the house the odd time. He's a dacent man. He likes a wee drink. He goes into town most Sundays before dinner time.'

'I see. What age man is he?'

'Oh, I'd say about thirty-five. It wouldn't be Pat anyway.'

'Right. I'll tell you what I'm going to do.'

He got up, went to a press and got out the petty-cash box.

'Go round to Mum and get me a needle.'

He had a fair idea what his father was up to. His mother got out her sewing box. He remembered the Christmas cake the tin box had contained. It was a gift given to his father by a publican years before he was transferred to Butlershill. A fruity homemade cake laced with whiskey. It was reduced slice by slice through January until there was nothing left but crumbs.

'Just what I want,' his mother had said, 'for my bits and bobs.'

She had filled it full with needles, spools of thread, a bag of buttons, her silver thimble, lengths of elastic, bits of material, zips, a few spare buttons for his father's uniform, a Bohemian safety razor blade in its paper sheath. The paper was red and black, the writing white: 'These blades are made of finest surgical steel on most modern machinery and are tested most carefully before leaving the factory. Made in the Republic of Ireland.' His father used it to pare his bunions.

When he went back to the office, there was a

ten-shilling note on the table. The colour of a robin's breast. His father took the needle and pricked the note in one corner and in the corner diagonally opposite.

'Now, Tamper, you have witnessed me making these holes; so have you, Danny. Next Sunday morning before you go to Mass, put this note under the clock as per usual. If, when you come back, it's missing, come and report it to me immediately. Immediately. Understand? Right? Okay? That's essential.'

'Aye, Sergeant.' He nodded but looked dubious.

'If you could just sign this receipt that you received a ten-shilling note from me. Good man.' His father dipped a nib pen into a ceramic inkwell.

Tamper signed slowly in big childish letters.

'What if it's stolen? Do I have to pay it back?'

'We'll cross that bridge when we come to it.'

Tamper went to the door but before leaving the office said, 'But . . . I can't understand how . . . I mean — '

His father cut him off. 'Just do as I said, like a good man.'

'And, Tamper, if I may, could you inform as many of your friends as possible that I have no intention or the slightest interest in discovering, training, riding the next Caughoo or any similar beast now or in the immediate future. I like horses. Preferably if they are in the next field. Or on the wireless.'

'Aye? I backed Caughoo. I had a shilling on him. They told me right enough you had the makings of a jockey, more luck to you.'

His rate of chewing quickened before, with an explosive phtt and the accuracy of a marksman, he spat his squid of plug across the office table and into the tiny fireplace.

He gently closed the door after him.

'If you got a shot of that in the eye he'd blind you.'

'You've sent him away not knowing whether he's coming or going. You have this knack of twisting things. I don't know what we're going to do with you. And me and Mum don't like the way you strut about.'

'What? She never mentioned anything to me.'

'We do have the occasional private conversation. Yes, strutting around like an Orangeman on the 12th of July.'

'Since I spent the first part of my life crawling, I thought it was time I walked erect. In the world outside Ireland it's a well-accepted evolutionary step.'

'You have neither trade nor calling and yet you think the world owes you a living. Go back in to Mum and leave me alone.'

He did. But he didn't mention the strutting. That day anyway.

Caughoo had won the Grand National at Aintree in 1947. 100/1. The second horse home was Lough Conn. That's why he remembered. His mother's old school, Gortnor Abbey, was on the shores of Lough Conn in County Mayo.

'If only it had won. I backed it with the egg money. It wasn't to be. You'd think once in a while you'd win something, wouldn't you? If

384

only I drew a ticket in the Sweep. Even a raffle ticket pulled out of the hat. I played whist. All I ever won was a packet of fags. I still dream of winning the Sweep. Wouldn't it be wonderful? All that money. Good God wouldn't I love to be spending it? I'd get a new rig-out for a start. From head to heels. You need a new suit too. To be going out in the world. And pyjamas. You have no idea what it's like to be my age and not have one single penny in my pocket.'

★ ★ ★

The Dress Dance had a lot riding on it. It was a taste for a few hours of a dream come true. The dance was on the Saturday night. Guard Sullivan would be coming out for them in the squad car. Jim Reilly, the publican, would give them a lift home. As well as members of the legal profession, publicans patronised the event, it being in their interest to keep in with the Garda. So too county footballers, doctors, bank managers, smugglers, politicians, teachers, clerks, nurses, shopkeepers and pig farmers. Local thieves might even dodge in, hoping to bum free drink in the private bar at the back of the bandstand. These petty criminals were tolerated for the night. Without them the policemen would be redundant.

From the Saturday afternoon until Sullivan came for them at eight o'clock, his mother and father turned the house upside down getting ready. His mother put the long dress on and off several times, always finding little faults and putting them right.

'It's not a dress, by the way, it's a gown.'

He polished his father's dancing shoes but when he tried them out he complained about the left one pinching.

'Where's the Bohemian blade? I've got a damn welt on the side of my big toe.' A welt was a corn.

He commanded his son to deal with the corn.

'You with the delicate hands.'

He had to let him rest his leg across his knees so he could pare the corn. He hated his big naked foot on his knees and he dreaded cutting him and drawing blood.

'After I retire, I wouldn't mind taking up chiropody.'

'Yes, Dad, you told us before. Don't. People would be leaving your surgery a foot shorter than when they went in.'

His father held the bits of skin in his hand and when the job was done he threw them on top of the range and watched them frazzle and smoke.

'God grant we don't end up in Hell.'

'You won't be going to Hell, Dad. Old Nick doesn't allow Garda sergeants in. It costs a fortune trying to burn your tough old leathery hides.'

'Do you hear that, Mum?'

'Don't be annoying me. This necklace won't fasten. Danny, fix the clasp at the back, will you?'

By the time he had located a pliers and closed the link next to the clasp, his father was wrestling with his shirt and separate shirt collar. All thumbs, he couldn't get the collar studs into position.

'If I put this shirt on, will you secure the collar with the stud?'

'How about I hammer it to your neck with a six-inch nail?'

'Don't be so smart.'

The kitchen was a jumble of discarded clothes — tunic, trousers, shirt, a skirt, a petticoat, cardigans, socks, nylons, apron, boxes, tissue paper, string. At five o'clock his mother bundled the lot in her arms and dumped them in the spare room. She made the tea — bread and boiled egg — wearing her dressing gown. His father, in long johns and woollen vest only, sat in the armchair reading the *Irish Independent*. He looked ridiculous. The gown hung from one corner of the mantelpiece, the dress suit jacket from the other corner. The dress trousers were draped over the back of a chair. The dress shirt hung from the key in one of the glass doors of the dresser. The key was never turned. The collar and studs lay on the sewing machine.

After tea the two of them went to their rooms and didn't emerge until fifteen minutes to eight. He could hear his father grunting and moaning and toppling into the wardrobe as he lost his balance trying to get his legs into the trousers. His mother was pleased with herself: she was singing. When fully dressed, they came into the kitchen.

Standing together, shoulder to shoulder, smiling shyly, they waited for him to comment.

The long black dress tightly contained his mother's hips, tummy, bosom. She had a white knitted shawl round her shoulders. Her hair was short and swept back. She wore her necklace and earrings. He could just see the toes of her high heels under the dress. She looked serious. She was a fine woman, in her eyes a world of amusement. The most amazing thing was the long black gloves she wore. They went right up to her elbows. She was also clutching an envelope-shaped handbag.

The first thing he noticed about his father was the width of his shoulders. He stood square but at a slightly extrovert angle. He was tall and powerful-looking. The black suit, white shirt and bow tie and the shiny shoes seemed to have found the perfect physique. He was smiling like he knew he looked good and didn't care what anyone else thought. In the drab kitchen, he was actually posing. Swaggering, moving slightly on the balls of his feet, sticking his chest out like he was having his photograph taken.

He didn't know what he thought, deep down, about his father. He didn't think he liked him, he wasn't even sure he loved him, but he was as close to him as a coat of paint on a door.

He was utterly proud of them both.

'Mum and Dad, God's honest truth, if there's a better-looking pair on that dance floor tonight, they've come down from Heaven on a moonbeam.'

They laughed and broke apart, and his father poured a glass of milk and swigged it back.

'That's because he'll be drinking tonight. Don't make an ass out of yourself,' his mother said.

'All we need now is for Sullivan to turn up.'

He took out a big white handkerchief and dabbed his lips. Then he put his hand into a pocket and revealed his Scott Medal. There was a small safety pin in the green, white and orange ribbon. He pinned it on his left lapel.

He and his mother were shocked.

'What are you doing, O'Hay? Why are you putting that on?'

'I've got a strange feeling tonight might be my swansong. So . . . '

'But, Dad, it's against regulations. You're not allowed to wear that except on official ceremonial occasions. The *Code* — Chapter 21.10. You can only wear it when in uniform.'

'Chapter 21.13. There'll be fellahs there tonight wearing All-Ireland football medals, St Christopher medals, fáinnes, Pioneer pins . . . Every woman in the place will have an Immaculate Conception medal sewed into her garments. This country is awash with medals. I'm going to be the only one there wearing a Scott Medal. And if The Bully Barry or any other man says anything, by the time I'm finished with them they'll wish they hadn't.'

'Jesus, Mary and Joseph, if you're going to ruin the evening, I'm not going to go. You can go on your own.'

'Now, now, Lizzie, calm down. It'll be okay.'

He smiled like a small boy to her and held out his hands in appeal. But he didn't remove the medal.

They heard a knock on the door. Right on time: Guard Sullivan.

'Are ye right?'

389

'Bedad we are, Tim.'

'Janey, missus, you look a picture.'

'Don't be coddin' me,' she said, still annoyed, but they could tell she was pleased too.

'Are you not going to the dance, Tim?'

'I am, boyo. Drop your parents off and then away home to change. I'm not going to miss the night of the year.'

His very pale face was excited. His face was the colour of wet flour. The medal impressed him.

'I doubt I'll ever be brave enough to earn one of them.'

'Ah now, if you're called upon, I can tell you won't be found wanting. Make sure you come and see me tonight. I want to buy you a drink. You're very good coming out for the two of us.'

'Arrah, not at all, Sergeant. It's a pleasure.'

'We better be going, if we're going,' his mother said. 'We can't keep Peggy Dell waiting.'

The squad car was a Zephyr Zodiac with the Garda sign on the roof. His mother sat into the back seat, then elegantly drew her legs in. His father sat in the front and gave a salute as they moved off.

He went back into married quarters. Without the two of them the kitchen never felt emptier. Despite the finery, he couldn't help noticing his parents were getting old. He'd always thought his mother was a very young woman. The evening clothes, though endowing great dignity, emphasised her years. His father's hair, Brylcreemed and neatly parted, was turning grey. And he had put on some weight and seemed to be slower and stiff. The harsh climate, the damp Garda Station — arthritis took hold like moss on stone.

They were getting old right enough but they had each other. Familiarity, or love or whatever it was, had taken root and they were inseparable and always had been from the moment they first met. If her family hadn't imploded, they wouldn't have met at all. Society was like dak, the sticky gluey stuff boys put on the branches of trees to trap songbirds. It was easier not to try escaping. It was all in the lap of the gods.

As he sat alone in the kitchen, he didn't feel so cocky. The waiting world seemed immense. The two of them would be dancing, his mother laughing over his shoulder. She was a good dancer, his father adequate by effort.

She had mentioned Peggy Dell and the night in Turners Hill. Peggy Dell's all-female orchestra was playing in a marquee in his native town. They had told him they were going to the dance for a few hours and not to worry, he'd be asleep and they'd be back soon.

He was five. He woke up in pitch-black night and she wasn't there beside him. He padded into his father's room; he wasn't there either. The marquee was only down the street, near the handball alley. He dragged a chair to the hall door, stood up on it and managed to work the lock and let himself out. Dressed only in his pyjamas, he went barefoot over the grassy bank to find them. The raised bank, next to the house, led down to the road. Tall dock leaves came up to his knees. He was worried he might step on a leprechaun. He often searched under the leaves for the little man with a crock of gold.

When he came on to the road the tarmac was warm. He was lonely. He wanted his mother. He missed the two of them. He wasn't a bit scared. Turners Hill was his home, he knew everyone in it and they knew him. He could see the coloured lights of the marquee and the shadowy figures milling about at the entrance and he could hear the music. It looked like a picture in a book and he was hurrying into it. The night was warm and fresh and as good if not better than day.

When the people in charge saw him approach, they laughed and some of the big girls he knew kissed him and Moggy Gargan went 'Ah' and ruffled his hair. Moggy Gargan had piles of auburn hair and was the best fun in the world. She got him to say 'sausages' because she knew he pronounced it 'sau-sa-da-duds'. They all laughed and Moggy led him into the marquee. It was like crashing into a wall of sound and a forest of legs. He was so small most of the crowd didn't see him and he was afraid of getting walked on. As if he were a leprechaun. There was a piano playing and a woman singing and the dancers joining in as if they were shouting: 'Open the door Richard . . . ' Way out in the middle of the floor, he got a glimpse of his mother. He tried to get to her but the legs were in the way. She was laughing over his father's shoulder. He waded into the river of sound and they didn't see him until he got between them and tugged at her dress and wrapped himself around her legs. The music stopped. She lifted him into her arms and, laughing, hugged him and his father said, 'What are you doing here?' and he was laughing too and all the dancers were round them and touching his curls and laughing and after a while Moggy Gargan took him home and put him back in bed.

The fourteen years in Turners Hill, his mother always said, were the happiest years of her life.

He was going to wait up for them to come home. He listened to someone on the wireless saying that Catholics weren't allowed to vote for Communists and Mr Khrushchev wasn't allowed into Disneyland. He wondered did that mean Donald Duck and Mickey Mouse were Catholics? He decided to go to bed. He thought he heard a car pull up but it wasn't them. There was a clock in the room. He wound it up and set the time. Midnight. He didn't have a wristwatch. At his age, he didn't even own a wristwatch. If he . . . when he . . . went to England, first thing he'd do would be to buy a . . . He fell asleep.

★ ★ ★

Someone turned the light on. His mother. Three o'clock. He sat up in the bed.

'We're back. Go to sleep.'

'You wake me up to tell me to go back to sleep? What's up? Have you been crying?'

'He made a holy show of himself. He threw the medal at them.'

'Why?' Her face was red and wet and the tears had made a pathway down her face powder.

'They told him they're definitely closing the

393

Station. He went mad. There was a bar at the back of the hall. Jim Reilly and young Sullivan and a few others had to hold him back. I was so ashamed. He's retiring as soon as he can. The whole lovely night ruined.'

'Who has the medal now?'

'I have. The Bully Barry gave it back to me. Mr Barry is a very nice man and so is his wife. She's from Mayo too.'

'Where is he now?'

'I managed to get him into bed. The Jameson went straight to his head. Not to mention all the Guinness. He ripped a lapel on his dress jacket and he's lost the dickie bow. I'm mortified.'

'He's retiring or resigning?'

'Does it matter? They said the Troubles are over. Butlershill is the first station along the Border to be shut. He went mad. It wasn't very nice, was it, telling us at the Annual Dance? He even tried to sing. 'The West's Awake'. There was no one left listening to him. Young Guard Sullivan drove us home. There's hope for the country when there's young men like him around.'

She wiped her eyes with a glove. Even though he was well away from his father's room he could get the reek of alcohol.

'I thought Jim Reilly was driving you home?'

'He was so drunk the Guards let him sleep in the cell for the night. He wasn't the only one. Half the legal profession of Cavan were along with him. Goodnight, darling.'

'See you in the morning, Mum. Everything will be okay, don't worry.' She turned the light out. He knew she had woken him to reassure him, never forgetting the night in Turners Hill. He could hear a bluebottle whanging about the room. He eventually fell asleep.

★ ★ ★

There was a ferocious knocking or noise of some kind and a voice calling. It had to be his father. He jumped out of bed. He was surprised to see it was morning. Late. Ten o'clock. His mother was usually up first thing on a Sunday. He made for her room to see was she all right. She was asleep. What the hell was his father up to? He too was asleep and reeking still of booze. The noise started again. It was the hall door being banged. Tamper Conlon was outside, all of a lather.

'The money's gone. Where's your father? I got back from first Mass — it's gone. He towl me to tell him straightaway.'

'Right, right, okay, Tamper, I'll tell him.'

'Will I wait on him?'

'No, no, that's not necessary. You can go home now and stay there until further notice. He will be pleased at your prompt action and will no doubt confirm the same personally.'

He closed the door on Tamper's impressed expectant ovoid face.

His father came out of the bedroom. He had his uniform trousers on and a vest. He clutched the trousers round his waist to keep them up. He looked rough as a beagle after the hunt.

'You couldn't resist giving Tamper a lick of your glib tongue. I heard you.'

'What about your tongue last night?'

'I told you it was my swansong. The swan sings before he dies. How is Mum?'

'She's still asleep. Do you want breakfast?'

'Yes. I'm not receiving today.'

Receiving was going to Holy Communion. He boiled an egg for him and wet the tea, whilst he shaved.

'Mammy said you made a holy show of yourself. You went into the town hall your chest swelling all the more because you had the medal on it. Am I right? And you can't drink.'

'It was fine until they told me they were closing me down. The Station. The Chief, the Super, any amount of inspectors, the oul District Justice himself — they were all there, looking at me. Next thing I knew, there she was . . . out on the floor dancing with The Bully Barry.'

'Mum?'

'Mum.'

'Betcha that was when you ripped the medal off and flung it at him. Am I right?'

He sat in to the table and cracked the boiled egg and, lost in thought, kept hitting at it with the spoon far longer than necessary.

He was a jealous man. His wife dancing with another man troubled him far more than the Station closing. She was as faithful to him as could be, yet he would consider it a betrayal. She wouldn't talk to him for the rest of the day until he apologised. He dreaded when the two of them weren't friends.

'What are you going to do about Tamper? You told him he had to come to you immediately

. . . you're nowhere near ready.'

'Shut down. Closed. I often wondered how it would all end.'

'Are you going to bother at all with Tamper?'

'Yes, yes. I am. I'm not retired yet. Get the bikes ready. You can come with me. It could be me last case.'

'It's not exactly a murder case, is it?'

'To catch a common thief is just as sweet.'

'You haven't caught him yet.'

'No, no. We'll see.'

★ ★ ★

They rode out into the countryside, up past the chapel and past Tamper Conlon's stone cottage and came to a stop at a narrow spot in the middle of nowhere on the road to Cavan town. His father dismounted and stood in the road and told him to do the same. He didn't speak. On either side were fields of ragwort, dock, thistles, nettles, fern, rock, whin and a few cattle mooching about, searching out the grass.

'What's up?'

He didn't reply. He was probably mulling over the events in the town hall. It struck him he'd better be kind to him. After all, apart from his wife dancing with Chief Superintendent Barry, he'd been told he was redundant. Surplus to requirements. Goodbye, old chap.

'Dad, what are we waiting here for?'

'I don't know. We'll see.'

In his dark-blue uniform, cap, black boots, baton hanging from his belt, shiny buttons, whistle and chain and gripping the handlebars of his old tank of a bicycle, he looked a formidable obstruction on the public road, no matter who came along. Because it was Sunday and first Mass long over, there wasn't anybody about or cars on the road.

They were on a hill and looking back the way they had come but they were just round a bend in the road. Anyone coming from the direction of the village wouldn't see them until the last moment. His father was always a mystery to him but this time he didn't really have the slightest clue what he was up to. It was amazing he could stand so still, so in his own world . . . so, so, so . . . unflinching.

'Sssh.' He'd heard something. The rattle of a bike, the easy grunt of a man pedalling hard up the hill . . . when the cyclist came round the bend he was going very slowly and had to stop anyway because the Sergeant was in the middle of the narrow road.

'Ah, good man yourself,' his father said, 'that's a grand morning.'

'It is, Sergeant, not bad.'

'Heading for town?'

'I am. The football match is on later.'

'I wish I was going with you. Do you think they'll win?'

'I'll put it this way — they'll be hard bet.'

'I think the very same. You're Petey Brady, aren't you, am I right, Petey?'

'No, Sergeant, Pat Reilly.'

'Ah, sorry, sorry, Pat, of course, how are things, Pat?'

'Oh, the best.'

'That's good, that's good, Pat. Well, I suppose you better be on your way. We can't stay gas-baggin' all day.'

Pat Reilly was in his forties and wearing a brown suit, brown shoes and a shirt and tie. His trouser bottoms were bicycle-clipped. His fair hair was thick and well combed. He had a funny way of twitching his right shoulder. As if it was stiff. Or itchy. As he was about to get on his bike and head for Cavan, he paused and felt his back tyre.

'Do you need a pump, Pat?' his father asked him.

'No, I think she's hard enough to get me there.'

'How much is it into the match today by the way?'

'It's enough. I wouldn't like to have to pay for anybody but meself.'

'You're a man like's a drink or two as well, I'd say. How much have you on you, Pat, not meaning to be personal?'

'Just a few quid, Sergeant. Thirty bob in fact.' He thumbed his breast pocket and they could see the outline of a wallet.

Before he could ride away his father said, 'Would you mind me having a look, Pat?'

The man looked at his father, his head moving in surprise.

'Why? I towl you how much I have.'

'Of course, of course, but I'd like to just the same. It'll only take a second or two. Head-quarters tell us to do this all the time. Sure there's no need to worry at all, man. You see, if you don't let me have a look I'll have to bring you into the Garda Station and search you there. It means you'll be coming with me just as all the people are coming out of second Mass. The whole parish will know something's up. That's right, Pat, isn't it?'

The fear of the shame was all over his face. He took out his wallet and handed it over.

'You're a decent man, Pat,' his father said.

The wallet was the same colour as his suit — deep brown. His father's big fingers poked into it and he felt the notes before withdrawing them. A pound note and a ten-shilling note. He turned them over and back, his face glum.

'Exactly as you said, Pat, thirty bob, you're no liar anyway.'

As he watched on he was afraid his father had the wrong man. The suspect looked relieved.

His father, still glum, stared at him but then inexplicably began to smile.

'How did you earn this money? What kind of work do you do?'

'I was footin' turf the last couple a days for a man. That's what he gave me.'

'It's little enough, Pat, hard earned.'

Pat looked at the Sergeant, not quite sure where he stood but beginning to believe he'd soon be on his way. He held his hand out for the wallet but quickly withdrew it and ran his fingers through his hair. His father now looked as relaxed as an angler in the river playing with a well-hooked trout.

'Well, Pat, you may have earned the pound note but the ten-shilling note — you never lost any sweat getting that. I tell you what I'm going to do. The two of us are going to call on Bill Agnew, the Peace Commissioner. Being a Sunday, he's the man we need to see. I'll give him the facts of the case: you're a thief, you stole this ten-shilling note from Tamper Conlon's house. Bill will read you your rights and you'll be bound over to appear at Belturbet District Court in a few weeks' time.'

Pat Reilly gulped, blinked and looked very shifty.

'I didn't steal that ten-bob note, Sergeant, as God is me judge, I didn't, I swear it. Who said I did? What proof have you?'

'I marked it with a pinprick in two places. There they are, see? I wrote down the serial number as well, oh bedad I did. We better be on our way so you can avoid the people coming out from Mass.'

The three of them rode back towards the village at a gentle pace. They could have been a party out for a spin in the country. The hedges were full of songbirds. Wrens and finches scudded along in the bushes and a cock robin, his ten-bob waistcoat on show, alighted on a twig, observing them for worms.

His father had caught his man with one of the oldest tricks in the book. And the casual, almost bumbling way he got into conversation with the suspect was a classic tactic. He always said the best policeman was a stupid policeman.

'Lull them into a false sense of security. Let them think they're smarter than you. Then, when ready, pounce.'

His wife had danced with the hated Bully Barry, he was hungover, tired, ashamed and they were closing him down, but work came first. Crime. The people had to be protected. Only the Force stood between good and evil. Nothing was more important than justice. Ten shillings or ten thousand pounds — it was all the same to him.

★ ★ ★

That night as they knelt to say the Rosary, he apologised for causing trouble at the dance but blamed it on the drink and swore he'd never touch another drop 'except for medicinal reasons'. Likewise with cigarettes. When sitting on the Elsan can in the lavatory, a cigarette relaxed the bowel and the smoke purified the air.

He and his mother hadn't spoken all day.

'I'm sorry. I apologise.'

'Apology accepted.' His mother looked pleased. An apology meant she'd won and the silence was over. She gave him his biscuits and hot milk and then set about repairing the damage to the dress suit. The lapel was practically ripped off. He asked for Milk of Magnesia. It looked like potato spray — without the blue. He swallowed a large spoonful — 'For my stomach's sake.'

'Are you going to put in to be transferred to another station, Dad? You could still serve a few more years, couldn't you?'

'I've served enough. I'm resigning. The end.'

'The end,' echoed his mother. 'The Troubles are over, thanks be to God.'

'When the powers that be put that border

there, it was like a man had an eye stolen out of his head. He'll never give up looking for it. The Troubles will never be over, say what they like. That's my solid opinion.'

'What are we going to do? Where are we going to live, Daddy?'

'Me and Mum saved every penny we could. We gave you the best education affordable, in the circumstances. We stinted ourselves. For the future. For this very day. We kept it a secret.'

'Kept what a secret?'

'The day you were born I bought twenty-five acres of land near Dublin. I couldn't risk telling you. A serving member isn't supposed to own property. We're going to build a house on it. I've already spoken to a builder I know. He's going to start right away. Our own house.'

'Our own home. A bungalow. With a proper bathroom. And a kitchen with a serving hatch.'

He had heard her talking about a serving hatch from time to time. Apparently it was a hatch in the wall with doors and you could hand in plates and cups of tea into an adjoining room. The *Irish Independent* said it was very modern.

'Why don't we go back to Turners Hill? We were always happy there. I was happy there every day of my life.'

'It's never the same. Look at all the stations I've served in. I've never gone back to one of them.'

'And I've never gone back to Mayo.'

His father was a peasant at heart and had a peasant's cunning. The land was in his blood and he was only happy with clay under his boots. His own clay. All these years he had twenty-five acres in Dublin and never said a word about it. The stone-cold silence of the Famine was in his genes.

★ ★ ★

They began, each of them, preparing for leaving. All the stuff that had to be moved could wait. The house in Dublin wouldn't be ready for six months at least. But the wrench of again saying goodbye to a part of your life was painful to contemplate. Hands would have to be shook, friendly eyes looked into, backs turned, a new road faced. Saying goodbye was a funeral without a corpse.

His father carried on with his police work and in the evenings dug the garden as if he was going to be there for ever. The clay spoke to him. The clay was honest. He dug it for truth.

His mother made lists — things she had to pack, things she could throw away.

'And we're going to buy a new armchair.'

'And I'm going to go to England.'

'And a carpet for the sitting room.'

'There'll be loads of girls there.'

'And a television as well. With doors. To match the hatch.'

★ ★ ★

Word spread quickly that the Station was closing. In Jim Reilly's pub the pros and cons were discussed endlessly.

'Jaysus, gauson, we're going to miss you. Just when you were turning into a half-dacent footballer.'

Lady Sarah Butler-Coote sent for his father. Despite her once glorious demesne and Georgian mansion, all within miles of high wall, she had ended up old, alone, abandoned by her steward and servants save for a local woman who went in and fed her every evening and, before leaving, prepared her breakfast for the following morning.

He and his father were driven into the demesne by Guard Sullivan in the squad car. The driveway was overgrown, the potholes unfilled, the atmosphere of abandonment complete. A heap of years lay on the place like a heavy sack on a beggar's back. They knocked on the door and waited for ages until they heard a pained shuffling inside.

'Lord God, Sergeant,' Sullivan said quietly, 'how the mighty have fallen.'

After much fumbling with locks, keys and bolts, Lady Sarah, leaning on a stick, grey and wrinkled, stood blinking at them through the bottle-thick spectacle lenses he remembered from when he was boy. She looked at him, puzzled.

'Is this your boy, Sergeant?'

'No longer a boy, Lady Sarah. The years have passed us by.'

'And who is this?'

'This is Guard Tim Sullivan. When I go, he'll look after you if you're ever in trouble.'

Sullivan smiled timidly.

'He's quite nice,' she said in a surprised tone. 'Do come in. I abhor the report of closure.'

They sat in the kitchen, which was spacious but rundown with a wide lump of plaster and paper hanging from a wall. The oil lamps and candlestick holders from a previous age were still in place. The door of the range was open but he sensed a fire hadn't been lit in it for many a day. The once vibrant woman, in her decrepitude, was an echo of the house or the house was echoing her. Her heavy grey stockings sagged on her thin legs and her mottled hands gripping the top of her walking stick were incredibly wrinkled. She was never good-looking enough to get a man and too intelligent to marry a fool. Her inheritance from Nature didn't match her beautiful estate.

'I have over the past weeks been aware of rumblings in the night. Down here. Somewhere. I spend most of my hours upstairs in my bedroom. I came down today because you have responded to my summons.' Her tone was still imperial. His father and Sullivan exchanged looks. Their uniforms were alien in a house still hung with pictures of dead royalty and wall-plates with inscriptions commemorating royal birthdays and anniversaries.

'Sullivan,' his father said, 'take a look in the rooms, see is there anything amiss.'

'The rooms are under lock and key. Access is impossible.' Her accent, in a very long life, never lost its cut-glass edge.

'I see. Well, go outside and take a look round and about.'

'Rightio. Excuse me, Lady Sarah.'

She watched him go and, her head doddering, said, 'I like him enormously.'

'Yes. He's stationed in Cavan but the squad car will be on patrol at all times. I'll see to it that they keep a constant watch for you. After I retire.'

'It's too bad, Sergeant, too bad. How is your dear spouse?'

'Ah, oh, she's very well, thank you, Lady Sarah.' When she wasn't looking, amused, his father winked to him. Spouse. It was from a Latin word meaning 'to promise.'

She seemed to be wearing the same brown tweed skirt and jacket she wore when as a boy he first saw her. Instead of brown brogues she was in bedroom slippers.

'Do you regret at all, Lady Sarah, not declaring for the matrimonial stakes?' His father enjoyed sailing close to ethical winds. He made it sound like a race meeting. He also spoke in an affected accent.

'Rude of you to ask, Sergeant, if I may be so bold. There were no alternatives to a solitary state. Suitors were very dull English or mad Irish.'

Sullivan came back in and reported nothing amiss apart from a rear sash window that wasn't locked on the inside. His father was instantly engaged.

'Hm. I see. Did you gain entry?'

'No, I didn't go into the room. If that's what you mean.'

'Can you escort me upstairs, Sergeant, with

407

the help of Guard Saloman?'

'Sullivan.'

'I am never coming down again. I am unable. Mrs Reilly will attend me daily. Come along.'

She led them into the hallway and to the bottom of the winding staircase. In the old days it shone with polish. The walls had paintings of bewhiskered vicars and an impressive one of a hideous-looking Queen Elizabeth I. He knew it was Elizabeth I — it said so in peeling letters. An ugly old mad-woman at her wits' end, chopping off her friends' heads, in a Court that was an asylum full of psychopaths.

A large dinner-gong sat on a table. He picked up the drumstick and crisply struck it. His father turned and glowered but Lady Sarah didn't react.

The two men got her up as far as the landing, where, panting, she paused.

'I intend selling. Provided I am allowed to see out my days here. Shouldn't be long. Going to auction in a month.'

'Gosh,' said his father, 'what an upheaval for you.'

More than once, working in Jim Reilly's bar, he had heard Reilly say that one day she'd have to sell. And he was prepared to buy. He had the money.

'Jim Reilly would buy it from you, Lady Sarah. And he'd be very happy to let you live on here for ever.' For ever was a euphemism for a few years at most. Lady Sarah was in her late eighties.

She turned and looked at him — he was down a few steps.

'No Papist will ever own Butlershill Demesne.' Her understated tone was superb and deadlier than if she'd screamed the words.

'Never is a long time,' Sullivan said, almost apologetically.

His father and Sullivan escorted her into her bedroom. The bed was a four-poster and on the walls were pictures of geese and goslings, ducks and drakes, sheep and horses. On a small side-table was a toasted crust and an eggshell. There was a good view out into the demesne — giant Californian cedar, the lake, the winding drive, the drumlin hill at the centre of it all. At the edge of what once was a perfect lawn was a tree which was supposed to be where native chieftains met their sixteenth-century end. Locals called it the hanging tree.

They bade her goodbye. She told them not to worry about closing the hall door, the woman would be coming soon to attend to her needs. His father promised to call on her very soon again and not to worry, he'd see to it she was looked after.

When they got outside he asked their opinion of what she'd said about a Papist never owning the place.

'It sounds harsh enough,' his father said, 'but sure she doesn't really mean it deep down. She's trapped in her history like we're trapped in ours.'

'The poor woman isn't long for this world,' Sullivan said.

He was amazed at how cool and calm they were. His father said if you can't change a thing don't waste your breath ranting about it. Just before they got back into the squad car, he decided to go round the back of the house and have a look for himself at the unlocked window.

The window was in a gable end near a minor untarred public road the other side of a big iron gate — a rear entrance to the demesne. The heavy curtains were drawn so you couldn't see into the room. His father prised up the lower half of the window and pushed the curtains aside. Light flooded in. The room, a study, hadn't been used for some considerable time. Some of the furniture was covered with sheets. A large sofa was turned upside down near the fireplace. There was a bag like a doctor's bag beneath the window. His father reached in and when he opened it, discovered, a hammer, a chisel, a set of keys and a jemmy. Quietly he put the bag down on the ground. He was staring at the upturned sofa and listening hard.

'Come out! You're nabbed, me bucko. I'll count to three and if you're not out by then I'll come in for you.'

He couldn't understand what his father was up to and neither could Sullivan.

'One . . . two . . . '

The sofa shifted and a man crawled out from under it. On all fours he stared up at them. He got to his feet. He was about thirty years of age, slightly built, wiry, wearing white plimsolls, flannel trousers and a white shirt. He had wavy hair and a plump, unshaven sullen face.

'Well, be the holy hammers of Hell,' his father said. 'Ginger Jordan, the Clones burglar. Come here 'til I arrest you.'

Guard Sullivan fetched a pair of handcuffs from the car and slipped them on to the man's wrists.

'I was doin' nothin' wrong. I was just sleeping in the place. Temp'rey like. I never went near the oul doxy.'

'Caught red-handed.'

'I've done nothing wrong. You can't charge me with anythin'.'

'You that's supple, hop in there and see what's behind the sofa.'

Under the Chesterfield sofa he found a pile of blankets and a suitcase. When it was opened, it contained a silver salver, a cigarette case, a hip flask, a chalice, a gentleman's watch, a tiepin, cufflinks, a silver tea tray, a pair of binoculars, golf balls.

'Who did you rob last night, Ginger — a parish priest?'

'I'm telling you nothin', Sergeant.'

His father took him round the front of the house and in the hall door and up the stairs to Lady Sarah's bedroom. He knocked loudly on the door.

'Lady Sarah, don't be afraid, it's only me again. We found the source of those rumblings in the night. Are you there?'

'Come in.'

She lay on the bed, a big book on her chest. An Old Testament. It looked as if it was squashing her.

When she saw the strange handcuffed man, she looked aghast.

'This is the notorious Ginger Jordan, the

411

Clones burglar. He's been using the room with the unlocked window as a den. Sleeping during the day and coming and going through the night. I wanted you to see him and to reassure you it won't happen again, Lady Sarah.'

'I never touched the old bag. Let me go. I know nothin' about that suitcase. You can't prove a thing.'

His eyes checked every item in the room. He was quick as a ferret.

'He's a rather disagreeable sort. Show no mercy, Sergeant. Is it likely he'll be hanged?'

'Not for breaking and entry, Lady Sarah.'

'More's the pity. Take him out of my sight. Thank you so much, Sergeant. What shall we do without you?'

The burglar stuck his tongue out at her. He had a reputation for doing the same thing when sentenced by a judge.

'You can rest easy tonight at any rate, Lady Sarah. Slán leat.'

Her remark about hanging may have been humorous. His father's farewell in Gaelic certainly was.

The burglar was gasping for a cigarette. Sullivan gave him one of his Sweet Aftons. And back at the Station, his father brought him into married quarters, where his mother made him a mug of tea and a ham sandwich.

'You have two lovely eyes, missus. If I could, I'd rob them.'

The compliment, even a burglar's compliment, pleased her enormously. Soon she was going round the house singing ' . . . The roses all

412

have left your cheek, I've watched them fade away and die, Your voice is sad when e'er you speak, And tears bedim your loving eyes . . . '

* * *

At the next sitting of the District Court in Belturbet, the judge praised his father for his ingenuity in the Tamper Conlon case and for the shrewd arrest of that 'notorious criminal' Ginger Jordan, the Clones burglar. Having had a satisfying lunch, followed by a few glasses of port, the judge was in benevolent mood. He gave Jordan a mere two months.

When his father was mentioned in the *Anglo-Celt*, they bought three copies to send to his sisters in America.

From time to time he accompanied his father to Dublin, to see how the building of the house was progressing. It was up a winding country road not far from the airport. He walked the three fields with him and saw how proud he was of having had the foresight to buy it all those years before. In the sky above, two buzzards, in sweeping ever-rising circles, called to each other in plaintive peep-peeps.

It would be best, he thought, to reach for the skies rather than plod the earth. When the world ended, the birds would have the hop on man.

In Butlershill his mother visited the neighbours well before they left, as a way of gently easing away.

The Station was to close in December and the house would be ready the same month.

He would go with his parents to Dublin and after Christmas flee the new nest. England. That much he had decided.

★ ★ ★

At the end of November it snowed heavily and after a few days the roads were clogged with frozen slush. One Friday morning, he took a walk out into the country along the road past the football field, now covered in snow. The set of goalposts nearest to him, aslant in the bitter wind, looked like a trapezium about to collapse. Across the fields on the other side was the lake where he swam with his father. A hot summer's day after a game, he and all the team raced down through the meadow and shouting and laughing plunged into the cooling turfy water. He was missing those friends already.

Walking in the snow was hard going but he was in the mood to stick at it. He came up on to the main Cavan—Clones road at Gannon's Cross. Turning left, the crusty frozen snow crackling underfoot, he walked on but very soon heard a car or a lorry coming from behind. For safety he got up on the hedge bank. It was twice the height from the fall of snow. To his left he saw the squad car from Cavan approaching. When he looked to his right he saw a cattle lorry, the engine roaring as it tried to get up the slight hill to the crossroads. When it breasted the hill it gathered speed. He'd never know what happened but the driver of the squad car must have seen him standing up on the ditch. Despite the fact

414

that he was accoutred in overcoat, scarf and a cap, he may have recognised him. He definitely braked and went into an immediate skid. The driver of the lorry braked as well. The two vehicles crashed head-on. The lorry was loaded with bawling cattle. The squad car hit the lorry at amazing speed because of the icy road. The sound was like someone smashing a bucket with a sledgehammer. The car flipped over and righted itself in a field gateway. The windows had shattered and the body of the car caved in.

The lorry managed to stop. When the driver jumped out of the cab he saw it was Ginger Jordan, the Clones burglar. They went to the squad car and wrenched a wrecked door open. There was a uniformed Garda in the passenger seat. He was badly injured, unconscious but somehow looked alive. The driver was Tim Sullivan. He was dead. There wasn't a mark on him . . . but he was dead. His face was pale as snow.

He stood staring into the wreck, frozen with fear and shock. And guilt. If he hadn't gone for a walk, it might never have happened. Ginger Jordan, despite the weather, was wearing his silly white plimsolls. Gannon's Cross was in the middle of nowhere and with the blanket of snow and ice it might as well have been the North Pole. There was a lake nearby — frozen over. A grey crow landed on it. The wind was so sharp you could see its feathers ruffling.

'The wife made me take the job,' Jordan said. 'A few quid. Good job the lorry didn't turn over. All them cattle, yah know?' His ferret head

415

jerked as he spoke. His feet must have been freezing. The accident wasn't his fault.

Rinty Maguire, who lived down from the crossroads, had heard the smash and knew immediately there had been an accident. He phoned the Sergeant, who alerted the County ambulance and arrived himself on the scene not long afterwards.

The injured Garda was taken to Cavan Surgical and Tim Sullivan was taken to the Surgical morgue. By evening people started calling to the morgue to pay their respects.

'Ah, poor Tim,' his mother said, 'the Lord have mercy on his gentle soul. There's not a mark on him true enough.'

The fatal blow had been delivered to the back of his head, where it couldn't be seen.

The parents arrived up from Limerick. It was a long journey in a country half-stopped with ice. They were crippled with grief. The father had the same pale face as the son.

He stood back from them all, stricken with guilt. In his heart where none could see it. Why had he gone for that damn walk? He was convinced Sullivan braked suddenly because of him. He watched as the parents were introduced to his father, who was in full uniform. He wondered how he was going to handle the situation. What could he say in the face of a horrible reality?

Taking the mother's hand in both his hands, his father said, 'Mrs Sullivan, you can be proud of your boy. He died on duty in the service of his country. He's a great loss. Had he lived I have no doubt he'd have risen up the ranks. We'll never forget him in our prayers.' He said it straight and true, without a scintilla of false emotion.

The weeping mother replied, 'You're very kind, Sergeant. Tim loved all his friends.'

A dark-haired girl came to the morgue. She had arranged a date with Sullivan for the next night. Another girl, in a white raincoat, arrived. She'd had a date with him the night before. On either side of his corpse, they looked each other up and down and soon worked out the situation. They shook hands and went off down the town together.

He remembered the remark Sullivan made about Lady Sarah not being long for this world and it was another irony that the lorry driver was the Clones burglar. The owner of the cattle lorry couldn't get anyone else to drive for him that day, because of the icy conditions.

★ ★ ★

His father was put in charge of the Cavan end of the funeral. He did it according to the book. The *Garda Síochána Code*, Chapter 17.11: 'Rank of deceased: Guard . . . Party: 1 sergeant, 12 guards . . . The funeral parade will be in the following order: (a) hearse, (b) funeral party with the officer in charge in front, (c) chief mourners followed by the general public.'

Even in death the *Code* couldn't be escaped. The cathedral was packed for the funeral Mass. An aunt of the deceased sang 'There Is An Isle', a song synonymous with Limerick despite its

417

Scottish origins. Gardaí from all over the Division attended, from all over the country. Tim Sullivan was young and popular, his death untimely. When the coffin, covered with the tricolour, was carried out of the cathedral, on the many steps leading up to the main doors his father had placed two ranks of men. It was an impressive sight. A stickler for detail, he'd also arranged for the steps to be salted. Local townspeople packed the street, many of them dabbing their eyes with handkerchiefs. Only the good died young.

Maybe there was a lot to be said for dying bad and old. Lady Sarah was good and old. Was it a consolation to her? Trapped upstairs in her lonely bedroom with a burglar secretly living below? Lying in bed with what had been an ancestor's Bible almost too heavy for her aged arms to lift?

All the time it seemed to him that his position up on the snowy ditch may have been the cause of Sullivan's death and though he saw the two vehicles approach and had somehow sensed they were going to collide head-on, he was unable to intervene. He had hoisted himself on the horns of a philosophically impossible dilemma. It was cruel luck. Blind fate. Yet his eyes had been wide open.

In Christian Science, the teacher had spoken about Jesus in the Garden of Gethsemane seeing every person who was going to enter Heaven. It was a discussion about free will. Someone said, 'What's the point of me trying to be good when God knows already I'm going to be bad?' The teacher likened it to a man standing on a high

418

rock who sees two cars approaching each other on a narrow mountain road. They are going to crash. It's inevitable. But the man on the rock cannot interfere. Neither does God interfere in the affairs of men. Though he can see what is going to happen. Each person has free will.

His father said, 'How could it be your fault? You didn't put your foot on the brake, did you? You didn't physically and you didn't mentally. So shut up about it. Why torture yourself over something you couldn't control?'

He shut up about it but how could he forget?

★ ★ ★

One morning in December he watched his father out at the back of married quarters washing himself. He was stripped to the waist though it was so cold he had to smash the ice on the water barrel with the hatchet. His skin was white and in places had moles and red spots he'd never noticed before. He was ageing, his skin collecting the evidence with each advancing year. He had thickened around the girth and when he bent to pick up the towel which had fallen on the ground, he groaned. But he stood facing the wind and a watery sun and took the freezing air deep into his lungs, as if defying the temperature.

That night he came in having patrolled his sub-district for the last time. Then for the last time, after thirty-five years, he took off his uniform jacket and cap. Inside the cap in white paint was his number — 4447. He held the cap for a few moments, staring at it, then tossed it away on top of the dresser.

They watched him, his mother smiling.

'That's it,' he said.

He shook his father's hand, surprised at his own emotion. He was emotional because his father wasn't. His father had a boyish simplicity — he expected nothing much. The world wasn't going to change. It would carry on without him. He was surprised his mother didn't kiss or embrace him. In essence they had become two of a kind. They were so unalike, so alone and yet the years of isolated geography closed the gap between them.

'I never let the side down,' he said.

'You did not, a grá, never once.'

'I remember joining up in 1925. I got on the train at Woodlawn, in Galway. There was only one other person in the compartment. A young fellow like myself. We journeyed the whole way to Dublin — Broadstone Station. We never exchanged one single word. Lo and behold — wasn't he joining the Force as well? We met up in the Phoenix Park after. That'll give you an idea of the atmosphere in the country. After the Civil War. You couldn't trust a soul.'

'Yeah, I know, Dad, you told us before.' It was a hurtful remark and he felt immediately repentant. His mother clucked her tongue reproachfully.

'Sorry, Dad.'

'How could you understand?'

That was it. He had his hot milk and biscuits and they went to bed.

The house in Dublin was ready. The furniture would be removed by a reputable firm at the government's expense. But all the stuff in the shed was to go in Rinty Maguire's lorry. All the hens as well. The *Code* stated that fowl would not be paid for.

His mother was to travel in the furniture van. He would go with his father and Rinty.

The night before the departure, Jim Reilly had a party for him in the pub. His football-team friends were there and so too were Chisholm Flood and his brother, Squealer, and Tamper Conlon and the dark-haired girl who had the date with Sullivan and a load more. As he was leaving them, Chisholm said, 'You'll hardly be missed. You weren't worth the shootin'.'

Walking home he was stone-cold sober with the loneliness. He could have screamed with anger at having to leave the lovely drumlin hills, the pregnant country cloaked under velvet green, a lake in every pocket, a river up every sleeve.

When the furniture removal men had stripped married quarters bare, he walked with his mother from room to room. Their voices rang and the walls and floors now looked even colder and drabber. His mother gave a shiver and hurried out. The men had forgotten one item — the picture of Pius XI. The Apostolic Blessing on his parents' marriage. It was leaning against the wall of a recess by the small fireplace. He picked it up.

Piled on Rinty's lorry was the accumulated

paraphernalia of a life so far ... Thirty corrugated-iron sheets, most of them rusty, a good deal of them from the dismantled hen-house. Five other sheets which before his father somehow hammered them flat had been tar barrels. Loose loops of barbed wire, old half-rotten wooden stakes, thin knobbly ash poles cut out of hedges. Netting wire. Pots, pans, buckets gardening tools, his cobbler's box, his carpentry box, the wooden wheelbarrow which still hadn't been repaired from the last move. The tilley lamp, a Primus stove, the earthenware hot-water bottle, two riddles — one of them busted, a pile of unchopped logs, a bag of coal, a load of loose turf, three tea-chests and four hessian sacks containing the hens and the big Rhode Island Red rooster. The tin bath, the cross-cut saw with the golden solder, any amount of handsaws, half of them with worn useless teeth. The sledgehammer and a clunking bag of wedges. Twelve sheets of plasterboard, the corners of which were broken and all of them covered with hen dung. Two warped bike wheels. A stout tin watering can and an Elsan can and a couple of tins of hopelessly congealed paint. Two sacks of wrinkled potatoes he'd grown in the garden and a bag of withered cabbage. Last to be loaded was his father's bicycle. And a sack of corn — a mouse hopped out of it. Almost forgotten, his father's long-handled shovel, the handle the same colour as his weather-beaten hands. The whole lot lashed together with Tully's rope.

Mr and Mrs Gregg, the next-door neighbours,

waved them goodbye and the farmers taking their milk to the creamery waved as well. When the lorry moved off, the old rooster started crowing.

Acknowledgements

Stephen Rea

Lisa Cook   Faith O'Grady   Tracey Elliston

Brian Og Connaughton Sean McElhinney Sean Doris

Eoin McHugh (C)   Brian Langan

Padraig McPhillips Jim McCorry Hughie McInerney

Sean Conlon   Gerry McMahon   Mattie Kennedy

Other titles published by Ulverscroft:

A BORDER STATION

Shane Connaughton

For the son of the local sergeant in an isolated Garda station on the border between Cavan and Fermanagh, life is balanced between the brooding, taciturn presence of his father, whom he loves and fears in equal measure, and the reassurance of his warm and witty mother. His world is narrowed to lakes, woods, hayfields, country lanes and the amazing characters he encounters — tinkers, drinkers, publicans, policemen, farmers and the tantalising older sister of his Protestant friend. Amidst the drumlins and bogs, the boy's imagination roams free and unfettered. And at night, lulled by the rhythm of his mother's fleecy breathing, he finds solace. But change is coming. It's time to grow up . . .

COLD FEET: THE LOST YEARS

Carmel Harrington

Reeling from the sudden death of Rachel, his beloved wife, Adam has no time to grieve. He has to keep going, for the sake of their baby son . . . Jenny moves back in with her ex-husband Pete, eight and a half months pregnant with another man's child. Can their relationship overcome past jealousies? And Karen and David agree to an amicable divorce — but that's before he sleeps with the divorce lawyer . . . From Manchester to Belfast and back, these tales of the original characters from the hit TV show bridge the gap between the old series and the new — with plenty of tears, laughter and friendship in true *Cold Feet* style.

THIS BEAUTIFUL LIFE

Katie Marsh

Abi Cooper is living her happy ending. She's in remission and is ready to make the most of her second chance. But during her illness, her family has fallen apart. Her husband John has made decisions that are about to come back to haunt him, while her teenage son Seb is battling with a secret of his own. Set to the songs on Abi's survival playlist, this is the story of what happens when she tries to put her family back together — and of why life, and love, are worth fighting for.